Praise for

In the Name of Friendship

"French continues to write about the inner lives of women with insight and intimacy." —*NEW YORK TIMES BOOK REVIEW*

"Marilyn French is brilliant . . . full of life and passions that ring true as crystal." —THE *WASHINGTON POST*

"French brings a novelist's eye, a scholar's sense of detail and a feminist's worldview . . . [this is] a novel for women with a progressive perspective on gender bias and an old-fashioned fondness for discussing the curveballs life lobs." —*PUBLISHERS WEEKLY*

From Eve to Dawn: A History of Women in the World

"No history you will read, post-French, will ever look the same again." —MARGARET ATWOOD

"One day, no history will be written without the female half of the world. Until then, we have the unique scholarship of Marilyn French in *From Eve to Dawn*. No home or library or hopeful reader should be without it." —GLORIA STEINEM

"[Marilyn French] still knows how to keep the pages turning." —*TIME OUT NEW YORK*

"In four ambitious volumes under the title *From Eve to Dawn*, [French] surveys world history from a staunchly feminist perspective. . . . Readers can profit greatly from her brisk and passionate prose." —*MS.* MAGAZINE

Books by Marilyn French

Fiction

The Women's Room

The Bleeding Heart

Her Mother's Daughter

Our Father

My Summer with George

In the Name of Friendship

The Love Children

Nonfiction

The Book as World: James Joyce's Ulysses

Shakespeare's Division of Experience

Beyond Power: On Women, Men, and Morals

Women in India

The War Against Women

A Season in Hell: A Memoir

From Eve to Dawn: A History of Women in the World
Volumes One–Four

the

Love Children

MARILYN FRENCH

THE FEMINIST PRESS
AT THE CITY UNIVERSITY OF NEW YORK
FEMINISTPRESS.ORG

Published in 2009 by the Feminist Press
at the City University of New York
The Graduate Center
365 Fifth Avenue
New York, NY 10016
feministpress.org

13 12 11 10 09   5 4 3 2 1

Library of Congress Cataloging-in-Publication Data

French, Marilyn, 1929-2009
The love children / by Marilyn French.
    p. cm.
ISBN 978-1-55861-606-6
I. Title.
PS3556.R42L68 2009
813'.54—dc22

                              2009010439

Cover design by Faith Hutchinson
Text design by Drew Stevens

the Love Children

so smug denouncing "gooks" and "Commies." They were the same kids who were delighted when Robert Kennedy was assassinated; they were laughing—"Two down, one to go."

When I dared to argue, it was as a pacifist; I was against killing anyone. I was pro-McCarthy, shocked by the Democratic convention and devastated by the assassination of Robert Kennedy and Martin Luther King Jr.: I felt that we were murdering all our decent leaders, leaving only wild-eyed crazies and dullards to run the country. But I was young and didn't have much knowledge, just lots of emotion.

In 1968, the year I started senior high school, we had more than a half million troops in Vietnam, killing with abandon and dying like flies—we learned in biology that flies have a lifespan of twenty-four hours; the lifespan of a new ground soldier in Vietnam seemed to be about the same. War had come to mean something to me. I read how army sergeants bullied and harassed young boys and taught them to hate the enemy. And when I read history, it seemed as if wars didn't really accomplish anything. They might make one man a big deal for a few years—like Alexander the Great or Napoleon or Hitler or Stalin—but he always died in the end, and his empire always fell apart, and meanwhile millions of people had died for him. Half the time warring countries ended up friends, like the Catholics and the Protestants in Europe, after hundreds of years of disemboweling each other's babies and burning each other to death. War meant a lot of people getting killed or dying of disease or starvation and houses and schools and churches or whole cities getting burned down. I thought that the man or group who wanted power enough to go to war should do the fighting in a bullring, and leave the rest of us out of it.

Mostly I didn't think about war, though. I lived in a dream of a happy life. I painted a set of pictures of it when I was six: in the first, a little blonde, blue-eyed girl dances toward a woman with brown hair and wearing an apron whose back is to the viewer. Then the girl hands the woman a garland, which she tries to hang on the barren branch of a tree under the eye of a savage sun. My mother framed my pictures and hung them in the kitchen.

I gleaned my sense of happiness from books, especially from the pictures in them, and from glimpses of my own family at charmed moments, like when my father spoke with love in his voice or my mother made an affectionate gesture toward him. Such things filled me with as much happiness as drinking a glass of chocolate milk. But by the time I was nine or ten, my father was in a rage pretty much all the time—at least when he was home. Willa Cather quoted a French saying about husbands and fathers who were "Joy of the street, sorrow of the home." That was my father: always amiable in public but a horror at home. He did have an occasional moment of lightheartedness; he might be full of jokes at Christmas or after a trip to New York. Because these occasions were rare, they were always a surprise, and a relief. Mom would get silly with pleasure. He won gold stars just for being pleasant.

Most of the time, though, his voice hurled through the house like clanging metal. He harried Mom over some glance she'd dropped, some word mislaid, creating a complex weave of betrayal and infidelity. Or he would yell at me for some terrible sin I couldn't remember committing—putting my hand on the wall or using the wrong fork. Then Mom, trying to deflect him from me, or just trying to shut him up, would yell back, and the two of them would be off, the house reverberating with curses and yells, their fury bouncing off the walls.

When that happened, I was grateful for my books. I retreated to them, lying on my bed submerged in the tales of Mary Norton's Borrowers series, about tiny people concealed under the floorboards, or thrilled by Edith Nesbit's *The Enchanted Castle*, eased by the healing beauties of Rumer Godden. I was especially enthralled by the harmonious family life and salubrious hard work of Laura Ingalls Wilder's families. I read all nine of her Little House books, reread them, lived them.

Besides books, I had friends. I always had friends. I'd stick to one girl, cling to her, my life raft in the heaving ocean of childhood, with its huge pull of Mommy and Daddy. Mommy and Daddy had friends and seemed to always know what to do and be able to do it: I was just an offshoot. But when I was with my friend, I was almost myself. I wasn't allowed to cross the street or leave the block or go anywhere exciting, such as a candy store or ice cream parlor, so having a friend was a kind of declaration of independence. I took friendship seriously and always thought my present friend would be my friend forever.

I was ecstatic with each step I took toward some vague horizon I could not even see—crossing the street alone, walking to the ice cream store on Broadway, walking to school alone, and eventually, going to the movie house on Brattle Street with my friend. I savored each revolutionary event as a major rite of passage into the state I longed for: adulthood. I resented being a child; it was outrageous that I, who had a perfectly good mind and will, should have to obey other people just because I was small! It was an indignity to have to get permission, or hold someone's hand, just to do what I wanted to do.

Sandy Lipkin was the first friend I could be completely— almost completely—independent with. By the time we met in tenth grade, we were fifteen, we had some money, and could go to the movies. We both had driver's permits. The only thing remaining was to earn money on our own, and that would happen soon. We were very proud of ourselves. We wore our hair long, forgetting to comb it, and never wore anything but blue jeans. We felt as new sprung as Botticelli's Aphrodite from seafoam, but no modest virgins we, using our hands to conceal our pubes; no, we were part of the new world, the miracle of a chosen generation, which made us miracles too. We were proud of our pubes. Well, we wanted to be. Well, we knew we would be when we were grown up.

Sandy was tall, with light brown eyes, dark blonde hair, and long arms and legs. I have light blonde hair and blue eyes and people always said I was beautiful, but to my sorrow I was and still am short and have a tendency to bustiness that I deplore. I wore oversize T-shirts and sweaters to avoid comments on the street.

Sandy and I were smart enough that we didn't have to spend much time on our homework. So was Bishop, our friend. His father was the police commissioner in Cambridge. He was taller than Sandy and gangly, with eyes as pale as water. His skin was pearly, giving off light. He was a butterfly, flitting from one thing to another. He would stop and sip, leaving behind a tinge of sweetness. Both Sandy and I were in love with him. None of us ever made out with each other, although we thought about it.

Most of my friends and I started out in the Cambridge public schools, but for high school we were sent to Barnes, a private school. Barnes was housed in an ivy-covered stone mansion in the wealthy part of Cambridge north of Brattle Street, within walking distance of Harvard Yard and the Square. With our small classes and smart teachers, we were ahead of the public school kids even though we cut school fairly often, as did the public school kids.

In the fall of 1968, when I started at Barnes, Harvard students took over the Yard. It had been an eventful year, beginning with the Tet Offensive, and followed by a Viet Cong attack on Saigon and Hue. Events on campus were set against life-and-death matters in the larger world, and it was exciting to walk through the Yard, with hordes of students milling around the administration building, people yelling through loudspeakers, students sitting in, everybody protesting the Vietnam War. The same thing was happening in other schools but I wasn't all that up on the news; most of us weren't, except Bishop, who was kind of crazy on the subject. His jaw would set and his mouth get almost mean when he talked about the war. I admired his seriousness and tried to equal his passion. But I knew I was a "flibbertigibbet," as my father constantly reminded me.

When, in October 1968, our government began to negotiate with the Vietnamese in Paris, we were all sure that it was student protest—our movement!—that had forced it to act and that the war would be over in a few months. We believed that we, our generation, had provoked this. It was heady, a triumphant affirmation of our power. We would not have believed then that the war would drag on for another seven years. It's hard for people who weren't there to imagine that scene now. None of the many wars since—in Grenada, Panama, the Balkans, Afghanistan, the Gulf, and Iraq—have aroused anything like that degree of sustained protest.

The air in Cambridge in those days was fragrant with the scent of weed as my pals and I happily walked the streets for hours. A bunch of us would gather in my kitchen after our travels, sitting around the table, on the armchairs, and the floor, talking and drinking Coke. My friends always left to go home for dinner about the time my mother came home to start cooking.

Few parents were willing to put up with the whole crowd. We could go to Phoebe Marx's apartment in a fancy building. It was always empty, because both her parents worked, but it was dark because it was on the first floor, and there was never anything to drink except water; her mother was a doctor and refused to buy sweet drinks. We could go to Sandy's, but she lived way out in Belmont—too far to walk. She took a bus to school, or her mother or father drove her. Her house was a wide brick colonial with big windows. Light streamed into all the rooms, and I loved that. They had wall-to-wall carpeting in every room, not old-fashioned Persian and Indian rugs like ours. But the atmosphere was so refined, so quiet and mannerly and beige, like the furniture, that we didn't really feel comfortable there. We didn't go to Bishop's that often either. His parents had built a rec room in the basement for the kids, and his younger brothers were always around, playing pool or just running and yelling, so boisterous and present that we didn't love being there. I was an only child, my father was rarely in the house, and if my mother was home she was in her study, so my house became our usual destination.

I see now that most of us were well-off, but I didn't realize that at the time. We weren't considered wealthy in our own society, so it escaped us that we were among the privileged of the world. Our parents probably did think about the bills, yet they could afford to hire people to clean their houses and wash and iron their clothes, take care of their lawns and gardens, cater their parties. They bought good clothes—Sandy and I had our worst quarrels with our mothers over clothes. They would buy sweet little dresses for us and beg us to wear them to cousin Lily's wedding or Great-Grandma's funeral, but we stormed out of rooms and slammed doors, loudly lamenting that destiny had provided us with such square parents. We refused on point of death to compromise our principles.

My family lived a few blocks from Harvard Yard. I had no idea that our smallish house, whose lack of modernity embarrassed me, was something other people might envy. Parts had been built in the eighteenth century: there were exposed beams in the ceilings of the living and dining rooms, and the kitchen had open wooden shelves that I hated and my mother loved. The fireplace was old, and the downstairs had wide-board wooden floors. Downstairs were the living room, dining room, and kitchen; an ancestor had tacked a porch on the side and there was a big old pantry behind the kitchen, part of which my mother had converted into a bathroom. Upstairs there were two bedrooms and my mother's study. Our house wasn't fancy, like the nineteenth-century castle on Garden Street where Bishop lived, with its high ceilings and sculpted moldings and its sliding walnut pocket doors between the downstairs rooms. It had a gallery all around the front and side, nine bedrooms, and two parlors.

What was nice about our house was the backyard, which sprawled into a stand of trees. It had a garage that my father had put a second story on and made into his studio. It had huge windows to the south and east, and a beautiful wooden floor. Back when life was happier around there, he worked in his studio and slept with Mom in the double bed in the big bedroom. I wasn't sure when or why that changed; it happened in whispers behind my back. I was thirteen when Dad announced one night at dinner that he couldn't paint here; Cambridge drove him crazy, Harvard drove him crazy, the Harvard art department drove him crazy, and he was going to move to Vermont, to the cabin up there that we used for summer vacations. It was a shack, really; it didn't have indoor plumbing, and it was isolated out in the woods.

"I just got my PhD, Pat!" My mother cried. "What am I supposed to do with it up there? There's nothing there! I just signed a contract with Harvard!"

"That's nothing!" he countered. "Just tear it up!"

Mom sat back. "I don't want to."

"We'll rough it," he urged. "It'll be fun!"

"Fun for who?" my mother challenged.

"Tsk, tsk, your grammar." Dad laughed. "And you with a PhD!"

She ignored that. "*I'll* be the one roughing it. You'll be in your studio painting, as always. Whereas *I* will have to do the laundry on a washboard, hang the clothes on a line, empty the chamber-pots, wash the dishes by hand, and be a general dogsbody! I won't become a slave!"

"Slave? Slave! It's called being a wife! It's what a wife is sup-posed to do."

"According to your family." Mom's face changed. "Let's not fight in front of Jess," she said. He shut up then, but both their mouths looked zipped.

After dinner I went to my room to do homework. After I fin-ished, I crept out and sat on the top step, listening. They argued in low, urgent voices. A few days later, as Dad packed his stuff into his car, Mom watched him in silence. When he left, he kissed me good-bye and told me he'd see me pretty soon. It would be months.

I loved my dad and I knew he loved me. Sometimes, when he thought I was being fresh, he'd snarl at me like a dog; but other times he'd chuckle, as if he thought I was cute. Sometimes he looked at me with kind eyes, and he hugged me once in a while. When he was gone the house was quieter. After that, every once in a while he'd descend on us from Vermont. He never called ahead, he just came, annoying Mom. Her reaction bothered me. It was as if he didn't have the right to come to his own house. I loved Mom, but I wished she was nicer to Dad. The main reason she was annoyed was that she hadn't bought enough food for his dinner. But also she knew he was trying to catch her at something.

The Vermont cabin was tiny, with a main room and a narrow bedroom and bath on one side and a loft over them, where I slept. The bathroom had a sink and a wonderful huge old claw-foot tub, but no toilet. Dad absolutely refused to put one in—we had to use the outhouse. The whole place was heated by a wood stove. I loved the cabin; it was beautiful. It was in deep woods, facing a lake, and had no neighbors. There was a canoe Dad's father had built, and a rowboat and a sailboat and an outboard motor. Wood for the stove was stacked in a shed attached to the house, and wildflowers grew all around. I loved to go out at night and lie on the grass, looking at the sky. It was so dark, the stars were like diamonds, hovering over the lake. For me it had a mysterious resonance with the Little House books I had read, with a dream of an America built by good, hardworking, disciplined people living in a nature that was gorgeous, if harsh.

One day, Dad called from the cabin. I was in my room doing homework when Mom answered the phone, and she called up to say that Dad was on the phone, and if I wanted to talk to him, I should get on the extension. I ran into her bedroom and picked up the phone; I heard him announce to my mother, "I fixed the kitchen for you!"

"For me?" she asked, surprised.

"Yes, of course for you. Who else?"

A little excitement made its way into her voice. "You mean you put in a dishwasher? A washing machine? A dryer?"

"No," he said angrily. "I put in a gas stove and a new sink. An expensive sink, one of those stainless steel jobbies." I could picture his set mouth. I could hear the lecture on the environment, on not polluting the lake.

"You didn't take out the wood stove, did you?" I asked.

"No, Jess. It's still there," he assured me.

"And did you put in a toilet?" Mom asked quickly.

"No, I didn't," he said. "You know how I feel about that." He hated toilets on principle.

"And you know how *I* feel about that."

"Why do you have to be so petty?"

"I don't think it's petty to care about how you spend your life. What you spend your life doing."

"You know damn well those things harm the environment."

"I'm not coming to live there, Pat."

"You are such a bitch!" he shouted. "You bitch, you slut, you whore!" I hung up. Dad rarely called Mom by her name; he usually called her "honey" or "sweetie." But whenever he was angry, he called her those other names.

We didn't hear from him for another month. The next time he called, I didn't pick up the extension. My mother listened and murmured something that I couldn't hear. When she hung up, she said in an odd tone of voice, "He's finished his studio up there."

"But he has such a nice one here!" I lamented. I wanted him to come back. I didn't want to live in Vermont any more than Mom did. I loved Barnes, I loved my friends, I loved Cambridge. I didn't want to move. If we lived in Vermont, Mom would have to drive me to and from school every day. I'd never see friends, if I even had any. But if Dad had built a studio there, he was serious.

A few years earlier, he had bought an old barn and had it transported to a meadow near the cabin. Now he'd dug a foundation for it and put in a new floor and electric heat. He'd broken through the walls to insert huge windows, one facing the lake and another facing the meadow. I remembered how dark the cabin was, tucked in the woods, and I pictured light streaming into the barn. In history we were reading a book about ancient Athens that said that the men spent their days in the bright agora, or light, open-sided public buildings, while the women were locked away in the house, running home factories, doing all the work. It gave me some insight into how Mom felt about being in Vermont.

About a month later, Dad came back to Cambridge again. Mom came home from work to find him and me sitting at the kitchen table. Dad had a whiskey and soda; I was drinking a cola. Mom stopped dead in the doorway and said in a flat voice that there were only leftovers for dinner and only enough for two. "What do you want to do for dinner, Pat?"

He looked at her lazily. "I can just have eggs. You know I don't care about food. You got any bacon?"

"No."

He shrugged. "You can make me a cheese omelet."

She came in and took off her coat and poured herself a drink. She put the scotch bottle beside the bottle of Canadian Club whiskey on the counter. That was a common sight. "Would it kill you to call and let me know you're coming?"

"What's the matter, you had other plans for tonight?"

Mom rarely went out at night except to political meetings. Dad knew that. She grimaced.

She made him an omelet and gave him the same salad we had, Boston lettuce, asparagus, and white beans. I liked all Mom's dinners, except eggplant parmesan. I hated eggplant in those days, and because of that, Mom hardly ever made it.

It got to be a custom: when he came home, they'd have one serious talk. They'd be in the kitchen. Mom would be cooking and Dad would sit on the kitchen counter over by the washing machine. He would have a drink in his hand, and he would say they had to have a talk. And she would say, "Ummm." Then Dad would say a wife's first duty was to her husband, in a pronouncement from on high. Mom would exclaim, "Whooa! Listen to the man! The ghost speaks!"

She was referring to his ancestor. Dad was related way back to the poet Coventry Patmore, author of *The Angel in the House*, whose thesis was that wives were created to make little heavens on earth for men in the home. I'd never read it and I'm not sure Dad had either. Dad's full name was Patmore Leighton. He used to tell me I had the right to join the Daughters of the American Revolution because his forebears had fought in the Revolution. When he said that, Mom would snarl that the DAR were a bunch of bigots too ignorant to let the great Marian Anderson sing. I didn't know what that fight was about, exactly, but I knew enough never to join the Daughters, whoever they were. Mom came from a Lithuanian family that had settled in Rhode Island; she still had some cousins in Providence. Her name was Andrea Paulauskas Leighton. Whenever Dad started quoting his ancestor, she would say that a woman's first duty is to herself, that she was a free being, not a possession. I'd disappear then: I couldn't stand those arguments. Dinner would be late that night.

They would have one long talk, and that was it. No matter how long Dad stayed, they'd never talk again and they'd both act mad afterward, walking around barely speaking to each other until he disappeared again. As the years passed, they grew more and more hostile, more fixed in their positions. I couldn't understand why they had stopped loving each other.

My mother was smart and my father was talented. He painted large, energetic squares of color, two or three to a canvas, cerise and gray and yellow, or blue and that same cerise, sometimes with a squiggle or two connecting them. For many years he didn't make any money from his artwork, and we lived on their Harvard salaries. Dad was an adjunct, and Mom just a teaching fellow, and the two combined made hardly any money. At the time I didn't know how hard up we were for money; we had the house Daddy had inherited from his great-uncle, and Mom could turn a cheap cut of meat into a feast.

But when I was eight or nine, Daddy was "discovered." An important art critic wrote about him, and after that galleries called and then articles and reviews proliferated. Museums and collectors bought his work. I was proud that he was famous.

One thing we never talked about, Sandy and me, that was sort of a secret bond between us, was our pride in our parents. It separated us from the others in our gang. Nobody talked about their parents—that would have been tacky. But Sandy often quoted things her father had said and I quoted my mother all the time. Bishop's father was famous too; he was a politico in Cambridge, he was deputy police commissioner or something and he knew the governor and Tip O'Neill. Bishop never quoted him though. Still, we knew he used to adore his father, who was a friendly, laughing man full of good humor even at home. Only these days, Bishop barely spoke to him because they disagreed about the war. His parents supported it: well, two of his brothers were in the service.

We knew little about the other kids' parents, and most of what we did know was bad. Like we knew that there was something weird about our friend Dolores's father and maybe her mother too. I had also met a guy named Steve Jackson, who went to Cambridge High and Latin. Once we met, Steve and I were together all the time: he would hang around Barnes waiting for me after school, or he'd call and tell me to wait for him after school at Cambridge High. Steve didn't like to talk about the fact that he didn't live with his parents. He only told me after a long time that his mother was dead, and he lived with an old woman he called his grandmother, who wasn't any relation at all. She kept him for money from the welfare people, he told my mother at dinner one night. She had three boys living in her apartment, sleeping in bunk beds in one room. Once a week she cooked a huge pot of spaghetti, leaving it on the stove for them to help themselves, all week long. After hearing that, my mother invited Steve for dinner every time she laid eyes on him.

Actually Steve's father was alive, but living with a new wife and a couple of new kids. When Steve was a freshman in high school, he used to spy on his dad. He'd stand in a doorway across the street from his apartment on Mass Ave and just watch. He loved to see his dad come breezing out, brilliant white shirt tucked into tight black jeans, hair in a huge Afro, jingling change in his pocket. He always headed for the T. Finally, Steve got up the nerve to approach him. He crossed the street, walked right up to the man, and said, "I'm your son, Steven."

The man stopped, surveyed him with cold eyes. "So what," he said, and walked on.

Steve was even more terrified of him after that.

Sandy and Bishop were one center of our group. It was a big group, thirty or more kids, and we didn't always all hang out together. It was a huge, shape-changing cell with several nuclei. Sandy and Bishop were one nucleus—the intellectuals I guess. Before I met them, I was best friends with Phoebe.

Phoebe Marx's father, like Sandy's, was a professor at Harvard. My mother was a professor at Harvard too—or so I thought. I suspect that Phoebe knew even then that Mom was merely a lowly teaching fellow—there was always an edge of scorn on her face when I talked about my mother. Her father probably knew my mother's job title and told Phoebe. Throughout my sophomore year, I spent many of my afternoons with Phoebe in Cambridge.

Phoebe liked to shop—whether window-shopping or shoplifting, it was her favorite thing to do. My mother disapproved of magazines like *Vogue* and *Mademoiselle* and wouldn't give me money to buy them. So I stole them. I stole lipsticks and nail polish, although I never wore either, and stockings in their cellophane packages; ditto. We stole cigarettes, which we did use, constantly.

Everybody smoked in those days. My father always had a cigarette dangling from his lips when he painted and when he drank—his two favorite things to do. My mother had a cigarette going when she washed dishes; she smoked even in the bathtub. Phoebe's mother, who was a doctor, smoked constantly. She was Chinese and was pretty, dark-haired, and intense. She was a terrible cook. She said cooking wasn't built into the X chromosome. When she did cook, Phoebe said, she'd make things like lima bean casserole, or a tian, a tasteless pie of rice and eggs and zucchini. Usually they had TV dinners in little tin trays. I loved these— they were a treat for me: my mother wouldn't buy TV dinners; she disapproved of them. So I was thrilled when Phoebe's father asked me to stay for dinner with Phoebe when the Marxes were going out. Phoebe was adopted, which made her special. She said her parents had told her that most children are just *had*, but she was *chosen*, which meant they really loved her.

Phoebe's father was a doctor too, but not the medical kind. He took us out for dinner sometimes. He loved Chinese food, although he wasn't Chinese. There was a great Chinese restaurant in Cambridge in those days, Joyce Chen; we all loved the *moo shu* pork there, shredded pork and vegetables in a pancake. Mom and I couldn't afford to eat out. I didn't understand that either because people said my father sold his paintings for lots of money.

I didn't care about money in those days. I never wore anything but jeans and stole the few expensive things I wanted. But Phoebe loved money. She never had enough, despite her ten-dollar weekly allowance. Phoebe's and Sandy's fathers loved them, and I always felt a little pull of something I didn't want to feel when I saw the way their dads looked at them. My father was hardly ever around, and when he was, he and my mother squabbled. He was nice to me when he remembered I was there. When he hugged me, though, tears would come to his eyes.

Phoebe never showed interest in the boys in our gang, though she was very interested in sex. A couple of times, we went to the Friday night dances at the YMCA and picked up boys and went outside and made out. We did this a few times and it was fun, but once I stayed out later than usual, and my mother came looking for me in her car and couldn't find me; when I got home at four in the morning, she was wild with rage. When I told her where I'd been and what I was doing, she shrieked. She yelled that it was dangerous, that terrible things could happen to me. After that, I lied about where we were going and made sure to get home by one.

Phoebe was much more sophisticated than I was. I usually followed her lead; we did things I'd never think of and wouldn't have done without her. Phoebe and I were never caught in the act of shoplifting, but my mother did find out one day. I had just got home and was in my room emptying my big shoulder bag when there was a light knock on the door and it opened. Mom stood there, about to say something, when she faltered, having processed what she was looking at: me emptying my bag of stockings and bras I'd stolen a half hour before. Caught holding the bag, I thought ironically. Mom was speechless for a minute, then she strode over and took the packages I was holding in my hands and studied them: two sets of queen-size nylon stockings and a bra, 36D, all still wrapped in plastic. I wore a size 4 dress and a 32C bra. She surmised the rest.

She sank down on the bed. "Why, Jessamin?"

I stood there. I stared back at her, as hard as I could. I made my expression defiant. I concentrated on the fact that it was all her fault for not giving me more spending money.

"I wanted them!" I said loudly.

"No, you didn't," she said sadly. "That's the thing. That's really the thing. You're risking—do you know what could happen to you if you got caught? Cops grab you, pull you into the office. You know, cops treat kids like dirt. They might drag you down to the police station. You might even be prosecuted if the owners knew you, had spotted you before. You could be sent away to a juvenile detention center. You would hate the way the cops treated you; you'd hate the way the storekeeper spoke to you. You would really hate detention. You would hate your life. And you would have courted this, asked for it, your own self! For what? Queen-size hose and a huge bra? Things you can't wear, don't need? Why?"

I just stared at her. I tried to keep up the defiant look.

"Think about it," she urged, then got up and started out of the room. She turned back. "It would be good if you saw less of Phoebe."

"How did you know it was Phoebe?"

She moved her head, as if indicating something invisible at the windows. "It's obvious," she said.

I was amazed, but then I'd been amazed at my mother before. Little kids think their mothers have eyes in the back of their head, and I used to think my mother could see me wherever I was. I needed to get away from her.

I sank down on the bed and I thought about what she had said. It did seem stupid. Why was I doing it, anyway?

I think that may have been the moment when I made up my mind about something nameless but important, something I didn't so much think as feel. About how to live my life. I didn't know that at the time. I made up my mind not to steal anymore. Not that I'd ever let my mother know she'd influenced me.

I vowed hotly to see Phoebe all I wanted, but in fact I stopped wanting to see her so much. When she would sidle up to me and ask in that sneaky way of hers if I wanted to hang out, I'd say I couldn't that afternoon. After a few weeks she stopped asking, and by Christmas we barely spoke to each other.

That fall I got an after-school job rehanging clothes in an expensive dress shop on Brattle Street. I made twenty dollars a week, so I could afford to buy my magazines and cigarettes. I never stole again.

2 **Funny how deeply** those high school years are engraved on my memory. College is a flash; I barely remember the name of the first boy I made love with, and my twenties are only a blur. But the three years of senior high sprawl across my brain, taking up nearly all the room there is.

I do remember a time before that. I think it was happy; I remember summer days at the cabin, swimming in the lake, paddling with Daddy in the canoe. Sometimes Mom would invite my best friend of the moment to stay with us for a few weeks. I recall good times in Cambridge too, when there were visitors on a Sunday afternoon. Daddy was always nice when other people were around, and he would cook chicken or hamburgers on the grill, and Mom would make ratatouille or potato salad or macaroni and cheese, serving the food on paper plates on the patio or the porch. If they had company on a Saturday night, Mom would cook for two or three days and serve a fancy meal in the dining room with candles on the table and would let me help her.

They often invited Annette and Ted Fields, who lived in Newton, to visit. The Fields were as good looking as movie stars. Annette was tall, with a beautiful shape and curly golden red hair and creamy skin and big blue eyes; she looked like a dancer. Ted was tall too, with glossy black hair and brilliant blue eyes and very white skin. They were the most beautiful grown-ups I'd ever seen.

Their children—they had three, Lisa, Derek, and Marguerite—were not like them. Lisa was pale, with crooked teeth and close-set eyes. She was smart and athletic. She was younger than I was, but we played Ping-Pong together in our garage, or croquet, if Dad or Ted would set it up for us on the lawn.

But their next two children suffered from terrible problems. The Fields talked about it to Mom and Dad in low voices, saying they wouldn't dare to have another child. Derek, who was ten, never looked at anybody; he didn't speak and was deaf. He couldn't walk very well. They had a red wagon for him, with a back he could lean against. They would settle the wagon in a corner of a room with a complicated puzzle spread out on a board they had fitted across the wagon, and he would be happily absorbed for hours. He was brilliant; he could do the most impossible puzzles. Marguerite was even worse off. Her eyes did not work together, so she walked unsteadily, taking one direction, then another. She would work her way to where she wanted to go with amazing persistence, knocking things off tables trying to keep herself steady. When the Fields visited, Mom would put all the breakable things on the mantelpiece or in the hutch. At seven years old, Marguerite still had to be diapered and was fed in a high chair. Her speech was a kind of growling. Only Annette understood what these noises meant. When the Fields brought the younger children with them to visit, they tried to keep Marguerite in her high chair, but she would cry to get out. You could understand she was frustrated, and Annette would lift her out and try to keep her on her lap, but she would squirm loose. Annette would hand her to Ted, who would lean forward to take her, with such love that I couldn't get over it. They never seemed annoyed or impatient. Once in a while they hired a woman to watch the two younger children and came without them, but they had trouble finding anyone willing to stay with them.

These children could not have been more unlike their gorgeous, smart parents. Ted was an engineer and Annette had studied to be a librarian. Later on, she went back to school and got a degree so she could teach disabled children. Daddy really liked Annette; he paid a lot of attention to her. She liked him too, but she was so taken up by her kids that nothing else got her attention for very long. In those days, she would get this odd expression on her face when people talked to her, as if she were surprised at hearing a foreign language. When I mentioned this to Mom, she said, "Just imagine what her days are like. She's in a totally different world. You have to be kind to her no matter what she does."

Mom had a couple of friends she saw alone, among them Eve Goodman. Like Mom, Eve was studying for a PhD, Eve's in psychology. She was tall and thin with an oval face and long, straight hair. I loved to look at her, she was so lovely; she wore long beads and tight tops and hip-huggers with bell bottoms, when Mom was still wearing plain old jeans. She brought me presents once in a while, often books with beautiful, sophisticated pictures in them.

Eve lived with a psychiatrist in Boston. Mom said he was funny and loud and a little vulgar; Eve would quote him and make Mom laugh. She always whispered these jokes.

She and Mom spent hours analyzing people, including Eve herself, who had had a terrible childhood. I sat on the floor just outside the kitchen listening; I learned that her father had committed suicide when she was just three or four years old and that her family then acted as if her father had never existed. Then her mother had married a man who owned a gun and who hated Eve. It scared me just listening to the stories. As I lay in bed at night, I would imagine this man with a gun threatening me. I assured myself that

I would yell so loud he'd be scared of me. Sometimes I'd pretend I was Eve's sister, and I'd yell at the ogre and make him stop scaring Eve. By the time I was ten, I was wishing that the man was still alive, so I could find him and tell him how bad he was.

Mom had a friend she talked about for years, but whom I only saw once, when I was six or seven, named Kathy. I remember her because she brought a baby, and I was enchanted with the baby. She was pretty too, with freckles and a pug nose and curly brown hair and a giddy laugh. I remember her talking all day about Sean, I thought it was spelled Shawn of course, it was Shawn, Shawn, Shawn, and I wondered who he was and how he was so wonderful. Mom often mentioned Kathy, and a couple of times she went to visit her in South Boston. Something was wrong in Kathy's life, I didn't know what, and Mom worried about her and made a nasty mouth when she said Sean's name.

When I was seven or eight, Kathy fell down the stairs or something, Mom was vague about it, and was badly hurt. Mom raced to a hospital to see Kathy, but she died. Mom's eyes were red for days afterward. When she went to visit Eileen, Kathy's sister, she'd always take clothes or a cake, or something, for Kathy's children. I never heard what happened to Sean.

There were other friends who came and went; I don't remember them all. But I do remember that when I was about nine, some man came to visit, a very important man, from New York. Mom was nervous about him and asked Daddy to take off his paint-stained pants, but he wouldn't. The man went out to Dad's studio and stayed there a long time. Afterward, he had drinks with Mom and Dad in the living room.

The man talked about Daddy's work. Daddy got very quiet and after the man left, Mom cried and embraced Daddy, and Daddy got drunk. It was then that Daddy became famous. That man came back once or twice, and sometimes he brought other people with him. They never paid any attention to me.

After Daddy became famous, they didn't have people to dinner anymore. Daddy went to New York a lot without Mom. And then, when I was thirteen and got my period and Mom gave me a party, Dad got annoyed about it. Then he went to Vermont to live and there was no more "social life," as Mom called it, though she did still see Eve and the Fields and other friends.

I try to remember only the happy times. I was building my life, with my own friends, and I wanted to be happy. In high school I got closer to Sandy and Bishop and Dolores. I picture us in 1968, Sandy and Bishop and Dolores and me, tramping the Cambridge streets, our breath puffing out in front of us. The world is exploding around us: Martin Luther King Jr. is assassinated in April, and there is a presidential campaign. We're for Eugene McCarthy or George McGovern or Robert Kennedy, and people are teargassed on the streets of Chicago as they gather for the Democratic convention and lots of people say they will not vote for Hubert Humphrey because of that and people are pouring gasoline over themselves and setting themselves alight on city streets.

We are talking about the meaning of life. Bishop is saying life has no meaning at all, it simply is, that we are as transient as butterflies, hovering for our instant, and that God is breath, a warm breeze caressing our faces. While he says these things, he leaps over a hydrant, trips over a curb, flies into the air at the sight of a child with a balloon, puts his arms around Sandy's neck and smooths her hair, kisses my forehead, pats Dolores's arm (she hates to be hugged or kissed), pulls out a chocolate bar and passes it around.

Sandy says life has to have meaning, how could suffering be meaningless? She walks steadily, staring straight ahead, speaking in a low, calm voice. Sandy is always calm and sure. She talks about *The Brothers Karamazov*. She says, "Remember Ivan Karamazov and his scrapbook of clippings? He insisted suffering had to have a purpose, it had to make us better, or why would God have created it?"

She takes a bite of Bishop's chocolate bar and smiles. "Ummm," she murmurs, and we all smile. Sandy loves chocolate.

Dolores doesn't say anything. She looks at us with her large eyes that always seem to be on the edge of tears. She's our listener but I know she doesn't think there's a god at all. Neither do I.

I say that Ivan Karamazov goes crazy because he realizes that suffering has no purpose. I say that my mother says the only good thing about suffering is that it sometimes teaches people to care about each other, but that on the whole pain is bad for the soul and often teaches people to be unkind. Words explode out of me; everything comes out of me like a protest; my voice is too loud; I can hear that myself. I don't want to talk that way, but I can't help it. I say (and I know I sound angry saying it), Why did Sandy think a god created anything, life was too complex and multitudinous to come out of a single brain, it had to just evolve gradually, chemically, one system after another. And I say, When you think about all the horrible things that have happened in history, who'd want to worship a god who made things like that happen?

We think we are being brilliant. We feel profound; we feel that no one else on earth has ever had such discussions. We question whether we should write down our ideas, publish them in the school newspaper. But no one wants to bother doing it. I wonder if my daughter had discussions like that. When she was thirteen, she came home with a brand new volume of Kahlil Gibran, not knowing that I had an old one in the attic in the same box with one that belonged to my grandmother, that my mother found when she was thirteen or so, and took as her Bible.

It's amazing to me that babies are still born utterly helpless and ignorant. You would think that with all the other progress humans have made, there would be some change in infants too, that by now they would be born able to walk and feed themselves, and knowing how to use a computer. But every one of us still has to go through every one of the same damned steps, the same time-consuming, tedious progressions: learning to walk, to dance, and to march; to come to love Kahlil Gibran and to abandon him to the attic.

One day in November 1968, Sandy, Bishop, Dolores and I were walking around near Porter Square. Nixon had just won the election and the more radical kids were saying that this would cause a revolution. I didn't believe that. I thought nothing would change. It was freezing cold, the kind of day when your breath turns to fog, and we were broke. We longed to go someplace where we could get warm, but we didn't know where to go. We were miles from our homes. We passed an empty store. Bishop stopped. But he was always stopping short or leaping in the air and we paid no attention until he cried, "Hey!" and waved his arms in the air.

"I bet I could get us in there," he said, pointing.

It was an ordinary store, empty, its owner gone. It had once sold picture frames: the word *gallery* still fluttered on its torn awning.

"Let's walk around to the back. Saunter," Bishop ordered, "casually."

There was a parking lot behind the stores, and we cut through it to the back of the gallery. The door was secured by a hanging lock. Bishop reached into his backpack and fished out a hammer.

A hammer?

He looked around furtively, then slammed at the lock. After a couple of hits, it fell open. He removed the lock, opened the hasp, and tried the door. It opened. We crept in. It was dark and cobwebby inside, but somewhat warmer than outdoors. Bishop found the light switch, and the lights came on. We gazed around, awestruck.

Sandy said, "There's a deli down the block. I'll get a couple of coffees for us to share."

"I'll go with you."

When we returned, Dolores said wistfully, "I wish we had a place like this to hang out in."

"Why don't we just appropriate it?" Sandy asked.

"We could have a kind of club room," I suggested.

"Or an art gallery," Dolores offered. "It says *gallery* on the sign."

"We even have electricity! We could install a heater," Bishop said.

At school the next day, we spread the word. We brought brushes and soap and buckets and washed down the walls and windows; one kid brought some paint from his father's store and we painted the place white. Dolores hung artwork contributed by all of us. We stole candles from home, and cushions, and even a couple of rugs from our parents' attics. Dolores found—we don't know how—an electric heater. She brought in pillows and a blanket and began to sleep there. We noticed an improvement in her after that.

We had an opening shortly before Thanksgiving; we invited just about everybody in our class and some kids we knew from other classes. They had to bring drinks and food, and everyone did—soda or potato chips or Doritos or Twinkies; a few guys brought beer. After that, we had a place to go afternoons. We used it all that winter. I don't know who got the electric bills. One day, the landlord stumbled onto our arrangements when he was showing the space to a prospective renter, and that was the end of that. But by then it was spring, and warm.

One afternoon after Thanksgiving that year, my father showed up. When I came home from my after-school job at the dress shop, there he was, sitting at the kitchen table with the newspaper, drinking a whiskey and smoking.

"Hi, Jess," he said, hugging me with one arm when I went over to him.

"Hi, Daddy." I touched his face. "You growing a beard?"

He shrugged. "No. Not intentionally. Maybe. Who knows?"

I giggled. "You mean you've just been too lazy to shave."

"Got it in one." He smiled. "Where's your mother?"

"At work."

"She sure spends a lot of time at that place for someone who only teaches two courses."

"She has independent study too. Two students. They're writing senior theses. And she's doing research."

"*Research?* Research?" He asked sarcastically. "Who's that when he's at home, huh? What the hell do you mean, research?"

"She reads," I said.

"Why the fuck are you crying?"

"You're yelling at me."

"For Christ's sake, I am not! I just want to know what this exalted stuff is, research!"

I took a can of soda from the fridge and started out of the room.

"Jess!"

"Ask her!" I screamed. "Ask Mom!"

I let the door swing shut behind me. He pushed it open, hard, and followed me to the stairwell.

"So what does she have, twenty-two students?"

I hated that tone of voice. "I don't know," I said, as flatly as I could, climbing the stairs to my room. It was clear he had come to Cambridge to fight.

"Jessamin!" he barked.

I stopped.

"I'm sorry I yelled. I just want to know, what the hell is research?"

I sniffled. "She's reading books and articles, you know? She's writing a book."

"She's writing a book?"

"Yes."

"What does she know enough about to write a book on?"

"Emily Dickinson."

"Why the fuck are you still crying?"

"I can't stand your barking at me like this. Like you hate me. You're my father. You're supposed to love me."

He staggered backward so suddenly he knocked into a chair, which fell over. I started at the noise.

"Oh, Christ!" He walked up four steps and put his arms around me. I flinched; I thought he was going to hit me. But he patted me, hard. "I'm sorry. I'm not angry with you. I'm angry with your mother and taking it out on you. Sorry."

"Okay," I said faintly. I just wanted to go. He released me and I ran upstairs.

I guess it was understandable that my father was mad at my mother because she wouldn't live in Vermont with him. I thought it was odd too, us not living with him, but I liked living in Cambridge. Vermont was pretty, but the cabin was primitive, and there wasn't much to do up there. My mother said the only thing she could do in Vermont was work in a cheese store. My father would hold forth on what she should do, reciting his rules, but she would get the look of a bulldog on her face and say he was being macho.

That day, I hadn't got home until a little after five; Mom was usually home by then, but she was late. I was taking a nap and was woken by a roaring sound. I didn't want to hear it. I didn't want to see what was happening. I didn't want to know. But they were in the kitchen and I couldn't avoid hearing them. My father was shouting: "You're crazy if you think I'm going to keep on sending you money to spend on other guys!"

"What other guys, you idiot!" my mother yelled. Then she said—and I winced, hearing her; she had to know it was fatal— "Money is the only thing binding us now. You stop supporting your daughter, and there's nothing between us at all!"

There was dead silence. Then my father rumbled something threateningly and she yelled, "Go ahead! The amount you give me is laughable! You think two hundred dollars a month keeps Jess? Where do you live, in the 1950s? Her food alone costs more than that. You always used money as a weapon, you bastard!"

I could foresee ruination; we were going to be really poor. I knew what that meant, I saw how Steve and his friends lived.

My parents had lowered their voices. Then my father boomed, "I will!" and my heart stopped. I knew it was my life they were arguing over.

I darted down the stairs and into the kitchen and stood there glaring at them. Daddy was sitting at the kitchen table, flushed, and Mom was standing by the fridge, still in her coat. When she saw me, she took it off, and put the kettle on for tea.

"Hi, Jess," she said.

"If you're disposing of me, I have the right to a say," I burst out. I hated that they were discussing me like the loot from a robbery.

"How'd you like to live with me in Vermont?" Dad asked me, showing his teeth, in a kind of smile.

Mom looked at the floor.

I looked at both of them. "You don't mind ripping me in half, is that it?" I said bitterly.

They both looked abashed.

— 36 —

"You like Vermont," Dad urged.

"I like Cambridge better," I said. "And I like Barnes, and my friends. I've spent my whole life here. I don't want to move in my sophomore year!"

"If I say you're living in Vermont, you're living in Vermont!" he thundered. "I'm your father."

"I'll just run away," I said as coldly as I could.

Mom looked at me, a long look. Did I imagine the hint of a smile on her face?

My father burst out crying. Oh, God.

I went to him, putting my arms around him. My mother turned her head away.

He kept crying. I remembered him crying on other nights, when he was drunk, and gradually I pulled away from him.

"Are we going to eat tonight?" I asked my mother.

"Good idea," she said, moving away from the fridge door, where she had been leaning. "Food," she sighed. She opened the refrigerator and pulled out stuff. She had made a ton of meatballs the other night, and we were having them with spaghetti and a salad of Boston lettuce and avocado with thin slices of parmesan on top. While she and I cooked, my father went into the living room and threw himself on the couch. When I went to call him to dinner, I found him sound asleep. He seemed dazed during dinner, not saying a word; afterward he went to bed—in my mother's bed. I knew she'd end up sleeping in her study. She and I cleaned up the kitchen.

"He can't make me go to Vermont, can he?" I asked her.

"He may have the legal right to order you. I'm not sure. He would if we got divorced and he fought for custody in court and won—which he might because he has a lot of money and I have none. I can't even afford a lawyer. But you're almost sixteen, for God's sake. He couldn't force you to stay there. On the other hand, how could you live if he doesn't support you?"

"I don't want to go! I want to stay with my friends!" I almost screamed.

"I don't think it will come to that. He loves you. He doesn't want to make you unhappy. He's just pissed tonight. You know how he is when he's drinking. He's a tender creature, basically. Still, I think I'd better look for a job."

"You *have* a job."

"I mean a real job."

"Your job isn't real?"

"Honey, I'm part time. I get slave wages."

"Tell the department head you need a full-time job."

"He can't do anything. Harvard doesn't hire women in full-time, tenure-track positions."

"But you *went* to Harvard!"

"Yes, but even letting us in was a concession. You read about what the president said, complaining that the war has left them with 'the lame, the halt, and the women?'"

I didn't know what she was talking about.

I was more disappointed in her than I could say. I felt it was her fault. She had let me down.

That evening, I hated both my parents.

3 **My father stayed on**, and for a while we were a family again. I prayed we would stay that way. I closed my eyes tight and wished really hard that he would stay and not go back to Vermont, but also stop getting angry all the time. I don't know who was supposed to be listening to the wishes and I don't know why I wanted him to stay, with the way things were. He didn't stop getting mad, and he didn't even work in his studio; he sat in the kitchen every day, drinking. By the time I got home from my job at the dress shop, he was pretty sloshed. Mom took to working in her office until six every night, which really pissed me off. I felt like she was dumping him on me. I got home a little after five, and I didn't like arriving there before she did, because he didn't care whether he blasted Mom or me. Either of us would do; since I had started my period, we seemed to be the same person in his mind.

It was just before my menstruation party that Dad first talked to me in a nasty way. I was thirteen, almost fourteen; many of my friends had had their periods, and I was beginning to worry. But it finally came and Mom said I was a woman now and we had to have a party to celebrate. Dad didn't like the idea, and it was a strange party: Mom invited *her* friends, not mine, as if her friends were good fairies come to shower gifts. And they all did bring me presents, really nice ones, beautiful books and a leather three-ring binder and a gold locket and a fountain pen. Mom even had a cake made. I was mortified at the idea, thinking it would say "Happy Menstruation!" or "Congratulations for Falling off the Roof!" But it just said "Good Luck, Jess." Dad went out for the whole day and never said anything to me. And soon after that he left. So what was I supposed to think?

Now, every night he would be sitting in the kitchen, reading the newspaper, ready to jump down my throat as soon as I walked in the door. Whatever I did was wrong. And he smelled of booze and slurred his words and was disgusting. After he passed out one night after dinner, I gave my mother an ultimatum.

"I can't take this anymore. Daddy's always yelling at me for something, he's always sloshed, and he's mean. I'm going to stay at Sandy's for a while."

I'd already asked Sandy. She never even asked why. "I have twin beds," she said. "My parents love you. Come for a while."

But my mother looked stricken. "Oh, honey, I'm so sorry. What can I do to make things better?"

"You could come home a little earlier," I said indignantly.

"I'll do that. I didn't know. . . . I'll get home by five every night. Promise."

I considered asking her to be a little nicer to him, but didn't know whether this would hurt her feelings. I felt so sorry for my father, I don't know why exactly—he seemed so . . . hurt. I didn't know how to fix him, but I was sure my mother did. In the end, I just blurted it out. "You could be nicer to him, you know."

"Well, he could be nicer to me too," she said angrily. I closed my eyes in despair. She turned away from me. "I'll try," she mumbled.

"I feel like he's dying," I said.

She shrugged. "Jess, our relationship is dying. It hurts. We were crazy about each other once."

"Does it hurt you?" I asked incredulously. She sure didn't act as though it did.

But her eyes filled up. If they loved each other, what were they fighting about?

"If I were nicer to him, he'd think we still had a chance. But we don't. Too much has happened."

"What has happened?"

She grimaced. "Oh, you wouldn't understand."

"Maybe I would."

She lit a cigarette. "I'll come home earlier, Jess. Will that help?"

"I hope so. It's going to be an awful Christmas if he's like this."

"I'll have a talk with him. Tomorrow. Before I leave, before he starts drinking. I'll tell him how upset you are."

"Don't put it all on me!"

"He has to see he's distressing you. He's distressing me too, but he wants to do that. I can't believe he wants to distress you, though."

"Okay. But Christmas is a week from Sunday. Are we going to celebrate it?"

She stared at me. For the first time, I saw how pale and strained her face was. I never thought my mother could be hurt. She had seemed impervious, impermeable, invulnerable.

"We *should* do something, shouldn't we? Invite people." She named some of her friends. "Okay? Want to invite Sandy and Bishop?"

I began to feel a little better. My father didn't act up in front of other people. It was against his code of manners. I'd already bought Mom and Dad their Christmas presents, and I'd bought a Hanukkah present for Sandy. I got a little thing, a toy car, for Bishop, as a joke Christmas gift, something small, because I was afraid he wouldn't think to get me anything and I didn't want to make him feel bad. It was nice having a little money, and working near the Square, near the Harvard Coop and all the other stores. I smiled. "Okay," I said.

My mother must have spoken to my father, because he wasn't drunk when I got home the next day; he wasn't even there. He came in at about six, crowing about the Monets in the Museum of Fine Arts. My parents had dragged me to museums when I was little, back when they did things together, so I knew the museum and those Monets. He was full of enthusiasm, but it seemed to be an act. It didn't feel real. At least he wasn't drunk—although the first thing he did when he walked into the house was pour a whiskey on the rocks. The next day, he went to the Isabella Gardner Museum, and then came home in a rage about the way things were organized there. The day after that, he went to the Fogg Museum and raved about the Rembrandts. I began to wonder if he had really gone to these museums, or if he was spending his days in a bar on Mass Ave.

Mom did get home every day before me, and cooked dinner, just like the old days. Every afternoon, I found her standing there, smiling, in an apron, which was how I liked her most: safely tucked away in motherhood. I have to laugh at myself, looking back. Now I'm the one in the apron. We had delicious meals, and they slept in the same bed at night, and there were no quarrels that I heard. But the house was full of tension, and at times I wished I'd gone to Sandy's after all. But I felt I'd made a bargain with Mom. She'd looked so hurt at the thought I'd leave.

How had my powerful parents turned into these hurt birds? I didn't like it; it made me feel like a big bad wolf.

Christmas was nice, though. The Wednesday before Christmas Day, Dad brought home a tree, and the two of us decorated it, the way we used to when I was little. For Christmas dinner, Mom cooked a ham and roast beef and made scalloped potatoes, which I love, and lots of vegetables and everybody brought dessert.

Mom had invited Sandy's family—her parents, her two sisters, and her brother—although the Lipkins didn't celebrate

Christmas. Only Sandy and her parents and her sister Naomi came—Naomi was twelve and cute—since her other sister and brother were in grad school. I liked them all a lot. The whole family was tall; the four of them looked funny getting out of their car, a Volvo, like clowns in the circus, one giant after another getting out of this little car.

My parents had invited Annette and Ted Fields also. The Lipkins and the Fields didn't really mix, but being mannerly, they didn't collide either, so the afternoon was filled with little fits and starts of conversation that dribbled off into nothing, as if they kept trying but failed to find one song they could sing together. Of course they would have had something to talk about if the Fields had told the Lipkins about their disabled children, Derek and Marguerite, but they didn't. Or maybe if the Lipkins had told the Fields about how bad they felt about Israel being militaristic, but they didn't either. Or if anybody had brought up Vietnam, but everybody stayed away from that. Ted and Dr. Lipkin talked about music, about composers I'd never heard of who lived before Bach; Annette and Mrs. Lipkin talked about volunteer work, which Mrs. Lipkin did a lot of, and Annette would have liked to do but couldn't. Mom and Mrs. Lipkin talked about books, because Mrs. Lipkin read a lot. So did Dr. Lipkin, but the books he read no one else in the room had ever heard of, on physics and astronomy and mathematics.

The meal was delicious, and everybody brought a little gift for Mom or me; and Mom had small gifts for all the young people, and the grown-ups drank wine and got mellower, and at the end of the afternoon the atmosphere was convivial. Thank goodness, because Dad had had enough wine that his manners were beginning to slip. All it would take would be if some man looked at Mom the wrong way.

Bishop didn't come; he spent Christmas with his family. He had invited me the night before to Christmas Eve mass. The Connollys and five of their seven sons all went, with a few guests, including Sandy and me. We took up a whole pew in the church. Mr. Connolly was a big burly man with white hair and a red face. He was much older than my father: Bishop's sister, Maggie, was thirty-one and married and had four children of her own. Bishop's two oldest brothers were in Vietnam; Michael was in his first year at Holy Cross, and Bishop and the others ranged down from him. The Connollys were nice, but you couldn't tell what they thought about anything. Mrs. Connolly was constantly worried about something and asking one of the kids if this or that had been done. You could see she had been pretty once, but she now looked worn down.

The church was decorated with statues and embroidered linens and flowers everywhere. It had stained-glass windows and it was beautiful. I'd never been to a mass before. It was pretty long and you had to stay alert to know when to stand up or kneel or sit down. Afterward, we went back to Bishop's house and there was cocoa with whipped cream, then a huge feast, spread out on the dining-room table. A lot of the people who had been at the mass came to the house afterward; it was a big party. There were two maids and a man in a black suit to serve drinks, and there were two Christmas trees, one really tall one in the front parlor and a smaller one in the back parlor, both elaborately decorated. After the midnight supper, the grown-ups stood around drinking, and Sandy had to go home. Her father came for her. Bishop took me up to his parents' room—they had their own living room upstairs, connected to their bedroom, and they had their own television up there, Bishop said, to avoid the arguments the boys always got into over the other two, one in the living room and one in the rec room in the basement. Before Bishop, I'd never known anybody with three television sets. Bishop's older brother had gone out with friends and the younger ones had gone to bed, so we sat up there and he gave me a Christmas present, a little silver bracelet; it was really beautiful, and I was so embarrassed because all I had for him was that stupid toy car. But he loved it, or he said he did, and hugged me. I kissed him and told him I loved him, and he said he loved me too.

It was a great Christmas, except for the fact that I was dreading what was going to happen when it was over. But then it *was* over. Time is so strange; events approach so slowly and go by so quickly. After Christmas, Dad went back to Vermont and our lives settled down again.

4 **I don't know when** I realized there was another war going on, right here in our own country. I should have known the year John Kennedy was killed, because Medgar Evers was murdered that same year, and white people bombed a church in Birmingham, killing four little girls at Sunday school. I should have remembered how upset Mom got when Malcolm X was killed in 1965. But I didn't read newspapers, not even after Martin Luther King Jr. was killed in 1968. It wasn't until Steve explained it all to me that I saw it—all of a sudden, in one glimpse. It all made perfect sense to me then. I'd been seeing it without noticing all my life. I was fifteen by then, old enough to know how white people treated black people. I'd often thought that if I were black, I would be mad as hell at white people. I was pretty mad anyway. I just didn't realize it was a full-fledged war.

Steve went to public school, but through me he became part of our group—well, sort of. Sandy and Bishop really liked him, but there were kids in my school who didn't want to hang out with him. I didn't care about them. Neither did Steve—he had plenty of friends of his own.

We didn't do much. We hung out, we smoked weed, we talked a lot. We shared books and music, and we went to parties, all over the place. Steve had friends everywhere. He had to support himself and soon after New Year's, in 1969, he got a job in

Monaghan's, a little store on Bow Street that sold cigarettes, newspapers, magazines and, it was rumored, drugs. Maybe because of the drugs, he didn't want me to visit him there. He said cops watched the place and it wouldn't be good for me to be associated with it. I worked afternoons myself now, so the only time I could hang out with my friends—unless we cut school— was on weekends. I hardly saw Phoebe anymore. Every time we got together she wanted to shoplift or shop; I didn't want to steal and I couldn't afford to shop all the time, and it got tired. I wondered why she had to shop so much. She didn't need more clothes, I thought; her closets were bursting. So I started to hang out mainly with Steve or with Sandy, Bishop, and Dolores. After we started the gallery, kids showed up there afternoons and weekends, wandering in at odd times. Most of the time, the air mattress in the corner had sheets and blankets folded neatly on it, a sign that Dolores was hiding out there again. Poor Dolores. We just didn't know what to do to help her. We didn't even know what was wrong.

One rainy Saturday Steve and I were alone there. We were sitting against the wall, drinking Coke and smoking and listening to music, when Steve said, "Want to try something weird?"

"Sure."

He pulled a little plastic bag with something brown in it out of his pocket.

"It looks like chopped-up mushrooms," I said.

"That's what it is. Magical mushrooms." He grinned. "Take a handful. Eat them." He washed them down with Coke. I imitated him, chewing the tasteless things.

"Now just wait." He fiddled with his big portable radio until he found a station playing the Beatles. You could always find one eventually: the Beatles were constantly on. They were playing "Strawberry Fields Forever."

We sat close to each other, our legs jiggling in time to the music, letting the mushrooms settle in. After a little while, I could see the strawberry fields. I was wandering in sunlight, delighted at the tiny red berries nestled in the deep green leaves all around me. All my pores were open to the sun, and I was a cauldron of fire.

"I am fire and air!" I cried. "I have immortal longings in me!"

We were reading *Antony and Cleopatra* in junior English.

"I am open to the universe!" I cried. Steve tried to hush me. He hugged me lightly, told me to calm down.

But I pulled away from him and ran outside. I was burning up. I threw open my coat; I put my face up to the rain and tried to drink it. It was amazing how hard it was to get the drops to fall in your mouth.

"Jess! Jessamin! Stop!" Steve urged from the door. "Suppose a cop sees you!"

I stopped. That remark had penetrated my haze. I turned to him proudly. "I am open to everything!" I announced, holding my wrists out in front of me for the cuffs.

"You idiot." He laughed and grabbed me. He pulled me back inside and sat me down and sat next to me and kept stroking my forehead and uttering calming words, for a long time.

He said, "No more mushrooms for you," but after that I clamored to try everything Steve came up with. One time Bishop had some pills—God knows what they were—and I took them; I scrawled for hours in my notebook, poem after poem bubbling up into my head. Sometimes a whole group of us would take something together, and we'd compare visions. Everything looked so weird with the pills, it felt as if you were seeing the very bones of life, the skeleton under the surface. The trees looked like fingers drawn by Van Gogh; my own hand was a continent filled with ships and land and bodies of water. We would lie around in the gallery, everybody offering his or her picture. We were full of love for each other; we were adored babies in the laps of the gods.

Over that winter and spring, we regularly experimented—that's how we thought about it, as experimenting; we saw ourselves as Timothy Leary and Aldous Huxley. We took mescaline and acid, pills that made you soar. Some people took downers, just to see what they were like; I didn't. We always smoked pot when we had it, and we almost always had it. It was easier to get than alcohol, which stores weren't supposed to sell us, though some kids could get it. Bishop could always get beer and even whiskey from one of his older brothers' friends or even his sister's husband. He could take it out of the family liquor cabinet if he wanted. His family—well, the men in it (and it was mostly men)—believed in drinking. It was the best part of life for them.

But most of us preferred drugs. And until the cops kicked us out of the gallery, what a time we had! We'd lie around on the floor in states of benign passivity. We were experimenting with altered moods, and our experiments made us broader, more tolerant, more generous people. That was what it meant to be part of the new generation; we were each a *love child*.

We thought that we were a miracle generation born to create a new way of seeing and feeling, a different morality. We had the sense that for generations, for eons, maybe, people had thought war was a great thing, killing was heroic, and domination noble. But we knew that killing was awful, domination miserable for dominated and dominator, and war a horror. We were against the Vietnam War, yes, but also all war, all violence, and racism. We were convinced that if the people of the world took drugs instead of alcohol, and preferred peace to war, violence would disappear in a haze of well-being. It filled me with terror to think of Bishop or Steve or any of my friends having to go to the jungles of Vietnam with a gun, to kill or be killed. What mattered was connection: getting in touch with your feelings and with other people, seeing the beauty in other people, loving them. Relatedness. We were fond of quoting E. M. Forster: "Only connect." We were incredulous that anyone on earth would deny the truth of our ideas. We spoke in wonder of people who did, the over-thirty or over-forty generation. We couldn't grasp their mentality. I couldn't comprehend the men in the government, Robert McNamara, say, but I also knew that not everybody over thirty agreed with them. My mother was over thirty, but she thought war was used by elites to maintain their power over the rest of us. My father supported the war, but not because he thought war was wonderful. He thought it was inevitable. He bragged about Leightons fighting in all this country's wars—he felt they had sacrificed themselves. But I didn't see him signing up for Vietnam, and Mom said he hadn't wanted to fight in Korea either. Sandy's parents didn't support the war, but Bishop's did. They didn't change their minds even after their second-oldest son was killed in Vietnam.

A lot of people didn't like our ideas. When I look back on those days, I see how naive we were, how simpleminded. People today talk about the sixties as a crazy time; they say we were foolish, deluded, a wasted, drugged-out generation of losers. But our experiments with drugs were part of our sensibility, one aspect of our enlightenment. We were open to discovering our inner being, instead of driving drunk or fighting each other with fists, or metaphorically killing each other on the floor of the stock exchange. We tried on altered states of being, and the truth is, my friends were a sweet bunch of kids who mostly turned into a sweet bunch of adults. We really were the beginning of the brave new world. If you tell that to anybody today, they smirk. But I say it's true.

Of course, some of us got lost along the way.

Steve and I often cut school. One day that spring he came over to Barnes and found me in the hall on my way to French class.

He asked if I wanted to cut. I nodded and we darted out a side door just before the bell rang. He'd promised to hang out with his friend Jeffrey, so we walked back to Cambridge High and Latin to get him. Steve would go into the school at the period break to find Jeffrey. We stood across the street having a smoke on the sidewalk while we waited for the period bell. We were in front of the house of some lady who didn't like us (she'd chased us away before), when we saw a squad of police with riot shields and helmets charging down the street. We looked at each other: were they coming for us? Had the lady called the police on us like she'd said she would? And they were coming for us with riot shields? We started to walk quickly, trying not to look like we were running, toward town. But even after we were a hundred yards from the lady's house, the police kept running in our direction, batons in their right hands, shields in their left. They looked absolutely terrifying, like robot medieval knights. We finally stopped dead on the sidewalk, but they went on running past us and into the school. They disappeared, and after a little while kids came running out, white faced. Some were crying. No one we asked seemed to know what was going on. We didn't see Jeffrey.

Steve said, "Let's go get my car. Then we can take off if we need to." He had earned enough at his job at Monaghan's to buy himself a red-and-white Chevy, a couple of years old but shiny and nice.

We ran toward Bow Street. The car was parked in the lot behind Monaghan's. We got in Steve's car and crouched down in the backseat. We were both panting from running and were very thirsty. Steve jumped out and went in the back door of Monaghan's and came out with some bottles of water and a little bag of weed. We sat on the floor of the backseat and gulped water, then Steve rolled a joint. He licked three little skins, and pressed their edges together to make a big one, then laid the dried-dung-looking tobacco leaves into a crease, spreading it out along the paper. Dexterously, he curled the paper up into a cylinder, slid in a tiny piece of cardboard, and twisted the end of the paper. He lit it and passed it to me. I inhaled deeply. Oh, it was good.

While he worked, Steve joked about the owner of Monaghan's, Varashimi Agni, who had two daughters named Jolly and Jett. Steve was doubled over laughing about Jolly and Jett, and I was laughing too and told him I knew someone who had a sister named Brie. I said maybe when I grew up and had a daughter I'd call her Cheddar.

He said, "Or Jarlsberg!"

And I said, "Or Bleu!"

He exploded: he had a friend named Blue! At this point, we were both laughing so hard we had to pee, and he ran into Monaghan's again, then I did. I knew we were both laughing off our nervousness from seeing the cops. A vision had flashed through my mind of being arrested by those robots in plastic helmets, booked, lined up against a wall, shot. For a moment, it had seemed possible.

We had another joint and calmed down, and then we started to make out, and I, well, we'd made out before, and I loved Steve, I really loved him, but before that day I hadn't felt quite so, well, something was new, something was squirming inside me, it was like the time I ate the mushroom, I was painfully open, hungrily open, and I let him touch me and I touched him and he came in my hand. He'd never done that before, and I was kind of overwhelmed, it was a little disgusting, I didn't know it'd be like that. I cried out and sat up. And he turned away and wiped himself off and said he was sorry but he couldn't help it. I kissed him and tried to pretend I didn't mind, but I felt a little sick.

I went home after that. Mom was home although it was only a little after four and she was surprised that I had skipped work. I didn't tell her I'd also skipped French and math. The minute she laid eyes on me, she could tell something was wrong, so I told her about the cops. I said I didn't feel well.

She looked at me with concern and felt my forehead, and I had this idea she was smelling my breath. I could still taste the pot in my mouth and wondered if she could smell it, but she didn't say anything. She told me to lie down and she'd bring me some tea. In a little while, I drifted off to sleep. But after that, I thought she acted just a little bit odd. Something was bothering her. I could tell by the set of her neck. And a few days after that, she told me she thought I should spend the summer with Dad. She had decided this all on her own. She asked Dad to get me a job and he called a couple of nights later to say I could be a waitress at some bistro there a friend of his owned, and together he and Mom hustled me up there, giving me no say whatever about it. I was livid.

I admit it was heading to be a lonely summer anyway. Sandy was going to the summer camp she'd gone to for years in Maine, this year as a paid counselor. Bishop was going to the dude ranch in Nevada that his uncle owned, also to work for pay. The only kids who would be around over the summer were Dolores, and probably Steve. Steve was going to be working full time but he'd be around nights and I could see him on weekends. I didn't want to go to Vermont and protested vociferously. It did me no good. Mom was determined to get rid of me. Steve thought she knew what we'd done in the car—I think he thought I told her—and that she wanted to separate us. I didn't see how she could know about that, but then I didn't see how she could know about the drugs, either. That she knew something seemed clear.

Or maybe Dad had been right all these years and she did have a lover and wanted to get me out of the way. The idea had crossed my mind before. Or maybe it was because she was trying to find a new job. Ever since Daddy left after Christmas, I'd been hearing her phone her friends to ask if they knew of anything. She had made up a résumé and had it photocopied in the Square and sent it to a hundred colleges. She did most of this in her cubicle in Holyoke Center, where she kept an electric typewriter, so Daddy wouldn't know what she was doing—we never knew when he might appear, and whenever he was home, he searched her desk and trash basket. He wasn't the least bit embarrassed to do this, even if I saw him. I'd told her about it. He'd always done it, even before he left.

Mom did find a job, late in June, right before I was to leave for Vermont. She was hired at Moseley in Boston, luckily, starting in the fall. The night they called to offer her the job, we were in the kitchen together, preparing vegetables. She dried her hands and took the phone. She didn't say much, and when she hung up, she stood there for a while, as though thinking deeply. Then she said, "I got a job, Jess."

"Great! Where?"

"Right here," she was almost crying. "In Boston. Moseley."

"Terrific!" I meant it.

She took off her apron. She poured a scotch. She sat down at the table. "Sit with me, Jess."

I put down the leek I'd been about to slice.

"You know I wanted to get a full-time job, a tenure-track job, so I could earn enough to support us."

I knew.

"I'm going to be paid thirteen thousand dollars," she said. "We can live on that."

"Great."

"That means I can divorce Daddy."

"No!" I cried.

She sat there in silence as I bent forward, crying. My heart was broken.

"I'm really sorry, honey."

"It will kill him. Do you have to? Do you have to?"

"It won't kill him. And I do have to. You know why. His constant rage . . . It makes me hate him. And living with someone you hate is unhealthy. It makes me hate myself. It's bad for my health. And it's bad for you. And I want a happy life. I'm thirty-eight years old. I still have a chance for a happy life."

"It will kill him!"

"No, it won't. He'll think it will, but it won't. He'll find someone else to rage at fast enough."

"I won't ever see him!" My voice rose.

"We'll try to fix it so you do," she said.

But I was inconsolable, and she had to finish making dinner all by herself. I went up to my room and lay on my bed. In the end, I came down. I was hungry, and we were having veal chops with a puree invented by Alice Waters, a great chef in California, of leeks, potatoes, celeriac, and white turnips, something I really love. And stewed tomatoes.

She made the divorce another reason for me to go up to Vermont. She said I should be with Dad while I could. He didn't know she was intending to divorce him. I sure wasn't going to tell him: I didn't want to pay for her sins. Not only did she make me go, she sent me up there by *bus*.

As it happened, that summer in Vermont wasn't so bad. Dad was easier when Mom wasn't around. He stayed out in his studio from about ten in the morning until eight or nine at night. His housekeeper would carry out a sandwich and a beer and some cookies around one in the afternoon, and she left food on the stove when she left in the afternoons at about three, when her kids finished school. He was supposed to heat the food up for his dinner, but he never did; he ate it lukewarm, right out of the pot. But at least food was available. I heated it up when I came in from work, and always thought of Steve. It wasn't spaghetti like his grandma's, it wasn't bad, and maybe it was even good, but heated-over food is never delicious, and I was used to delicious food.

Dad would come in around nine, pour a stiff drink, and sit down. He'd just sit there, staring into space for a while, drinking fast, pouring drink after drink. After a while, his soul would come back into his eyes, and he'd get up and grab a pot and a fork and sink into a kitchen chair and eat. He'd slice off a hunk of meat and eat it with his fingers. He ate this way when he was alone—he thought I didn't know. When I was in the room, he used a knife and fork. Whether he finished something or not, he left the pot on the stove. Unless I happened to go in and see the leftover food and wrap it in foil and put it in the fridge, it would get so dried out that the housekeeper, Mrs. Thacker, would have to throw it out the next day. I thought about my mother's horror of waste and shuddered, but I knew it was useless to say anything to my father. He was in another world. Like Mrs. Blake said about Mr. Blake, he was always in paradise. Only I felt my father wasn't in paradise but maybe hell. It made me feel so bad for him. Like being an artist was some terrible doom.

After he ate, he'd pour a fresh drink. I'd hear the ice cubes tinkling in the glass when he came into the living room, and I'd look up from my book or the TV and say, "Hi, Dad," and he'd say, "Hi, Jess," and sink into his armchair and after a while he'd fall asleep. I'd wake him before I went to bed and tell him to go to bed. He either did or he didn't. I couldn't stand the way he lived, but he didn't give me a hard time. He always spoke gently to me, always seemed a little surprised that I was there.

Working at the café, which I had dreaded, was fun. It drew college kids from New York who spent summers in Vermont. I made some friends and became pals with a girl called Gail, who lived in Manhattan and went to Brearley. She came in every day for a cappuccino. She smoked pot right out in public. She reminded me of Phoebe a little. When we met after work, we usually shared a joint or two, and often I just stayed at the café, hanging out with Gail and some other kids. There was nothing else to do there.

Mom called me every week. At first I wouldn't talk to her; I was so mad at her for sending me up there. But after a while I relented; I knew she missed me and was sad without me. I never told Dad she'd got a job, or said anything about her wanting a divorce. Some things you just didn't mention to my father; it would be like lighting dynamite. At the end of August, she called to say that she was flying to Mexico in a few days to get a divorce. I asked if Dad knew and she said no. I didn't understand how she could get a divorce without his knowing, and she said he'd signed a power of attorney. She said that when he had been home at Christmas, he'd been in a rational state of mind for a few days and she could talk to him about their separation without his having a tantrum. She even got him to go with her to see a lawyer; she'd borrowed five hundred dollars to pay him. The lawyer called Dad and asked him to come into the office to sign a separation agreement, and Dad did. But judging from how he acted later, he must never have believed Mom would go through with it.

Dad was always a paradox: he regularly blew up at her or me, shrieking absolutely hateful things in tantrums that lasted whole weekends, but when she would mention divorce, he would laugh. He would say how happy they were together and that he never loved anybody but her. He constantly suspected her of infidelity, but even when he was in a rage, he assumed she was utterly bound to him and would not leave him, no matter how horribly he behaved. At the meeting with the lawyer, he promised to give Mom generous child support. She and the lawyer urged Dad to get his own lawyer; he refused. He signed the papers and stormed out of the office.

Mom knew he'd never pay the child support. That was why she knew she had to get a better job before she left. I was happy

I had a job, so I could buy my own clothes and not ask Mom to do that, knowing how thin she was stretched. It's odd to think of money being love. Someone told me that Freud said money was shit, but that's crazy. It's love, doled out or withheld. It made me wonder how my father felt about me that he wouldn't send Mom enough money to even feed me, as though I was the one who had divorced him.

At the end of August, my mother flew down to El Paso and crossed the border in a van to get a Mexican divorce. The night before, she called my father from Texas to tell him what she was doing. I was asleep when the phone rang, which it did a few times before I was able to pull myself out of sleep; I went to the top of the stairs, preparing to run down and pick it up. Dad must have been sleeping in his chair; he answered the phone and quickly exploded in curses, calling Mom horrible names. I ran back to my bed. He stayed awhile on the phone; I couldn't believe Mom would remain on the line to be called those names. Then I heard loud noises. Dad was clattering and clanking around, throwing things, it sounded like. Suddenly he appeared at the top of the stairs.

"Did you know about this?"

I sat upright in bed. "What?"

"Shit!" he cried, and stomped back down the stairs.

The next morning, as I got ready to go to work, he threw some things in a bag and tore out of the house, yelling at me not to burn it down. He got in his truck and drove away, fast. When I was sure he was gone, I called Mom to see if she knew what had happened. But there was no answer. I tried to think of who else I could call, who else might know. I called Annette Fields, but she wasn't home.

The next evening as I was sitting down at the table to eat the dinner Mrs. Thacker had left, my father burst in through the back door.

He took one look at me and shouted, "Did she tell you?"

"What?" I asked, hating the tremor in my voice.

"The *divorce*, bitch!" he screamed.

Bitch?

He stomped past me and went to the pantry and opened a fresh bottle of Canadian Club, poured himself a glass, and sank down at the table.

"She divorced you?" I asked timorously.

"She tried," he muttered. "But I fixed her."

I waited. I didn't dare ask. But he couldn't contain himself.

"She thinks I'm a dummy. She thinks she can use my power of attorney. But I sent a telegram to Mexico, revoking it. Hah!"

"How did you know where to send it? How did you know the address?"

"Americans get divorced in Juarez," he said. "They stay in El Paso and cross the border in a van. That's the cheapo way to do it. That's what she'd do. I know your mother. Oh, yes! I called the court there."

"So what does that mean?"

"Means she thinks she's divorced, but she isn't!" he grinned. "And then I met her at Logan and told her so! Fixed her wagon. That bitch!"

"You met her at Logan? How did you know what flight she'd be on?"

"There's only one flight a day from El Paso to Logan. Had to be on it." He smiled that sick grin again and poured whiskey down his throat.

I hadn't realized my father was that resourceful. I always thought of him as an innocent, an artist with his head in the clouds, who just couldn't help being inadequate in daily life. That was why he drank; everybody knew artists and writers drank because making art was so hard. Jackson Pollock and William Faulkner and Ernest Hemingway and Scott Fitzgerald—you didn't expect them to be able to deal with daily life, fixing a faucet or mowing the lawn. But Daddy could work with his hands—he built all his studios.

"What did she do?"

"Nothing," he shrugged, "what could she do? It's a fait accompli!" He smiled again.

Somehow I couldn't picture my mother standing there silent for this. Not that I wasn't dismayed that she'd divorced my dad. Why did she have to do that? And why did she have to do it while I was living with him?

"She must have done something," I insisted.

"Bitch," he swore.

"Are you calling *me* a bitch?"

"You act just like her sometimes."

That did it. I stood up.

"What's the matter with you?" he cried.

I didn't know myself. I ran up to my room and packed my stuff in my duffel bag, then counted my money. I'd been saving my wages over the summer, and with tips and no expenses for living, I'd accumulated a few hundred dollars. I'd never had that much money in my possession before, and it made me feel strong. Since my friends and I looked down on materialism, I knew I'd have to think about this, but later, not now. At least I was sure I had enough for a bus ticket to Cambridge. When I got downstairs, the kitchen was empty. My father had disappeared, along with the bottle of Canadian Club. Either he'd gone out to the studio or was in bed. I refused to look for him, refused to ask him to drive me into town, not after the way he'd spoken to me. And I was too angry to leave him a note. Let him worry. If he even noticed I was gone.

I walked to the road and hitched into town. I had to sit in the bus station for a couple of hours, but I had a paperback of Doris Lessing's *The Golden Notebook* with me. It was near midnight when I got home; Mom was sitting in the kitchen over a drink. I groaned, but she wasn't drunk. She looked ravaged. We hugged each other. We didn't talk at all. I wanted to yell at her for what she'd done, but she looked too wasted. It would have to wait.

The next day, she looked okay. We were both home, neither of us had work to go to. So we dawdled in the way we both liked to in the morning. I liked to drink coffee and sprawl on the old armchair we kept in the kitchen and read. I was loving *The Golden Notebook*. Mom liked to make coffee and read her newspapers— the *New York Times* and the *Boston Globe*. It took her hours to get going in the morning.

So we were lolling there in the kitchen, reading, and I decided to plunge in.

"Dad was very upset yesterday."

She looked up. "I hope he didn't take it out on you."

"Of course he did. You knew he would!"

She put her newspaper down and looked at me. "I'm sorry, Jess."

"Yeah. He said he met you at Logan."

She grimaced. "Yes."

"What did you do?"

She shrugged. "It was so stupid. He said . . ." She sighed and stopped. "I don't know how to explain . . ."

"I know what he said. He told me."

"Oh. Well, it was so stupid. The chances are his telegram didn't go to the right place, and in Mexico . . . Things are so confused there anyway . . . There's little chance that he did actually cancel the power of attorney. Anyway, I think I am really divorced. I have papers. . . . But even if I'm not, it doesn't matter. I mean, he understands that we're not together anymore, not husband and wife anymore. That's all that matters to me. That we are legally divorced matters only if one of us wanted to marry again, and I won't, I wouldn't put myself in that situation again, *ever*. For me, marriage was too horrible. But not for him; he'll marry again. So if he did mess things up, it's himself he messed up, not me. I told him that. He'll be the bigamist, not me."

She lit a cigarette and breathed in deeply, then glanced at my mug. "More coffee?" She stood and went to the stove and poured a mug for herself. I held mine out and she filled it.

"What makes you think Dad will marry again?"

"He was happy being married; he wasn't unhappy being married to me."

"But you were?" I couldn't help sounding a little accusing.

"Of course. You know what his tantrums were like. He went into such rages . . . even before he started drinking so much. I was thinking about divorce long before he went to Vermont. His living up there probably kept the marriage alive for a few more years."

"How can you be sure you won't marry again?"

She smiled. "I'm sure, honey. Very sure."

She was right, Dad did marry again, twice. A few years after he married for the third time, he died, at fifty-nine, from lung cancer. And Mom was right about herself, too. She never married again. She had a recurring dream, she told me—long afterward, when I was in my forties—that she had somehow married Daddy again. She would discover this and cry out in grief and rage, "How could I do that? I was free of him, how could I let myself marry him again?" In the dream, she was frustrated to tears that she had blown her chance at freedom. I like to think that if she had lived long enough, she would have got over her fear of marriage and let herself have a companion again, but she died at sixty-two, also of cancer.

The whole event—Mom sending me up to Vermont and then secretly getting a divorce, my father's dreary way of life and the way he acted toward me at the end—all of it did something to me. It didn't turn me against my parents, exactly, but it changed where I stood in regard to them, as if a giant hand had picked me up and set me down again at a different place on the globe, farther away from my family, my friends, my country. I began to see them as if they were not my parents, but just people. It felt disloyal. But it also gave me a sense of *freedom*. They weren't me, I wasn't bound by them, I wasn't like them and didn't want to be.

Mostly, it made me decide that no matter what, I wouldn't live like them. I would be careful whom I married and I would do whatever I had to do to have a happy marriage. I would never drink too much. I would live *right*.

5 **Over that summer**, my friends seemed to change, too. They were more distant. Or maybe I was the distant one. But it shook me up that when I told them that my parents had divorced, they just murmured sympathetically, as if it wasn't a disaster. I'll bet they'd think it was if it happened to them, I thought. They probably just didn't know what to say, but it felt as though they didn't care. The truth is, I was not unique. All of a sudden, everybody was getting divorced. It was a tidal wave. I'd never heard of *anyone* getting divorced before, except my mother's friend Alyssa, who acted as if her divorce was a major tragedy and whispered about it.

Nobody was really interested in my problems. Just after the term started, there were massive demonstrations across the country against the war; everybody was up in arms about it. Nixon had made a peace offer, but those of us who were against the war thought he wasn't serious. People seemed to be getting more and more angry and were blaming us for all the problems. It seemed like the four of us—Sandy, Dolores, Bishop and I— symbolized everything the conservatives hated. We all had long hair. Almost everybody in our school had long hair. And wherever we went, into the little stores that lined Mass Ave or the shops on the side streets, storekeepers and cops and shoppers practically hissed at us, especially Bishop. They railed at him as if his hair was *their* business. Even the portly ladies in hats and gloves who never raised their voices would make nasty cracks about our dirty jeans, our dirty hair. It was as though the country was at war, not with the North Vietnamese, but with long-haired kids.

One day we were sitting together on a bench facing the Charles River, just smoking and watching people crossing the bridge and talking about the war. It was warm out, even though it was December, and I was wearing sandals, and when I wiggled my feet, my shoes fell off. A huge cop came storming over—luckily we weren't smoking pot—and commanded me to put my shoes on immediately. Sandy glared at him, asking, "Is it against the law not to have shoes on?" But he didn't even let her finish. He boomed, "It's a law that you be covered up, yes, smart-ass, now shut your mouth or I'll arrest you!" She was so shocked, she shut up. The four of us looked at each other and just got up and walked to my house. We didn't feel safe outside.

In any case, we were getting older and had to start thinking seriously about ourselves. For years, we'd discussed questions like infinity versus finity and what was outside the universe, if anything, and the existence of god and the nature of evil, but we'd never thought about what we'd do day to day for the rest of our lives. We assumed that would take care of itself, and suddenly it came to us that it would not.

Most of the boys I knew were scared. They were nervous even talking about their alternatives, because they weren't sure what was legal and what wasn't. They thought they could get arrested just for talking about getting out of the draft, and they were unsure about the rights and wrongs of doing that. Was it morally acceptable to go to college to escape the draft, or to Canada? Was it unpatriotic? Was it all right to drop out, or cut off a finger or a toe, or claim to be a conscientious objector? Did you have to enlist and kill Vietnamese to be a good American? Because, of course, however defiant people sounded, everybody really wanted to do the right thing, to be patriotic. But how could it be right to kill people for no reason at all? People felt they would be cowardly if they tried to escape the draft, and they didn't want to be cowardly, but they also didn't want to go to a place they had no reason to go to, to kill people who hadn't done anything to them—innocent people, babies, grandmas, hardworking farmers. And a lot of the boys knew they'd be killed there. Had they been born and loved by their parents and fed and taught and grown up healthy and strong just to be killed in a war over nothing?

Going to Canada seemed almost as bad as going to war. They'd have to leave their families, their friends, their neighborhoods behind, they might never see them again. They'd have to live in a place where they knew no one, getting whatever low-paid job they could find without training or legitimacy, and without being sure they'd ever be able to come home again.

Dropping out was the worst. They'd have to run away, like criminals, and live furtively until the war was over, and maybe they wouldn't be able to come home even then but have to live marginal lives, on the streets. These were middle-class boys, they slept in comfortable beds with clean sheets and ate three good meals every day and had no useful knowledge of how to survive in the great big dark world outside.

A few boys bragged that they were going to enlist, maybe hoping we'd admire their courage. But when they announced this, their voices sounded hollow. They weren't sure whether enlisting made them heroes or villains in the eyes of other kids. In my crowd, it made them villains. We hated war, and we turned away from them. Looking back now, I see that for us it was a matter of class. Those boys who thought they were doing the right thing by enlisting were the ones who were sacrificed. They went, and they hated what they did and learned to hate themselves. An awful lot of them got hooked on dope; some couldn't live with the terrible things they'd been taught to do. They came back ruined people with ruined lives. And for what? To bolster the egos of a few people in Washington who were sorry later on anyway.

People edged into wildness. Everybody was ready to explode. In New York, the great writer Grace Paley spent six days in jail for sitting down in front of a police horse. Middle-class people were sent to jail for counseling young men about the draft; young men were jailed for burning draft cards.

At Barnes, kids protested the curriculum, saying it was irrelevant. They wouldn't have dreamed of doing that a couple of years earlier, not even in advanced junior English, when we spent the whole damn term working through a long list of works, from *Beowulf* to *The Waste Land*. Talk about irrelevance. Kids showed up for class high or stoned. I was not the only one who cut classes.

I experimented with alternate states more rarely. I had decided that my mother had smelled the marijuana on me and that was why she had sent me to Vermont. I was afraid to ask her about it, but one day I finally did: "Mom, why did you send me to Dad's last summer?" I asked.

And she, who always said she was honest with me, mumbled that she thought I'd enjoy it, I always loved Vermont in the summer, and she wanted me to be closer to Dad.

So I didn't know any more than I knew before, and I was afraid she'd send me up there again. And after the way Daddy had acted toward me, I didn't want to go there now. I felt like he hated me. So I began to be careful; whenever I smoked weed, I made sure to eat something or suck on a mint afterward, and I took uppers only when I knew I'd be out for the whole night. I still hung out with Sandy and Bishop—I still loved them—but everything that was going on, especially the divorce, put me into a different stance toward what I'd known and done before. It was as if a shadow now intervened between the old and the new me, saying, Wait! You don't have to be this, or do that. It isn't what you want to be, it's only one alternative. Not that I knew what I did want to be.

Mom was now working full time. She taught three courses, had three independent studies, was on committees, and held office hours. But she was home by six most nights, and she always cooked dinner, and afterward she'd say, "Finish your homework, honey, before you watch TV," and I would, or at least I fiddled with my books, so there was some kind of order in our lives.

I'd quit my job at the dress shop when I went to Vermont. When I came back, I got a job at Sonny's, a restaurant on Mass Ave. I now had experience waitressing. I worked weekday afternoons from 3:30 to 5:30 and eight to two on Saturdays. Sonny paid me practically nothing—fifty cents per hour—but I still made more money waiting tables than at the dress shop, because of the tips. Waiting tables is hard work and demeaning, but I always felt avenged when I took home a hundred dollars or more at the end of the week.

Mom was having a pretty lonely time. People didn't invite divorced women to dinners or parties. Annette and Ted Fields were still her friends, but they never entertained and nowadays never visited. The children had grown too big and heavy to travel with. Mom saw Eve Goodman a lot until late fall, when Eve's lover, Daniel LaMariana, was diagnosed with ALS. Mom said it was an absolutely terrible disease; it would waste his body away in just a few years. After the diagnosis, Eve decided to marry him. Mom cried when she heard that. She said Eve would never have time for her again, because she would have to spend all her time with Daniel. He would deteriorate quickly, to the point where Eve would have to do everything for him. I wondered why Eve would want to marry someone who was about to become a vegetable.

"She wants to make him feel safe," Mom said, "to make him

feel loved." She said Eve would get swallowed up in taking care of him, but that was her choice because she was self-sacrificing, a saint. The way she said it, I thought Mom wouldn't want to be a saint herself.

She said her friend Alyssa was a saint too; she said lots of women were—too many. These days she hardly ever saw Alyssa, who was too tired from sitting in the hospital all day with her son Tim, who had leukemia. Mom said Tim might *die*. I couldn't picture a kid dying.

In the summer and fall, Mom sometimes went to doctors' offices or labs with Alyssa, to sit with her while Tim had one test or another. And sometimes she picked up groceries or went to the bank for Alyssa, but after Christmas, Tim went to Sloan-Kettering in New York for treatment. Alyssa moved to New York and lived with her sister in her big apartment on Central Park West. After that, Mom and Alyssa only spoke on the phone every couple of weeks.

I wondered whether my mother's friends just had bad luck, or whether she chose people with some kind of fatal flaw. I believed that some people were immune to such sorrowful things, that there were people whose lives went easily, happily, all the time. I was sure there had to be people like that, and I wanted to be one of them. I felt that my friends and I might be. I knew that Dolores wasn't, but I thought Sandy and Bishop were. I made a secret decision to be a lucky person for the rest of my life.

Mom specialized in nineteenth- and early twentieth-century American literature; she taught seminars on Wallace Stevens and William Carlos Williams. She was researching a book on Emily Dickinson, but they wouldn't let her give a seminar on Dickinson: she was "not important enough." Mom was outraged. She considered Dickinson the greatest American poet ever, but there was nothing she could do except keep urging her department to allow it. It took them until 1980 to change their minds, but she won eventually. In 1975, she got them to let her offer a course on women writers of her period—Edith Wharton, Ellen Glasgow, Willa Cather, Kate Chopin, and others. She had always offered a lecture course on the men of that period—Theodore Dreiser, Sinclair Lewis, Upton Sinclair, William Dean Howells—and she would sneak some Cather and Glasgow in. I read all the books Mom taught. I liked them all; I even liked Dreiser, whose books, like Thomas Hardy's, I found long and depressing. Both seemed to feel that human beings didn't have a chance, that God, the odds, the environment, sexual desire, or something else had stacked things hopelessly against them. Still, bits of truth glittered in them, and I liked reading about the way things had been in times past. Some of those writers I loved, among them Willa Cather. She was so clean and open, and she loved the land. I felt that she and E. M. Forster were poets of topography; the way he loved the landscape of England, she was thrilled by every clod of earth, every reed and thistle, every stream and hill in the United States. It was exhilarating to read them. But most of all I adored Emily Dickinson. When I read Dickinson, I felt that I was being hit with one truth after another by a soft little voice using shimmering language.

One afternoon in October, a Tuesday, my period was really heavy and I was in a lot of pain. Midol wasn't helping that day, and I went home from school to lie down, skipping French. I figured I'd call the restaurant from home, say I was sick.

I was not only sick, I was also upset. I'd seen Steve the afternoon before, in the fifteen minutes between the end of school and the start of my shift at Sonny's. His car was parked behind the restaurant, and we did some heavy petting in the backseat. I hate rushing things like that, but my body—it acted the way it had the day we'd seen the armed police—something was different inside me. I responded to him in a way that scared me. So I thought superstitiously, in a way typical of a person who was ignorant of sex, that these menstrual pains were punishment for this new fervor. I knew I was edging close to something major. I *wanted*. I felt that my inside was a gaping abyss starving to be filled. The feeling terrified me, and despite my "liberated" upbringing, I felt sinful, bad.

I unlocked my front door with a heavy heart and then was shocked to hear strange sounds in the house. My heart stopped. Mom wasn't supposed to be home yet. Who was there? A burglar? Maybe Daddy had come home. His car would be back in the driveway, by the garage, and I wouldn't see it from the front door. I peered into the living room. There was my mother on the couch with a man I'd never seen before. She was naked, straddling him where he sat on the couch, and he was moaning.

I flew up to my room and curled up in a fetal position on my bed, aching physically and mentally. A while later, Mom knocked on my door and came in, her clothes askew. She put out her hand. "Honey," she said, "come out."

I walked out, attached to her hand.

"I'm sorry to shock you, Jess. But come and meet Philo."

The man was sitting on the couch, his clothes in place. His face was flushed.

"Jess, this is Philo Milovič. Philo, this is my daughter, Jess."

We said hello, both mortified. I examined him furtively. He was pale, with dark hair and the most beautiful face I'd ever seen on a man, better looking than even Ted. And he was very young, in his twenties, much younger than my mother. Closer to my age.

That night, Mom asked Philo to stay for dinner. She made crêpes stuffed with chicken and mushrooms, one of my favorites. I felt better after a nap, and I chopped shallots while she made sauce. With it we had rice and a sliced tomato from a local farm, the only kind Mom would buy. There were still a few late ones left. Philo set the table, then sat in the kitchen with us, sipping a scotch and talking to Mom about Moseley gossip and asking me about Barnes. It felt nice, like a family. Mom had a drink too, and she was sipping it, not gulping it down the way she did around Dad. We talked, laughed. The kitchen television set was on low, broadcasting the evening news. It was like I used to think a family could be, but ours never was.

I wondered how long they'd known each other. I kept remembering my father's suspicions. My imagination leapt back to when Dad was home last year, when Mom didn't get home until after six day after day, and acted so . . . I don't know . . . strange. I couldn't help wondering if she'd known Philo then. But I decided finally that I didn't want to know. She was entitled to some happiness. And in truth, Philo acted as though he didn't know Mom all that well. He was nice; he didn't try to act like my father, but behaved more like a brother. And I'd always wanted a brother.

Philo went home that night, but came back again on Saturday. He had dinner with us; Mom made a blanquette de veau, one of her specialties. Dinner was so nice and the talk so interesting that I was not enthusiastic about going out, but Sandy, Bishop, and I were going to the movies. When I got home at one in the morning, the house was dark. I peered around the corner and saw that Philo's car, a maroon Buick convertible, was still in the driveway. My heart skipped a beat.

The next morning, I awoke before they did. I prepared the ingredients for omelets—boiled ham, leftover boiled potatoes, Swiss cheese, basil, parsley, and chives. They still weren't up, so I made breakfast menus. I used Mom's gray typing paper; I folded it in half and tore it against a ruler so the edges were frayed, then, using my most elegant calligraphic script, I wrote out a menu for each of them, decorating the edges with floral designs. I listed things in an attractive way:

Orange or Tomato Juice

Omelets: ham and cheese, fines herbes, ham, onion, potato

Soft rolls, rye or white toast (found in the freezer)

Butter, Jam

Coffee, Tea

When I got tired of waiting, I made coffee, hoping the aroma would wake them up. Mom came down about ten-thirty, and when she saw what I'd done, I thought she was going to cry. Philo came down laughing about not having a toothbrush and having to use his fingers to brush his teeth, and that was the end of her teariness. You could tell he was young, his spirits were so high. It was nice, having company. They both said they wanted everything in their omelets, and everybody ate every scrap and talked and laughed the whole while.

It was the happiest I'd been for a long time.

Then Mom said we should go to Walden Pond and take a walk. We started out with Mom walking with Philo and me sort of hanging behind them; then Philo dropped back and told me to walk with Mom for a while, so I did. On the way back, Mom called to us to go ahead; she wanted to look at some shrub. Philo and I started off. Philo talked to me like a friend. He asked me what classes I was taking and what I was reading, and I told him about Doris Lessing. He'd never read her, but he seemed interested. He taught seventeenth-century literature—Sir Thomas Browne, Robert Burton, Robert Herrick, and Francis Bacon. I had never heard of any of them. I knew John Milton and Andrew Marvell: in English I'd read one of Marvell's poems, "To His Coy Mistress." I'd loved it so I remembered some of it and quoted it to Philo: "Had we but world enough, and time, / This coyness, lady, were no crime" and "But at my back I always hear / Time's winged chariot hurrying near." Philo was very impressed that I remembered that much.

Philo recited another poem by Marvell he said I might like. It was long, and he didn't recite all of it, but one stanza really struck me:

> Meanwhile the Mind, from pleasure less,
> Withdraws into its happiness:
> The mind, that ocean where each kind
> Does straight its own resemblance find;
> Yet it creates, transcending these,
> Far other Worlds, and other seas;
> Annihilating all that's made
> To a green thought in a green shade.

That really knocked me out. A green thought in a green shade. That was great, just like where we were in the woods, where the very light turned green from the leaves above us. And the sugar maples had turned dark, in a spiral, a corkscrew of gold and red that colored the air copper. I loved Philo for introducing me to that poem.

He talked more about Marvell and Milton and Herrick and other poets, and pretty soon I was feeling stupid. And he stopped talking suddenly, and asked me which authors I liked.

"Emily Dickinson and Virginia Woolf," I responded.

"Virginia Woolf!" He was surprised. He said he'd never read her. I was shocked that anyone hadn't read Virginia Woolf; I felt a huge relief. He couldn't think I was stupid if he hadn't read Virginia Woolf! He didn't even seem to know how great she was!

It was a beautiful day. Almost, but not yet "bare ruined choirs." I remembered Mom quoting from Shakespeare's sonnet years before when Dad and she and I took a walk through Walden, Dad grimacing and making some joke about her showing off. She got tears in her eyes. I had been angry with Dad for that. I loved it when my mother recited poems. And that sonnet had seemed so right to me. "Bare ruined choirs, where late the sweet birds sang" in the almost leafless woods.

That night I asked Mom how she'd met Philo. She said he was an adjunct at Boston University, finishing up his doctorate there, writing on Marvell. She had met him at a Harvard party given by a teaching fellow she knew.

"When?" I asked, hating myself.

"Oh . . ." She was vague. "A month or so ago." I let it go. I didn't want to pin her down and make her lie to me. So what if she hadn't been faithful to my father? Still, I knew I'd never do that. Never.

"How come you paid for dinner tonight?" I asked. "Isn't the man supposed to pay? You never paid when Daddy took us out."

"Daddy has money now," she said. "When we first knew each other, he was broke. I paid for things all the time. Before you were born, I supported us. And Philo doesn't earn much."

"He has a nice car," I retorted. "Nicer than yours."

"Yes," she agreed with some surprise. "I imagine his family bought it for him." She thought, then said, "What do you mean, nicer than mine? Mine's a Volvo."

I laughed. "A hundred-year-old Volvo."

"Oh. I guess it is." She didn't pay attention to things like that.

The next time Philo came over—he visited most Saturday nights—he brought me a tiny book of Marvell's poems with a beautiful lavender cover, a book you could read holding in one hand. It was a facsimile, with the original spellings. I loved it, although some of the poems were in Latin, which I couldn't read. But I read the whole poem about the green thought in a green shade. I had a little trouble understanding it, but I clung to what

I did understand. And I found another poem I loved, called "The Definition of Love." It begins:

> My Love is of a birth as rare
> As 'tis for object strange and high:
> It was begotten by Despair
> Upon Impossibility.

That poem hit me hard, but I didn't know why. It wasn't as if I was in love with anybody in that way or could even imagine it, yet it felt familiar, something I'd always known. It felt *right*, as though maybe all love was like that. I memorized it and recited it to Mom, who smiled and said she'd always liked that poem too.

Sometimes Philo stayed the whole weekend, but some Sundays he went to his family's home for dinner. He was Croatian; his grandfather had got out of Yugoslavia after World War II. He disappeared into his family quite frequently. But we never met them. Funny.

Steve and I pulled back from each other after the day we petted in his car. I never could seek him out: either he waited for me outside Barnes or I didn't see him. I'd never thought about his inaccessibility until he stopped showing up. I suppose I could have looked for him at Cambridge High and Latin, but I had no idea which exit he used or what his schedule was. He'd long ago asked me not to call him at home; his grandmother was old and tired and didn't like answering the phone. And he never called me. Sometimes I thought he was afraid of Mom answering the phone, but I couldn't figure out why. She was always nice to him and always asked him to dinner when she saw him and listened to him when he talked and asked him questions. And Steve liked Mom, I could tell. But he thought she had sent me to Vermont to get me away from him, and no matter how nice she was to him, he believed that she didn't really want him in my life. I didn't think that was true, but maybe it was. And even if it wasn't, I didn't know how to get him to stop thinking it.

The thought of having sex, really doing it, made me nervous. Lots of kids were doing it, I knew. I could tell Dolores knew about sex, just from little things she would say, but I didn't know how she found out about it. Sandy and Bishop both seemed a little apprehensive about it. I was sixteen now, which was probably old enough to start having sex. I decided to talk to Sandy.

We were sitting in Bailey's, having a Coke, and I said, "My mother has a boyfriend."

She looked horrified. "Really? How is that?"

I shrugged. I didn't like the look on her face. As if she was disgusted with Mom. As if Mom was a terrible person compared with Sandy's proper, polite mother. "It's okay. He's nice."

"Really?" She lit a cigarette. "Doesn't it feel weird?"

"No," I said. I was annoyed with her. As if my mom was doing something . . . wrong. My mother was divorced. She was allowed to have a love life.

Sandy knew she'd stepped over the line. She exhaled smoke. "So, what is he like?"

"Very good looking. He's twenty-two. And he's very smart." I knew this would carry weight with her. "We had a long conversation about Andrew Marvell one day, and then he brought me a book of Marvell's poems."

"Oh!" She was impressed. "What does he do?"

"He's teaching at BU. He's getting his doctorate."

"Oh." I could tell by her tone exactly what she was thinking. I knew BU was not as classy as Berkeley, where her sister went, and certainly not in the same league as the Institute for Advanced Studies at Princeton, where her brother worked. But it was a university, not a garage. I mean, it had some cachet. And Sandy fought against her own snobbery the way I did. So she smiled and said, "It must be nice to have someone like that around." I wondered if she was thinking, "After your drunken father." But then I realized she didn't know Daddy drank. I'd never told her.

"How old is your Mom?" Sandy asked.

"Thirty-eight."

She raised her eyebrows. "He's closer to your age."

"Yes." I made my face look unconcerned.

"Is he cute?"

"Gorgeous."

"Your mother can pick 'em. Your father is a hunk too."

"You think so? He's a little flabby."

"No. He's really nice looking. And charming."

"Your father is too," I said.

She smiled. "Yeah, he's adorable, isn't he? Your mother is nice looking too. Of course, not as gorgeous as you. Nobody is as gorgeous as you."

Sandy always said that.

I liked hearing it but I never knew what to say. I didn't want to say, "Thank you," because that would sound as if I agreed. I didn't want to say, "No, I'm not," because that would sound coy. I lit a cigarette.

"I look like my father's great-grandaunt," I said.

"Wow! You can trace your family back that far?"

"My father's family, yes. We have pictures. And a genealogy book."

"Cool. We don't. We only have one picture of one grandfather—the one who survived the Nazis—and one aunt, and that was when they were old, after they got out. All the other pictures were lost."

Many members of Sandy's family had been lost in the Holocaust, and every time I thought about that, I felt tears welling. It had all happened before we were even born, but it was in our hearts when we sat around smoking and feeling bad; it grieved us, along with slavery in the United States and Hiroshima and the war in Vietnam, part of the pain that we carried everywhere we went.

Sandy saw me falling into the bleak mood that overcame me whenever I started to think about this, and she changed the subject.

"How's Steve?"

I shrugged. "I think he's given up on me."

"He wouldn't! He loves you!"

"Yeah, but maybe he's tired of waiting," I said miserably. "You know."

She gazed at me.

"He wants me to get birth control, but I can't seem to get it together."

"That means you're not ready for sex," she said with supreme assurance. "That's what my father says. The summer my sister was going to summer camp as a counselor, he asked her if she wanted birth control. And she said no. And he said that she probably wasn't ready for sex, and that was okay, not to worry. He said he was really proud of her for knowing you shouldn't do it when you're not ready. 'Because if you do it against your will, you are violating yourself,' he said. He says when you're ready, you'll know. She told me about it when I turned sixteen, after my birthday dinner. I thought he was amazing."

"But if she wanted it, it was okay to do it?"

"Yeah. He says ours is the first generation raised in sexual freedom. He says when he was young, sex was taboo for unmarried people, that it was considered dirty. He said that was one reason he became a psychoanalyst. He said they got over it, but he doesn't want us to have that happen to us."

"But how do you know when you're ready?"

"I'm not sure. He told Rhoda she would know, and I guess she did, because she and Roger definitely get it on now."

"How old is Rhoda now?"

"Twenty-four. She'll get her PhD in June. She finished her dissertation. It's on this really weird French guy called Derrida. It may even be published!"

We moved on to other things, but the subject of Philo really interested Sandy and she returned to him repeatedly. The next time I saw her, she asked about him. And the time after that too.

I was still distressed about Steve. I loved him, but I had these odd feelings about sex, with him or anybody else. I loved Bishop; his gangly body and disconnected air drew me like a magnet, but he didn't seem interested in sex and I wasn't sure I was either. In all the years I'd loved Bishop, he'd kissed me hello and good-bye plenty of times, but he never came on to me or to Sandy either. Although we were both in love with him, he was off limits. But if I'd found out that he had come on to Sandy, it would have broken my heart or corroded it with jealousy.

These confused sexual feelings lived like a nest of worms in my poor brain. They had me nearly sick sometimes; I didn't know what to do with myself. I was relieved when Steve wasn't around and I could spend Saturday nights or Sunday afternoons with Sandy, Bishop, and Dolores. Of course, it was getting so just hanging out and talking wasn't enough for the boys—they wanted something more. And they always knew how to get it. Steve always had dope, Bishop always had booze. Actually, Bishop always had dope too. We'd meet at the west gate of Harvard Yard and walk down to the Charles and sit on a bench and smoke and get mellow. We'd see guys sculling on the river, and masses of people walking across the bridge, and sometimes a sailboat would pass. I would think about a line from T. S. Eliot, and it made me mad at myself: "I had not thought death had undone so many." Why did I always think that, when these people were alive? We'd watch them until it got too cold to sit around outside.

Then we'd go to my house or gather in Bishop's basement. They had a pool table in their rec room and Bishop taught us how to play. We couldn't smoke dope there, but we could smoke cigarettes. We could have sodas or beer or even hard liquor if we wanted it, but we girls never drank. We didn't like it. Bishop's father was police commissioner and they had lots of money. His mother ordered cases of soda and had them delivered by the liquor store along with booze and wine and beer every week. I envied them, this big Catholic family, so easygoing, always joking around, just as I envied Sandy her cool, refined, sophisticated Jewish parents. Just goes to show you how crazy envy is. What did the Greeks say? Call no man happy until he's dead and you know the ending. Well, if you knew their endings, you wouldn't envy anybody. Ever.

6 **Toward the end** of my junior year, on May 1, 1970, the United States invaded Cambodia. I couldn't believe it. Here we were all marching and protesting, saying, End the war, and the government decides to extend it. A few days later, there was a huge demonstration, a peace march. My friends and I went; even some of our teachers went. My mother went with her friends. Not all her friends went—some taught at BU and BU's president was very conservative, not to say reactionary, and punished people who were antiwar by withholding raises, even though they were legally entitled to them. Some were too intimidated to show up, Mom said. But lots went anyway, like Philo and a history professor Mom knew from her antiwar group, who she said was really brilliant and a wonderful historian and had written a groundbreaking book, but he never got a raise the whole time he worked at BU, forty years or something. He was tenured, so the president couldn't fire him, but he punished him.

All along the route of the march there were men watching us. It made me nervous. Some of them seemed like FBI or CIA or DEA or whatever, with cameras, but some looked more like construction workers, and they were the ones I was afraid of. I imagined they might suddenly attack us. People's rage was so blatant that you could imagine extreme actions. And lots of people in the march were openly smoking pot. Smoking weed in those days was a badge of subversion. We walked until we reached the Common and then we spread out across the grass. We looked like millions of people, but everyone was peaceful, I wasn't scared at all when I looked around. I could smell the dope in the air. People stood up and gave speeches against the war—which was great. But the greatest thing was the *feeling*, the sense that we were together, thousands of people, fighting for tolerance and peace, an end to mass killing. We were a peace-loving crowd, the love children, here to uphold life and freedom not just in our own country but in Vietnam and Cambodia too. We were here to testify that life was not just a matter of competition for power and grabbing for money; that there were other ways to live, ways that made people happy, not miserable.

When it ended, we drifted away. It was an easy end, people sauntering across the bridges, down Commonwealth Avenue, up to the T. I ended up at Bishop's friend's house, a member of his church named Walter. His parents were in Europe. They had a big old house on Brattle Street, and we sat in the kitchen, smoking and eating stuff his mom had left for him in the freezer—hamburgers and hot dogs, canned beans and spaghetti. We discussed the war, well, some of us did, the ones who read the newspapers, like Sandy and Bishop and Walter, who knew what was happening. We were so mellow by the end of the day we were nearly paralyzed, but around nine I wandered home, where Mom and Philo were pretty mellow too. I thought all of life could be like this if people just let themselves love each other.

The good feelings from the peace march were still hanging in the air when the next thing happened, and that should have taught me the way life is, except I wasn't ready to learn it. It leaped out at us from television one night; we saw it just the way we'd seen Jack Ruby kill Lee Harvey Oswald, the way, years later, we'd see bombs exploding in Iraq and an airplane fly into the

World Trade Center and not know if we were seeing something real or a movie.

What we saw on TV was a college campus, with young, bloody bodies strewn across it. The government itself, the government of the state of Ohio, had sent soldiers to shoot these college students at Kent State, for protesting. Everyone was horrified: we were on the phone all evening and the next day. For days, no one talked about anything else. My friends and I kept thinking that those kids who were shot could have been us; Mom was thinking the same thing. It changed the minds of lots of people who before had not been against the war. The worst thing was that Kent State happened so soon after the peace march. Was this a foreshadowing of what was going to happen in the war? Would the government punish us for protesting the war by prolonging it? Or by shooting more of us?

Yet ordinary life continued, as it always does. I love that poem "Musée des Beaux Arts" by W. H. Auden about the Breughel painting of Icarus. The painter shows Icarus in the sky falling, far off in the distance, while in the foreground a peasant pushes a plow through the dark soil. He's sweaty and tired, paying no attention at all to the tiny figure falling behind him, and Auden says they were right, the old masters, because they knew that life goes on as always, no matter how terrible events may be. When my generation of ordinary kids weren't worrying about the draft, they just worried about getting into college and which college to choose. At the time, it seemed a world-shaking choice and many of us planned to spend the summer taking car trips with our parents to various schools. The serious world was inching closer to us, and we felt it with excitement and cold dread, an open door leading, we hoped, to heaven; we feared, to hell. We were also taking exams that would brand us for what felt then like the rest of our lives; we were about to be put in categories we might never be able to alter.

I was applying to Simmons, in Boston, so I went over there on the T and looked around. It was a nice place, and I started to get excited, but Mom thought it would be good for me to go away from home, and I liked that idea too. On the one hand, staying home would allow me more freedom, because some colleges still made girls obey strict rules—no smoking in the dorm, no drinking, getting in by ten at night and midnight on weekends. I hated rules in general, but I was willing to obey them if everybody else had to. What annoyed me was that *boys* didn't, only girls. Did the people in charge think that girls were too simpleminded to be in charge of themselves? On the other hand, if I stayed in Cambridge with all my friends gone, I'd feel forsaken. The idea of going away was exciting. Mom's college would pay half my tuition and Dad said he'd pay the rest, so I didn't have to worry about money, like Dolores and Steve.

Dolores's father didn't want her to go to college. He wanted her to stay home and get a job to help out and take care of the house because her mother was kind of broken down and didn't do much housework. But Dolores rebelled and said she'd run away if he didn't let her go to college, and so finally he said he'd pay tuition, but nothing else. So she had to go locally. UMass in Boston was the cheapest place because it was a state school; and it was pretty good too. She cried at the thought of going to college on the T, but her grades had fallen so precipitously in the past two years that she was lucky to get in there. She used to be one of the smart kids. As it turned out, she didn't go to college for very long. But that's another story.

Sandy's father drove her to Smith, Bryn Mawr, and Vassar, and she loved them all, but she finally decided on Smith, where Rhoda had gone. Bishop visited Wesleyan, Amherst, and Yale; I knew all along he'd choose Yale. And Steve got into Harvard.

He had been hanging around outside Barnes one day when I came out. I thought maybe he missed me after all. When I saw him at the side door we always used, my heart jumped a little. He must have still loved me a little or he wouldn't have been there. And I was embarrassed too. I felt I'd let him down . . .

I had to work that afternoon, but I invited him for dinner and he said he would come. It turned out we were having pasta that night. Mom would never have planned pasta if she'd known Steve was coming, and she apologized as I set the table. "It's what I have," she said, "What can I do?"

"He'll like it, Mom," I said. She simmered tomatoes with garlic and added fresh basil leaves at the end; her sauce always tasted fresh. And we had veal chops with it and a wonderful salad with avocado and red onion. Steve ate with gusto, saying the spaghetti was delicious, nothing like his grandmother's. Then he wiped his mouth with his napkin and put down his fork and said, "Mrs. Leighton, I got into Harvard."

"That's great, Steve!" she cried.

"Yeah," he said. "I got in because I'm black."

"What do you mean?"

"I get C's. I got in because I'm black." He said this as though he was throwing it at her.

She was almost angry. "Don't knock it, Steve," she said. "You may not think it's fair, but it's an attempt to make up for hundreds of years of a different kind of unfairness. You should have more respect for yourself and for Harvard: you're very bright, and somebody at Harvard saw that. Lots of the kids that get in, kids whose fathers went to Harvard and boys from rich families, like the Kennedys, don't have great grades either."

"And Kennedy cheated."

"Maybe."

"You really think that?"

"What, that he cheated?"

"No. That someone there thought I was smart?"

"Of course!" she nearly exploded. "You think every black kid who applies gets in?"

Steve thought about that for a while. "I guess not."

"You're letting the arguments of resentful white people determine your values. Don't let them define you. Make the most of your chance!" she urged.

Steve nodded. I wasn't sure he understood her argument. I wasn't sure I did. But there was something in Steve, something hard and stubborn that wouldn't let him feel good about himself. I tried to build him up all the time; when we first met, I was sure that I could improve his confidence. But I knew better now.

Mom and I had gone on the college tour in June after my junior year. We visited Vassar and Mount Holyoke and UMass at Amherst, but the place I loved was Andrews, a small college in northern Vermont known for its arts programs and liberal dorm regulations. The campus was small and pretty, dotted with birch, pine, maple, and oak trees, and the dorms were coed! They were really ahead of the times. The girls were as free as the boys, allowed to come and go as they chose, and they had a great faculty—artists, composers, and writers. I thought I wanted to write; I imagined becoming a poet. I wrote poetry on and off, especially when I was high. You could write a novel or a long poem for your senior thesis. No other college allowed that in those days.

When we got home, I had a long talk with Philo about college. He wanted me to go to Barnard or Smith or Wellesley or Harvard, even though it was local, someplace, he said, "seriously intellectual." I was flattered that he thought of me that way, but that wasn't the way I thought of myself. I said I didn't think I was that smart. He insisted I was. "How many kids your age know Emily Dickinson the way you do? Or have ever heard of Marvell?"

"Umm," I mumbled. It was one thing to like poetry, another

to be a physicist. He was thinking of me as if I could be a physicist, and I couldn't. I knew that. But I liked that he thought I was so smart. I said I'd think about it, but of course I didn't.

Sandy planned to be pre-med, and Bishop to study political science. He wanted to go into politics, or maybe teach it. We had meandering conversations about what we wanted to be. We were all pretty happy, thinking about going away, and we strode through the Cambridge streets laughing aloud. Knowing that we would soon be separated gave an edge to our feelings. We said we'd never forget each other, no matter what. Once we were in college, we'd visit each other for long weekends, sleeping on the floor of each others' dorm rooms, and call or write each other regularly.

"We can write a chain letter," Bishop suggested. "I'll start it. I'll send it to Sandy, who will add on and send it to Jess, who will add on and send it to me. Then I'll add on and send it to Jess, who will add on and send it to Sandy. What do you think?"

"Terrific!"

"When it gets too long, we'll put the old pages in a binder and save the entire thing. For years!"

"We'll be famous! Like Virginia Woolf and T. S. Eliot!" Sandy was breathless at the thought.

It didn't seem inconceivable to me. If there was any justice in the world, they would grow up to do great things and get famous. Sandy would become a doctor and cure some terrible disease and win the Nobel Prize; Bishop would become president of the United States, or at least governor of Massachusetts or mayor of Boston for sure. He was already president of our senior class. And I would be a poet and wear a long straight gown and a big hat, and be invited to read from the stage like Marianne Moore, who came to Barnes one time. Wouldn't it be great to have our own little world like Virginia and Leonard Woolf and all their friends, people like—my God!—T. S. Eliot and E. M. Forster! That's what I longed for: a life in which I'd know sophisticated people who understood life and literature and art and were smart and nice and everybody loved each other.

Philo had become an installation at our house. It was cool the way he wove himself into our lives. On weekends when we didn't go anywhere, Mom worked in her study, and he sat in the living room reading, or worked at the dining-room table, note cards and books spread out, until dinner time. They could work for hours at a time, not seeing each other or talking, yet taking pleasure in knowing the other was there. That's the kind of man I wanted to marry, someone who could be with me in silent pleasure.

At dinnertime, Mom would come downstairs to start cooking, and Philo would pack up his notes and go into the kitchen, offering to help. If I was home, I went to the kitchen too. I liked to be part of it, the three of us peeling and chopping vegetables together, setting the table, stirring the sauce. We'd put the news on television, or music on the radio, or a record on the stereo. Philo loved Mozart and Dvořák and Mom loved Bach and Richard Strauss and Mahler, and they'd take turns in what they listened to. Philo said Mom's music made him want to lie down. She said Philo didn't love music, he just loved to dance, and he did tend to hop around when his music was on. Their arguments were dotted with laughter.

Sometimes we went to the movies together, and once, when Philo was flush, he took Mom and me out to dinner. I was often included in whatever they did. Philo taught me to play chess, not that I really learned. But he tried. And he gave me books to read. There was the Marvell, and one by Richard Fariña. It was called *Been Down So Long It Looks Like up to Me*. I loved that book, and I fell in love with its author. Philo said he was killed in an accident soon after he published that book. Sandy met Philo one night when she was at our house for dinner, and she thought he was cute. Steve liked him too.

One Saturday when Philo arrived, I was so happy to see him, I hugged him. He hugged me back and we talked a little bit. I sat there with him—Mom had gone to the market—and I asked him about some lines in a Marvell poem. Philo transformed himself into a kindly teacher and sat there with me patiently explaining words and syntax and talking about Marvell's philosophy. I gazed at his beautiful face, and suddenly realized I was in love with Philo. He was talking about Milton's *Areopagitica*, against censorship, which he said was really great. He pulled a book from his briefcase and began reading it aloud. It was amazing. What metaphors! I was struck by "five Imprimaturs are seen together dialoguewise in the Piazza of one Title page, complementing and ducking each to other with shav'n reverences, whether the Author, who stands by in perplexity at the foot of his Epistle, shall to the Presse or to the spunge." He read the famous one "I cannot praise a fugitive and cloistered Vertue"—at least it was famous when I was a girl; I bet nobody knows it now. I asked if I could borrow the book. He said he needed it for a class the next day, but he'd bring me a copy if I wanted to read it through.

Philo and Mom were going to a party that night given by somebody in the English department at Moseley. I went out too, with Steve and his friends Lonny and Beck, to a party in Roxbury. It was wild, lots of dope, and I think there was even heroin, great music on the stereo, and people dancing. I danced a few times, not that I'm good at it, or even decent. I'm uptight, repressed, Sandy would call it, but I can't help it. Still, it was fun. I loved the people there, they were so full of life, and didn't act fake.

All of us were kind of hungover the next day, Mom and Philo from wine, me from all the smoke, excitement, and weed, and we lay around the house like sick dogs. In the afternoon Mom insisted we had to go for a walk, so we drove to the coast and walked on the beach at Manchester. We weren't really allowed to walk there: the people who live in those towns reserved the beaches for themselves. Manchester was a rich town, like most of the coastal towns, and the townspeople didn't want outsiders coming in. But Mom said no one has the right to own the beach, that it should be for all the people, and we used to sneak in. The problem was parking, but Mom would drop us off with all our gear, and then she'd drive down to the supermarket and park in their lot and walk back up. We'd never been caught except the time I brought Steve. One look at him and they knew we didn't live there; they threw us out. But this day, we were all white and the only ones on the beach. It was winter, and we walked in the wind; I felt the wind was cleansing me. We held on to each other so the wind didn't blow us over, and we talked and laughed and watched the gulls and the ridges in the purple sand and listened to it sing in the wind.

The following weekend, Philo brought me another lavender book, much bigger than the Marvell, this one with Milton's prose. It included *Areopagitica*, which I read all the way through. Philo explained censorship to me: I knew what the word meant, of course, but I didn't really understand why it was important. Philo said that rulers always tried to increase their power as much as they could, by taking power away from anybody else that had it, like nobles or the clergy. The common people, of course, had no power at all. To succeed, rulers had to keep people from knowing what they were doing; if they could keep people ignorant, they would never protest, but only bow their heads. They had people say or write the story the way they wanted it known. When people got tired of lies and told the rulers they wanted a voice in their own lives, like in Milton's time, and in the American Revolution, the rulers refused and they had to rebel. The "shav'n reverences" in Milton's essay were priests in the Catholic Church, which censored writing in Europe so no one would question the church. Milton was telling his fellow revolutionaries not to build a society like the Catholic Church, which went on banning books and plays and even movies right into the twentieth century. What really shocked me was that the year after Milton wrote the *Areopagitica*, he became the head censor of England. You think when a person writes something as magnificent as *Areopagitica* that there would never be censorship again. But Philo told me there was censorship even here, now, in our country!

Mom had once said that love was mean, but Philo never was. I don't think he ever made Mom cry. She made *him* cry, but not by being mean. I found out about this one hot night that summer. It was stifling and we had both left our bedroom doors open, as well as the door to the screened porch downstairs. Fans in Mom's room and mine were whirring but still I could hear Mom and Philo talking in bed. I was reading Trollope, a treasure from a trove I had found in the attic. I loved the little old books you could hold in one hand and the onionskin pages that smelled of the library, of glue and paper, that crinkled when you turned them and felt sacred. Mom's voice was a murmur and Philo would every once in a while mumble a question. Then at one point, her voice rose a little and got thick and I could hear her sob, and I perked up, trying to hear what she was saying. I thought Philo was making Mom cry. But then she cried out, "You marry so young and live together so long, you get trained. You are educated—it's like postgraduate work—in adapting to your partner. And if you're married to someone who has no control over his rage, you train yourself not to react to rage, not to feel, not to respond, to stay calm and in control at all times. And that ruins you; it kills your soul! You get numb! When I met you, my feelings were dead. I couldn't feel anything. I didn't know if I'd ever be able to feel again! And I'm not sure I do!"

I sat up sharply. Was that true? Then Mom was sobbing, and in a little while, there was a chord, another voice sobbing with her, almost in harmony with her. Philo was crying with her!

I pictured the two of them, Philo lying across the foot of the bed the way he did when they talked, Mom leaning back against her pillows, Philo hugging her feet close to his body, then crawling up to hug her. Was she saying she didn't love Philo? I felt like crying myself, but then I had to laugh, what a family! The family that cries together stays together?

The sounds of that night lingered with me, and as time went on, it came to me that that was exactly what I wanted, someone who would feel with me, who would share my sorrow like that. I wondered if Steve would, or Bishop. I had never really asked much of them. I had thought before about asking Steve to give me something I needed. I knew I had given him what he needed; I became furious at our country when we talked about what happened to black people here, about the different things, terrible things that had happened to Steve and his friends. But nothing terrible had ever happened to me except my parents getting divorced, and I could hardly ask Steve to feel bad for me about that, when his mother had died when he was seven and his father didn't even want to know him. And by now I was used to my parents being divorced and in truth I didn't feel that bad about it anymore. Mostly what I felt bad about was Daddy, the way Daddy was. But if marrying Daddy made Mom not feel, what did it do to me to have parents who were always screaming at each other? Maybe I didn't feel anything either.

I was working the breakfast-and-lunch shift at Sonny's one Saturday when Steve stopped into the restaurant around two o'clock. He asked if I wanted to go to his place after work. He said his grandmother was going to visit her cousin in Roxbury and wouldn't be there, so I could finally see where he lived. I said sure and he hung around until my shift ended at two thirty, which really meant almost three. I didn't want to show it, but I was very excited: I felt that this was a mark of serious trust. Steve had never taken me to his apartment before; he'd never even shown me where it was.

He drove us over toward MIT, where there were a lot of factories, nothing like Harvard. One of them was a yellow-brick twelve-story apartment building surrounded by a high chain-link fence and with a concrete yard, which looked like a prison yard, with no trees or flowers or grass. Children were playing in the yard, but they had no swings or seesaws or slide. The base of the building was covered with graffiti, most of it telling you to go fuck yourself. We opened a heavy brown door with a barred window in it and the letter *D* on it, entering a hall whose beige paint was almost completely obliterated by more graffiti. Garbage was scattered everywhere. There was a smell of urine and liquor and rotten food. We got on the elevator, which heaved its way up to the tenth floor. Steve held my hand all the way; I guess he knew I was nervous. It felt strange being in a place where people hate where they live so much that they scrawl "fuck you" on the walls and pee on the floor and strew garbage around. I'd read that animals never foul their own nests, so why would humans? I knew that a girl in Steve's building had had a baby last year and thrown it down the incinerator shaft. Steve had shown me the article in the paper, saying it had happened in his building. I figured the girl must have felt like garbage herself. Did the people who lived here think they were garbage? It made me want to cry. What had to happen to people to make them feel like garbage?

The hallways were concrete, painted light brown, the doors dark brown. Up here there wasn't so much graffiti. Once we were inside Steve's grandmother's apartment, I felt better. The living room had a beige couch and two green chairs and in front of the TV was a wooden rocking chair with a beige cushion. There was an end table next to the couch and a standing lamp behind the rocker. Pictures of flowers cut from magazines were thumb-tacked to the walls, and nylon lace curtains hung at the windows. There was a statue of Jesus on the television set and a painting of him on one wall. The carpet had dark green leaves on a lighter green background. The walls were white. The color combination was nice.

"It's nice," I said to Steve.

He smiled stiffly. I felt he didn't like my saying that. Maybe he thought I was patronizing him. Was I? Or maybe he thought I was surprised that it was nice. But I hadn't known what to expect. He had commented on our furniture the first time he came to my house. It had never occurred to me that our furniture was beauti-ful, just that it was old-fashioned. But he raved about it, said it was gorgeous. No way a black person could afford to buy antique furniture like ours, he said.

Steve's apartment had a kitchen, a living room, and two bed-rooms. His Grandma Josie's room had a double bed covered with a crocheted bedspread, an old bureau, a rocker, an old rag rug, and lace curtains. It was really nice, a quiet old-fashioned room where you could feel the peace. A photograph of what I guessed were her mother and father stood in a silver frame on her dresser; they looked incredibly old, wizened and nearly toothless. The boys' room was small and crowded, with two sets of bunk beds, one against each wall. There was a window at the back wall in the narrow space between them, with a sheer nylon curtain over it, and a blue shag rug on the floor. Their storage was in four big drawers, two in the base of each bed. The beds were covered in dark blue cotton bedspreads that I wondered if his grandma had made herself; they looked handmade. She had tried. You could see that. But the room stank. Well, three boys lived in it, two younger than Steve, and there were clothes everywhere, soiled underwear and smelly socks and sneakers. Books, balls, comic books, little toy cars were scattered on the beds and floor. The closet door was open, showing coats and jeans and shirts hung precariously on crooked hangers and schoolbooks piled on the floor.

"She does the laundry on Sunday, her day off," Steve said, as if he was embarrassed. Then he put his arms around me. I nestled against him, but I was a little uncomfortable in that room. I couldn't take the smell. I knew I was being snobbish, and I tried to get beyond myself. I reminded myself how terrific Steve was, what a great person, and how much I loved him. I relaxed a little.

We lay down on his bunk, the lower one on the right. Near our feet, a ladder leaned against the upper bunk, and we stared up at the board that held the mattress above us. We were lying on a thin mattress on a board too, so the bed was very hard. Probably good for the back, I thought.

We turned toward each other and started to kiss, and I got into it a little, I started feeling shoots of electricity, pangs, oh, I did love Steve, and he tried to slide my sweater off, and I had to help him, then we took off his sweater. He had on an undershirt and I had on a bra, and we had to get those off too. There wasn't much room in the bunk, and we started to giggle. I grabbed him and kissed him, he was so cute. All that undressing wore us out, but we still had to get off pants, with his belt, and his underpants. Getting those off was a real project, but we finally did it, we were down to our socks, but we didn't bother taking those off, we were hot now and pressed up against each other and our hearts were beating madly in among the clothes and I was moaning a little, and he was hard and big against my leg, and he started to pull his body up, and get on top of me, when we heard the front door open and slam shut.

We both fell back, aghast.

Steve looked at me, put a finger on his lips. We listened. We could hear sounds, soft and slow. Not one of the boys. Steve heaved a great sigh. He pulled up his trousers and zipped them up. He put his sweater back on. His underwear lay mixed with mine amid the sheets. He got up silently and put on his shoes. He called out, "Gram? Josie?"

He went out into the living room and walked toward the kitchen. "Gram? What happened? Thought you were going to visit Eleanor."

I heard an old woman's voice saying that Eleanor wasn't feeling well and didn't want company, so she just went to the grocery store. It sounded as if she was in the kitchen, putting groceries away. I could hear cupboard doors open and close. He stayed with her for a while, the two of them talking. Then she must have walked into the living room. I heard the TV switch on. I heard a body settle itself into an armchair.

"Umm, there's a girl in the bedroom, Gram," Steve said. I could hear him better now they were in the next room.

"A girl? In the bedroom?"

"Yeah. Jess. My friend from school. I was showing her the apartment and she started to feel sick, so she lay down."

"Well, I can't take care of her, Steven," she said, sounding alarmed. "You better take her home."

"No, no, I know. As soon as she's feeling better, I will."

"All right, boy."

A game show took over the living room. Steve suddenly appeared in the bedroom. He smiled at me. "How you feeling?"

I rolled my eyes at him.

"Better? Don't get up till you feel better, y'hear?"

I grimaced and felt around for my underwear. I couldn't find my bra.

"Where's my bra?" I mouthed at him. He put his hand over his mouth, stifling a laugh, and came over to the bed to look around.

Between us, we found it, tangled in the sheet. He helped me put it on. We found the rest of my clothes and I struggled into them, still lying there. Finally I got up. I started to make the bed.

"Don't bother," he whispered.

"A sick person would leave a bed looking like this?" I hissed into his ear.

He laughed so hard you could hear him, and he said, out loud, "I'm glad you're feeling better, Jess."

We pulled the sheet neatly over the mattress, pulled the blanket and spread up to where it might have been. Then we tried to leave the room, but Steve had to wait a minute to stop laughing and calm himself.

We went out into the living room. "Gram, this is Jess. Jess, this is my Gramma Josie," Steve said, smiling.

Josie turned her head and stared at me—and froze. Her face changed, her color changed, her whole body changed. She looked at me, then at Steve. Then she turned away from us, her head moving very slowly. The image hung before me, her old worn face, its grooves deep with sorrow, her eyes empty, their life gone.

"I don't know what you think you're doing, boy," she said, tonelessly.

We stood there, transfixed. Then Steve took my hand and led me out, and wordlessly we went back down in the elevator and got in his car, and wordlessly he drove me home.

My senior year I waited tables at the café, but only breakfasts and lunches. Sonny wanted guys to work the dinner shift; he thought it was classier, and of course the guys liked it because dinner had the best tips. I was always off after three and often shopped for my family. I tried to buy things I knew Philo liked. Mom and I liked almost everything, but Philo didn't—he was used to a different diet and he didn't care much for unusual vegetables or fish or salads, so we reserved them for nights he wasn't there. His mother was a wonderful cook, he said, and she cooked the specialties of her own country, spicy meatballs he couldn't describe beyond to say they were delicious, and chicken or veal with paprika.

"Ummm," Mom said, "can you get me the recipes?"

He looked at her falteringly.

"Just ask your mother. Jot them down. I'd love to try them."

He sat there blinking.

"Philo! What's the matter? Is that so hard?"

"She won't give them to me," he finally wrenched out.

"Good heavens, why not?"

He wouldn't meet her eyes.

Now she was really curious. "What is it, Fi?"

"She wouldn't give me a recipe to give you," he said.

"Why not?"

His teeth barely moved. "She thinks you're a bad woman."

"Oh." I could see that many things became clear for my mother in that instant. Her brow clouded.

Philo watched her miserably. "I'm sorry, Andy. She's old-fashioned."

"So that's why we haven't met your family," she said. Her mouth was tight.

"Yes."

"Were you ever going to tell me?"

"No."

Mom burst out laughing then, and I breathed out.

In the spring of 1971, a lot of bad things happened. In March we found out about the My Lai massacre. It had happened a couple of years before, and some people had known about it earlier, but most of us found out about it then. The military was blaming a soldier named Calley. I felt bad for him: maybe he had been a killer that day, but that's what he'd been trained to do—he was just a boy who had been turned into a weapon, doing what his superiors told him to do. He wasn't like Eichmann, an educated man with connections who would know how to transfer himself out of an untenable situation. He was a grunt. Killing those people certainly hadn't been his own idea. My friends and I thought there should be a court somewhere to put the president, the head of the army, the secretary of defense, and the secretary of state on trial. Everybody was disgusted with the war and with our leaders, but no one seemed to think we could do anything about them.

Nixon was ordering a lot of bombing and there was a protest in Washington by soldiers who had fought in Vietnam. Men who had been acclaimed heroes threw their medals back at the government, saying they had suffered and killed for nothing. The government was slowly, almost silently bringing men back from Vietnam, but in the middle of June, there was a huge explosion after the *New York Times* published the papers taken from the Pentagon that showed that the government had been giving covert assistance to Vietnam since 1954. The papers showed how useless American efforts—the sacrifice of the limbs and lives of the men like the ones who had thrown back their medals—had been. All these things made us sick. We were sick about being Americans, responsible for these horrors.

The Pentagon Papers appeared the month I graduated from high school. Graduation was no big deal, especially in these circumstances. I mean, we may have been the peasant walking behind the plow, but the figure in the sky behind us wasn't tiny and was making a lot of noise. Graduation probably wouldn't have meant much to me even if all that other stuff hadn't been going on. Finishing high school was a major event once upon a time, but at that point it was just one more occasion for a party.

One Sunday in June, Mom and Philo were sitting in the living room reading the *New York Times* and arguing, or rather discussing, the war passionately, as usual. It was around noon but I was still in my pajamas, sitting on the porch with a cup of coffee, when the doorbell rang and Philo jumped up—he was the only one dressed—and let Annette and Ted Fields into the house. I went inside. Nobody was saying anything. The Fields had Lisa with them. Annette, her hand resting on Ted's arm, said in a trembling voice, "Andy, we've just left Marguerite and Derek at a school in Maine. A live-in school near the New Hampshire border. They'll stay there now. Forever."

Then she burst into tears.

We all jumped up. Mom and Philo and I all hugged her, hugged Ted, hugged Lisa. We kept patting them and making them sit down and Philo ran to get them drinks. Mom asked Lisa if she would like to play Ping-Pong or something. She nodded, so I ran upstairs and dressed quickly, then took her out to the garage, both of us carrying sodas. I don't know what the grown-ups did after that, except I knew there was crying. It made me think about the time I went to church with Bishop one day and saw a sign that read *camera lacrimosa*. I asked Bishop what that was and he said it was a crying room. I asked him, "What for?" and he looked at me as if I was an idiot. As if life was about crying and I should have known that at the age of seventeen. But I couldn't imagine reserving a room to cry in.

I felt really bad for Annette and Ted. They had been unlucky. Many people would find Marguerite and Derek strange and difficult but to their parents they were beloved. Annette and Ted just couldn't manage them anymore. They had to take them to a place where they could be cared for. They would not see them much anymore, or maybe not at all, because the people at the school said it was better for the children if they just forgot their parents. It was breaking their hearts. I didn't want to think about it.

Mom asked them to stay for dinner. Of course, they didn't know it was supposed to be my graduation day celebration dinner—graduation had been the day before—and they accepted. They were desperate for comfort. Mom came out to the garage and asked me if I minded if she scrapped the original dinner she'd planned, which was rib lamb chops, my very favorite, and made "a more healing dinner." I said sure, and she asked if I'd go to Savenor's and get a couple of chickens. She was going to make the meal she always made when one of us was sick, chicken in broth with leeks and angel hair pasta. Lisa wanted to go along, so we both got in the car. I could drive now; I had my license. That was a major step. I felt so grown-up the first time I took the car out by myself. Mom begged me to drive especially carefully. I could see in her face that she was telling me, This is the one precious child to them.

By now, Lisa, having beat me in two out of three games of Ping-Pong, had cheered up and was laughing. And only once, when I turned away from her to choose the leeks, did I notice her staring blankly into space. I pointed out old Momma Savenor, who'd been sitting at that same cash register for fifty years, and I said what a sweet old thing she was—although I didn't even know if that was true. She was old, and that seemed to be enough to qualify for sweetness. Anyway, it cheered Lisa up to think that that old woman and her children and grandchildren were still in the same place, making a good living and being comfortable for all those years, and she was okay again.

Philo kept trying to amuse them and the Fields tried to be cheerful all through dinner. Annette and Ted kept exclaiming how delicious it was, as if they never had dinners that good. We had this wonderful healing meal with a chocolate layer cake I'd bought, knowing that chocolate made people feel better. After they left, I was upset. I asked Mom if they'd ever recover. She said they'd get over it eventually but never completely, and I shivered with fear of becoming one of the unlucky ones.

But they did get better. Within a year Annette and Ted were

able to laugh and get upset over little things without bursting into tears, and a few years later you wouldn't have known by looking at them that they had had such sorrow in their lives. After the children left, they threw themselves into the antiwar movement and kept it up until the war ended. Annette had majored in art history in college, but once Lisa was in college, Annette signed up for courses to learn how to teach disabled children, and after that, she got a job teaching kids who were like hers but a little more able to learn. It made her feel better, doing that. When Lisa graduated summa cum laude from Yale, she wanted to work at the State Department: she wanted to be a diplomat. But her parents' antiwar history was held against her and she ended up teaching political science in Madison, Wisconsin. She was extremely upset at first, but got over it in time. It wasn't a terrible fate, I thought: life can have a happy ending, even if you're unlucky.

I thought about things like that a lot because so many of Mom's friends had bad luck. Her friend Kathy was beaten to death by her husband, and Alyssa's son Tim died of cancer. After he died, Alyssa got a job and went to work every day selling dresses at Bergdorf's. After work she went home, got into bed, ate snacks she'd bought on the way home, and watched TV until she drifted to sleep. She had no other life. Mom said she was a walking dead person, killed by grief.

Eve Goodman took good care of her husband, Dan, who, with his ALS, became increasingly helpless, but lived for almost a decade. A long time, Mom said, for someone with that illness. Eve hired a young woman to help her and concealed the disgust she occasionally felt at what was required of her. At the end, Dan didn't succumb passively. He took his own life. He had told Eve, when he could still talk, to help him when the time came, but when it did, he didn't want to do it. We hold on to life even when it's unendurable. But finally he drank a potion of drugs, and then Eve went to pieces.

So many people had something terrible happen to them that it began to seem to me that everybody did. It made me so nervous. I was terrified about what was going to happen to me. Even the sweet Gross family next door, who were graced with good luck and happiness with their three sons, fell to pieces when their oldest son was killed in Vietnam. His mother, Lenny, never got over it. Whenever she mentioned his name, or anybody referred to the war, her eyes teared up.

I don't believe the people who insist that if you obey God's rules (how can anyone know what God's rules are?) you will be safe. What can make you safe in the world? People have searched for something magical to make them safe, but they've never found it. It's understandable that people would want to believe that there is someone or something who can protect them from the terrible things that happen. But there isn't, and I don't even think about that. What I think about is how people get over the terrible things that do happen to them. How come terrible things don't just end your life? Could you let yourself trust again, relax again, in somebody's arms? Could you really believe that the future will be happy? Did the people who endured the Holocaust ever get over it? Did their children? Could Annette and Ted ever forget, no matter how old they got, Derek and Marguerite, and the days of their birth and the discovery of their impediments, and the day upon day of anxious tedium and dull, endless love they spent taking care of them?

Does life really go on? How?

I hadn't seen Steve since the day we went to his apartment. We hadn't talked and I hadn't been able to talk to anyone else about it—Sandy was at camp and Bishop at his uncle's dude ranch. But as the weeks went on and college came nearer, Steve receded from my mind. It was as if some door had shut. And it came to me in a slow wave that the person I really loved was Philo. I mulled this over and finally decided I had to act.

I waited until a night Philo was at his mother's house. Mom and I had shrimp and peas and rice for dinner that night. It was nice being alone; much as I loved Philo, it was also good when he wasn't there. We sat smoking together as darkness gathered outside. "Mom," I began.

"Yes, sweetie."

"I'm in love with Philo."

"I know you love Philo."

"No. I'm in love with him."

She turned toward me. I could see the outline of her head, but not her face. She couldn't see mine either.

"I think you should give him to me."

She was silent for a while. Finally she said, "He's not a piece of meat to be handed over."

"No. But if you told him it was okay, he'd want me. He wants me."

She stared at me. It was a long time before she said anything. "He well may."

"But he won't act on it unless you say it's okay."

"No."

"So I think you should."

Again, a long silence. By now, my pulse was beating so hard it seemed my heartbeat drummed the beat for the insect chorus outside. But I contained myself. I didn't say another word.

After a long time, she tamped out her cigarette and stood up. "I'll think about this, Jess." She piled dishes on a tray and went into the kitchen. I didn't help. I left the rest of the dishes on the table and just sat there. I lit another cigarette.

As time passed, I watched Mom suspiciously. I wasn't about to let her just drop the whole subject. After I left for college, there was no point in her giving me Philo. I wanted him now; I wanted him to bond with me so he would drive up to Andrews to see me on weekends, the way he drove to Cambridge on weekends to see Mom. I couldn't tell what she was thinking, but she waited weeks before she said anything. After dinner one night she said, "Jess, we need to talk."

I was all attention.

We both lit cigarettes. You did that in those days, as if smoking was a preamble to personal drama. They did it in the movies, like a curtain going up, an overture.

"I've been thinking about what you said," she began. "At first I thought maybe I should do what you want, at least give Philo the choice. You're seventeen now and old enough to have a relationship. Maybe I should step out of your way and let Philo decide what he wants to do."

By now, I was grinning.

"But then I thought more about it. And I've decided it's a bad idea. I know Philo loves you; I can see that. And that you love him. But he's been my lover, and you're my daughter. And no matter how the three of us try to avoid it, we will draw comparisons. You'll always be asking him or at least wondering if you are better than I was. He'll always compare the two of us; he can't help doing that. And no matter how hard I try not to, if he chooses you, I will feel resentful. And if he chooses me, you will. It would be bad for our relationship, yours and mine. It would be bad for Philo and his relationship with both of us. It's a bad idea, Jess, and I'm not going to do it."

I just sat there and said, "Okay." Okay! As if it was okay! I didn't get angry, I didn't cry, I didn't do anything! I said, "Okay," and then, Goody Two-Shoes, I helped Mom do the dishes. I didn't think. That's, of course, my solution to everything—don't think about it. But actually, while I'm not thinking, part of my mind is working away like mad, planning, planning. When I was in college, I read that Catherine de Medici was a clever woman who would say, "Hate and wait." I didn't hate my mom. But I also knew that I was the one with the time to wait, and I could. I'd wait.

I ran the household that summer to the point where I worried about how Mom and Philo would manage when I went away to school. Mom had finished most of her research and was writing her book. Now that Dad had stopped coming around, she often worked at home. Her study tables were covered with papers and card files and journals taken from the library. She used an IBM Selectric typewriter I envied deeply. I had to type my school papers on the old manual Royal portable I'd inherited from her. I kept hinting for a typewriter as a graduation present, but I knew they were expensive. Philo was still doing research, taking notes in longhand on five-by-seven cards he filed in a gray metal box.

Either Mom and I did the marketing together or I did it alone. Both Mom and I shopped with Philo in mind because he was at our house almost all the time that summer. He had become a member of the family, and that made me extremely happy. I waited tables for money for clothes and books and to save for all the expenses I'd have at college next year. Dad hadn't sent any child support since he'd remarried. We hadn't known he had remarried—we just knew he wasn't sending money—until we had a phone call from Irene Templer. Mom had met Irene and Dan Templer years ago when we spent summers in Vermont. They lived up there year round, in a big old house on a hill. Dan was a doctor. Mom thought he was wonderful because he still made house calls. Irene was an artist. She painted in watercolors, Vermonty pictures of old houses and barns and gardens, selling them to tourists, and did very well.

Mom liked Irene, but they only saw each other when Mom was in Vermont, so she was surprised when Irene called us in Cambridge one night. Irene sounded upset. She said she knew a young woman named Julie, a waitress at the bistro. Irene and Julie had become friendly, and last week, while Irene was waiting for her club sandwich and Coke, Julie told her she was getting married.

"That's wonderful!" Irene said. "Who are you marrying?"

And Julie said Pat Leighton.

Irene was shocked. "You can't marry Pat Leighton!" she scolded. "He's already married, and his wife is a friend of mine!"

"Oh, they're divorced," Julie said vaguely.

Was that possible? Irene had wanted to know. Was it true? How horrible!

I guess Dad must have been lonely. That was really fast. And Julie was only twenty and hardly his intellectual or emotional equal—or at least so Irene said. Irene said Julie was nice enough and had finished high school but that then she went to work as a waitress. She worked in the same café I'd worked at, which felt a little strange. Dad never called to tell me he was getting married or to invite me to his wedding. But maybe he didn't really have a wedding.

Mom made a face and said, "Poor girl, having to live in a house without a toilet." Irene said he was putting one in for Julie. When she heard that, Mom was hopping mad. She didn't give a damn that he was getting married, she said; she was mad that he'd put in a toilet for someone he'd just met when all those years he'd protested that he loved her above anything on earth, but he wouldn't put in a toilet for her.

Maybe out of guilt, Dad sent a check for my support in July, and Mom wrote him a thank you note. In it she asked if by marrying again he was sure he wasn't committing bigamy. But she said the real reason she wrote was to let him know I'd be at Andrews next September. I guessed she said it in a way that he would think that I was going there to be nearer to him—a complete fabrication. "So it isn't just governments that lie," I said to her. And she answered—just like a government—that it was a strategic move. In truth, northern Vermont, where my college was, was farther from him than Cambridge. But Mom wanted him to pay more attention to me, to spend time with me. She seemed to think I wanted that. Or needed it. Every time he called to beg her to come back, she'd urge him to call me or come and see me—that is, if she could, before he began cursing her. I'd hear her talking in her room as I came up the stairs to start my homework, or even from my room. I always knew it was him. Her voice became strained in a way it didn't with anybody else. And it usually ended with her slamming down the phone.

One time I overheard her saying, "She needs you. She cares about you. You never call or write her. It hurts her."

I bit my tongue, I was so mad. How dare she talk about me like that to him! I stormed down the hall to her room, ready to shout. She was already hanging up the phone.

"How could you do that!" I shrieked.

She looked at me.

"Beg him to see me! How could you?"

"Begging? Oh, Jess . . ." She reached her arms out to me, but I stayed in the doorway, arms folded hard against my chest.

"You made me sound pathetic!"

"You know, sweetheart, it may sound that way to you, but it doesn't to him. He doesn't hear me begging. He's so sure you hate him, that I hate him . . . He's paranoid, honey, you know that. I was trying to reassure him that you love him. And you do, don't you?"

I hated that my eyes filled up so I couldn't see. "No, he's right! I hate him!" I screamed, then ran out of the room. I went back to my room and slumped on my window seat. I lit a cigarette and gazed out though the screen. A young man walked on the sidewalk by the house down below, all alone in the night, and my heart curled up with longing, as if he were my long-lost brother.

His heels sounded on the concrete, all the way down the block as he disappeared. As the sound vanished, I felt my heart break.

Dad called the house from time to time, before he remarried, begging Mom to come back to him, saying how he loved her, telling her he'd changed, he was different now. Then, when she'd say she wasn't coming back, he'd start yelling and call her terrible names. The last time he called, we already knew he was getting married again. He called to beg Mom to come back to him. She said, "Pat! How can you ask me that when you're getting married!"

He shrieked, "Bitch! Slut! Whore!" and slammed down the phone.

I knew this because I'd accidentally picked up the phone at the same moment Mom did. I felt overcome by what he'd said. I covered my face with my hands. My eyes were wet. I wondered what was the matter with my father. He was an ache, worse than a toothache, worse than a pulled muscle in my insides.

I dragged myself into Mom's room. She was sitting in bed with a book, smoking a cigarette. She didn't seem upset at all.

"Mom?"

She looked up, then her eyes opened in alarm. "What's wrong, Jess?"

"I don't know . . ."

I sat down on the edge of her bed. "Is Daddy . . . ?"

"Did you pick up the phone?"

I nodded.

"What's the matter with Daddy, Mom?"

"I don't know, sweetheart. You know, he's obsessed with me. Not that he loves me, or even likes me . . . He's just obsessed. It's beyond his control."

"Is that crazy?"

She thought for a while. "It's a pocket of craziness. We probably all have one or two, you know, places where we're a little off . . ."

I wanted to cry but I couldn't. I wanted to scream but I didn't.

Mom began to talk in a monotonous tone. She was talking about Andrews and how it would be there and what we needed to do before I went. I wasn't paying attention, but after a while she began to talk about clothes, and I began to think about what I needed for school, and I started to get a little excited.

After a time, Mom went back to her book and I went back to mine. A few days later I got a letter from Dad, with a check for five hundred dollars. For clothes for school, he said. At first, I was furious. Did he think he could buy my love? But then I thought, well, Mom shows love with her cooking; Dad does it with money. Maybe it was all right. Part of me was thrilled to get the money, but the rest of me hated that I was thrilled to get the money and blamed him for sending it.

Dad had written a real letter. He mentioned Andrews, which was a long trip from there to Brattleboro, which was near Dad's place. But he wrote that he'd come and get me any weekend I wanted. He said he was remodeling the house, and had built a real room for me upstairs, but he would wait for me to say what I wanted done to my room—as if it was some sacrosanct space dedicated to me and not just a bare space.

I could see how Mom's divorcing him made him feel as though I was leaving him too. Maybe that's why he acted the way he did when he called me that name. And I could see that he might feel that our leaving him meant we both thought he was a worthless human being. I just didn't want him to be crazy. I was terrified that he might be crazy, because I loved him as much as I loved Mom, even if he made me cry.

7 **My birthday was** at the end of August, and after my friends came back from their summer away, Mom gave me a combination eighteenth birthday–going away party. She let us have beer as well as soda, because we were all eighteen by then. She stayed up in her room with her door shut and promised me she wouldn't come out unless there was trouble. My friends smoked, and I had to go around opening windows and waving towels around to get rid of the smell of weed after they'd left, but Mom didn't say boo to that.

I said good-bye to Dolores and Bishop at my party. Dolores was all teary; she'd been teary for a couple of years now. I was annoyed with her for always being so distraught. She was going to UMass but she wasn't happy, not at all. "I have to live at *home!*" she said, as if that was the worst thing in the world. I thought I might have been a little sad too if I was going to school locally, but I could see *some* advantages to it. I thought she always looked on the dark side. She used to be so brilliant. And she was still a wonderful artist when she put her mind to it. But she'd gained weight and these days she wore too much makeup and flirted outrageously, things you really didn't do in our crowd. The night of my party, she kept crying, all night long. She said she would miss us horribly, and we said she'd make new friends right away, that everybody would love her, and she burst out crying again.

I guess we were all sort of volatile that night, happy and sad at the same time, excited and frightened and unsure about what we were getting into, but I had a feeling that none of us would keep up with Dolores, that we'd sort of let her go.

Steve didn't come to the party. I didn't know where or how he was. I couldn't find him. I didn't dare to call him and he hadn't come around to Barnes in a while, or to my house.

It was as if Josie's look had ended things for us. She had finished something for me, I know. I couldn't bear the thought that I was causing her more suffering, when I could see in her face and her body that her life had been spent mainly suffering. And I think Steve felt that too.

But one day just before I was to leave for college, Steve came round to Sonny's and asked me if I wanted to go for a drive after work. We drove out to Revere, to the beach, and sat there talking. I asked him if he was going to Harvard and he said he didn't know. He held my hand and kissed me on the cheek as though he was saying good-bye. My eyes filled with tears; he was such a sweetheart, and I sensed I wouldn't see him much anymore. Then he drove me home.

Early one morning in September, Philo, Mom, and I packed up the car. When we were done, Philo and I stood gazing at each other, and then he grabbed me and gave me a great big hug and a kiss on the cheek and I clung to him. Then Mom and I set off for Andrews. I was flying. I hated to leave Philo; it hurt me to think I wouldn't see him for a long time, but I was so thrilled to be going away that you'd think I was escaping from the Soviet Union. We drove for hours, Mom and I spelling each other. She offered to stop at Dad's so I could have lunch with him, while she ate in town alone. But I wasn't sure he'd want to stop working to have lunch with me; he never had when I lived with him. And besides, I knew there would be fireworks if he knew she was anywhere near, so we bypassed him.

We stopped for lunch at a small coffee shop off the main road—Mom prefered any grungy thing to the fast food on highways. We had bowls of a delicious chili with not-very-good bread. Mom said bad bread was par for the course in America. Europeans, she said, really know their bread and have delicious bread everywhere. That made me want to go to Europe.

We reached Andrews in the afternoon. My dormitory was at Lester Hall, an old rambling three-story house with twenty bedrooms. We carried load after load of stuff up long staircases to my room on the third floor. There were an awful lot of stairs, but one of my roommates, a girl named Sheri, who was already there and settled in, helped us. Once everything was in the room, I had no idea what to do next and was grateful Mom was there. She whipped a tape measure out of her bag and did some measuring. Then we drove back into town. It was a tiny town, a cute little place with a Woolworth's that had a creaky wooden floor. Mom kept oohing and aahing, saying, "God, it smells just the same!" as the five-and-tens from when she was a kid. She bought a hammer, a drill, and a screwdriver, saying I'd find uses for them. I couldn't imagine what. She also bought curtain rods, shelving paper, a bathmat, and toothpaste—I'd forgotten to pack mine.

We drove back to the dorm, and she climbed up on my desk chair and made holes in the woodwork with the drill, then used the screwdriver to attach brackets for the curtain rods and put them up. Aha! That was what the tools were for. She had brought up some Indian cottons she'd bought in the Square months ago, big pieces of fabric that could have been tablecloths, bedspreads, or maybe even saris. She'd made wide hems on two of them with iron-on tape and now she stuck the curtain rods through the hems and, presto! They were drapes! She threw the fifth, unhemmed one on my bed as a bedspread, so everything matched. We'd made my bed with the blankets I'd brought. I arranged my books in the bookcase, and she hung my clothes neatly in the closet—

the only time all year they were neat. She put my lamp on the desk, and with enormous pride I laid my heavy new Selectric (my graduation present from Mom and Philo after all) on the desk. That really thrilled me, I have to say! And the room was done! Just like that!

Mom arranged my desk drawers too, being a neatness nut like her father, as she said. She said his garage and cellar and attic were "filed." While she was being neat, I was bouncing around with Sheri, a big girl with a big laugh whom I wasn't sure I would like at first.

I was sharing a suite with Sheri and another girl, Patsy. I loved Patsy the minute she arrived, her parents behind her, loaded down with bags and boxes just like us. The sight of each other made us all laugh. She was tall and dark haired, with a wry sense of humor like Sandy's. I had been assigned the single room, Sheri and Patsy the double; the three of us shared the bath between. When she heard that three boys had the suite next door, Mom told me to lock my door at night. I thought she was being paranoid, but when night came, I did lock the door, anyway.

I loved my room. Its wide window faced the quad, a broad lawn at the center of the campus. Beyond that were college buildings, built in squares around green areas. Stands of birch and pine trees reached into the far distance. Beyond them rose a mountain, green dotted with rust and yellow, an image by Cézanne. The view made me extremely happy.

Registration was Friday and Saturday, and classes started Monday. I had to choose my courses and make up my schedule. All this was frightening. I'd never been allowed to choose my own courses or make up my own schedule, and it felt liberating but scary and made me a little hysterical. I think Sheri and Patsy were scared too.

When I didn't hear from Steve before I left, I calmed myself down by telling myself I'd be home at Thanksgiving and would see him then. Of course, by the time Thanksgiving came around, I was deeply immersed in my new life with new friends and didn't even miss my home. I was enthralled with my roommates, and I met a girl I'd befriended when I worked at the café near Dad's. Gail had transferred to Andrews for her sophomore year, and we stumbled into each other on campus. She'd taken a year off to go to Baja, California to get to know her father. She was brought up by her grandmother in Queens, New York. Her mother was a private detective; her parents were divorced. Her dad lived in Baja with his second wife. She was crazy about him and stayed out there for a whole year. She loved it there; she swam every day and got really tan. She said she was a pro at indolence, but that there was really nothing for her in Baja and in the end she had to come back. Her mother wanted her to finish college. Her dad didn't care, she said: he was a happy guy who drank a lot and sat in the sun and played a banjo, living on his dividends.

Hearing this inspired me to call Dad, and he drove up to fetch me one weekend. He drove me back to the cabin, which had become a house since I had last seen it, with a real kitchen and a bathroom—with a toilet! I couldn't help saying that if he'd been willing to put it in a little sooner, he might have kept Mom. I said this even though I didn't think it was true; I think Mom had about had it when they split up. He snapped at me not to be a smart-ass, but I didn't care. In the car as he was driving me back to Montpelier, it came to me that I wasn't afraid of him anymore. I didn't know why I'd been afraid. He yelled, but he never hit me or anything. Still, I was glad to feel easier with him.

What I'd realized was that Dad had three personalities. The first was the man who had Dad's usual demeanor, the one he used with people outside the family—a really nice guy, amiable and sweet, with a self-deprecating sense of humor. You had to love him; he turned everything into a joke. From things she'd said, I'd gathered he was the one Mom married.

The second didn't appear right away, although soon enough, Mom said. That one was explosive, with a red face, eyes popping out of his head, and a booming voice so loud it hurt your ears. This guy could not hear over the sound of his own yelling, and he made himself madder and madder in tantrums that went on for a whole day, or a weekend sometimes.

The third was a zombie. Dad became this when he felt defeated. He would walk around looking numb and not speaking, not present in his body. He could stay that way for a whole weekend, although often enough zombiedom led to explosion. He'd been a zombie the summer I lived with him in Vermont. I thought maybe that was why he got married again. It must have felt awful to be a zombie.

In whatever persona he was in, though, he was deaf. He couldn't take anything in from the outside. When he was in the first, you could talk to him and think he was hearing you, but he really wasn't. He was locked in and all he could do was repeat himself, shifting from gear to gear, grinding them sometimes. I kept thinking there was a "real Daddy," a person who loved Mom and me, who thought about us, but I never did find him. There was a person who claimed to love us and cried when he talked about it, but I think he was always crying for himself. Mom said once he probably really needed to cry for himself, but never knew he was doing it. She said something terrible had happened to him when he was a boy—his parents abandoned him when his sister died, and he never got over it.

I was thinking about all this, lying in bed one night at Andrews, and I decided it was silly to feel hurt when he got angry with me or called me names because it wasn't intentional. He wasn't seeing me; he was seeing some figment that looked like me. I wasn't real to him anymore—if I ever had been. Maybe no one was. Maybe real people merged with—who knows who?—his parents, maybe, his dead sister, kids he knew when he was young, people he'd read about in books or comics or seen in movies. As though he made everybody up. So when he yelled it was just because an object—me—was in his way. He was a tornado, beyond his own control, and whatever was in his path got blown to smithereens.

The first persona had probably asked Julie to marry him, but when I visited them, he had shifted into the third. I didn't know if Julie had met the second yet. She was nice but a lightweight and she would probably freak out if the second came up to her out of the darkness. You could see her trying to adjust to third when she kept expecting first, but because she didn't understand what he was doing, she didn't know what she was doing either. She always tried to be agreeable.

I liked Julie because she didn't try to be a mother to me. She tried to be my girlfriend: she was young and pretty and bubbly and she painted china. Dad looked at her—when he did look at her—with a kind of amused patience, very different from the way he was with Mom, all intense and raging. He added a room on the back of the house to give Julie a studio, with big windows and electric heat. She spent her days there painting flowers and birds on cups and saucers and plates. They were pretty, her dishes; she sold them through a local cheese shop, not enough to support her, though. It gave her something to do.

She asked me to choose colors and fabrics to decorate my room; she was eager to have the whole house finished, everything with dried flowers and pink bows and Laura Ashley fabrics and painted china everywhere you looked. I was shocked that Dad could stand to live in this environment and once I saw the rest of the house, I didn't want my room done. I was afraid she'd turn it into another one of the cutesy magazine rooms that inspired her, like the picture of a kitchen that she'd put up on her bulletin board. So I got stubborn and said I wanted my room painted white and left alone. I had a brown-and-orange Navaho rug and an antique lamp with an orange globe on my desk and that was that. Julie was really frustrated, but Dad was amused and commanded her to leave me alone. I was pleased that he defended me, but sorry to see her hurt reaction.

Dad worked in his studio during the day, so the only time I saw him that weekend was at meals. We did talk at dinner. Friday night Julie broiled chicken until it was truly dead and baked potatoes and made frozen peas. Dad gulped it in huge mouthfuls. After Mom's cooking, you'd think he'd know it was bad, but he didn't seem to. He asked me what I was going to major in, and when I said literature, he made a face. I said I wanted to be a poet, and he said I couldn't be serious. And I said, "As serious as you were about being an artist."

"How are you going to live?" he asked.

"How did you?" I retorted.

He made a face. "Stop being a smart-ass. You know you can't count on a man supporting you anymore," he boomed.

"Like you supported Mom?" I said, wincing inside.

"Yeah. She got the car and I got the car payments," he snarled. He looked absolutely disgusted and plunged into his drink as if my nastiness had driven him to it.

Saturday night he took us to a local restaurant, where he ordered a large steak, a baked potato with sour cream, and a lot of whiskey. He often looked flushed these days, and I wondered if that was healthy. That night he asked me about Andrews. I was careful in my answers. I felt guilty for being snarky the night before, and had vowed to try to be nicer. Of course, I never knew what would set him off, but I tried to soft-pedal the more liberal aspects of the place. I talked about its arts programs, the great writers on its faculty, the beauty of the campus. I figured he would like my being in Vermont. I tried to bring up as many names as possible because I knew that the one thing that would make him like Andrews was hearing the name of someone he knew on its faculty, but no name I mentioned seemed familiar to him. It seemed I just generally annoyed him, and he lost himself in his drinks the same as he had the night before.

It didn't matter about my room, because I didn't go back to that house very often. Julie did eventually turn it into a doll-house room. Well, why not? It was her house. I felt like a stranger there. I could only skirt my father's life: he did almost no talking. He stayed in zombie gear most of the time he lived with Julie; if he erupted into his second persona, I didn't see it. But maybe he did, because Julie left him a few years later. Until then, when you went there, you were really visiting Julie—who wasn't all that interesting.

He loved me; I kept reminding myself of that. But his mind was elsewhere. It wasn't with Julie or Mom or me. Maybe it was with his painting. Maybe he saw colors. Or maybe he was thinking about smoking and drinking. What he felt for me was something he'd buried deep in his heart, years ago. Every time I thought about him, my heart broke again. What broke my heart wasn't anything he was doing to me, or even anything he was doing to himself; it was just what he was. I don't know how to explain this, even now; I didn't know then, and couldn't have spoken about it to anyone, not even Sandy, not even Mom. I felt as though he was a walking ruin of something that wanted to be, that started out to be fine and noble and good. But he collapsed, imploded.

Still, it was on that visit that I got my first insight into his painting. I went into his studio one morning before he'd staggered out there with his mug of coffee, and I walked around and looked at all the paintings in different stages of completion and a few that were finished and leaned, drying, against the wall. They were big paintings, at that time almost all cerise and gray, with purple or black streaks and sometimes a yellow patch.

And suddenly I was overwhelmed by them. I felt them rushing at me, like nature overflowing, like rage pouring out of my father. They expressed uncontainable, animal energy. I began to see why people said he was great; and it came to me that maybe he was and that maybe it was worth it to him to pay for it with his life.

It would not be worth it to me. Did that mean I would never be a poet?

Sandy, Bishop, and I had exchanged a round of letters before the first intimations of disaster began to ripple, right around Thanksgiving, when I was home for the holidays. At first, the story had no connection with anyone I knew: several weeks earlier a Cambridge cop had been charged with taking bribes. A man who had just been promoted to captain of the police force was ordered to investigate long-standing rumors of police involvement in a drug ring in the city. An ambitious idealist, he followed his orders scrupulously and so became the first cop to look into the drug rumors seriously. His efforts gained him an ally, a political columnist for a Boston paper. The columnist had a team of informants, and he publicized the campaign. At Thanksgiving, he hinted that upper-level Cambridge cops were involved. I wasn't very interested in local news. I read this article only because Mom had called it to my attention, knowing that Bishop's father was police commissioner. When I went back to Andrews, I asked Mom to follow the story and send me clippings if anything more happened.

In the next weeks, she sent me a few clippings. To save himself, a cop who had been accused agreed to inform on a ring of other officers taking bribes from drug dealers. Actually, if you thought about it, it was obvious that this was happening. Otherwise, why would it be so easy to get drugs in Cambridge? Or any place? There had to be whole systems of people passing them on, each stop skimming a little from the pot, and the police had to be agreeing not to notice. At Monaghan's, where Steve worked, you could get weed, mushrooms, amphetamines, anything at all.

When I came home again a few days before Christmas, Mom met me at the bus station and told me that the columnist was hinting that the commissioner of police was implicated—Bishop's father! The papers were full of talk about the ring of cops and rumors of higher-ups involved.

For dinner that night, Mom and I made a navarin. We stood in the kitchen together peeling tiny white onions and thin green beans. As it simmered, I called Bishop. He answered the phone, the same vague, dreamy Bishop, and I realized I didn't know what to say. I was home, I said, and how was he, and had he seen Sandy, and how was Yale and had he seen Steve and would he like to get together. I didn't mention his father. He said everything was okay, yeah, he just hadn't had time to write, he was so busy. Yale was great, he hadn't seen Sandy, he hadn't seen Steve either, he didn't know if Steve was going to Harvard or not, he never went into Monaghan's. Sure, we should get together, but he had promised his mother he'd drive her around this week to do her Christmas chores—getting the tree, ordering food, buying presents. He'd call me when he had some free time.

I put the phone down with a bad feeling. Bishop had always had time for me.

Always.

I called Sandy.

No, she hadn't called Bishop, she was too nervous, didn't want to upset him, didn't know what the situation was. Sure, she could have lunch with me tomorrow, she had loads to tell me, Smith was great! Really great! She loved it, loved her roommate!

We met at Bailey's, our usual place, and giggled and told truths through a three-hour lunch of a cheese sandwich and three cups of coffee. Our poor roommates' every secret lay revealed before we were through. Neither of us knew anything new about Bishop or his family.

Bishop's father was arrested in March, so Sandy and I weren't around to give Bishop attention. Our mothers kept us informed, and we both called him, first at Yale, and then at home. He wasn't at Yale, and nobody answered the phone at the Cambridge house. The newspapers were full of Commissioner Connolly, who was accused of receiving payoffs over many years. He said he was innocent, but the headlines screamed corruption and there were photographs of him showing up at court with a fake smile on his face, and his lawyer beside him and little Mrs. Connolly clutching his arm, smiling also, right on the front page of all the Boston newspapers. I called on and off all week, hard as it was to call long distance from the dorm (the phone was on the wall of the common room on the first floor), calling Sandy in between. She was having no luck either. By early June, there was a weird machine hooked up to the Connolly's phone, some new invention, a machine answering the telephone! I didn't recognize the voice on the machine; I think it must have been Bishop's brother-in-law, Francis, saying the Connollys were unavailable but to please leave a message and they would return your call and to wait until the signal to start talking. The first time we heard this, we both just hung up in shock, but after that we spoke into the mechanical device. Bishop never called us back, so finally Sandy and I each wrote Bishop a letter and sent it to the Cambridge house.

Neither of us heard from him again. He vanished out of our lives. People said that the family had sold their house and that Mrs. Connolly and the younger boys lived in an apartment outside Boston and that she had a job working in a school cafeteria. We didn't know if this was true. By the end of the summer, Mr. Connolly was in jail. He had pleaded no contest and been sentenced to five years in a minimum security prison. It was horrible to picture cheerful Mr. Connolly in jail. It was horrible to picture poor overworked Mrs. Connolly with her worried forehead, standing all day behind a steam table ladling food onto plates, then going home to her many sons in a cramped apartment.

Then we heard that Patrick, the second-oldest son, had been killed in Vietnam.

My heart hurt thinking about all of them, remembering how, when our gang would pile into their house, they always welcomed us with smiles. They'd urge us to have a Coke, a beer, some peanuts. They were a golden family, full of well-being, affection, and generosity. It was the Connollys I thought of when I read *War and Peace* and came to the Rostovs. It was the Connollys who had strengthened my belief that if people lived the right way, they could have happiness and good luck all their days.

Now suddenly, I couldn't offer to help, couldn't find them to tell them I was sorry about what happened to them. Sandy and I clung to each other, telephoning each other and writing every week, but after a few months we forgot it, or I did, being the fickle thing I am.

8 **I loved college,** everything about it: the beauty of the Green Mountains, the freedom of living without a mother or father around, the thrilling new people I met who shimmered with the glamour of the unknown. Above all I loved what I was learning. I encountered books by authors I hadn't known existed—they weren't from long ago, like Austen or Trollope or Henry James, or new, like Lessing and Solzhenitsyn, but in between—I read Arthur Koestler's *Darkness at Noon* and André Malraux's *Man's Fate*. They were about recent times, times when I was alive yet knew nothing about. They opened up whole new worlds to me. They put the Vietnam War in a new context and made me realize how innocent—ignorant, really—my protesting had been. I was still against war after reading those books, but not as I had been. Somebody had to fight against the horrors described in these books, just like my father had said. Even my mother agreed that Hitler had to be defeated. It had never occurred to me that some wars were, if not good, necessary, and some were not. I was fundamentally against war itself, against humans trying to dominate other humans, but after I read these writers, the problem seemed more complicated.

Freshmen couldn't take creative writing courses, but I joined the poetry club. I never got up the nerve to read anything of my own aloud, but my juices flowed with the stimulus of being there, and I was writing poems at a hectic pace. Different kids showed up there each week, but the core of it was five girls (including me) and three guys, one named Christopher Hurley. The guys were snobs, mocking almost everybody. They looked down on the girls, which made me nervous. But they were all really nice to me for some reason. I especially liked Christopher. He was older than me, a junior, and he wrote poems about science, culling it for metaphors, especially about time and space. To me he seemed profound. I knew the concept: time and space were a continuum, two ways of looking at the same phenomenon. I wasn't sure I really understood it, but I loved to listen to him read and I tried to talk to him when we all went out for drinks together after the meeting. He didn't seem to particularly notice me. Still, I believed he liked me without knowing it. He was very serious.

I had a terrific lit teacher, Dr. Ruth Stauffer, a dynamic woman around Mom's age and, like Mom, good looking and with a nice figure and nice clothes; she wore pants to class. There weren't many women on the faculty, and the few there were wore skirts. I wore jeans; everybody did, with boots and sweaters. That was our uniform. Ruth (she told us to call her Ruth) had us read Christina Stead's *The Man Who Loved Children*, Günter Grass's *The Tin Drum*, and Christa Wolf's *The Quest for Christa T.*, which knocked me out. We read Lessing's *The Four-Gated City*, which was great, and then *In Pursuit of the English*, which was a hoot. We had such lively discussions in lit class that we groaned when the class bell rang, and we often hung around afterward.

Ruth started "Fridays at Four," an informal gathering for us to discuss books or anything else we wanted to talk about. She invited faculty members and students to come and talk about their favorite writer or poet or artist or whatever else they were interested in. Professors who were boring in class came alive when they started to talk about their passions. There was a biology professor who loved Gerard Manley Hopkins and read his poetry to us in a velvety voice. A math professor came with slides of the beautiful little boxes by Joseph Cornell. A French professor who loved George Sand but never got to teach her talked for over an hour one afternoon and kept us all rapt. He told us about Sand's involvement in the 1848 French Revolution and how she left her husband and went to Paris and dressed as a man so she could go to the theater and feel free in the streets. She took lots of lovers, among them Chopin and Alfred de Musset. We learned that her writing influenced all of Europe and America, inspiring Marx, Bakunin, Dostoevsky, Walt Whitman, Balzac, and Flaubert. She was the first author to write about poor people. The professor read from a novel about the poor, *Francois le Champi*, *The Country Waif* in English. I was so excited by Sand that I ran to the bookstore to get all her books. But they didn't have any—not one. There were two in the library; I read them both.

Afternoons like that were inspiring, and I felt that this was what college was supposed to be. After lectures, Ruth served sherry and cheese, which made us feel grown up and civilized. The glasses were tiny and there were as many faculty as students, so no one drank too much.

I also took political science, a survey of different forms and theories of government. Unfortunately the teacher was boring, and my mind would drift to Bishop, who had intended to major in poli sci. It was an early class, nine a.m., so I often cut. Nobody took attendance at Andrews, so it didn't matter. I wondered if Bishop liked Yale; I wondered if he felt comfortable there and if he was taking the same poli sci course as I was. I would have liked to write him long letters about it, to ask what he thought about these theories of government. I did start a letter to him, writing three or four pages, but lost it before I could mail it.

During my freshman year, I fell in love every couple of weeks. My attitude toward sex was evolving, and I decided that I had to get over my hesitations and just do it. A number of guys were pursuing me; the most ardent and indefatigable was Donny Karl. He looked somewhat depraved; he had a thin face with sunken cheeks and cold eyes that I imagined glittered with desire. He looked so sophisticated that I thought he must know all about love. I wasn't crazy about him, but his wicked appearance and his infatuation with me seemed enough. I warned my roommates what was coming and, one rainy Saturday afternoon, locked both my doors and went to bed with him. Afterward, I was shocked: this was the great thing everybody panted for?

When I told Patsy it was a big nothing, she said that if I was disappointed, Donny hadn't known what he was doing. I denied I was disappointed; I insisted I was just not impressed. But her words stayed in my mind, and I started to review Donny's acts and realized he had been sort of clumsy and stupid. Maybe his looks were deceiving?

She had said, "You know what an orgasm is, don't you? You masturbate, right?"

I said, "Sure." But masturbate! Certainly not! What an idea!

Not that I hadn't done a little exploration of my body. But whenever I began to feel something ripple through my flesh, when my heartbeat speeded up and my loins began to throb, I pulled back, because I felt I was doing something bad. But what Patsy said made me think about this and the next time it happened, I let my hands continue their activity, and even exercised some ingenuity, and before long, *Whammo*!

So that's what it was all about.

I abandoned Donny and looked for partners I felt more about, not that there's really any way to be sure sex will be good with anybody. I just thought it would be better if I felt something for the guy, which hadn't been the case with poor Donny. At eighteen, though, I seemed to feel things for an awful lot of guys, and I couldn't tell which feelings mattered and which didn't. Everybody was attractive! I wondered if there was something wrong with me. Maybe I was oversexed? I was crazy about some girls too. It was common at Andrews for girls to get together with each other. It had cachet—a girl could be a lesbian one year and straight the next. It wasn't as acceptable for boys. My fickle heart sent me roaming, never settling anywhere for long.

Toward the end of the spring term, Dad called and said he'd come and get me and lug me and my stuff to Cambridge. That was so thoughtful, so unusual for him, that I felt almost teary, but I just said casually, "Sure, okay." We set a day and time, and there he was, bright and early on a Friday at the end of May. He had his truck, which held all my stuff easily. It was amazing how much stuff I had—almost twice as much as I'd come up with. I didn't think I'd bought much over the year, some books, a couple of lipsticks, that's all, I thought, but I'd gotten a new stereo for Christmas and a lot of clothes and books, tons of books. He packed all the stuff up and I got in the cab with him and we drove off. After we'd been on the road for what seemed like ages, I was pretty hungry, but he was driving with grim intensity and I didn't dare to suggest stopping. Finally, as we approached Marlboro, he pulled into the driveway of a little restaurant. "Want some lunch?"

"Yeah!" I said fervently.

We got out. Dad stretched and we went in. They knew him in this place. He liked to be known and greeted; it put him in a good mood. That put me in a good mood. We both had huge hamburgers topped with sliced raw onion on a delicious bun. I had a cola and Dad had two Manhattans. That worried me, but he did have coffee after lunch. Still, I was leery of driving with him, but he drove calmly as we left, seeming not to be in a hurry. He pulled into a place—it looked like a car dealership—and I wondered if he was having trouble with the truck.

"Out," he ordered. I shrugged and obeyed. We walked into the dealer's office.

"Mr. Leighton!" a booming voice welcomed him.

"Harry!" he boomed back.

They chatted like old friends. I just stood there until Dad turned to me. "And this is my daughter, Jessamin."

Harry turned on me what he probably thought of as his charm. It felt like a blast of heat. He turned away and we followed him out the side door, and he said something to a boy in a grease-stained uniform, who ran off. He and Dad went on blustering to each other, while I stood there trying to figure out if my father had gone completely over the edge, or what was happening. Pretty soon, a little red Fiat convertible pulled up in front of us.

"There she is," Harry boomed cheerfully.

"Cute as a bug," my father grinned. He looked at me. "Get in, Jess. It's yours."

That day glows in my mind still. They say money can't buy happiness, and it's true that after a few years the car didn't affect my spirits at all, but that day and for a long time afterward, I floated in joy. Daddy said he'd bought it because it was a pain in the neck to drive all the way up to Andrews to get me and then drive me back again whenever I visited him. But I'd only visited him once the whole year and I wondered why he had to spoil his generosity by being mean. He told Harry what I'd heard him say to other men, that I was a drag on him, costing him money and time, especially my college education; maybe that's how he felt, but then why was there always a tinge of pride in his voice when he said it? And why was he always laughing while he said it? And they would nod their heads and laugh too. Were his jokes a cover-up for affection for me that he was, for some reason, ashamed of? Was it not manly to love your daughter? My father's sense of things often seemed to me to reflect an upside-down world.

He ordered me to follow him on the highway, but sometimes he'd get behind me as we drove together the rest of the way to

Cambridge. We arrived late in the afternoon; Mom was there but not Philo—I'd called to warn her that Daddy was bringing me home. He took her out to see the car, and as he preened, she seized up with worry. "It's so tiny!" I heard her whisper to him. "If she has an accident, Pat, she's dead."

"She won't," he said.

She didn't ask him to stay to dinner, which I thought was mean, since he'd been so kind all day, and he was surely tired, especially after those Manhattans, and now he would have to drive all the way back to Marlboro. I was appalled at her unkindness, until I realized that if he stayed, he'd have got drunk and maybe become abusive; he'd have wanted to stay the night and she'd have had to let him, drunk as he was. So maybe she was right. Still, it seemed sad that my mother could not even manage to be a decent human being for my father. Or he for her, I guess. I clung to him before he left: he'd been so nice to me, he'd never been so nice, and I had a terrible premonition that I'd never see him again. I begged him to call me when he got home and he promised he would, but I waited up late and he didn't. I didn't dare call Julie too late at night, so I called the next day and she said he'd come in at two in the morning, sloshed but in a good mood. So that was okay.

I got good grades my first year, all A's, even in political science. My mother was pleased, and I guess I was too, but down deep, I didn't care. What would good grades do for me? I wasn't planning to go to graduate school. I was in college to learn about life; that was what mattered. I thought about Aristotle and his pupils, wandering around Athens talking and arguing without ever even having heard of grades or degrees or a curriculum, just learning to think.

That summer in Cambridge the air was full of schadenfreude. Men associated with Richard Nixon had broken into the Democratic Party headquarters in Washington, and Nixon was in trouble. I went to see Sonny, who hired me for the summer. I was happy to get the job, because even with my new car I figured I was going to be pretty lonely that summer. Sandy was supposed to be a camp counselor again and Bishop, Dolores, and Steve had disappeared. The only things I could think of to occupy me besides work was going to the movies or a concert with Mom and talking to Philo on the weekends. I loved to see Philo, but I was sad that Mom had put him out of my reach.

But Sandy called as soon as she got home from school, bursting with news. We planned lunch, although not at Bailey's, Sandy having become a vegetarian. We went to Aragon, a little Spanish restaurant that offered a vegetable plate—a rarity in those days. Aragon had white tablecloths and guitar music played low on the stereo, and we each had the vegetable plate and a small glass of red wine and felt terribly sophisticated.

In a portentous tone, Sandy announced that she was gay. She was madly in love with a woman named Sarah, who lived in her dorm. Sarah came from Marblehead, from a WASP family who were very rich and very proper but eccentric and just a little alcoholic (martinis every day at six, wine with dinner, cognac afterward) and traced their ancestors to the Mayflower. They did not care for Jews. Sarah didn't agree with them. Sarah was brave.

Hearing this, I confessed that I might be gay too, because I was involved with a girl named Melanie, who lived in my dorm and came from New Jersey, from a small lakeside town called Greenpond. Melanie was often melancholy; at other times she got so giggly that I couldn't stop laughing. For some reason, Melanie looked up to me. She seemed to think I was decisive. Actually, I wasn't sure I was in love with her, but it felt modern and daring to be with her just then. So when Melanie had problems with her roommate, I invited her to share my room. She leaped to be with me and I felt a tremendous gush of something I thought was love. And the thing was, we gave each other orgasms *every time*.

Sandy and I showed each other pictures of our new friends and laughed at the fact that our discoveries had occurred at the same time. Then we started to talk about Bishop. I told her how dumb I felt about the Connollys. I said I felt naive and thought my values were shallow.

Sandy said, "I felt the same way. I don't think that was stupid. They were a great family. Why shouldn't you think that they were happy? They *were* happy!"

"Yes, but look at them now."

"That doesn't mean they weren't happy then. Just because a bad thing happened, something that made them unhappy, that doesn't erase the happiness they had."

"Except that the whole time Mr. Connolly was taking bribe money."

"Umm." She lit a cigarette. "You mean, Mr. Connolly wouldn't have been happy because he was doing a bad thing and knew it? But maybe he was. Maybe he didn't feel bad about what he was doing. And the rest of them didn't know it, so they were happy as clams."

"He couldn't have been happy doing an illegal thing," I argued.

She pondered. "Why not?"

"You just can't. You have to be scared you'll be caught. Even if you don't let yourself think about it, your body is scared all the time. How can you call them a happy family if he wasn't happy too?"

She studied me. "You mean," she said slowly, "in a happy family, everybody has to be happy?"

"Of course. Otherwise it isn't a happy family. It's a happy person. But not a happy family. Could you say my family was happy and only count me? Or Mom and me? You could say we were happy when Dad wasn't around. But that makes the phrase meaningless, *happy family*."

She thought for a while, then laughed. "Well, *you* have a gift for happiness."

"Do I? Really? Oh, I wish I could share it with Bishop."

"I heard he dropped out of Yale."

"Oh, no!"

"Well, they probably couldn't afford to keep him there."

"Oh?" I hadn't thought of that. "Yeah."

"I wish he'd call. Or write. Let us know where he is."

"Yeah."

We both fell into gloom then.

"Things fall apart; the centre cannot hold," Sandy intoned.

One reason I always loved Sandy was that she knew poetry.

"But do things *always* fall apart?"

"No. Not everything," she assured me. "We aren't falling apart."

"Let's not," I urged. "You and me."

She put her hand across the table and took mine. "We won't."

"We made the same pact with Bishop," I said.

"I know."

A week later, Sandy's plans completely changed. She had just heard that Sarah had got a job in Boston for the summer, as an intern at Houghton Mifflin. Could Sandy leave if Sarah was coming to Boston? Yet Sandy knew her parents would disapprove of her abandoning her summer job. They were very principled. "They'll say I have an obligation to make good on my promise. And I do feel bad letting down the people who run the camp. But Sarah is more important, don't you think? Love is more important than duty, isn't it?"

"Love *is* more important," I said with certainty.

Of course love won. This made me happy; I began to hope I might have fun that summer after all, with Sandy and Sarah. The women's movement was burgeoning. Women all over town were starting new enterprises—a restaurant called Bread and Roses, with a vegetarian menu, good soups and breads and salads, and extremely low prices; a couple of terrific women's newspapers; and a medical clinic for poor women. The clinic was set up by female students in the med schools at Harvard and UMass and other local colleges and was located in the Portuguese part of Cambridge. It was funded by a grant and the women who worked there took very little pay. They treated any woman who walked in for a minimal fee, or for free if she were really poor. Sandy's sister Rhoda had gone to undergraduate school with one of the women who was working there now as a doctor, and she told Sandy about it. So Sandy applied for a job as a receptionist and was hired. In the end, she became much more than a receptionist—she was a coordinator, a nurse, a secretary, a babysitter: she did everything. She was paid the same as the doctors—everyone got seventy-five dollars a week. That was how the women wanted to do things: everyone was paid the same pittance. But she was doing it for love, so she didn't care. Besides, when her father found out what she was doing, he was so proud of her that he increased her allowance.

Then Sandy had news about the Connollys. Her mother had a cousin who lived near Dorchester and sometimes shopped at the Star Market there. This cousin, Lily, recognized Mrs. Connolly because there had been joint charity projects between her chapter of B'nai Brith and the women who helped Catholic Charities in Mrs. Connolly's parish. Mrs. Connolly had been a leader in that group; she had spoken at some of their meetings, so Lily knew who she was. And of course she had followed their story in the papers. So when she saw Mrs. Connolly in the Star Market one day, she mentioned it to Mrs. Lipkin, who told her that Sandy would dearly like to know where they were living. The next time Lily saw Mrs. Connolly, she followed her out of the store and watched which way she walked.

So did I want to go with Sandy to try to find them?

I would drive us, I said. Then came the question, Should we take things?

We pondered. We wanted to take as much as we could—food, clothes, wine—but we didn't want to humiliate Mrs. Connolly. We decided to take only a few toys for the boys and a box of candy and a basket of fruit for Mrs. Connolly—sparse recompense for all the hospitality they had offered us over the years. We bought a street map of South Boston and set a date and time. It was a beautiful June morning, a Saturday, when Mrs. Connolly would not be working at the school. We drove to South Boston, to a neighborhood of shabby three-deckers with cracked sidewalks, dilapidated stores, and a few scrawny trees. We found the Star Market and drove a few blocks in the direction that Sandy's mother's cousin had seen Mrs. Connolly walk. Then we got out of the car and wandered around. We rang some doorbells and asked for the Connollys. We told people we had been to school with Bishop and were trying to find him. Most people were sympathetic. The folks in that neighborhood were often on the outs with the cops and saw the Connollys as just another persecuted Irish family. We knew people would know them: they were famous. And eventually we were pointed to the right house—an old three-decker with stained brown siding and a front yard full of weeds and broken bike pieces. We climbed the front stairs and found their name on the bell. We rang it.

We were sick with nervousness.

Lloyd Connolly answered the door. We had last seen him at a Christmas party when he was seven; he not only was taller now, but also had a hard expression on his face.

"Hi," he said, puzzled, surprised.

"Hi, Lloyd. You remember us? Sandy and Jessamin. We were friends of Bishop's and we used to be at your house a lot."

"Yeah."

"We came to visit your mother."

"Uh. Oh. Well, okay," he said, letting us in. He ran up the stairs and we followed him up two flights to the third floor. Near the top, he began to yell. "Mom! Company!"

She came to the apartment door, looking bewildered. We stood, paralyzed. She was old, white-haired and wrinkled. She was wearing a shapeless cotton dress and smoking a filter-tip cigarette.

"Mrs. Connolly!" Sandy gushed. "It's Sandy and Jess, remember us?"

"Girls," she faltered. "Bishop isn't . . ."

"No, we came to see you," I said in a false cheery voice.

"Oh, well, come in, come in, girls, do."

We held our gifts out in front of us like armor. Sandy handed the toys to Lloyd, who was still standing behind his mother.

"These are for you and your brothers," she said, and he cried, "Okay!" and went charging off, yelling for Philip. "And these are for you," I said, handing Mrs. Connolly the fruit and candy. We followed her into the front room.

The dingy white walls of the apartment were cracked crazily. Elegant furniture from the old house, shabbier than I remembered, crowded the room. The tables were dusty and the doilies a little gray, and a huge television set from the old house dominated the small space.

"Can I offer you some tea, girls?" Mrs. Connolly asked.

"Oh, no thanks!" we chimed.

"Oh, you have to have tea! Lloyd!" she called out, "Put the kettle on!"

"How are you?" I asked her, searching her face. "All of you?"

She shrugged. "Sure, we're fine. We lost Patrick, you know. Last year. Of course you hardly knew him, but . . ." She pulled a hanky out of her dress top and wiped her eyes. "And Gus was wounded. In the leg. This terrible war! But he's fine, he's a major now and they're promising to send him home soon. He's going to stay in; he might as well, he has so much time in now. He'll be stationed in California. He's a good boy, he helps us out. John— Mr. Connolly—he'll be home in a few months, we think. Things should pick up then. And Maggie and Francis and their little ones are glorious, thanks be to God. Francis works for the bursar at Boston College, you know," she offered, sounding deeply impressed. "Maggie's over here regular, our godsend. Michael graduated from Holy Cross this June, thanks be to God, and he's living out in Framingham; he has a job in an insurance company there. Billy's in his last year of high school and Eugene's a sophomore. They have jobs at the Star Market, so they're not home now. So there's only Lloyd left, who's nine, and Philip, who's seven now. And that's all of them. We're managing fine."

Throughout this conversation, Mrs. Connolly had been twisting her hands together almost constantly, so while her face bore a small smile, her hands countered the message.

"And how is Bishop?"

Her hands stopped dead. She looked at the wall. "Sure, he's fine," she said.

"Where is he? We've been calling and writing . . ." Sandy began.

"Ach, I know you've been faithful friends. I gave him your letters, girls, last time I saw him. But he's taken all this very hard. You know, he was a bit on the outs with his dad, back when the war . . . even before all our troubles . . . and then, when . . . he felt his dad had let us down, betrayed the family, Oh, he's a sensitive boy, you know . . ."

"So where is he living?" Sandy pursued relentlessly.

"He's livin' in a sort of commune place, you know? Up in western Massachusetts somewhere. In the far mountains. I've never seen it, it's out of the way, we have to send his mail to a post office box. They have horses, and he's good with horses. Bunch of hippies," she lamented, "on a farm."

Sandy and I looked at each other.

"Oh, that's good," Sandy said. "He's safe, then."

"He's neglecting his education. Bishop was the smartest of the boys. He had a scholarship, and they would have given him another one, surely."

"Probably he'll go back," Sandy reassured her. "Someday."

"You think so? John had such hopes for him . . ."

"Oh, I think so. He's too smart not to," Sandy insisted.

She seemed to relax for the first time since we arrived. "Well, you were his best friends, girls. If you think so . . ." Her forehead smoothed a little.

Lloyd appeared, carrying a heavy tray bearing a teapot, cups, saucers, and a plate of vanilla wafers. He set the tray down on the coffee table in front of his mother. Her silver spoons had given way to cheap stainless, but she still had the lace-edged tea napkins. The teapot was her beautiful old Minton china. The top was a little chipped, so she couldn't have sold it. The cups and saucers were glass. She poured tea for us as formally as the girls' dean of students at Smith, the one time I visited Sandy, adding cream and sugar after asking. Sandy and I each took a single cookie, nibbling politely.

"So! How are you girls doin'?" she asked, her chore complete.

"We're fine," I said. "Sandy's studying pre-med at Smith, and I'm at Andrews. We're fine, but we miss Bishop and we've been worried about him."

"Sure and I'll tell him next time I write. They aren't on the phone up there, and I'm not the best writer, you know. Billy writes sometimes though."

"We hope your family will all be together again soon," Sandy said.

I thought, not for the first time, how tactful and gracious she was. I would never have thought to put it that way. My thought was, "I hope the old man gets out of the joint real soon, I hope he'll be able to call in markers from some of his old graft buddies to give him a decent job and get you out of this shithouse," but it wasn't something I would say aloud.

We said the polite things and left. We'd taken action and it had been successful: at last we knew what had happened. Bishop had blamed his father for his disgrace and the ruination of the family. And there had been a terrible family fight and he had stalked off and hitched to Massachusetts to join a guy he'd met at the dude ranch a couple of years ago. Brad d'Alessio was an idealist, a philosophy student who had dropped out of UCLA and started a commune in the mountains near Becket, Massachusetts, where his mother's parents had lived a generation ago. We remembered Bishop saying what a great idea the commune was, people living together in an egalitarian community in a big old house in the mountains. They could turn their backs on the hideous world and create an ideal world of their own, where everybody was equal, where nature was respected, where the power of money and social status were irrelevant. The commune had horses. The commune members trained them for show, boarded them for rich folks in the area, and rented them out for rides by the hour. The members raised soy and corn. They had no electricity and no phone and refused to pay taxes.

We had sighed over the thought of it, back when Bishop told us about it. And now, it made sense that after the family catastrophe he'd run there; Bishop was safe and in a place he ought to be, no matter how his mother felt about it. We knew we'd find him again someday.

Sandy did stay in town that summer, but after that I barely saw her. She was always working or with Sarah. They were caught up in each other and rarely thought to invite me along. Sarah was staying in Beacon Hill, in an apartment owned by her cousin Polly, who was in England studying art. She and Sandy had Polly's small but luxurious apartment all to themselves. They invited me one Saturday night for dinner. Neither of them knew how to cook. They got takeout from Legal Sea Foods and we gorged ourselves on shrimp cocktail and cherrystone clams and lobsters and salad.

The two of them were always laughing—everything struck them as funny. They told me that the previous weekend they'd driven up to Marblehead to go to the beach, but it was a strain because Sarah's parents were wary of Sandy, acting as if she came from a different race. They kept asking if she could eat certain things, then served lobster—which Jews who keep kosher do not eat—without any apology. Sandy's family did not keep kosher. Sarah's mother seemed to expect that Sandy would wear a wig.

Sarah insisted that once her family actually got to know Sandy, they would be impressed. Sandy looked unsure at this. Sarah laughed and started to describe what they expected a Jew to look and act like, but Sandy looked even more uncomfortable and Sarah stopped.

Physically, Sarah was like another Sandy: tallish and slim, with long, curly hair and a long, pale face. She wasn't as restrained and not nearly as smart as Sandy. She was cute and funny; she had a deep gurgling laugh. She didn't know about art and literature and politics, like Sandy, but she was very athletic—she was a championship swimmer and a tennis ace, and she played volleyball and golf. Sandy was very proud of Sarah's tennis cups and her golf and swimming prizes.

A couple of weekends, Sarah came over to Belmont and stayed at Sandy's house, and once the three of us went out together. It was almost like old times with Bishop and Dolores. It saved the summer from total misery. I loved their relationship. Sandy lent Sarah books and showed her prints and taught her about books and art; and Sarah taught Sandy to play tennis. I thought that that was the ideal—two people who made each other larger, better. That's what I wanted too.

I tried to find Dolores, but she was gone, we didn't know where. We couldn't get information from her family; when we called and reached her father, he shouted that she wasn't there and hung up on us. Her mother sounded just as angry, saying that Dolores was "away." None of our friends knew where Dolores had gone, only that she had dropped out of UMass.

I couldn't find Steve, either. Breaking his taboo, I went into Monaghan's and asked about him. The place was grungy, and the guys who hung out there seemed to belong to gangs. The man behind the counter said Steve didn't work there anymore and he didn't know where he was or what he was doing. I thought of driving to the building where Steve had lived and seeing if his grandmother was still there, but just thinking of her desolate face was enough to stop me. Even if I found her, she wouldn't tell me where Steve was. She didn't want me in his life.

So most of the time I was alone. I was feeling pretty abandoned and wishing I was back at Andrews. Then, one Wednesday at the end of July, I was walking home after work—I never drove to work, there was no place to park—and I saw someone, a male, unwind himself from our front doorstep. He stood, stretching, for a moment, and I stopped, my mouth falling open. It was Christopher Hurley! He had come down to Cambridge to see me! So he did like me! I was so excited I could hardly talk. I invited him for dinner and when Mom came in—she was teaching summer school—introduced him enthusiastically as the poet I'd told her about. But Mom, who usually liked my other friends, disliked him on sight. I could see that. I didn't know why, but I suspected she was being bourgeois and judgmental. He didn't bathe too often. But Mom supposedly knew things like that weren't important; she wasn't usually so narrow. I had told her what a wonderful poet he was—you'd think that alone would make her like him. That he came all the way to Cambridge just to see me was important to me. But she never relented.

He slept on our couch that night; Mom said he couldn't stay permanently. I made him shower the next morning, but his clothes still smelled. I took him into work with me anyway. Sonny gave him a job in the restaurant, but ordered him to wash his clothes. I was pissed that Sonny was going to pay him more per hour than he paid me. I complained, but he said Christopher needed it; he was a guy.

I tried to understand that.

Sonny said, "Listen, when you go out with a guy, who pays?"

"Both of us," I said.

"Bah!" he responded. "The man pays. Always. The man pays. He needs more!"

That was the end of it. In my mind, I argued with Sonny. I wanted to tell him that my mother supported me and that she usually paid for her and Philo. But Sonny didn't know my mother, and besides, I'd seen him blow up at other girls and was a little afraid of him. And I knew Sonny was a Greek American, like Christopher.

We found a laundromat and Chris washed some of his clothes, but the ones he was wearing were still unpleasantly fragrant. He found a bed in a student hostel. He couldn't leave his stuff there during the day, so he had to carry everything he owned around in his backpack, a huge unwieldy canvas sack on an aluminum frame. I would sneak him into our house when Mom was out and let him have a shower and do his laundry in our machines. Once in a while I asked him to stay to dinner.

The hostel wouldn't allow me to stay with him there, so there was no way for us to get together, which both of us really, really wanted to do. So on the afternoons we both had off, I would drive us out to the beach at Revere. It was fun driving there in my cute little red Fiat with the top down. I could tell Christopher was really impressed by it. I would park under some trees, isolated from the other cars, and we'd put the top up and Christopher and I would make out. It was tight quarters in that little car, and sometimes we got out and threw a blanket on the grass between the car and the trees, where we felt hidden.

That summer I was convinced that Chris was it for me. He was handsome, in his unwashed way—long black curls, a chin that never looked fully shaved. He was very tall and thin and although his name sounded Irish, it was an anglicized form of a Greek name. That gave him a certain cachet at Waspy Andrews. His hands were El Greco hands. He always hung back, looking at life from a distance. This aloofness made him glamorous. The Andrews girls thought he was the coolest thing. The only thing that upset me about him was he didn't want to read my poetry, and when I read it to him, he seemed not to listen. My heart sank each time this happened. It hurt so much that I stopped trying. But I loved to listen to him read his poems, which he constantly revised. He enjoyed reading them to me each time he changed them and I was honored that he cared about my opinion. I loved his metaphors.

We hung out together just about every day, because Sonny started him working days. If he stayed long enough, Sonny would give him nights and then we'd never see each other. But I didn't want to think about that. We wandered through Cambridge or went to the movies or for rides in my car. I introduced him to Sandy. She didn't seem to respond to him. She wasn't into men just then. I understood that Sandy was distracted, but that wasn't Mom's trouble. She was just being negative. I wondered if she was jealous that I had a lover. She could have made things so much better if she'd let him live at our house, but she absolutely refused.

Still, the summer had soared after all, and I was riding high.

Then, one day in mid-August, I came out of the restaurant at the end of my shift to see Steve standing outside. He was clearly waiting for me—he had probably spotted me through the big front window of Sonny's restaurant. I screamed and ran to him and we grabbed each other in a huge hug.

I wanted to know everything about him, and he wanted to know everything about me. We stood there jabbering wildly for a long time, and finally Steve said, "Hey, why don't we go grab a cup of coffee?"

We went back inside. Sonny had moved Chris to the male-dominated night shift; two to ten. Steve and I sat at a booth in front, talking. When I spotted Chris serving in the back, I waved to him to come over. When he finally approached us, I introduced him and Steve. I told Chris that Steve was an old friend and Steve that Chris was a new friend. Steve smiled at me with love in his eyes. Chris seemed absent; he had to go back to work.

Steve was nervous about something, and finally it burst out: he had not gone to Harvard after all. He didn't know why. "Jess, it was too much for me, I wasn't up to it, I knew I wasn't, I knew I'd be miserable."

I had no trouble understanding that. I felt the same way about Harvard and Yale and Smith and Vassar. I admired people who went to them, but I knew I couldn't do it, I wouldn't be comfortable there.

"I understand that, I'm the same way. I know, I really know, Steve. That's why I went to Andrews. I didn't even apply to those places. I knew I wasn't up to it."

It seemed really important to Steve that I understood. He took my hand in two of his and told me he loved me as much as ever.

Then he said, "So I applied to UMass."

"That's great!" I exclaimed. I realized that I had had a secret nightmare about Steve. I knew how easy it would be for him to just start dealing drugs after working at Monaghan's; I knew he could slide into a life that would sink him. I'd never let myself fully envision it, but it was curled up at the bottom of my fears along with a lot of other things I'd never let myself think about.

Instead, he was doing well in college: during his freshman year, he got A's and B's and was on the dean's list. He'd had to move out of his grandma's house, because once he was eighteen, the state no longer paid her to keep him and she could not afford to. She had to get another young boy. He felt bad about that.

"I worry about the boys, you know. Gram is old, she doesn't know how to control them. When I lived there, I always knew what they were up to; I made sure to keep them out of trouble. But now . . ."

He went back to see them occasionally, and as far as he knew, they were still okay.

Steve still got some assistance from the state, and he could afford to rent a room in Boston near the campus. He had a job in a copy shop near the school to earn spending money. And he had a girlfriend, Lila.

"Oh," I said.

He'd looked happy for me when I introduced Chris. Why couldn't I be happy for him about Lila?

Who was pregnant.

Oh.

They were planning to get married one of these days.

My voice was stiff when I asked about her, but Steve either didn't notice or preferred to ignore it. He said she was twenty, his age (Steve was a little older than me), and beautiful, creamy colored and skinny, with tight little cornrows in her hair. She was at UMass too, studying media. She wanted to be a television producer. I was awed. I couldn't even imagine wanting something like that.

Then Steve changed the subject, a little abruptly, I thought, to ask about me. He listened with such attention that I felt myself unfold and expand. I chattered the way I used to, about Andrews and Sheri and Patsy and Gail and Donny and Christopher and my lit class and Fridays at Four and the campus and my father's remarriage and Philo's getting his PhD and Mom's book getting published and Philo publishing an article on Marvell in this really important academic journal, and Dad buying me a car and . . .

It was like a faucet had opened after months of being turned off.

At the end, I tried to take Steve home with me. "Mom will be thrilled to see you. She always asks about where you are and how you are."

He looked a little shamefaced. "Aw, I'd be embarrassed, Jess."

"Why?"

He shrugged. "I didn't go to Harvard."

"Mom will understand."

He shook his head. "Not today. I got things to do. Lila's expecting me."

We were standing in the street outside the restaurant, and I grabbed him by the shoulders. "Don't get lost on me again! Keep in touch!"

He laughed and hugged me. He promised. He gave me his phone number. He said he'd catch me another day. Then he left.

I almost flew down the street, a smile pasted across my idiot face. I knew Mom would be happy to hear that I'd seen Steve and to know he was okay. And she was. All my anger at her vanished; I chattered all through dinner. I watched television afterward because Chris was working that night. It was after eleven; I had gone to bed and was reading when a shower of pebbles hit my window. I leaped up and looked out: Chris was standing downstairs.

I ran down smiling and opened the door. What a surprise! I felt so loved! First Steve, now Chris! Chris slipped in the door. Mom had heard something and was coming downstairs in her robe. When she saw who it was, she said stiffly, "Oh, hi, Chris." He could tell she didn't like him; he'd known for a while. She turned around and went back upstairs but left her door open.

I was still grinning, expecting Chris to embrace me or something, but he stood like a ramrod, hardly moving his lips.

"Who was that guy?" he asked accusingly.

"Steve? I told you. He was my friend in high school. I've known him for years. I haven't seen him in a whole year, and he found me today! It was so great . . ."

"He kissed you!"

"Of course he kissed me. He's an old friend. I kissed him too."

"I can't believe you did that. I can't believe it."

"What?"

He stared at me from a foot above me, his eyes icy green. "You're a slut!" he hissed. "I thought you were my girl!" He turned and walked out the door, leaving it open.

I stood there, my heart pounding. What had he called me? I couldn't believe it. My mind clutched at words, trying to frame my wondering. I considered running after him and dragging him back, but I was too shocked. After a while, I went upstairs. Mom heard and called me from her room. "Jess?"

I pushed her door farther open and stood in the doorway.

"What's the matter?"

"Nothing."

"Is Christopher gone?"

"Yes."

She gazed at me for a minute. "What happened? Why did he come here so late at night? It's nearly midnight."

"I know. He just finished his shift. He was upset about Steve. Jealous."

"Oh," she said, gazing at me. "Are you upset?"

"No. I'm going to bed."

"Okay. Good night, honey."

I barely mumbled good night. It was all her fault. She had pushed him away from me.

9 **I went back to school** that fall feeling older and a little shopworn. I drove myself up, unpacked by myself, and arranged my room quickly, an old salt used to keeping things shipshape. This semester I was rooming with Melanie; Sheri had transferred to Sarah Lawrence to study drama, and Patsy was in France for the year. I missed them, and I wasn't sure how I felt about Melanie. Before we parted in May, she'd said she didn't want to be lovers anymore. She wasn't sure she was really a lesbian. Well, I wasn't either, so it was okay with me. We'd talked on the phone over the summer, but I hadn't seen her. She'd been in South Carolina with her mother all summer.

When she appeared, she was the same old Melanie, and I felt okay toward her, but something in me was distant, was holding back real affection. I just felt cool toward her, toward everybody. I couldn't get over the scene with Chris. Nothing quite so bad had ever happened to me. Things that happen to you take time to digest. You have to process things that cut your heart to ribbons. I was angry with Chris for walking out on me, and for the way he did it. But I couldn't get over the feeling it was really Mom's fault, and I was furious at her irrational dislike of him. If she'd welcomed him and let him live with us, maybe he wouldn't have been so jealous.

Melanie and I slept in separate beds that semester. Sleeping with Melanie had been nice because we always brought each other to orgasm, but in some other way, it repelled me. I don't know why. As soon as the semester began, she started hanging out with Luke Burden, a skinny French major with bad skin. I thought she must not have cared very much about me if she could replace me with such a jerk. I saw Chris around the campus, but he would not speak to me. After a few tries at being friendly, I gave up, telling myself he was neurotic. He dominated the Poetry Club, and when he refused to speak to me, the others stopped too. That was really unpleasant, and I stopped going. I missed it, though, and I missed Sheri and Patsy. Once Melanie was involved with Luke, I missed her too. I missed Chris. I felt I was sinking in a swamp of misery. All that was left was Fridays at Four.

I distracted myself from all that by signing up for a course at Winship College, a small school a few miles away, where we could take courses not offered at Andrews. They had one called The Bible as Literature, which fascinated me, since I'd never read the Bible and had often wondered about it. It was taught by Dr. Munford, a Protestant minister, who, I thought, should be an expert.

I was enthralled with the Bible from the first day. We used the King James version. I loved the way it was written, so spare and resounding; the stories were so vivid that I could picture living long ago in a hot, dry, hilly place, among animal herders. I wondered what the people were like who wrote the stories, J and P and E. I would get excited in class and was constantly waving my arm in the air to ask questions, but Dr. Munford seemed reluctant to call on me. I thought maybe he was shy. I found amazing the tales of Abraham and Isaac and Jacob and Esau—and the women, who were barely mentioned, but still so vivid. Sarah laughed, it said. I loved that. And I loved that Jacob thought he could affect generation by putting twigs in the animals' drinking water.

That fall, posters appeared announcing a new organization, Queer Andrews, for gay men and lesbians. Their first meeting, on a Sunday morning (during chapel!) was to be held at the Hub, a local coffee house. Missing the Poetry Club, I decided to go to this meeting, to show solidarity with gay people like Sandy, and because I had been gay myself for a while and still thought I might be gay.

When I arrived at the Hub, half a dozen women and two or three guys were milling about. I didn't think there were only two gay men on campus: maybe boys were not too keen on being identified as gay. Everyone stared at me as though I was a foreigner, so I was a little uncomfortable. By eleven, when the meeting started, four more women had come in but no more men. A tall, slender, handsome woman with long hair and a light sprinkling of freckles across her nose stood at the front of the room and announced that the meeting was open. She gave a little speech, offering her name, Liz Reilly, and explaining why she and her friends felt that an organization was needed. Prejudice against homosexuals, she said, which was endemic in the nation and certainly in the state and even in the college, made it necessary. In the past, girls were expelled from college for any behavior that intimated same-sex affection, and everyone knew what had happened to Oscar Wilde. The group would dedicate itself to addressing issues of concern to gays and making its positions known to the college authorities. She asked for comments.

A short, stocky woman raised her hand. She stood and looked around the room. "My name is Frances Maniscalco," she said. "I think it's important that we know each other and that we all share the same values. We don't want reporters or administration spies poking their way in, so I think we should all identify ourselves."

"Okay," Liz agreed. "Let's go around the room, people."

Frances moved to the front of the room to stand with Liz.

People gave their names and their year. When it came to me, I did the same. Frances faced me. "Who did you say you were?"

I blinked and repeated. "I'm Jessamin Leighton, a sophomore. I live in Lester Hall."

"Why are you here?" Liz moved closer to Frances.

I know I turned red. No one else had been asked that question. "I . . . uh . . . wanted to show solidarity . . . I have gay friends . . . and I . . ." I was trying to think of how to explain that I'd been involved with Melanie without using her name (she'd be mortified), but I faltered.

"Solidarity? Are you gay?" Liz asked sarcastically.

"Maybe . . . I'm not sure."

"You don't know? You come here and you don't know? Aren't you a writer? Are you planning to write an exposé?"

"No!" I protested. "Well, yes, I'm a poet, but I don't write for the newspaper; I write poetry. Anyway, I thought you said anyone interested could come . . ."

"You're interested?" A third woman joined them—it now felt like a gang. "You?" she cried. "The school pump? Who will fuck any man at all, of any size, shape, or *color*, according to Chris Hurley! Who has worked her way through the male population of Andrews!"

They were staring at me with such hostility that I started to feel frightened. I realized that they all knew each other and thought they knew me. It was a closed circle I had intruded upon. I pulled on my jacket and said, "Sorry!" and fled from the room.

I ran to my room, locked my door, and threw myself on the bed, shivering. I lay there, not crying, not thinking, just trying to catch my breath, trying to understand why they hated me so much. What did I represent to them? What did they see when they looked at me? Had Chris really said that about me? How many guys did they think I'd fucked? School pump!

What a phrase! Well, I had slept with five or six guys last year. But how did they all know that? Was Chris angry because Steve was black?

The hurt of it didn't go away. For weeks afterward, I walked around the campus almost cowering, as though I was expecting to be hit, snarled at, called names. I'd be walking along and catch myself that way. School pump! I vowed not to sleep with another boy my entire time at Andrews. I thought of transferring out. I wanted to go home.

I threw myself into my courses, reading late into the night, working hard on my papers. I could actually forget the whole thing when I got into my papers. I was writing one on Sarah, on how she must have felt about Abraham taking Isaac off to sacrifice him, this child of her extreme old age, and her husband about to cut his throat; what did she think about that? Did he even tell her? What did she think about Abraham's god, who had made her laugh but who had given an order like that? And why were her feelings not in the story—weren't they important? Didn't she matter? I mean, she was his *mother*. I wrote with passion, envisioning her standing alone, watching them walk away from her, her husband and her precious boy, watching their backs as they headed out into the desert, walking for days toward a certain rock, the sun beating down malignantly . . .

I handed in my paper just before Thanksgiving, then packed a bag and drove to Dad's for the four-day break. I felt that since he had bought me the car, I had to visit him a few times, at least. Julie had some friends coming for Thanksgiving dinner, and she was thrilled to have me come too. I don't know why, but she liked me—so of course I liked her back.

She was proud of my old room, now the guest room, which she'd decorated with little baskets with pink bows and straw flowers and a flouncy pink bedspread. She took me upstairs, practically begging for my approval. And I discovered that I do not do

— 154 —

well in positions of power. I was just like my father. Julie constantly tried to placate Daddy, to keep him from getting angry, and the harder she tried, the worse Dad got. And she tried to please me too, and damn if I didn't get more and more negative and sullen. I just couldn't help it. The weekend gave me a new perspective on *Uncle Vanya*, which we had read in modern drama, and I vowed never to put myself in Julie's—Vanya's—position. When you need love desperately and show your neediness, you can count on people kicking you. The weekend gave me a new perspective on myself. I gave Julie a really hard time—about my room, about the meals she planned to serve, and about her cooking. I almost made her cry a couple of times. Daddy even looked over, a little surprised. Not that he would disapprove. Maybe the women at the meeting were right; maybe I was fundamentally rotten.

Driving back to school, my stomach kept twisting and I thought again of transferring out of Andrews. It didn't seem a welcoming place anymore. I told myself I was making a mountain out of a molehill, that what had happened was nothing. So a dozen people didn't like me, so what? They didn't even know me, they just thought they did. But I couldn't calm down.

There were only three weeks left in the semester. The term ended at Christmas break, after which I'd have almost a month off to decide what to do.

I had been back a week and was beginning to feel a little calmer, when Dr. Munford handed back our papers. I gaped at mine: I had an F. I had never received less than a B on any schoolwork. I examined it carefully. There were no markings on it, no comments. There wasn't even a spelling error. Just the F. My mind went blank, and after lying on my bed and rereading the paper several times, I picked up the phone. I hadn't been calling Mom very often; I was still upset with her about Chris. But I had to call her now; I didn't know what else to do. I told her what had happened. She was very sympathetic. She knew I wasn't an F student. What killed me was getting an F in a subject I was so interested in. How could that have happened? I'd never failed so abysmally! I asked her if I could read her my paper.

"Well?" I asked when I was through.

"I can hear your excitement about the subject," she said. "And I like that you were thinking for yourself. Just that alone is rare in a student paper. I would never give an F to an undergraduate who did independent thinking. And there are no grammatical errors and, I take it, no spelling errors. So there's no reason for an F."

"Yes, but?" I hung on her words, I could barely breathe.

"But you don't know much about the Bible, and you're a little incoherent sometimes—or maybe *enthusiastic* is a better word. If I got that paper, I'd probably give it a B or a B+. I certainly would never give it less than a C."

"Even when you were teaching at Harvard?"

"Even then."

I could breathe again. "So what do you think?"

"I don't know what to think. Maybe this man is rigidly religious or something . . ."

"Do I sound not religious?"

"Well, you're questioning the Bible a bit," she said. I could hear a smile. "Maybe he can't tolerate that."

Something in my heart eased. "Oh. Thanks, Mom. You're sure?"

"Sure. Positive. It's an interesting paper, honey. I like it."

"Thanks, Mom." I would never get angry at my mother again. Never.

The next day, as soon as my modern drama class ended, I boarded the shuttle bus for Winship. It took twenty minutes, and I had to stand in the hall for forty minutes until Munford arrived for his office hours. When he saw me there, he looked annoyed. But I steeled myself. I went in and sat down without being asked.

"Dr. Munford, can you tell me why you gave me an F on my paper? I've never received an F before, and I didn't think this was a failing paper. I was probably too excited about the material . . ."

"Really," he drawled sarcastically.

"Yes!" I insisted. "I find the Bible fascinating. That's why I was shocked by the grade. So I read the paper to my mother, who teaches at Harvard." Well, she used to. "And she said she wouldn't give it less than a C. So I wondered . . ."

He stood up so fast he knocked some papers off his desk. "You aggressive bitch!" he almost shouted. "Get out of my office!"

I stared at him, leaped up, and ran out. My heart was banging in my chest and I couldn't catch my breath. I sat panting on the bus, waiting for it to leave. What was the matter with me? What was I doing? Was I some monstrous person and just didn't know it? What did people see when they looked at me? Was I so stupid I didn't know how I was perceived? Was I unknowingly doing something obnoxious? Was I really so hideous in the eyes of people like Dr. Munford and Frances Maniscalco and Liz Reilly, from the meeting? If I was misunderstanding things, was there anything I could do about it? Was I responsible for it? Was there any way I could change how they saw me? And if not, how could I go on living in this world?

By the time I got back to Andrews, it was late afternoon and already getting dark. I went into my room, which was really messy, and beat myself up for being such a slob. I had to clean this place! I began to pick things up to put them away, but I put them, not in drawers or shelves, but in boxes and suitcases. I just kept doing it, putting everything away, out of sight, in something—everything, my clothes, books, electric typewriter, notes, radio, hair curlers. Then I carried load after load down the stairs and stacked them in my car. I didn't pass anyone I knew on any of these trips down and back; I knew that was a sign. When I had emptied my room, I got into the car and started the long drive home.

I got to the house very late that night. Mom was asleep and didn't hear me come in. I didn't unpack; I was exhausted and it was cold out, very cold for November. I dragged myself up to my room and, still dressed in my jeans and sweater and heavy jacket, crawled into bed. The next day, a Saturday, Mom was in the kitchen when I came down for coffee. She was startled to see me, and even more so when I burst into tears at the sight of her. She came over and held me; I stood there and just let her. We stood like that for a long time.

I didn't feel too good, and I couldn't think what would make me feel better.

I told Mom everything. She already knew the first part about the paper, but I told her about the gay and lesbian meeting, and I told her about Christopher. She listened to me, smoothed my hair, murmured, "My poor girl," and, "Poor baby," which I wanted to hear. She said she didn't understand what had happened; she insisted I hadn't done anything grotesque or ridiculous to other people. She said that things like that happened to every-body once in a while and that they were probably accidents. I had appeared in somebody's world at exactly the wrong moment for them. I'd been in a state of dread, driving home, imagining that Mom would be mad at me for leaving school like that, not even finishing the semester. But she said she didn't blame me for leaving and that I should never go back.

"When you go back to college, maybe you should go to a school that's a little better than Andrews. Where the students are more on your level," she said.

What was she saying?

"People have a hard time accepting someone who is clearly superior to them," she said. She was trying to make me feel better, but it didn't work. I didn't believe people were jealous of me. There was something I was doing.

We had coffee and cake and then sat smoking and talking. Mom seemed a little low, and finally she told me she'd broken up with Philo.

"No! How *could* you?" I burst out.

"I had to," she said. "It was time."

"What does that mean?"

She pondered. "It's hard to explain. He's so much younger than I am . . ."

"That never bothered you before!"

"Yes, it did, Jess. I just didn't talk about it. I told myself he'd mature over the years, but there's something about this relationship—I think my presence inhibits his growth. He isn't growing, isn't changing. I'm holding him back . . ."

"Don't lie!" I stormed. I wasn't going to let her lay the blame on *him*!

She looked at me. "You can try to understand. If you won't, I'll stop talking."

I sulked.

She got up and washed the breakfast dishes. Then she went up to her room to get dressed. I sat at the kitchen table, smoking. After a while, I bent double and wrenched out some huge sobs, crying in a way I hadn't probably since I was an infant in my crib.

The next weeks passed. I don't know what I did or thought or felt. I did some reading. I watched TV. I listened to some music. One day I got in my car and drove out to Lexington and Concord, but didn't even get out of the car when I got there. I played solitaire up in my room. I played Mom's music on my stereo, the last scene of Strauss's *Der Rosenkavalier*, which always made me cry. As if I believed that love invariably ends with renunciation. Maybe I did.

Sandy came home for the Christmas holidays. I didn't tell her what had happened to me at school or with Chris. I was humiliated, too ashamed to talk about it. But it was a strain not to talk about it, to get her opinion about what was happening, to share the worst event of my life with my best friend. Not telling Sandy also put me at a distance. I didn't like that but couldn't seem to change it. I was also at a distance from Mom, from everybody. From myself.

The one thing I was enthusiastic about, although Sandy took control, was visiting Mrs. Connolly over Christmas break. We wanted to take something useful this time. Sandy called some of Bishop's other friends from Barnes, who chipped in, and we bought two electric blankets, a turkey, fruit, and candy. We drove over there the Saturday before Christmas.

This time we'd called ahead and Mrs. Connolly was waiting for us. She seemed happy to see us and didn't seem to mind getting the turkey or the blankets, even if she was a little vague about them. She had prepared tea for us; she was bubbly: "John's getting out for Christmas, girls! He'll be home soon!"

He was getting out early. Someone must have paid somebody off or twisted somebody's arm to get him a reduced sentence. That was okay by us. We thought taking bribes was bad, but not seriously so. And we knew it was business as usual in the larger world, the part of the world we were barred from joining. We weren't opposed to his being punished but we didn't like seeing someone we knew and liked suffering. We'd been exultant when Spiro Agnew had had to resign in shame as Nixon's vice president, for taking bribes, but we thought he was an idiot, whereas we knew Mr. Connolly was a nice man, generous and kind to his family.

Thinking about Mr. Connolly took us back to our old discussions of good and evil. My friends and I tended to judge acts according to how we felt about the people who performed them, rather than on principle. One day in civics class in high school, Carl Hess, one of the smartest kids in our class, a whiz at science and math, had said that our thinking was plebian, that a Harvard professor had said that people with really good morals judged others according to principle. I argued back that what some people called "principles" often bore no relation to reality and were actually prejudices. I reminded him that Hitler persecuted Jews on the principle, accepted by many scientists of the period, that the races had particular traits and were ranked in a hierarchy, just as the Harvard professor was ranking us by morals.

In any case, principles in politics and business were as beyond our comprehension as government policy on drugs. Sandy, Bishop, Dolores, and I used to discuss that for hours. People wanted drugs and would pay for them. People said drugs were really bad for you, but we disagreed. We were pretty sure marijuana was not harmful at all, certainly less harmful than alcohol, and could even help people who were in pain or upset. Maybe heroin was bad for you, but didn't Freud take cocaine? Was heroin worse for you than automobile exhaust? Cars were legal.

To our adolescent eyes, such hypocrisies were absurd. We used to ask if there were things we felt were really immoral, and we all agreed that hurting people and stealing and killing were bad. But Bishop said, "My brothers have killed people in Vietnam." And Sandy said, "And the state executes people." The same contradictions applied to stealing and just about everything else. We couldn't get out of our conundrum.

There were no absolute guides to a good life, we decided, only tentative ones. But in our late teens, that was enough.

Maybe Mrs. Connolly sensed that we didn't judge; maybe that's why she didn't resent our poking our noses into her life. She sat on her shabby Victorian couch in her once stylish dress, with the diamond pin on her shoulder that her husband had given her for their twenty-fifth wedding anniversary. The diamond earrings he gave her for her fiftieth birthday sparkled through her pale blue hair, which looked professionally set. She wore blush and lipstick and mascara. She poured the tea with perfect manners, offering lemon or cream and passing us plates of cookies.

Maggie and Francis and the children were wonderful, she enthused, and had a new baby. They had just bought a house in Auburn, with lots of trees and a huge yard and a two-car garage and a big porch that girdled the house. "Wonderful!" she proclaimed, without reference to the mansion she'd lost. And Gus was back from Vietnam, with just the slightest limp. He was living in California, stationed at a base there. Married.

"Oh! Did you go to the wedding?" Sandy asked, smiling in delight.

"Oh, he got married on the other side," she said vaguely.

"In Vietnam?"

"Yes."

"Have you met her? His new wife? What's her name?"

"No. He'll bring her here to meet us when he gets leave. After John gets home."

"What's her name?" I repeated, relentlessly.

"Phuket."

Oh.

The other boys were fine: Eugene was still in high school, Billy was getting all A's in college.

Wonderful.

We chatted about the weather, asked more questions about the children, avoided politics, and only at the end slipped Bishop's name into the conversation. A shadow passed over her face. She did not say she was expecting him for Christmas. Her favorite son was gone.

We had parked right in front of the house this time, which was good, because it was freezing cold that day. Lloyd and Billy walked us down to the street and were fascinated by my little Fiat. When I told them about kids on my block who had come over to admire it and had lifted the car off the ground, laughing madly, they tried to do the same. But there were only two of them, and they couldn't get traction on the snowy street; they slipped and fell over the car and collapsed laughing. I glanced up at the third-floor windows and saw Mrs. Connolly standing there, watching us. She smiled when she saw me and waved, and I waved back, but I was embarrassed. I don't know why.

Mom tried to make Christmas cheerful for me by inviting people. But when she told me she'd asked Eve Goodman and Alyssa, I commented glumly that Christmas would be a day for ghouls: Eve was still mourning Danny, and Alyssa was still mourning Tim, who had died the year before. I said I might spend Christmas with Daddy. I threw this at her like a hardball, just to be mean. I didn't want to go to Daddy's and I don't know why I felt I had to punish Mom. I guess I was mad at her for hurting Philo.

She blanched and said, "Why don't you invite Sandy and her parents? And Steve, if you can find him. Whomever you want."

This soothed me a bit, and I set out to make something of the day. Luckily, Sandy and the rest of the Lipkin family had no plans for a holiday they didn't celebrate, and they were happy to come. Their presence saved the holiday for me. I couldn't find Steve; the number he'd given me had been disconnected. But when I called Dolores's house, amazingly, I got her! She sounded subdued, drugged out, but she said she'd love to come. Something told me not to invite her family. Mom also invited Annette and Ted and Lisa Fields. So we would be ten for dinner: a proper Christmas.

Mom and I planned the menu together. We decided to make cassoulet, and we allowed three days to cook it. We ordered a boned loin of pork and leg of lamb, a kielbasa, and a chunk of bacon. We decided to substitute a duck for the goose. We would serve braised vegetables with it—fennel, turnips, celery root, and carrots. And white potatoes and sweet potatoes. The Lipkins said they would bring a cake, Eve a pie, and Alyssa cheese and crackers and olives for appetizers.

The day before Christmas, while we cooked, Mom had talked about Eve and Alyssa and recovery. I said Alyssa had had a year and still hadn't recovered from losing Tim.

"No," she agreed. "She probably never will. It takes a lot of willpower to create happiness, and she's a sweet woman but not a strong one."

That stopped me dead. "What do you mean, *create* it?"

"Well, what do you think, it just happens?"

"Of course. Doesn't it?"

"Does it for you?"

I thought a bit. "It used to. I used to be happy most of the time."

"And what keeps you from being happy now?"

"The things people do . . ."

"Yes." She sighed.

We didn't talk for a while after that. The radio was playing a Mahler symphony, which sounded like anything but music for happiness.

"Does this music make you happy?" I asked finally.

"Yes."

"Why? It's so sad."

"Yes, it expresses sorrow," she explained. "Accurately. Profoundly."

"Hearing sorrow expressed makes you happy!" I cried incredulously.

"Hearing or seeing human emotion expressed is very satisfying to me. Isn't it to you?"

I had to think about that. "I guess so," I said finally.

"That's why we love art."

"So art creates happiness?"

"Oh, yes, honey, it does! Don't you feel refreshed after a great concert, a wonderful exhibition? Or even a great meal? Life is terrible. We just have to take that as a given. That there is no reason for unhappiness, no escape from pain, no justification for the ugly things that happen. That's the ground of human sorrow. But it's what you do in the face of that that determines what you are. To make something beautiful of it, that's grand."

"So how do you create happiness?"

She answered slowly. "I think it lies in the way you approach things. Finding a perspective that makes happiness possible. Lots of people invariably take perspectives that make happiness impossible."

"I don't understand."

"We're a family living in a poor country. A member of your family accidentally kills my son. What do I do?"

"Probably send out your brother to kill their son." I grimaced.

"Yes. Thereby precluding any hope of happiness for either of us, for as long as the vendetta lasts."

"Yeah . . ."

"But say you send your brother over with some gifts, a heartfelt apology, some money. Say you beg forgiveness. As people did in early societies, for hundreds of thousands of years."

"Yes. Maybe they'd forgive you."

"Yes, maybe. At least there's a chance. And even if they couldn't stop holding the accident against you, they might not act against you. This might make harmonious living—and even happiness—possible. Eventually."

"Yeah. But say people are attacking you and you don't know why."

"Well, you could stay and keep arguing with them. Or you could leave and find some other people."

"So what I did . . ."

"Was a choice. You are trying to create happiness in your life."

"Oh." I don't know why this made me feel better. It made me sound rational, not like a coward, which was how I felt.

Mom continued. "Say Sandy does something to hurt you."

"Yeah," I said tentatively. I didn't like this example.

"Whatever alternative you choose will determine your future relationship. To choose right, you have to know what you want. Do you?"

"Well, I love Sandy . . . I don't want to lose her."

"Okay, so what are your choices?"

"What are they?"

"You can go off mad and never speak to her again, you can scream at her in rage, you can sulk for a week."

"But I love Sandy, and I know the only way I'm going to be happy again is if the two of us get along. So instead of getting angry or screaming or sulking, I sit down with her and tell her how she hurt me and ask if she meant to do that."

"Exactly."

"And the chances are she didn't mean to hurt me at all, that the whole thing was a misunderstanding, and once she clarifies that, we can be friends again."

Mom smiled at me triumphantly.

"But suppose she did mean to hurt me. Suppose I did something five years ago that she's never forgiven, and she's been waiting all this time to get even. Or suppose something I did reminded her of something in her past, and she identifies me with something awful, and now I'm registered in her mind as something like a wicked stepmother?"

"Well, maybe talking it out can clear it up. Or maybe there's nothing you can do."

"And?"

"And you're going to be unhappy for a while."

"So you can't create happiness!"

"You can always try. You can't always succeed."

"Why don't people always try?"

She shrugged. "Oh, ego. A person might think, She can't do that to me, who does she think she is, I'll show her! They'd let ego get in the way of happiness. Or depression. They might think, Sandy hates me, everybody hates me, I'm just going to go home and stay there and I won't try to be friends with her anymore. Consuming rage can get in the way of friendship . . ."

"Ummm," I said uncomfortably, thinking that that was exactly how I had been feeling about the people I'd encountered at Andrews. I didn't want to get over it, maybe because I couldn't. When I was enraged with Mom, I wanted to be angry with her, wanted to stay angry. So did that mean I didn't want to be happy?

"All I think about these days," I said, "is that I don't know how to live to get what I want."

"What do you want?"

"Maybe that's the problem. I don't know," I wailed. "I can't figure it out."

"I can tell you what I want. I want to do good, interesting work and live in surroundings as beautiful as I can make them, and I want to love and be loved."

"So you throw Philo out?" I exclaimed.

"I didn't throw out love. I love you. I love Eve and Alyssa and Annette and Ted. And I still love Philo. I just don't want to be with him anymore."

I didn't want to argue with her about that. I mulled things over. "But how can people be happy when things happen to them like what happened to Annette and Ted, having those damaged babies?"

"Everybody suffers damage in life, everybody fucks up in some way, everybody is touched by tragedy."

"So how can anybody ever be happy?"

"It's a problem," she admitted.

Thanks a lot.

I decorated the house with holly and pine branches and red berries, hanging them from the mantelpiece and the newel post. I laid an arrangement of them, with candles, in the center of the dining-room table. We got a small tree and Mom and I set it up ourselves.

On Christmas Day, I put some of Mom's records on the stereo: Alfred Deller and a choir singing beautiful carols that were refreshingly unfamiliar and some madrigals by Gesualdo. Everything was lovely. It said what I wanted to say, that we were a happy family; we were together.

The day went well. Lisa was almost grown up, but not so much that she didn't want to have a couple of games of Ping-Pong, and we ran out to the garage in sweaters and turned on the electric heat. Running around playing quickly warmed us up. Lisa was old enough that I didn't feel I had to lose to her anymore, but she won anyway, four to two. We were out there when Sandy and her family arrived. She and Naomi came out to join us and we played doubles for a while.

The guests were drinking wine or scotch or gin when we went back in, and Sandy and I had wine. Eve and Alyssa were there. I was ashamed of myself for thinking of them as ghouls, because Eve was happy and laughing and very smart, like Mom had said she would be. Alyssa was a little sad; she always was. But she was so sweet you just wanted to curl your arms around her. Annette and Ted were full of Vietnam. Mrs. Lipkin was upset about it now too, and even Dr. Lipkin said something about it. Everyone had been outraged by My Lai, and Dr. Lipkin said it wasn't the only massacre, there had been others, for example, at My Khe 4. We discussed what would happen to Calley. Eve said he was just a poor soldier who did what he was told but Dr. Lipkin said that

that was what Eichmann had claimed. I wanted to argue but I was intimidated by Dr. Lipkin.

The cassoulet was wonderful. It had been a good choice. We wanted everyone to feel good, to feel happy, and we wanted food that would contribute to that feeling.

The only hard part was Dolores. She arrived late, looking strange. At graduation, she had been blowsy and fat, her breasts limp over a swelling stomach, her eyes teary, her face blotchy. She'd bleached her hair pale blonde and worn a trampish outfit, not the fashion in our crowd. She was much changed now. She had slimmed down and was dressed in a prim, matronly brown suit and brown shoes. Sandy and I had on jeans with sweaters and high boots; our hair was still long and natural. Dolores's hair was short and curled in a wave. She looked like her own mother. Sandy and I grabbed her as soon as she came in, gave her a glass of wine, and took her up to my room, where we could lie around and talk.

"Where have you been!" we exclaimed. "We couldn't find you."

She was subdued. She didn't look at us. "Yeah, I've been away."

"Where, Dolores?" I probed. "What was wrong?"

She looked up then. "I was in a hospital."

Suddenly everything made sense.

"What hospital?" Sandy asked warily.

"St. Katherine's."

A mental hospital in the suburbs. We looked at her questioningly. She lowered her head, studied her lap.

"I tried to kill my father," she said. "I stabbed him in the chest with the carving knife. I wounded him; he didn't die. They took me away, put me in the hospital. The state."

They hadn't charged her with anything. So she must have had

a good reason. We stared at her. Then I went over and embraced her. Of course—she liked to sleep in our gallery when she could. We should have known.

She began to cry, and I did too, and Sandy came and put her arms around both of us and rubbed her cheek against Dolores's.

"But you're out now," I said finally. "You're free." It was a question.

"Yes. And back at college. I live in a halfway house. It's part of my sentence. I have to stay there. I was at my parents' house the day you called just by accident. I went there to get the rest of my stuff. I'll never go back there again or see them, either of them, ever again."

"Both of them?" I asked. "Both of them?"

She exploded. "He fucked me and she was jealous! They fought over me all the time! She'd tell him nasty things about me, she'd nag him to beat me, and sometimes he did but sometimes he'd threaten to beat her, but he was always at me . . . Oh, God! My life wasn't worth living . . ."

"Oh, Dolores!"

I could see her go someplace in her head. She changed her breathing, slowed it down, breathed in deeply, exhaled hard. "It's okay now," she said. "I live in a group home. The kids there are great. You should hear their stories; I swear they're worse than mine! I love them! I'm starting my life over again. I hope you two will be part of my new life. I mean, you were always good to me. And so was Bishop. How is Bishop?"

We told her about Bishop. We couldn't stop hugging her, but we felt we had to go back downstairs and join the others. By then love for Dolores had lifted my heart.

After dinner, after the dishes were done, people were sitting drinking coffee or brandy or tea, talking in small groups. Sandy, Dolores, and I had dried the dishes and put them away. Now we sat in a corner of the kitchen.

"Do you know what you want in life?" I asked them.

"I do," Sandy said. "I want to be a doctor; I want to do research and find a cure for cancer. That's what I want most of all. I also want to live with Sarah—together, openly, in our own place. And I know it's ridiculous, but I am determined to live happily ever after." She laughed. "You know?"

"Yes. Me too," Dolores said.

"You should be able to have what you want," I said to Sandy, thinking that her plan sounded eminently realistic. She wasn't asking for too much, I thought.

She shrugged. "I think so too. What about you, Doe?"

"I want to get better and feel good sometimes. Feel good every day even. I want to get educated and help other girls with families like mine. And I will do it!"

I looked at her. She would, I was sure she would.

"How about you, Jess?" Dolores asked.

"I'm not sure. I don't seem to know for sure what I want."

"Well," Sandy gave a little laugh, "you for sure want a guy."

"What do you mean?'

"The right guy. The right man. You're always looking for him."

"I am?"

"Yes. Don't you know that?"

I gazed at her. "That's what you think of me?"

"Come on, Jess. We all search for love. You just do it . . . well . . . more ardently than most of us. In a more driven way, I guess. More passionate."

I wasn't sure I liked what she was saying at all. But I didn't want to have a fight with Sandy.

People started to leave. They were really mellow, their fare-wells hung on the cold air as we stood in the doorway, watching them get in their cars and drive off, waving. Sandy's parents left, but Sandy stayed, she and Dolores both. Mom left us alone in the living room and went into the kitchen to do a final cleaning up. Then she came in and kissed the three of us good night. That was nice. We sat with a bottle of cognac, for Dolores and me, and Southern Comfort, for Sandy, and talked and talked. I asked them to stay overnight but Dolores said she was fine to drive and they both left about three in the morning. I went up to bed, a smile on my face, a little woozy from the cognac, feeling that this was all I needed in life—my friends—to make me happy.

I had just drifted off when the phone rang. It was almost four in the morning! I leaped up and out of habit, forgetting I had my own phone, I ran into Mom's room. She'd already picked up the phone. I heard her say, sleepily, "Huh? Uh? Sandy?"

Oh, my God, Sandy! They were drinking, they had an accident, it's my fault, I gave them the booze, I thought. I grabbed the phone from Mom's hand. Sandy was screaming and sobbing into the telephone.

"Jess! My father! Daddy! He killed himself! He's dead!"

10 **Sandy's life fell apart** that night. There she is, a little high and giggly, dropped off by Dolores after a long evening getting tight with two old friends, smiling, full of good food and affection and Southern Comfort, standing in front of her family's neat brick Colonial. She stares in satisfaction at her home, framed by trees and stationed firmly against the cold, clear Belmont sky, when she notices a cloud hovering around the garage doors.

The sky is as dark as it gets in a place with streetlights, and in the grayish purple air, a fog rising in one spot seems strange. She slowly walks toward the garage, thinking her father has left the car running. How can that be? Her efficient father. Her heart races ahead of her brain as she approaches the closed garage doors and begins to hear a purr, the hum of a motor, and she is sure now that he did leave the motor running; how could he be so forgetful? Her systematic, scientific, careful father. Her thoughtful, quiet, unemotional father. She is running now, reaches the garage door. It is not locked, just shut, and she heaves it open. The smell of exhaust fumes is extreme. It is a smell she loves and used to breathe in when, as a child, she would stand in front of the garage waiting for her father to pull out. It fills her lungs and she remembers her mother telling her not to breathe it in because it is toxic and could make her pass out. She puts her hand over her face and darts inside. She opens the car door and sees a figure slumped over the wheel and doesn't know who it is. She reaches into the car and turns the key in the ignition and, blessedly, silence falls. It's over; her eyes close in prayer. She puts her hand on the figure's shoulder to wake him up; it's over, over now, get up, but his head falls back against the car seat; how could that slender, graceful, delicate man have become inanimate flesh?

Her thin scream is muffled by the hand that covers her mouth and nose, and she begins to cry in deep, heaving, silent sobs and doesn't know why she is crying because her father will wake up soon, she's sure. She runs into the house to get her mother, who will be able to wake her father, even though she, Sandy, cannot. She runs, sobbing, drops her keys and picks them up and drops them again, and finally gets the front door open and runs up the stairs to her parents' room where her mother is sleeping, floating in innocent sleep. I shouldn't wake her up, she doesn't know yet, leave her that way, but she does, nudging her mother, get up, get up, Mommy, Mommy, and Mommy does, bewildered. Sandy, what?

Sandy finds her mother's robe and slippers and puts them on her, unable to speak, holding her mouth closed to stop herself retching, pulls on her mother's hand, holding in her sobs like vomit, pulls her down the stairs and out the back door and down the driveway to the garage and in . . .

Sandy's mother gasps, covers her mouth, looks wildly around, finds Sandy and grabs her, holding her so both of them can cry out loud now. After a while, Sandy spots the note, written on a pale-blue credit card receipt, lying on the seat beside her father, scrawled with the words, "I can't go on," just that, nothing else, no good-bye, no love, no hope. The words end, the world too should end but it doesn't, not for any of them, only for him. It would be bearable if the world ended, but no, they have to trudge back inside, wake Naomi and tell her and watch as she runs out to the car, sobbing and screaming; they call for an ambulance on the off chance that there is some hope, though they both know, but you never know, maybe . . .

They have to go on living.

Sandy's first act was to call me. Mine was to cry in my mother's arms. He was my ideal father. My real father had already in some sense died, so this felt familiar. When it was light, I called Dolores at the group home. I knew she'd want to know. It was amazing how upset she was. You'd think Sandy's father was her father too. Maybe the Lipkins were the mother and father she'd have liked to have had, sweet, gentle, smart, tolerant people, ideal people, civilized people. Maybe Dr. Lipkin was father to those of us who didn't have one of our own, one we could use.

We both drove to the Lipkin house and between Dolores and me, we took care of things for the next week or so. When Seymour flew up from Princeton and Rhoda from Los Angeles, Dolores met them at the airport. When other relatives flew in from out of town, it was Dolores or I who met them. Dr. Lipkin was buried as soon as Rhoda arrived; then the family sat shiva, so the house had to be immaculate and food had to be available. Mrs. Lipkin lay in bed, dopey with sedatives. People visited her there, and she roused herself to sigh hello, then sank back into grief. Sandy and Naomi sat in the living room but did not inhabit their bodies; they were like shadows. They didn't rouse themselves even for Seymour. Seymour and Rhoda had to greet the many guests, an unfamiliar role for them. They were strained, polite, pale.

Friends and relatives brought food: platters of smoked salmon and stuffed grape leaves and hummus and pita and olives and figs and casseroles and meat and fish with noodles or rice that we put in the oven. People came every afternoon and evening for the next five days, and they ate the whole time. We were heating casseroles and putting out platters in the dining room, consolidating half-empty serving plates and cleaning away used dinner plates and putting them and the silverware in the dishwasher. It was tiring, but I found I was good at it, efficient. I'd learned something in all those years of helping Mom in the kitchen.

When it was over, the family had to face the silence. Rhoda and Seymour went back to their havens as fast as they could. From the way they acted, you'd think it hadn't been a happy family. They didn't want to stay with their mother; they didn't seem to want to deal with her at all. Naomi—they called her Nomi—pulled herself together first. She would be able to go back to school, to Barnes, after the holidays. She slept and ate almost normally from the first, and she worked on a paper due in her social studies class after the holidays and watched television, just like before.

But Mrs. Lipkin and Sandy remained prostrate. By this time, Dolores and I were going over only in the afternoon for a few hours. Dolores would go to the market and I would cook some dinner for them, but really, we went just to be company, to try to cheer them up. Neither of them was eating much; they both lost a lot of weight. They slept most of the time.

It was almost time for me to return to Andrews if I was going. It would be hard to pick up my life there—I had missed all my final exams. The new semester began the third week of January. I kept pushing away the thought, as though I didn't plan to go back. I guess I didn't: after all, I had brought all my stuff home with me. Besides, I was consumed with worry about what was happening to Sandy. I was afraid that she was close to suicide herself.

One gray afternoon, I made tea and carried the tray up to her room, where Sandy was lying on her bed, asleep. I had bought some black-and-white cookies, which I knew she loved, and put them on the tray. I knocked and went in. She looked up sleepily. I wondered if she was taking the same pills her mother took.

"How you doin'?"

"Okay," she mumbled, sitting up. She glanced at the tray. "Oooh . . . black-and-white cookies. Thank you. Where's Dolores?"

"She went to the market. To get stuff for dinner."

"Ummm."

I poured tea for both of us, pulled her armchair around toward the bed, and sat, facing her. "Sandy, it's getting to be time to go back to Smith."

"I know."

"I have to leave too."

She paled. "When?"

"Soon."

She turned away from me. "I'm not going back to Smith."

"Sandy!"

"I can't. It's pointless. I wanted to be a doctor—like him."

"You still can. Your uncle said he had a lot of life insurance, and had it long enough that the suicide clause doesn't affect it."

She shook her head. "It's not money."

I sipped. She munched on a cookie.

"I was thinking . . . maybe I'd go up to the commune where Bishop is. For a while."

Through the window, above the rooftops, the day seemed to grow lighter.

"Would you come with me?"

"Yes."

"I hate to leave my mother. But she . . . she blames herself, of course. I would too, if I were her."

"Your father must have been depressed."

"Probably. Who knows? We'll never know. He's just . . . gone!" She burst into tears. I let her cry until she stopped.

"The way he went. Just went. Like a light going out. I can't help my mother. Any more than I helped my father. But everything I wanted . . . it all seems futile, stupid, illusory . . . I just want to settle down quietly, far away from here. I want to put my hands in the earth, live naturally."

"Yes," I breathed, my eyes closed, picturing it.

"If you'll drive, I'll leave my car here for Nomi. So she can help Mom. Is that okay?"

"Of course. We only need one car."

"You don't mind not going back to Andrews?"

"I've been feeling the same way. That it's futile. Pointless. I wasn't really planning to go back anyway. Only I didn't know what else to do."

"Great. Do you think Dolores would want to go?"

"I don't think she can. She has to stay at the halfway house for a set period. But we can ask her."

Sandy tossed the blanket off her legs. She was dressed, in jeans and a sweater. She stood up and searched for her boots and put them on.

"Come on. We'll ask her."

I followed her downstairs, carrying the tray of jiggling dishes. Dolores wasn't back yet. I went into the kitchen to empty the tray and wash the dishes. It was easier to wash them than to put them in the dishwasher, which was already nearly full. It had just enough space for the dinner dishes, and I didn't want to fill it now and have to empty it before dinner. I was really tired of emptying the dishwasher. Sandy sat down at the kitchen table and lit a cigarette. She looked pale and thin. Her hair, usually alive and springy, was lank and greasy. We didn't speak. When I finished the dishes, I sat down with her and lit up too.

Dolores came in laden with bags. "Hey, you all!" she said, surprised to see Sandy downstairs. "Hey," we said. Dolores put the bags down on a counter and turned to us. "What's up?"

Sandy looked at me. I looked at her, then turned to Dolores. "Sandy is thinking of going to live on a commune for a while."

"Bishop's commune?"

"Yes."

Dolores stood gazing at Sandy.

"I'm thinking of going with her."

She transferred her gaze to me.

"We're wondering if you'd like to go."

Something crossed her face, not a smile, but like one, a ripple of gladness that then became a ripple of sorrow. "Oh, how I'd love that!" She turned toward the counter and pulled a pack of cigarettes out of her jeans pocket. Since she'd been hanging out with us again, she'd stopped wearing the stiff, formal clothes she'd worn after leaving the hospital, and was back to jeans and boots. She was thin again and her hair, which was still short, was puffy with little curls. She looked adorable. She lit a cigarette, laid it in an ashtray on the counter, and began unpacking the groceries. "But you know I can't go anywhere until . . . I have to stay at the halfway house for a full six months. After that, I can get a full-time job and go away weekends, but even then I have to live there." Her mouth twisted. "If I do what they say, they'll wipe my record clean. I won't go through life marked as someone who attempted parricide." She sat down, facing us. "But if you're still up there next year, I should be on my own by then. If I don't fuck up."

Dolores used the word *fuck* often. None of the rest of us did in those days.

"You won't," Sandy assured her.

"Oh, Sandy!" she wailed and tears came to her eyes. "How can you say that! I could—so easily! *Everybody* fucks up!"

We stared at each other and at her. "Dolores?"

"Oh, sorry," she said, blowing her nose. "Sorry! It's just . . . your father! You don't know what your family meant to me, just knowing he existed, you all existed, during those awful years . . . It's unbearable to me that he . . ."

Sandy looked at the floor.

"Well, of course it's unbearable for you too," Dolores admitted, calming down. She took a puff on her cigarette, then stood up and finished emptying the grocery bags.

"I thought I'd make your mother a vegetable soup tonight," I said, rising to help Dolores. "Do you think she'd like that?"

"Maybe. She's not crazy about vegetables," Sandy said. "Who knows? She's not eating much, as you know."

"Of course not. She's mad as hell," Dolores said. "I couldn't eat at all when I was so mad."

I turned to her in surprise. Given the mournful frailty of Sandy's mother these days, *mad* seemed a strange word to apply to her.

"Why do you say that?" Sandy sounded annoyed.

"Because I know she is. Remember when I used to be so weepy and helpless? I was really furious. At my father, at my mother. But I didn't think I could do anything about the situation. So I just cried. And when I ate, it was sweets, things with no nourishment, because they made me feel better."

"And you think my mother . . . is angry . . . at whom?" Sandy's voice was cold as ice. She sounded very like her father.

"At him. For killing himself. Aren't you? I mean, how could he do that to you? Terrible. And he didn't even say good-bye."

Sandy stared at Dolores. She put out her cigarette and started another. "So you can't go with us, Dolores," she said, coolly resuming the earlier conversation.

"No, I can't, Sandy, much as I'd like to." Dolores didn't seem to realize she'd been in any way tactless. "But I think it's a great idea. Bishop will be wild to see you."

I opened some cans of chicken broth and poured them into a pot. When the broth was boiling, I added the two chicken breasts Dolores had bought for dinner for Sandy and her mother. I lowered the heat so they could simmer while I peeled carrots, onions, green beans, and little white turnips. After half an hour, I took the breasts out and cut the meat off, then put the bones back in the broth. I tossed in a couple of handfuls of barley. I was making this up as I went.

I had asked Dolores to get asparagus, and now I washed and peeled and chopped it. I laid the vegetables on a platter together. They looked beautiful, and that was half my pleasure in cooking. Just looking at them made me happy. I was always happy when I cooked. Dolores and Sandy went on talking, but I had retreated when things had taken an unpleasant turn. I thought Dolores was right about Sandy's mother, but I knew Sandy did not like hearing that. I also knew that Sandy was angry at her mother, as if she were to blame for the suicide. I knew Sandy couldn't help what her mind was doing. When you're so horribly hurt, you cast around crazily looking for somebody to blame. I did that myself. I just hoped it would pass, for the sake of her relation with her mother, and for her mother's sake. Now Sandy was angry with Dolores. She was probably actually angry with her father, like Dolores said. But I didn't listen and barely heard them.

I removed the chicken bones from the broth and tossed the vegetables in. I opened a box of frozen peas and a can of cannelloni beans, which I drained. I would put these things in at the very end, along with the cooked chicken. I tasted the soup and added salt and pepper and a little thyme, tarragon, and basil. It was good, not great. I was disappointed. But maybe Sandy's mother would eat it.

When Mrs. Lipkin came down for dinner, I had the table set, the soup in a tureen, and crispy French bread hot from the oven in a basket. She ate a whole bowl of soup and some bread. And a black-and-white cookie afterward. I was deeply pleased. I went home happy.

I steeled myself on the drive home. I had been surprised by Mom's reaction to my coming home before Christmas, but I was sure she wanted me to go back to school, not to Andrews, but to some college or other. Maybe Moseley. She would want me to make up my finals at Andrews and finish the year someplace else. She would be horrified at my dropping out entirely.

But I had to go with Sandy. I couldn't leave her alone right now. Mom couldn't see what I could see, how close Sandy was to the edge—I didn't even want to think about it.

I tried to launch into the discussion tactfully, but Mom surprised me. She didn't argue. She must have sensed something. "Sweetheart, I admire your loyalty to your friend. And maybe this is the time for a break." She didn't even argue.

School seemed terribly unimportant right then, just something you invented to keep yourself busy. Taking care of Sandy seemed urgent. I had seen how upset she had become at Dolores, and I felt it was important to keep her from tilting over into rage. I was impressed by Dolores; she had learned a lot during her ordeal. But I wished she'd learned some diplomacy.

We planned to leave at the end of the week and Mrs. Lipkin had asked me to cook a special dinner for Sandy's (and my) last night at home. Naomi was speechless—with anger, I suppose—that Sandy was not only abandoning her but also leaving her with the responsibility for their mother; Mrs. Lipkin was still on tranquilizers and barely aware of what was happening around her. I didn't see how Sandy could leave, but I also didn't see how she could stay. The impossibility added to the urgency. I sensed she was running for her life.

On Wednesday night, I roasted a leg of lamb, potatoes, tomatoes, peppers, and eggplant, and everybody ate heartily. Even Mrs. Lipkin ate something. There was such a gentleness and grace about her. I felt sorry for her, but after a while, you expect a person to bounce back and start functioning, and if they don't, you begin to blame them. I'm not saying I was right, but that's what I felt. I thought, her daughters need her and it's her responsibility because she's the mommy. Obviously, I didn't think mommies had the right to break down, to fall apart, to fail their children. Daddies either, for that matter.

The next day, I packed my duffel and drove over to Sandy's, who had packed one too, and once more we set out to find a Connolly at an unknown address.

11 **So there we were**, on the road together in early January 1973, homing in on Bishop. I took the Mass Pike to Becket, a long, long ride through empty hills and sky. It was beautiful out there. When you grow up in an urban area, you don't realize how much open space there is in this country. Once we got off the Mass Pike, we had to go by feel. We went too far and stumbled into Monterey, a lovely town with a general store and a post office. We turned north again toward Becket. Snow was piled high at the roadside and on tree limbs and bushes. We reached a little town, Tyringham, and had lunch there, in a place my mother would have chosen, a little, locally-owned storefront restaurant called Ginger and Pepper. Ginger did the cooking, excellently, as it turned out. We had a delicious cream of asparagus soup and omelets with cheese and spinach. I told Ginger how much I liked her cooking and asked about Pepper. This endeared me to her and an hour and a half later, we were still there, Ginger leaning on her broom, telling us about her perfectly organized life, her four kids, her husband, and—the main focus of conversation—her worthless sister Pepper. She'd brought Pepper into the business to please her mother, but Pepper had contributed little and now did nothing at all, despite her name on the window.

I wanted to ask Ginger about the commune, but after listening to her commentary, I had doubts about how she'd receive such a question. Better Sandy should ask: she was dignified and ladylike, and Ginger would treat her gingerly, I thought, smirking at my own pun. I tried to signal Sandy to risk the question, but she wouldn't. So eventually I thought of a maneuver.

"You know, we're up here searching for a friend. A high school friend. There was a death in his family and he's out of touch with them, and we knew he'd want to know, so we're looking for him. He's somewhere in this area, on a commune. Do you know of one around here?"

Her face changed. "Commune? Bunch of hippies?" She examined us more carefully.

"Yes. That's what we heard. We don't know where it is. But we thought it was really important that he know," Sandy said with a mournful look.

"Oh, yeah." She thought it over. Our long hair and jeans made us questionable, but we were clean, well spoken, and polite. We had praised her cooking and sympathized about her sister. She decided in our favor.

"Well, there is one out toward Becket. You go down this road as far as the body shop, then turn right. Go about two miles until you come to a gas station. There's a little dirt road leading off to the left. Take it as far as a farm with chicken coops; you can't miss it. Then make a left and go, oh, I don't know, a few miles, until you see a fork in the road. There's a big oak tree in a triangle of grass, and you take the right fork. Just keep going until you see a red barn. Turn down the next driveway; that's them.

"They come into town sometimes, bringing eggs to the grocery store, trading them for laundry soap and whatnot. I don't deal with them. They live in sin. You girls don't stay there, just tell your friend what he has to know and get out, you hear? Smoking dope and living in sin, no life for decent girls."

Sandy and I gave each other frightened looks, which seemed to satisfy her, and paid the bill and left.

"I guess we won't be able to have lunch there anymore," Sandy said as we left. "Too bad—that soup was delicious."

Ignorant as we were about life on a commune, we had no idea that lunch in a restaurant would quickly become an unattainable luxury for us.

It took us longer than it should have, since we got lost and had to retrace our route and get directions from someone else, then got lost again, and might never have found the commune if we hadn't come across a UPS delivery man. Sandy ran up to him as he was getting back in his truck and, near tears, begged him for directions. He accommodatingly told us to follow him, and he drove us right to the commune. Around five in the afternoon, waving good-bye to him, we pulled into a long, muddy driveway that ran up to a ramshackle house with gray shingles, many turrets, and what had once been white trim. There was a red barn farther down the drive and some horses in a field.

We got out of the car and walked up the creaky wooden steps of the house. A storm door led to a glassed-in porch with some shabby furniture covered in old blankets. We opened the door and walked onto the porch; there didn't seem to be a doorbell. We knocked on the house door. Nothing happened. After a while, we tried the doorknob. The door was unlocked. We opened it, stepped over the threshold, and called, "Bishop? Anyone? Hello?"

Rock music—I recognized the Dead—was blaring. We walked into the small living room, which had a couch and a few chairs and a small stereo set on a table. We walked through the living room into a big kitchen, where two women stood at the stove, one stirring a pot, the other peeling apples. They glanced over at us. The kitchen was toasty warm, heated by a big wood stove in the middle of the room.

"Hi," we said uncertainly. "Sorry for the intrusion, but we knocked . . ."

"Oh, yeah. That's okay," one woman said. "When the radio's on, we don't hear anything." She was about my age, nineteen or twenty, and she was wearing a kerchief on her head. It made her look old-fashioned. Like a servant.

"We're looking for Bishop Connolly. Is this where he lives?"

"Yes. You're friends of Bishop's?"

"Yes. From Cambridge."

They both smiled at us. "Are you Jess and Sandy, by any chance?"

"Yes!"

"Does Bish know? He'll be over the moon! He talks about you two all the time. Take off your coats. This is the only room in the house that's warm." She laughed. "I'm Rebecca, and this is Bernice."

We made ourselves comfortable. The kitchen was big, with an old round wooden table in the center and a variety of chairs set around it. Old rockers and shabby armchairs were placed around the room; a breakfront stood against one wall, holding assorted dishes, many of them chipped or cracked. I guessed that this was the room they mostly lived in.

Rebecca was small and thin, with a delicate face, deep-set eyes, and dark, very curly hair. Bernice was taller and blonde, with a round face and small blue eyes.

They made coffee for us in a big aluminum drip pot, older than any coffeepot I had ever seen, and they chatted easily, working the whole time. They were preparing dinner—cabbage soup, millet and red beans with onions and chopped greens. Not too much work, except the millet, but they were also making a bunch of pies. I offered to help and ended up chopping apples and squash for the pies, which they were making with Crisco. My mother would have been outraged.

They told us about the other people in the commune. The oldest member, a founder, and someone we knew about, was Brad d'Alessio, whom Bishop had met in Nevada at the dude ranch. He was a dropout from UCLA and a friend of Bernice's. He had started the commune with Charlotte Kislik and Jerry Matthews, the three of them old UCLA friends. They had pooled their cash and had bought the old house for practically nothing, because it had no electricity or municipal water supply.

It was in terrible repair: in the first year they had to put a new roof on it. They were handy, and they got jobs in town and little by little made it livable. They installed a generator and began to plant the land, living in harmony until Charlotte and Jerry left to join some more radical friends who were impatient to change the country. They were now in hiding after a bomb they'd planted exploded at Enterprise University in Wisconsin, killing a night watchman. Bernice hinted that Brad knew where they were, and Rebecca told us, in whispered horror, that the FBI had been around, questioning him. But he claimed to know nothing.

Brad was a leftist, but against violence. He'd avoided the draft thus far and intended, if he was called up, to claim that he was a pacifist. Bernice insisted that he had never endorsed what Charlotte and Jerry had done. Not that we thought it was so terrible—except that they were careless about the watchman. After Charlotte and Jerry had left, Brad stayed on in the house alone, but he couldn't manage and was about to give up, when Bernice, Rebecca, and then Bishop arrived. I deduced from what Bernice said that Brad received them with despairing gratitude. He already had some horses—he knew a lot about horses—and he and Bishop developed a horse-training school and gave riding lessons. That kept them afloat for a while.

Bernice had left UCLA because of a failed love affair. During her sophomore year, her English professor, Gregory, had come on to her, and in time, she had fallen in love with him. But after a year, he dropped her for another student. She couldn't believe it and wouldn't back off gracefully. She hung around him constantly, visiting his apartment, haunting his office. She felt he had just made a mistake and would remember that he loved her if he just looked at her the right way.

"I couldn't help it. I hated myself, but I just kept showing up during his office hours, day after day. He told me he was going to call the police if I didn't leave him alone. But I just couldn't. Has anything like that ever happened to you?"

"It sounds like you really loved him," said Sandy, ever the diplomat.

"Oh, I adored him. I'd have died for him. I couldn't understand why he'd want to leave someone who loved him the way I did."

I thought anybody would want to leave a person who loved them that way.

"Brad and I were still corresponding. We were pals during freshman year, though he was older than I was. He convinced me that the way to Greg's heart was to leave him. If he was without me, he'd start to long for me, Brad said. So I thought I'd try it. I wrote a letter to Greg, telling him I was leaving, but giving him my home address. I went back to San Diego and waited for six months, but I never heard from him. And I was working at McDonald's, which is lethal, I kid you not! And my mother . . . well, she was pressuring me to go back to school. I didn't know what to do.

"Then Rebecca came to work at McDonald's—she'd dropped out of UCLA too." Bernice turned to Rebecca, who picked up the narrative.

"Yes, that was amazing! Kindred souls selling Big Macs! Actually, I ran out of money after my sophomore year. I was working to save up to go back to school. But some days it seemed like it wasn't worth it. Such disgusting work. I couldn't eat anything while I worked there. I lost fifteen pounds. The smell of grease . . ."

"And I told her about Brad and the commune, and she was fascinated . . ."

"It sounded ideal. I had always thought there should be another way to live. I didn't want to live like my parents. My father was a lawyer and I never saw him, he was always at work and he was so driven and, well, nasty, really. My mother was discontented even though she had this big house and fancy car and ladies to play golf with and a maid and all these clothes."

"Me too." Bernice said. "My father was very religious, a bulwark of the Episcopal Church. My mother was fragile, and he took care of her; he adored her. They were sweet, but it was so boring, their life, so repetitive; there was nothing in it, I felt. I wanted a little adventure, a little risk."

"And I felt there should be sharing and equality in life." Rebecca said. "Even before . . . well, my father got into some trouble. I don't know what he did exactly, but the government was after him for something, taxes maybe, hounding him, and he paid some fine. It was millions of dollars. He lost everything and then he had a heart attack and died, and my mother had to go on welfare and you should have heard her then!"

"Oh!" Sandy exclaimed in horror.

"Yeah. There wasn't even enough money for me to go to school, so I worked hard and got a scholarship, but my mother was in such bad straits, I quit after two years and got a job. I was living with her in San Diego, in a little apartment, and working in McDonald's, which was all I could get. It was horrendous; I hated it, but I was helping to support her.

"She felt horribly guilty making me quit college and do such disgusting work, and she pulled herself together and took a course to brush up on her skills. She got a job in a law office—before she met Daddy, she'd been a legal secretary. And before you knew it—bingo!—she landed herself another lawyer!" Rebecca laughed.

"Good for her!" Sandy exclaimed.

"We-ell," Rebecca said, "he was married. But he left his wife for her and bought her another nice house, if not as nice as the one my father had bought us, but she was grateful for it; she was happy. I think she did it for me. So I could leave. By then, Bernice and I were friends, and we decided to hitch out here and see the commune and maybe stay here."

Bernice picked it up. "I was scared to do it, but with Rebecca I was less scared, you know? So we came and I loved it here and Brad and I—well, we'd only been friends at school—but we hit it off when we met again. Maybe we were ready for each other. So I stayed."

"Bernice and I ran the farm in those days, not that we knew much about farming . . ."

"We learned. We learned a lot. But now more people have come, and we do everything. We help with the horses once in a while, with the farm most of the time, and in the house, often. Like now," she laughed, holding up a lump of pastry dough.

"Did Gregory ever write?" I wanted to know.

Bernice shook her head grimly. "Never. And don't tell Brad, but to this day I'm mad for him. How do you fall out of love with someone?"

It was an interesting question.

The newcomers were Stepan, Cynthia, and Lysanne, they said. Stepan was from the Soviet Union, Ukraine. He didn't have a green card and couldn't work legally. He had lived on a farm as a kid, before they sent him to engineering college, and he knew when to do what you had to do on a farm—plant, water, weed, whatever. He and Lysanne worked the farm while Bishop and Brad ran the horse ranch. They cared for the horses—fed them, exercised them, swept up the shit, and groomed them. Cynthia, who also helped with the labor of the animals, was in charge of the riding classes. She had been to school in England and had a

— 191 —

license. The classes were open to anyone in the area; there were seven students.

"The riding academy brings in about half of our cash," Rebecca explained, "not that it's very much. We charge fifteen dollars a lesson, which means we can count on about a hundred dollars a week, given absences. It's not really enough to keep us. We eat the vegetables we grow, but we need an awful lot of other things—oats and millet and brown rice, for instance—and we need money for things like toilet paper and gas for the truck and fuel for the generator. Just keeping the generator going is tough. We have enough trees for wood to keep us warm in this room; we take turns chopping it. She laughed, holding up her arm to show us the muscles.

The pies were almost finished baking and dinner was ready when the back door opened and the aroma of horse manure penetrated the kitchen.

"Phew!" Bernice cried.

"I know, I know!" a woman's voice called back. "I'll go back out." The door closed again.

"That's Cynthia. She cleans herself up in the stables, but sometimes there's horse shit on the path and it sticks to her boots."

The door opened again. "There! Is that better?" the voice cried.

"Yeah!" both girls yelled.

There was a rustle of clothes being removed and a third woman entered the kitchen. Cynthia was taller than Bernice, slender, and athletic. She had long hair and wore blue jeans on her long, skinny legs. She stopped in surprise when she saw us.

Rebecca introduced us.

"Bishop's friends?" she asked. "He'll flip!"

"Where is he?"

"He'll be coming in soon. He and Brad are repairing the north corral—a couple of logs rotted out. They're just finishing up."

The door opened again and a man and woman entered: Stepan and Lysanne, I guessed. Stepan was huge, tall and heavy, with a round face and thickish lips. He had large, pale blue eyes and was good-looking, with a sullen mouth that reminded me of Marlon Brando. Lysanne was small and very thin, but wiry; she looked strong enough to be a wrestler. She had bright pink cheeks and bright brown eyes and a happy expression, as if all the fresh air she worked in had cleansed her entire being. I liked her at first sight. I liked Stepan too; I wondered whose lover he was. It was going to take a while to sort out the dynamics of this place, I thought.

Then the back door opened again, revealing a tall, pale, skinny boy. There was electricity in the air as he entered. The whole kitchen stopped talking, watching his face, waiting. He looked around, a bit bewildered—what was going on? He spotted us, didn't take us in, then did, and his face exploded. He was smiling, then his body hurtled toward us; he was crying as he embraced us both, sobbing. We cried too, partly in shock—we'd never seen Bishop cry before. There was a loud clamor as everybody in the kitchen joined in talking or laughing or crying.

"How did you find me?"

"How are you?"

"Why did you come?"

"How are you?"

"Why didn't you write?"

"I knew he'd be thrilled!"

"How is my mother?"

"They're cute, aren't they? He said they were."

"Why did you abandon us? Didn't you know we'd stick by you no matter what?"

"I know, I know. I'm sorry. I was so ashamed."

"What's for dinner tonight?"

"Bishop, my father's dead!"

"What happened? Did he have a heart attack?"

The din in the kitchen went on as people pulled up chairs to the table and Rebecca, Bernice, and Cynthia prepared for the meal. Everyone was talking, laughing, babbling. We were still crying. Bishop tried to explain, Sandy tried to tell her story, I just kept stroking Bishop like a big dog I loved more than anything, and he kept touching Sandy and me, tears on his face.

"He killed himself, Bishop. With the car exhaust. He committed suicide. Can you believe it?"

"I can't believe *your* father did that. He was so calm, so gentle."

Sandy sobbed. Bishop held her while she wept. The others gave them some space, then talked around them. I sat with Sandy and Bishop.

"Why did he do it?"

"I don't know!" she wailed. "No one knows! He just said he couldn't go on."

"Had he read Beckett?" asked Rebecca, who was sitting beside Bishop. Sandy and I went on alert.

"Yes, why?"

"Oh, that's what his characters say. That they can't go on. Can't go on. But then they say they will go on."

Sandy's tears fell anew, and she left the table. Bishop followed her. The rest of us looked at each other. "Did I say something wrong?" Rebecca asked.

I shook my head.

Cynthia was setting the table—practically hurling things at it—and Rebecca and Bernice were putting out steaming bowls of vegetables and grains in the center. Then a bowl of cabbage soup was set on each plate.

"Should we put their plates in the oven?" Rebecca asked, referring to Sandy and Bishop.

"The food will dry out," Bernice said.

"But it'll get cold," Rebecca countered.

Bernice shrugged and Rebecca got up, covered the plates with a dish towel, and set them in the oven on a low heat.

Stepan and Brad wolfed their food down; I'd never seen people so hungry. The food was bearable. I could do better, I thought, but then had second thoughts—maybe not, with their ingredients. No meat or fish, no butter or cream—no luxuries of any sort. Maybe I couldn't do better. An electric lamp hung over the kitchen table; another hung over the sink, but in other parts of the room there were kerosene lamps. I asked why they had both.

"We have generator," Stepan answered me. "Expensive to run. We try save money. So we use kerosene. Cheaper."

For dessert we had one of the apple pies made with Crisco. It was nowhere near as good as Mom's, made with butter. Not as flaky, and the flavor was not as good. It filled the stomach; that's all you could say about it. Maybe I could add something to this commune if I stayed. But maybe they wouldn't care, or even notice.

After dinner we had more coffee, not very good coffee, either, weak, probably made with some mediocre grocery store brand with something added to bulk it out. Chickory?

Sandy and Bishop came back.

"Sorry," Sandy said.

"Sure," a couple of people reassured her. They got their plates from the oven, sat down, and ate quietly.

When they had finished eating, Brad stood up and spoke as if at a meeting. Formally, he announced, "We're really happy that Bishop's friends Sandy and Jess have joined us tonight," he said, as though he was the master of some ceremony.

Everyone chimed in, in agreement.

Brad turned to us then. "What are your plans? Have you come to visit, or to stay?"

I'm sure we looked dumb.

"Well, I mean, like, how long do you plan to stay?"

Sandy was embarrassed. She meant to stay, period. And I meant to stay as long as I felt she needed me. We were both non-committal, saying we were unsure.

"Well, whatever you two do is cool, man," Brad said, looking at Sandy and then at me. "I mean, you don't need a visa to come here. But the thing is, a commune has rules, it has to have rules. And our first rule is that anyone who wants to can come here and stay for one night free. But after that, to stay, you have to work."

"Oh, we want to work!" I exclaimed, having already chosen my job.

"Yes!" Sandy agreed.

"Okay, good. Glad to hear it. We have three areas of work: the chickens, the horses, and the farm. Three of us have the horses pretty well covered. I mean, we can always use an extra hand, but we can take care of most things without help. Bernice and Rebecca do most of the care of the chickens—feed them, clean up the shit, sweep the coop, give them water, put ointment in their eyes, collect eggs. There's not that much to do with chickens, so they also take most care of the house—the cooking and cleaning, although all of us pitch in with doing dishes and marketing and stuff, and we each take care of our own rooms, clean them and change our sheets twice a month. We all share kitchen and laundry duty, we have a schedule on the wall. Stepan and Lysanne do most of the farming; Rebecca and Bernice help too, and we all pitch in sometimes, but that's the area where we need the most help. Especially in the spring and fall. So most new people are asked to help out on the farm. Would you be willing to do that?"

Sandy and I agreed we would, although my heart sank. I really wanted to run the kitchen. I thought that would be fun and I thought I could make a difference there. Anyway, I wanted to try.

"Right now, of course, there's nothing happening with the farm. But in spring, it's mammoth work.

"The next thing is sleeping. There are seven bedrooms and seven of us, but some of us are doubled up right now, so three bedrooms are free, so you can have one or two, whichever you want."

Was everybody waiting, on edge, for our response? I must have been imagining it.

"Thanks," Sandy said, the first time she'd spoken in a full voice since dinner had begun.

"So which will it be?" Brad continued, gazing at us in the tense silence.

"Huh?"

"Will you need one room or two?"

Oh! That was the big question.

Sandy consulted me with her eyebrows. "Two, please?"

"Yes," I said. I wouldn't mind doubling with Sandy if they were pressed for space, but we both liked our privacy. Could it have been that everyone now relaxed? And that Brad and Stepan settled back with a look of satisfaction?

"Third problem is money. When we started the commune, Charlotte, Jerry, and I each put thirty-five hundred dollars in the kitty. That paid for the house—which was eight thousand—put on a new roof, and did a little other work necessary for livability. To buy the horses, fix up the barns and corrals, do the chicken coops, and install a generator, we had to take out a mortgage. When Jerry and Charlotte left, we couldn't afford to buy their shares back, but if the house is ever sold, they get a fraction of the purchase price.

"Bernice and Rebecca put two thousand dollars each in the kitty when they first came. We used that for a down payment on a plow. Lysanne put in three thousand, which paid off the plow. Stepan had no cash, but he chips in weekly. We all do—we have to chip in for food and fuel and water and paying off the mortgage and the plow, but Stepan chips in more than the rest of us because he had no buy-in money.

"He works at the post office three afternoons a week and six nights as a cleaner at the supermarket. The rest of us have part-time jobs. Stepan puts in a hundred dollars a week, which, with the ninety to a hundred dollars a week the riding academy earns, and the six-hundred-a-month board for the three horses, pays our overhead—fuel for the generator, the mortgage, and general repairs. Our money pays for groceries we don't grow. So how much can you girls chip in?"

"I could get three thousand dollars," Sandy said.

"That would be great!" Brad said warmly. "We really need it. We need a big dehumidifier for the basement and money to repair a leak down there. We may need a whole new foundation. We need a backhoe and a power mower to get in the hay."

"I can get something." I said. "I'm not sure how much." I was trying to imagine telling Dad I needed money to live on a commune. I could see his face flush and his eyes widen from where I was sitting; I could hear him shouting, calling me horrible names. I wondered if Mom could get her hands on some cash. I hadn't even thought about money before I came. You think *commune* and you think *free*.

"Anything would help," Brad continued. "We live from week to week, and we never have any luxuries. We have no capital."

"We sell our eggs every week to the grocery store," Lysanne informed us.

"They pay that money into our account, and we use it for cleaning supplies and flour and rice and stuff like that," Rebecca offered. "Peanut butter," she added.

"But it's never enough. We're always in debt to them. Coupla hundred bucks." Lysanne put in.

They were all extremely attentive during this discussion.

Obviously, it was a major subject for them. "I'll call my mom tonight," I said.

"You'll have to go to town. There's a pay phone outside the general store," Bernice remarked.

"I'll go with her," Sandy said. "I want to buy some wine. To celebrate being together again with Bishop and being with all of you. Do they sell wine in the general store?"

"Wine! Wow!" Bishop exclaimed. The whole group applauded in glee. Wine was a treat. "Yes, they do. I'll go with you, show you the way."

"Go ahead." Rebecca spoke as if giving us permission. "We'll clean up the kitchen."

A little chill crept down my spine. Was that how it was? You had to have group approval to do anything? Was that how it was going to be living on a commune?

12 **It was at the commune** that my adult life really began. It was after I set out with Sandy, with two hundred dollars in my pocket and a duffel bag packed with books, underwear, a spare pair of jeans, a pair of sandals, and a half dozen tops and sweaters, that I grew up. It's strange now to think how desirable it seemed, all through childhood, to be grown up; I equated adulthood with freedom and decisiveness, self-knowledge. But of course, these don't come automatically, as I'd imagined, and they are not synonymous. Being adult means you're responsible for yourself, which is burdensome, neither fun nor liberating. Still, I would not want to go back to being a child.

We settled in at Pax, the name given to the commune by its founders. Sandy got her mother to send her three thousand dollars, and my mother sent me fifteen hundred, all she had in the bank. We contributed the whole amount. With this money, the commune—we—voted to pay to have the foundation of the house firmed up and the leaks sealed. We bought a couple of big dehumidifiers for the basement, installed new gutters, and had the chimney cleaned so we could use the fireplace in the living room. That was nice: now we could sit in there on soft chairs, on special occasions, and be warm. We thought about buying an oil burner, but that was far too costly for us. The old coal furnace sat unused in the basement and we kept ourselves warm by the wood stove in the kitchen and the fireplace in the living room. The bed-rooms and dining room (which we never used) were freezing cold from October through May.

We also bought a stallion, a good one who would bring in stud fees. The dehumidifiers were a real improvement—the house had been starting to smell moldy—but also a real pain in the neck: they had to be emptied every damned day. We had a schedule for that, as we did for kitchen duty. We still needed money to buy seeds and a backhoe, and both Sandy and I got jobs in town. Since we were now living with the degenerates on the commune, I didn't dare approach Ginger, whose café would have been an ideal place for me to work. Sandy said it was her loss, but it was mine too. I got part-time work in the supermarket, which paid minimum wage and no tips, but my wages covered my share of Pax expenses and I had a few dollars a week left over for myself—just enough for cigarettes and tampons. For the first time in my life I was dependent on the library for books I wanted to read instead of being able to buy them.

The big question about bedrooms, I discovered later, was whether we were gay or not. Once we took separate bedrooms, everybody assumed we were both straight. Bishop hadn't known any different before he left; even Sandy didn't know until she met Sarah, though she may have suspected.

Sarah hadn't come to Sandy's house at all when Sandy's family was sitting shiva, and when I asked Sandy why, she acted vague, saying, "Oh, you know, she doesn't even know what it is, sitting shiva." I thought they had talked on the telephone a couple of times but I wasn't even sure about that. I privately thought it was awful that Sarah hadn't stood by Sandy at such a terrible time, but of course I didn't say so. I didn't know what had happened between them. I wasn't even sure if Sandy was writing to Sarah from Pax. I was afraid to ask, but it was on my mind often. We never discussed it. Nor did we discuss the fact that she had now simply left Sarah behind without a second thought. I took this as a measure of her desperation.

Sandy had pulled away a little, become a little secretive, almost reclusive. Maybe it was because on a commune, you are surrounded by other people all the time. You can't escape them except in your room at night. The others didn't seem to want to—most had partners, so they had company, including in bed, and they seemed to like that. At night, when I'd be alone in my room, grateful for the silence and the privacy, Bernice or Rebecca or Bishop would knock on my door, wanting to talk, wanting me to listen to music or their new poem, wanting to borrow a book. Sandy said this happened to her too. These people always wanted to be together. I was as nice as I could be about it, but for me it went against the grain. I needed solitude.

On the other hand, Sandy's new personality had appeared before we left for Pax—her prickliness, the feeling I sometimes had that she might hurt herself. As if she lived on the edge of something.

Sandy and I had it easy when we first got to the commune, because it was winter and the farm was in a dormant state. We helped out with the horses and chickens (shoveling manure, mostly) and by fixing fences. We bought paint and painted the downstairs rooms, which brightened the place a lot. Our spirits were high when, a few days after we arrived there, in January 1973, Nixon ended the war. By the beginning of April, all our soldiers had returned home, that is, all but the fifty-eight thousand who had been killed, including one Patrick Connolly. There were now more than three hundred thousand veterans in hospitals or homes, in wheelchairs, on crutches, wounded, maimed.

People at Pax talked about the war a lot, and all of them opposed it; it was all "us and them." It was generally assumed that we, as protestors, had ended the war. But I had different ideas. I didn't discuss them with anyone. I knew they would not like them, and I couldn't defend my bitterness—they were so sure we'd had an effect on things. I didn't want to have to fight with Brad, who was a little intimidating. My thinking was that this was the most protested war in American history. Bishop said that people protested other wars—the Civil War, the American Revolution. But people didn't protest any war as hard or for as long as they did this one. Yet this was the longest war the country had ever fought. If you counted from 1950, when Truman first sent American advisors there, it had gone on for twenty-three years. If you counted from 1954, when the government surreptitiously sent soldiers over there, then for nineteen. Or if you counted from 1960, when troop numbers started to escalate, it was thirteen years. And even if you only counted from 1964 and the fake reports about the Gulf of Tonkin, it still went on for nine years: much longer than the American Revolution, the Civil War, the War of 1812, or the French and Indian War. And to me that indicated how our government felt about us. As if they said, Okay, you go ahead and protest, we'll show you!

I didn't want to talk this over with my friends. I didn't want to hear one of them agree with me, to say, Yes, because we protested, the government prolonged the war. Just to show us who's boss. To put us in our place.

I couldn't have borne to hear that. I could hardly bear to think it.

Almost everyone at Pax hated the government, I knew. They thought government was an elite entity that took power only to increase it and had no interest in us. Some of them even thought it was okay to attack government installations, for example, nuclear bases. Only Bernice and Cynthia supported traditional parties and politics. I kept quiet mostly, because I just wasn't sure. But I yearned, oh, I longed, to believe the government was what I'd thought when I was little, a group of men (I had always imagined them as white men) who cared about the welfare of the country as a whole, who worked toward that, although they sometimes made mistakes.

So Watergate was especially fascinating for me. If ever there was proof that the government was not interested in the people, that was it. At the end of January, before all the troops came home from Vietnam, the Watergate burglars were convicted, and by that summer, the hearings had started. This caused an uproar in the commune, because most of us felt we absolutely had to have a television set to watch the proceedings. We could hear them on the radio, but we wanted to *see* them. But that would mean we'd have to buy a television set and then scrimp on all other uses of electricity, or pay whopping bills for generator fuel. In the end, we bought a set, put it in the kitchen, and that summer, kept running in to watch it. The farm did not get our full attention that year, but Watergate made us happy, very happy. It made us feel we did matter, we had some power, government could be called to account.

One person I was always happy to entertain in my room at night was Sandy, who started coming in to visit the first night we arrived. Much of what occupied us in our first months there was figuring out the sexual and social psychodynamics: how people felt about each other, what the buried lusts and resentments were, and most important, who was sleeping with whom. After the first week, we'd get together in her room or mine a couple times a week for an hour or two—not too long, we were beat at night—to smoke and talk things over.

We knew that Brad and Bernice were a couple but had no idea how they felt about each other. They treated each other so off-handedly. After a month, I decided that they slept together for comfort more than for sex, that they were old friends who were easy with each other but didn't have much desire for each other. Sometimes they didn't seem to like each other very much. Contempt would at times slide out of Brad's voice when he spoke to Bernice, and Bernice, who had told us she was still in love with Gregory, often seemed vacant and distracted around Brad. Sandy read them differently. She thought Bernice was shallow and foolish, whereas Brad was intelligent and responsible. She thought Brad's irritation with Bernice was a response to her denseness and that Bernice deserved some contempt for being stupid. But I said Bernice was a good-hearted woman, the most generous person there. And I felt that since Bernice was never hostile to Brad, as he was to her, his animosity made you dislike Brad, not Bernice.

On the other hand, Brad was very fond of Bishop. And Bishop admired Brad, which also made us like Brad. About Bishop, there was no question. He was adorable and sweet and lovely, just as he'd always been, and everyone at Pax loved him too.

Stepan and Cynthia spent their nights together, but rarely spoke during the day. She seemed almost supercilious toward him, her aristocratic manner and clipped speech more cutting around him than around anyone else. And he could be surly toward her.

The big surprise was Bishop and Rebecca. Bishop had never shown signs of sexuality in high school, but was clearly in love with Rebecca, who was obviously in love with him. They were the one proper couple: it was sweet to watch them together; he was tender and playful with her, she adoring and mothering to him. They were each others' babies, constantly making sure that the other was fed, warm, content. Bishop and Rebecca, or Bec, as he called her, were cute together, he very tall, she very short, both of them pale and smart. When they walked out toward the farm together, they held hands.

Lysanne stayed out of all this, seemingly unfazed by being without a partner, the odd woman out in the sexual game. She was a hearty, hard working woman with a loud, explosive laugh.

She was the soul of the farm. Sandy thought she was gay, but Sandy thought that about almost every woman.

When the group sat together in the evenings, especially if we had a jug of wine or, better, a little pot, it was in a loving and harmonious atmosphere. Everybody mellowed out, gazed at each other with affection, and discussed commune business with interest and energy. Certain subjects did trigger arguments, such as cleaning up the kitchen. The men, particularly Brad and Stepan, wanted the women to do all the housework. They hated to do it and slid out of or forgot their kitchen chores frequently. Brad insisted that men did most of the repair work on the house, so women should do the housework. But Sandy and I had painted the house by ourselves and Rebecca reminded them that she had hammered tiles on the roof right along with Brad and Bishop. Bernice did carpentry alongside Stepan to repair the chicken coops and Lysanne helped Brad install fence posts. The women refused to relent, and the conflict ended in an impasse, always.

I decided to improve our food, and cooking turned me toward farming. The food at Pax was pretty awful, bland and tasteless. Since we could not afford things like butter, cream, meat, or fish, I wanted to brighten our diet of grains and vegetables with herbs. We did not have much to do over the winter and I could spend hours in the library reading about herbs and spices and researching books I could borrow through the interlibrary system. The librarians became my pals; we searched together through *Books in Print* and other reference works, a laborious project in those days, before the Internet. The librarians, all local people, knew the farmers in the area, and knew which men and women were knowledgeable about herbs and vegetables. They often called people to ask if I could visit sometime to learn what they knew.

There were a lot of nettles growing on our place, down toward the stream. Brad tried to eradicate them, but they kept growing back. Stepan said they were useless, as did most of the Becket farmers I met. But I had a feeling about them; to me, they looked like plants, not weeds. Finally I met a farmer who had been stationed in Germany as a soldier in World War II, and had eaten them in soup. I found a traditional German cookbook—Stepan could read German—and found a recipe for nettle soup. So I cut some nettles and made a soup with mint and parsley, thickened with potatoes. The Pax gang loved it. Encouraged, I made flour dumplings stuffed with parsley, chive, thyme, and tiny chopped nettles, and everybody raved.

That's when I began to plan the herb garden.

Stepan and Lysanne knew a lot about plants. Stepan knew mainly traditional lore, from Russia, ideas that involved things modern farmers had forgotten, or had never known. Lysanne had been to an agricultural college in Oklahoma for a few years, and she was up on newer stuff, a kind of farming that had no name then, which we called "natural." Later, it was called "organic."

The Berkshire winter was long; the ground was frozen hard late into spring. For fear of frost, we couldn't plant until May, but I started my herbs in April in shallow plastic boxes I'd found in the supermarket's trash heap. I asked Stepan to dig up earth to fill them, then planted the seeds I'd collected over the winter. I set the boxes on sawhorse tables against the barn facing east. Lysanne built a lightweight wooden frame, to which we stapled a plastic sheet. I laid this over the herbs, tying the loose ends of the plastic to the sawhorse legs so the wind didn't blow it away. Being against the barn protected the boxes from the wind, being up on tables protected them from frost, and the plastic protected them from cold. I had to raise the frame every day to water them, which was awkward, and as I tended them, I was building a permanent greenhouse in my mind. But this would do for now.

In May, when my fear of frost lessened and the ground was

soft enough, I persuaded Bishop and Stepan to till a bed for me in front of the house, where the sun shone all morning. Then I began transplanting the seedlings. I had planned the bed carefully, consulting Stepan and Lysanne as well as books I had borrowed from the library over the winter. I planted the herbs according to affinity. I made patterns of Italian basil, dill, tarragon, oregano, chive, rosemary, thyme, cilantro, purslane, sorrel, bergamot, sage, lovage, cumin, lemon thyme, and mustard. I thought they looked beautiful. Stepan shrugged; he saw no romance in farming. But Bishop raved over it. I could always count on him to make me feel good. I planted tomatoes among the basil and put a big pot of mint at one corner of the bed. I put low-growing edible flowers like nasturtiums along the edges, to brighten the bed. At that point, Bishop and the women at least were enthusiastic.

It took me three days to plant all the seedlings, after which my entire body ached: my back, the backs of my thighs, my knees, my shoulders. I was one mass of pain. I'd worn a big floppy hat but my neck was sunburned anyway. I spent a night soaking in a tub with bath salts. I'd never been so tired or so achy. But I'd been ecstatic while doing it, and I was happier than I'd ever been in my life, whether people appreciated it or not.

As I sat in the bath, smiling with joy, I was mulling over Sandy, who had acted sour that night at dinner. I wondered if I was so high that I was casting everyone else in shadow, but it now occurred to me that Sandy had been low for some time. She hadn't been into my room to see me for over a week, but I'd been so engrossed in the garden that I hadn't even thought about it. Her mood had been wavering ever since her father had died, and for months, I'd been writing it off as grief. But it seemed to me that night that she was getting worse over time, walking around with a sour expression and snapping at people, even me. So after my bath, refreshed by its luxury (we didn't have enough hot water to bathe often), I went to her room with some chocolates I'd gotten at work. Sheila, our store manager, had been given a box of chocolates for her birthday a few days ago and had generously passed it around all day long. Each time it reached me, I took one, but I hid it in a tissue in my apron pocket instead of eating it. I had four chocolates, waiting for the right moment, and now I handed them to Sandy with a conspiratorial smile: "Look what I've got!"

"Oh!" She pounced. She took one.

"They're all for you," I said.

"Oh, Jess!" She had tears in her eyes. She'd really been deprived since we'd been here. She took the others, but leaving them in the tissue I'd wrapped them in, she stowed them in her duffle bag. I watched her, laughing.

"Not going to eat them?"

"No, I'll save them for nights when I'm especially down. Chocolate cheers me up."

"Any special reason? Why you're down, I mean?"

She looked at me under heavy brows. "You mean you've looked up long enough to notice?"

"What?"

"You're so busy coming on to Stepan, I didn't think you could see anything else."

"What?"

"Oh, come on, Jess. Don't play innocent with me."

"I haven't been coming on to Stepan. He's involved with Cynthia."

"Who practically spits when she looks at you."

I was shocked. "You're kidding."

"I'm not kidding. Don't you see what you're doing?"

"I haven't tried to come on to Stepan! I've just been so happy about the herb garden."

"Oh, Stepan, you big strong man, dig up a plot for me, please, pretty please?" she mimicked in a little-girl voice.

Blood rushed to my head. "I never said anything like that!" I cried.

"Your smile said it, your posture, your voice," she said, her face hard.

I burst into tears. She was making fun of me. She hated me. Sandy. Sandy!

She gasped. "Oh, Jess, I'm sorry. I'm feeling so hateful! I hate it here! I hate it! But I don't want to go back home with my tail between my legs. Forgive me! I'm sorry!"

"Why? Why do you hate me?"

"No, I don't hate you! I'm sorry! I love you. Really! But you have been flirty, maybe you don't realize it. You've got Stepan all excited. He's ready to leap on you, don't you see that? What I hate is being here. Especially Brad!"

"Brad! I thought you liked Brad. The last time we talked, you liked him!"

"That was before he started driving me crazy by hitting on me," she moaned.

I wiped my nose with my handkerchief. We had to use hankies here, we couldn't afford to buy tissues. I'd had Mom send me my hankies from home along with the flannel pajamas and woolen bathrobe and slippers I'd neglected to bring.

"You're kidding! What does he do?"

"Oh, don't you see him? Don't you hear him? Are you deaf? He's constantly pressuring me, all the time, whenever we're in the same room. I don't know why you don't see it, except you're too busy coming on to Stepan!" Then *she* burst into tears.

What a pair.

I let her cry, waiting until she blew her nose and calmed down.

"He comes on to you," I prompted.

"Hard. At the beginning, I said, 'No way, you're involved with Bernice.' And he said, 'Oh, she doesn't matter.' And I said, 'She does to me. I like her.' So he started treating her even worse than usual. You could see how hurt she was—she was stunned."

"I *did* notice that. How nasty he was to her."

"Well, she figured it out fast and essentially stopped talking to me. She thought *I* was coming on to *him*," she said bitterly.

"Oh, God," I lamented.

"I have to get out of here. I can't stand it."

"Why don't you just tell him you're gay?"

"Can you imagine how he'll react to that? Brad! I'll never have a peaceful moment in this place again. And Stepan would join in. And Cynthia, too."

"I thought you thought Cynthia was gay."

"Well, I've changed my mind. She's a man in disguise. She'll spew at me, just like them."

"Ummm." I could picture it.

"But how can I leave? I'm stuck here because of you!"

I started to cry again and she reached out and grabbed my arm. "Oh, Jess, I didn't mean that the way it sounded! I'm just so ugly because I'm so unhappy! What I mean is, I feel guilty. You came up here for my sake and I can't just abandon you here. I don't know what to do."

"What do you want to do? If I weren't here, what would you do?"

"I want to get out of here. It's too awful here. I'm uncomfortable in my skin. I want to scream. But I don't want to go home. I can't stand the thought of my mother. Maybe in Northampton or South Hadley or someplace else around Smith I'd find some women who would be sympathetic. I've heard there are a lot of lesbians there now because of all the girls' colleges. A lot of the girls my sister went to school with were so happy there they never left. They teach there now or work in administration at Smith or Mount Holyoke or UMass or Amherst. Maybe I could find a group to live with. I can't go back home . . ."

"Why?"

She shook her head.

"Why? Your poor mother . . ."

"The hell with her," Sandy said brusquely.

"Sandy!"

Her mouth hardened and she stared out the window. "Everybody had to be so nice in our house. So polite. When all the while . . . who knows what he was feeling? Why couldn't he tell her? Why didn't she see? It's her fault! She insisted we all be civilized, she used that word all the time, she forced us . . . She killed him!"

I gasped. "You're being awfully hard on her, San," I said quietly after a while. "He was a psychoanalyst. He was a doctor. He must've known he was depressed, or whatever it was. He must have had some idea what was wrong with him. He was a quiet, polite man too, it wasn't just her. He could have said something . . ."

"He didn't want to upset her! It would have upset her too much!" Sandy practically screamed. "You know how she gets!"

I shut my mouth. I let her cry again, just stroked her arm. When she calmed down a bit, I said, "Tomorrow's Sunday. I have to make breakfast but I have no chores after seven thirty, and I work at the store from eight to noon. I can drive you to Northampton after that and help you find the people you're looking for. See what's happening. I have practically the whole day off."

"Oh, Jess!" She threw her arms around me. I was feeling some resentment, and my body was stiff, unyielding. She didn't seem to notice, though. She let me go with a sudden smile, a wicked look. She opened her duffle bag, removed the tissue, and handed me a chocolate. "We'll share them. Tomorrow, a new start!"

We found Marty Teasdale in a house in South Hadley, where she lived with three other women. They had all attended colleges in the area and found each other through the lesbian networks that exist everywhere. For lesbians, the Connecticut River Valley was a paradise where they were accepted and could live without harassment. Marty had been a friend of Rhoda's at Smith, and Rhoda had told Sandy to look her up. Marty worked for a new feminist newspaper, a journal I found absolutely thrilling because it treated women and the things they did seriously, as though they mattered. It had a fairly wide circulation, and the group who had founded it were now beginning to publish feminist books too.

When Sandy had read Rhoda's letter a few weeks ago (she had been thinking of leaving for a long time, I saw now), she told me about this with some surprise: neither of us had ever imagined a feminist newspaper or publishing house. A new world had opened. And without telling me, Sandy had written Marty, who invited her down and promised to find someplace for her to live.

We rang Marty's doorbell at two thirty on Sunday afternoon. Marty was tall and very beautiful, with black hair and blue eyes. Two of her housemates were home that day, and they joined us for cocoa and cookies. Sandy described Brad's behavior, and they listened attentively. They had had similar experiences, they said; they knew how it felt to be pursued by an insistent male who would not accept polite refusal.

They said they had friends in a commune in Mount Tom that took in women in need of help. The members were involved in half a dozen different enterprises, and Sandy possibly could work in one of their projects. She would need a car. It was not possible to live there without one.

"I have a car," she said anxiously. "I can get my car."

"Good. I thought we'd go over today and introduce you," Marty said. "Then you can join them whenever you're ready."

We took Marty's car and drove a few miles to a small settlement of old houses, stopping in front of a tall, narrow Victorian, complete with a turret, peaked roofs, and a gallery. The front door was unlocked like ours at Pax, but this house could not have

— 213 —

been more different from where we'd been living. It was formal and immaculate, furnished with Victorian pieces—curved-back chairs with red velvet or striped red-and-silver seats, lace curtains, a red turkey rug, a round table covered with a lace cloth, and a red globe lamp. We stood in the foyer, near a staircase, and peered in at the living room.

"Wow!" Sandy breathed.

"Laura!" Marty called, and someone responded from upstairs, then came running down the dark wood staircase. The woman was heavyset and was wearing jeans and an embroidered shirt; she had short hair and a clean, open face. She greeted us boisterously.

"Hi, Marty, how're ya doin'? Sandy?" She moved toward me. I smiled and pointed to Sandy, and she changed direction. "I'm Laura. Hear you want to join us."

"If you'll have me."

"We will! At least for a time. I can't promise permanent membership—we have to have room, and we have to vote on you. But you can stay with us temporarily. We take any woman in need. And you certainly sound in need." She turned to Marty. "Sexual harassment, right?"

What was sexual harassment?

"Yes," Marty said, grimacing.

"Oh," Sandy said falteringly and I thought she was going to cry. "I'm so tired. It's been so exhausting. I hoped I could settle somewhere for good. Is there someplace else I can go?"

She *was* a different person, I thought, since her father died. As if she had all these years been standing on a platform called Daddy, and it had suddenly splintered under her feet, and she was flailing in the air, falling. Where was my calm, confident, dignified, cool-headed friend?

"Don't fret," Laura said in a motherly way. "You can settle with us for a while and if we don't take you permanently we'll find someplace else for you. When did you want to join us?"

Sandy gave a tiny smile of relief. "Really? Oh! Oh, as soon as I can! I'm living at Pax, a commune near Becket. I went up there with Jess"—Sandy nodded her head in my direction—"on New Year's Day. I have to go back there today to settle up. Otherwise I'd just stay here. I can't wait to get out of there. But I put in three thousand dollars to join, and I have to at least try to get something back. Will I need to put money in here?"

"No. This is not a formal commune. A professor of psychology at Mount Holyoke owns the house—Annette Collier—she has a private practice here, in the annex. It's toward the back. A little two-story cottage attached to the main house. It was originally built as a dower house, for the mother-in-law, you know? Annette pays the upkeep on the house. The main house has eight bedrooms, and right now six women live here. We're self-governing, except that Annette decides about repairs and any changes in the structure of the house. We have chores, there's a schedule, we make it up ourselves, and we each pay something every month toward the upkeep and our food. It's not a lot. She's not in this to make a profit; she wants to help women. If you get a job, you should be able to cover it. We never ask for lump sums. When we need to make repairs or redecorate, we use the emergency fund. Our monthly maintenance fee includes a few dollars for the emergency fund. But people who come here for shelter, like you, don't have to pay anything. After a week, we ask you to contribute to the food kitty, but that's all. If you can get some money back from Pax, good for you. But the chances are you won't. Especially if it's run by the guys who are harassing you. And you don't need it to come here."

"God. Money's all they talk about up there," Sandy said. When she said that, I realized it was true. But I had been used to hearing my parents talk about money problems in the years before my father got famous, and it had never bothered me. Sandy's family probably never talked about money. "It's constant." She laughed.

I felt that that wasn't entirely fair. Aside from politics, everything we talked about was mundane, because we worried about things that were broken or dirty, that needed attention. We worried about them because we could not afford to replace them, so talking about them was sensible, practical. We talked about what we would eat, when we would do the next baking, if the plumbing needed attention (as it regularly did with only one toilet and bathtub), how the horses were doing, the chickens, the land itself, and our bills, especially the one at the supermarket. But that was one of the things I liked about Pax: everything was practical, real. There was no time for fancifulness, daydreams, pretensions. No time for egos, preening, or psychology. Nothing superficial.

Sandy and Laura made their arrangements, then we drove back to Marty's place and picked up our car and I drove us back home. I was a little worried about how the group was going to react to hearing that I had helped Sandy plan her escape, and I was tense at dinner that night, when Sandy told them she was going to leave. They were stunned. At first no one said anything.

"Really?" Bernice said finally. She tried hard not to smile, but her mouth trembled. And I thought she liked Sandy!

"So soon?" Rebecca asked in dismay. "You just got here!" She looked hurt.

"Yes." Sandy set her mouth. "I've had problems here. I'm a lesbian," she said to the women, avoiding Brad, "and I'd be happier living without male harassment." There was no kindness in her voice.

Instantly, the rest of them turned to me. I kept my face impassive.

"Why didn't you tell us?" Lysanne protested.

"I was sure the guy harassing me would just get worse," Sandy said bitterly, not looking at Brad.

Brad glared at her. He stood up suddenly and thrust his chair back so hard it hit the wall. "Do as you damned well please. Who cares!" he growled.

"Brad!" Rebecca cried. She turned to Sandy. "Sandy, I'm so sorry. Have we been insensitive to you?"

"*You* haven't," Sandy said. "Some people have."

No one moved. They all must have known, seen it going on. All but stupid me.

"We're sorry, Sandy," Lysanne said.

Stepan looked hard at me. "You going too?"

"I'd rather stay," I said. Would they let me?

"Of course you'll stay," Bishop exploded. "Sandy too. Nobody will give you a hard time from now on, Sandy-andy! Anybody comes on to you, I'll beat 'em up for you, I'll take care of you!" That was the old Bishop. That Bishop always made us laugh. He did this time too—almost.

Sandy smiled at him. "Thanks, Bish. But I've made up my mind. I would like to get some of my three thousand dollars out, if I could."

"How? How?" Brad came charging back into the room. He must have been standing on the other side of the doorway. "We've spent it! It's in the house. The new part of the foundation wall. The dehumidifier."

"Is anything left?"

"We have a thousand in the bank."

"Give her that," Bishop said authoritatively.

"Eight hundred, actually," Rebecca said. "Plus change."

"Give it to her!"

"It'll break us! It's all we have," Brad argued.

"Do it," Bishop said in a low voice I had never heard before.

"Thanks, Bish," Sandy said, "but I don't want to leave you flat broke. Give me five hundred and a note for fifteen hundred against when the house is sold. A thousand should cover my share of rent for the four months I've been here."

"Is May," Stepan argued. "You come New Year."

"Four-plus months," Sandy amended, gazing coldly at Stepan. So it was agreed.

Sandy left the next day, Monday. I had to work at the market all day, so Bishop drove her to Pittsfield in the truck. She took a bus for Boston. She would get a cab from the bus terminal to Belmont, stay a couple of nights at her mother's house, pick up her car, and drive out to Northampton. She felt no guilt about that, she said: her mother could afford to buy Naomi a car of her own. But I lay awake late that night, my cheeks wet, feeling more alone than I knew I should feel, and more alone than I have ever felt since.

I stayed at Pax. I had become a farmer.

When we planned our spring planting, I urged that we use untreated seeds, and fertilize our crops only with compost. Stepan kept the compost heap, filled with our food waste and ashes. We also had a mulch pile, made up of our hay and choppings of the hairy vetch that grew down near our pond. Because I provided an extra hand, we were able to expand our planting area, and we put in corn, green beans, peas, zucchini, beets, asparagus, lettuce, spinach, turnips, potatoes, and soy. We used natural pest controls and watered with hoses—quite a chore! But after I tasted our spinach and sugar snap peas that summer, I was converted to the natural method forever.

With three of us working, we had enough yield to sell some. Bishop and Brad slapped some boards together and built a farm stand out front facing the road, and we made almost two thousand dollars that fall, selling corn, tomatoes, spinach, green beans, and herbs, as well as apples from our orchard. For the first time in Pax's existence, we were able to pay off our bill at the market, which gained us respect in the community. We were no longer dirty, long-haired hippies, but upstanding members of society who paid their debts.

I did a lot of cooking during the years I lived at Pax. I scorched dinners and skillets, I boiled soup away to a brown scum in the bottom of a huge pot, I overcooked and undercooked, overspiced and underspiced, and I learned. I can't say my cooking was great; our ingredients were too limited for that. But we had delectable fresh vegetables, and our eggs, always fresh and always fertilized, were scrumptious and plentiful. My vegetable omelets, soufflés, and scrambled eggs with herbs and potatoes were delicious; my soups were as good as soup can be when made without stock, which I did not often have. A couple of times a year on a special occasion, I would ask Bernice to kill a couple of chickens for dinner. She didn't mind doing it; she grabbed a chicken as if it were her former lover Gregory and wielded the ax with pleasure. Sometime that spring she had fallen out of love and into hate with Gregory; and whatever else Bernice was, she was steadfast in her feelings. Whenever we had chicken, I saved every bone and made a broth, and we'd have luscious soup based on it—for two nights at least.

Soon everyone in the house wanted me to cook every night because my cooking tasted better than anyone else's. And I wanted to do it, except when I was just too tired after planting or weeding all day. Then Bishop or Rebecca or Bernice would do it. That everyone groaned when I wasn't the cook gave me confidence, though I often enough found fault with my own cooking.

A few nights after Sandy left, Stepan came to my room, asking permission to enter. He was stiff and formal, sitting on the straight chair that functioned as my desk chair. I sat on the bed—there were no other chairs. He had his hands clasped between his legs, and he bent forward like a petitioner, which I suspected he was. We both lit cigarettes, which at Pax were a luxury rather than a habit.

He said he'd been wanting to get to know me since I'd arrived, but because he hadn't been sure about my relationship with Sandy, he hadn't wanted to intrude. I didn't believe this. I didn't think any of the guys had any suspicion whatever that Sandy was gay, and once we asked for separate rooms, we were both fair game. But I did think that Sandy being automatically my ally intimidated him a little. Now that she was gone and I was alone, he felt stronger.

I deduced this from his demeanor, and as I did, it dawned on me that I couldn't have been coming on to Stepan the way Sandy had said. Wouldn't he have noticed if I had? If he was interested in me, why didn't he act sooner, if I was being so flirty?

A terrible thought stopped me.

Could it be that Sandy was jealous of my attraction to him? Maybe she didn't want me to get involved with anyone, since she wasn't. Like both of us were attracted to Bishop, but neither of us had acted on it . . .

I didn't like these thoughts. I hadn't completely got over Sandy's attack on me. I knew she was sorry for it, but that didn't mean she didn't mean it. I couldn't bear to think about what it meant. My friendship with Sandy had been the one perfect thing in my life, the one relationship that had no subversive currents. It had proved to me that a beautiful friendship was possible. I would prefer to think that I was a flirty tease than to think that Sandy harbored animus against me. But whatever had happened to Sarah?

I couldn't think about this.

Anyway, I was happy to get involved with Stepan; he was sexy and warmhearted. His sullenness was that of a child whose parents don't listen to him; it made me feel tender toward him, as I would toward a small child. And maybe because he'd first heard about me from Bishop, he treated me with respect.

During the past months, without anyone to talk to intimately, without Mom or Steve, or even Sandy or Bishop, really, since the days of our intimacy seemed to be past, I had done some thinking about a number of things. I'd come to the conclusion that Christopher and the other guys I'd been involved with at Andrews didn't treat me with respect. Once they'd slept with me, they treated me in an offhand way. I didn't complain about it but it made me uncomfortable; it felt as if I had sunk in their regard. For example, Christopher's simply refusing to listen to my poetry, which, now that I thought about it, was probably as good as his. Steve had respected me, and Bishop, but I hadn't slept with them. I think I had just assumed that that was how boys treated girls they were sleeping with—that intimacy involved feeling so easy with the girl that a boy could talk to her as though she was his maid.

Another thing I realized was that people who are much younger than you are can be, oh, a little trying sometimes. A kid who worked with me at the supermarket, Tarak, was fifteen and beautiful—dark eyes and hair, pale skin—and had a crush on me. He was at me constantly, and I liked him, he was cute and funny, but he laughed at odd things, giggled, and he didn't understand when the manager, Sheila, felt blue. She'd been jilted by a guy she'd loved. Tarak just thought she was funny. Sometimes he got on my nerves. I'm not saying Philo was anything like him, but it made me think that maybe Mom might have had a reason to leave him. Since I'd been holding that against Mom ever since, in a hard place in my heart, it was a relief to understand that she might not have been acting like a witch.

These realizations made it easier for me to get together with Stepan that night. We pretty much stayed together after that.

Cynthia didn't seem to care at all; Stepan had said she wouldn't. She moved into a spare room, but I kept my room. I went into Stepan's once in a while; once in a while he came into mine. But we stayed separate.

That summer, I found out why Cynthia was the way she was. She and Stepan slept together sometimes, but for both of them, it was for comfort. They had never been in love with each other and had drifted together out of loneliness. Cynthia was actually in love with an unsuitable man she thought was unattainable, the father of one of her students. For months, they'd been eyeing each other. They then must have spoken, because over the summer, the door to the tack room—which had a couch—was sometimes closed and seemed to be locked and Mr. Howard's car would be in the driveway.

Stepan and I got along in a calm, sweet way. Both of us were mainly concerned with the farm, but we had desire for each other. My life settled into steady contented rhythms for the first time. I was almost twenty-one and thought I'd found the secret of a happy life.

13 **Soon after Sandy left**, a new guy arrived, Bert Stern, who had gone to high school with Hal Shaw, a cousin of Brad's from Alturas, in northern California. Raised in a strongly patriotic family, he'd enlisted in the army in 1969 and been sent to Vietnam. Hal wrote Brad that Bert had seen and suffered terrible things. Hal didn't know the details; he only knew that Bert's best friend, who had been in the same squad, had been wounded, treated, sent back to combat, and finally killed, along with everybody else in the squad. Bert never talked about Vietnam. He'd been wounded, how, we didn't know, but badly enough to be discharged. That wound apparently is what saved his life; the others he had fought with died in an action that occurred after he was airlifted to Tokyo. After the war, he couldn't seem to find anything he wanted to do; he just hung around Alturas, rummaging for drugs and lounging at bars and getting into fights. Hal told him about Brad and the commune, and he hitched across the country on the off chance that he'd be able to tolerate living with us.

Bert challenged all my prejudices. The minute I heard his history, I felt a certain contempt creeping up my spine. Then I realized that I was automatically adopting the attitude of my high school crowd, which was unfair and adolescent. I decided to keep an open mind, and when I studied his face and body, when he sat with us, saying he'd like to join Pax, I felt a wave of pity wash over me. He was three or four years older than I was, but he looked ten years older. And his face—there was something destroyed in it. The eyes, so cold, so carefully inexpressive, and the mouth, hard and set and bitter, but verging on a sob. He'd been in the midst of horror, had seen killing and maybe had killed himself. I found myself regarding him with great respect. He was a person who had suffered and survived; that gave him stature. I would not have admitted it, but he was a hero in my eyes.

He wasn't like anybody else I knew. Just the way he stood, with his stiff posture, and the expression in his eyes, marked him as different. He looked not just wary, but downright suspicious; his demeanor was hostile. I told myself—and I imagine the others did too—that this was a defensive posture that would ease up in time. He spoke between clenched teeth, and in low tones, so we all had to lean forward and try to read his lips to understand him. But he spoke so rarely that it did not become a problem.

Bert told us he was tired and needed to rest. He looked and sounded tired. His eyes were tired. But this didn't matter to the guys: when Brad and Stepan heard that he had experience with plumbing and electricity, they could have hugged him. Thrilled to have him join us, they carefully refrained from mentioning the virulent antiwar stance Pax had maintained for years. And the women, especially Bernice and Lysanne, took one look at him and were ready to open their arms and expose their breasts. He brought out the maternal in them; they too saw the hurt in him. I decided I didn't have any maternal side, because that's not how I felt; I just approached him very delicately, like somebody who could be broken easily.

So there was no argument when we voted on accepting him, although I could see that Bishop and Rebecca were not enthusiastic. I think that they felt that something was off about Bert, something that would make it hard for him to blend in—and that was our criterion, after all. I felt that too, but I thought that his being an injured man and a victim of war should override our doubts. When Cynthia suggested that accepting him was going back on our position against the war, I argued that, however opposed to war we were, we shouldn't blame the poor guys who'd been forced to fight it. Everybody agreed. In truth, now that the war was over, we rarely talked about it anymore.

Bert was more than tired; he was sick. He smoked cigarettes, as we all did, and pot, as we all did, but it seemed to me that he was constantly high on pot, and horribly edgy on the rare occasions when he wasn't. I didn't know how he could afford so much pot or where he got it. I wasn't sure what happened to your health when you took so much. But when the guys teased him about his sources, he would not be baited, and he had enough money to do as he liked. He bought his way in for three thousand dollars, twenty-two hundred of which Bishop forced Brad to send to Sandy—he felt she'd been taken by us. Bert always had pocket money and didn't need an outside job. I figured he got compensation from the government every month—which was only right, except I never discovered how he had been wounded. And he got his mail at a PO box, so I couldn't spy on him.

Bert should never have joined a commune, but that wasn't evident immediately. His rigidity, his stubbornness, and his need to dominate caused general bad feelings, a new experience at Pax. Before he arrived, people who had personal differences settled things by compromise; they made up because they *wanted* to get along, so the general tone was always harmonious. Why else join a commune? When someone got on my nerves, I reminded myself of what Mom would say about her friends' quirks: try to imagine what their days are like. If you imagine being another person, you quickly understand why they do most things they do. But no matter how hard I tried, I couldn't imagine being Bert; I couldn't fathom what could be going on in his mind. His expression scared me a little, when a cold hardness settled on his unshaven face, especially if it seemed directed at me. He almost never smiled and I never heard him laugh. He did more than his share of work, however, and with dogged thoroughness. And he impressed the guys, especially Brad, by being utterly self-contained. He rarely spoke to any of the women and rarely looked directly at anyone.

Brad, who was usually pretty cool except to Bishop, accepted Bert instantly. He didn't make overtures toward him, but offered silent, nodding agreement to anything Bert said. When Bert was engaged in a project, Brad always silently appeared to help, and when he needed help himself, he would glance over at Bert. If Bert nodded, so did Brad. They had a tacit concord. The rest of us, sensing this, warmed toward Bert. But he did not return our warmth.

Bishop had loved Brad from the first time he had met him in Nevada, and he still admired him. *L'affaire Sandy* had dented his regard for Brad a bit, but Bishop and Brad still worked together, and their friendship was continually reaffirmed. Bishop was impressed by Brad's knowledge of horses and tools, his expertise in what Bishop thought of as manly arts, and Brad's knowing big-brotherliness toward Bishop. But Brad treated the women at Pax—even Bernice, his lover—with some disdain. I sensed that Bishop was aware of this and didn't like it; he adored Rebecca and Sandy and me; he admired us, thought we were smart and deserving of respect. Maybe Rebecca had been offended by Brad's attitude and had said something and, in any case, I assumed that on their drive to Pittsfield Sandy had told Bishop how Brad had harassed her. And Bishop had to be upset that Brad had essentially driven one of his best friends out of Pax. But he showed nothing. This made me wonder: was Bishop a wimp? Or was he pulling away from Brad in small ways I could not see but that Brad felt? I think that was the case and that it made Brad even more open to Bert when he arrived—he needed a new ally. It was hard to know, because one thing happened on the heels of another. Sandy left in early May and Bert arrived in June, by which time Bishop was deeply involved in plans that affected all of us at Pax.

Not until supper one night in July 1973 did Bishop tell us his plans. He said, in his unpretentious way, that he had something to tell us. He had waited, he said, until the seeds were in—the biggest chore; the herb garden and vegetables were planted, and we were all relaxed. I was easy, happy. I'd got some free milk from the market (Sheila gave it to me because it was about to pass its sell-by date—she knew how hard things were for us and often did that), so I'd been able to make tapioca pudding for dessert. We ate it with the intense concentration we gave delicious food— always a treat for us—and we were sitting smoking afterward in the quiet that attends deep satisfaction.

Bishop glanced at Rebecca, who smiled encouragingly at him, and dread rose in my heart. They were leaving. I knew it.

Bishop began tentatively. "Uh, well, Bec and I, well, you all know how much we love you, and we love Pax, and the farm and the horses . . . But . . . maybe you feel the same way, there's this little nagging thing, this part of us that hurts and we've been discussing it for a while now . . ."

How long?

"And we started to think it might represent a part of us that isn't getting used. Like maybe our brains."

At this, everyone howled with laughter. We knew we all tended to veg out. People commented to each other, made jokes.

"Anyway, what we've decided is we need to go back to school."

Everybody else took this with calm understanding, but I knew the problem wasn't a simple matter of brain rot that could be solved by some Band-Aid solution. I sat, fists tight in my lap, lips pursed, pretending to smile.

They had both applied to UMass in Amherst and been accepted as part-time students.

"Hey!" people cried. "Congratulations!"

Fat chance, I thought. UMass is not a part-time place. It's too far away.

Bishop darted a look at Rebecca, who picked up the narrative. "We plan to commute. We'll leave every Monday after chores, around three or four, and spend Tuesday through Thursday there.

"And the greatest luck!" she interrupted herself enthusiastically. "We found a commune down there that is willing to have us just a couple of nights a week! We'll stay there Monday, Tuesday, and Wednesday nights, go to class Thursday, and then immediately drive back here. So we'll be here Thursday night, and the whole weekend.

"The commune down there will rent us a room for ten dollars a week, and we already have enough money saved up to pay for the year, plus expenses like books and stuff."

This was a stone dropped into my heart and, I think, all the hearts at the table. At that moment everyone saw how things would go. Everyone loved Bishop and Rebecca, who in some way were the core of Pax. We all knew how long the drive to Amherst was, how tiresome. I wasn't the only one who suspected that this was the beginning of the end of Bish and Bec at the commune. We put the best face on it, acted cheerful that they were getting their lives in order. But, I suspect, many at the table were broken-hearted.

I don't know how Brad felt. Six months earlier, he would have been crushed if Bishop left; but now he was more buddy-buddy with Bert, siding with him in family conflicts. There was something different in the way the two of them heard this news from how the rest of us took it. Having an ally had softened Bert a little, made him a little less rigid and insistent on doing things his own way. Maybe the two of them felt a bit relieved that their new bond would not be strained by Bishop's magnetism. Brad seemed to me to react with an edge of bitterness, as though he were a rejected lover. But maybe I was imagining it. Bert didn't seem to care, one way or another. Both of them turned away with something cold in their hearts, while the rest of us congratulated our favorite members, inwardly grieving and sympathizing with each other at losing them.

As for Bishop himself, I don't know if he was upset about the Brad-Bert alliance, but I was willing to bet he was relieved. He and Rebecca were so close, so loving, they really had no room for anyone else. And of course he had me too; I would take Bishop's side on any issue.

Bishop and Rebecca worked especially hard that summer, as if to prove that their hearts were still with us. They carefully avoided discussing their college plans, until after supper on a Monday night at the end of August. Then they went around the table telling each of us how special we were, then said good-bye, having quietly packed the night before. They took Rebecca's truck, leaving one less vehicle at the farm (that hurt), kissed us all, and promised to see us later in the week. We all stood out in front of the house. Tears streamed down my cheeks and Bernice's.

Bishop was resuming college in his sophomore year, Rebecca in her junior year. They were taking what was considered three-quarter time and planned to do their library research in Amherst, so they would bring almost nothing of college back to Pax with them. They tried to arrive in time for supper on Thursday evening, after which they worked and talked only of Pax matters. Their ambition was hopeless, of course, but they were as discreet about their schooling as if it were a love affair.

They both did well enough that UMass offered them full scholarships for the following year if they would attend full time. By then they had scouted the job market down there and found work. They could join the collective where they rented the room—of course the other commune had counted on that. They were such adorable people, everyone wanted them. They would have to leave Pax.

Bernice, Cynthia, Lysanne, and I cried, and even Stepan had wet cheeks on the Saturday morning in August 1974 when Bish and Bec packed their gear into the truck and left us for the last time. We had lost our sanest member, Rebecca, and our sweetest, Bishop. But in April that year, a new woman had arrived, Lolly Hunt, a southerner with great charm and with some knowledge of farming—she'd lived on a farm in Alabama as a youngster. So we went on.

During the year Bish and Bec were part time in Amherst, we finally had phone service installed. We needed it with them gone, to ask them things only they knew, like where the honing blade was and what medication to give the stallion when he was in a fit. Having a phone was great: Mom and I could now talk as well as write. I'd call and let the phone ring three times, then hang up. She'd know it was me and call back and we'd talk for an hour. I'd been writing her ten- and twelve-page letters since I'd arrived, but I missed hearing her voice. She drove up to see me the first summer I was away and stayed with us for a weekend; the next time she came she stayed at a motel in Great Barrington.

In 1974, soon after Nixon resigned, Mom got involved with a new man, Moss Halley, a divorced lawyer who practiced in Cambridge and had an apartment there and who, she said, had great humor. I was glad she had someone in her life, but his presence unavoidably became another wedge separating us. I was forgetting Mom!

I forgot Dad too. I hardly ever heard from him, although I wrote him every once in a while. He wrote me once, to tell me they were giving him a retrospective in New York, at the Guggenheim. That was a triumph for him and even Mom went to see it. Julie wrote me a sweet letter about nothing. Then, in 1975, I got a letter in which she apologized to me for leaving Dad, as if I would be angry with her for it. She said she had to leave because she couldn't make him happy. Irene Templer, Mom's friend from Vermont, told Mom that Julie had divorced him on the grounds of "abusive behavior." I didn't know exactly what that meant. By now, *sexual harassment* and *abusive behavior* were terms frequently seen in the papers, popularized by the women's liberation movement. But I didn't know what they meant specifically. Did she mean that Dad had gone completely off his rocker and hit her? Or that he was just his old yelling self, exploding every night over some imagined betrayal? Or was it that he retreated into sullen silence for days at a time? Whatever, she'd already left him. She was in New York, where her sister lived, and was taking a course at Pratt. She was a lighthearted person, and I knew she'd be fine wherever she was. I meant to answer her, but somehow never got around to it.

I lived so far outside the world that I had no interest in it. I was immersed in my plants and the people I lived with and I was completely satisfied, except for an occasional pang of guilt about selfishly cultivating my garden and ignoring my civic responsibilities, whatever they were. The only mirror at Pax was the small, cloudy one over the bathroom sink, and I rarely really looked at myself. But I felt that I radiated virtue. I believed that the commune was an innocent, pure world. Our virtue lay in our poverty, which was voluntary, and in our exercise of democracy in its truest form in our daily life. We were pure because we lived so austerely. My hands were calloused and red, I was sunburned all spring and summer (my face and neck and forearms at least), and maybe I looked older than I was, but I was utterly contented. I was living the life I had longed for when I was a little girl reading the Little House books. I remembered my satisfaction at helping to build a latrine one summer when I'd gone away to camp. Our life gave me that same joy. When you're encompassed by necessity, you don't suffer from ambiguity and doubt. They are luxurious diseases not caught by people who don't have leisure. I didn't miss them any more than I missed furs and jewels—which I'd never had or wanted.

From the first, even before they definitively left, I knew that Bishop and Rebecca were doing the right thing. They were too smart to spend their lives at Pax. It was a waste of their intellects. So what about mine? I had continued to write poetry, but with increasing dissatisfaction: I felt I didn't know enough to do it well. I decided to learn something about it.

My time could not be spared in the spring and early summer, but I had plenty in the winter. I didn't want to drive all the way to Amherst, so I signed up for a course in modern American poetry at a community college in Pittsfield, which was only about half an hour away. I went several times in the fall of 1974, but the class was poor. The level of teaching was too low, even for me. So in the spring semester I transferred to Simon's Rock in Great Barrington, a longer drive but not as far as Amherst.

Simon's Rock was designed for young students and I stuck out. But the teaching was better. We read Frost and Stevens and Williams and Moore and Lowell and Bishop. I decided that I would continue and study Yeats and Pound and Eliot. I took only one course at a time. Getting a degree was not important to me.

Meanwhile, as time went on, the impact of Bishop and Rebecca's departure became more evident. The mix had changed, and that seemed to change all the relationships. The two new people, Bert and Lolly, were so different from the people they replaced that we became a different community. Brad, who had the cachet of an original founder, and therefore maybe some more authority than the rest of us, had always been tempered by Bishop, softened by Bish's sweetness. Bert had the opposite effect on Brad, bringing out all his hard angles. Bert's silences were powerful; he didn't speak, but he looked a lot—and how he looked was askance. It was as if he disapproved of everything, all the time. But when I studied his eyes, I saw a life I wouldn't want to live; I saw a person who, when I thought of how he spent his days, I couldn't imagine. It was as though he was in hell and I could see it but couldn't reach him there, couldn't help to pull him out.

Bernice and Cynthia, who were rather dull, had been brightened by Rebecca's intelligence and kept in balance by her sanity. Lolly had neither; she had been wandering for years, and soon after she arrived it became clear that what she was seeking was an attachment to a man. I wondered if I had been like her once—just like Sandy had suggested. But whereas a man meant to me a center for my affection, a home, men meant power, even survival, to Lolly. This was the single piece of wisdom she'd filtered out of whatever her past had been. I watched her in fascination. Without a man, she would drown; you could see this in her empty blue eyes, the desperation of her carmine mouth—even on the commune, she was never without her dark red lipstick. She didn't attach herself to the women, but floated from one man to another. She tried Bishop first, but that was a waste of her time: he was impervious to flirtation, being as guileless as a three-year-old and utterly in love with Rebecca. So she tried Stepan, who was the most accessible of the others. He was flattered, wary, guilt-ridden, and afraid that I would explode. She played with him for a while, considering, but I gave her pretty strong competition, and besides, once she saw how the land lay at Pax, she moved to the hard men, who presumably had the power—whatever power she endowed them with in her mind. She didn't approach them directly; she hovered, observing them. They knew it and were flattered, but too steeped in steely manhood to respond.

I thought she would end up with Bert eventually, but I lost interest in the drama in all the activity of my poetry course and the impending departure of Bishop and Rebecca. And nothing changed until after they left. Then Lolly, I noticed, started to do more than her share of kitchen duty, seeming to show up when either Bert or Brad was on the roster. At first I assumed they had switched with her; later I decided they paid her to do their work (they both hated kitchen duty). She was penniless when she joined us and Brad suggested she pay a little more into the kitty every week than other people in lieu of an investment. Brad and Bert always had more spending money than other people, I never knew exactly how. But if they were paying her, they were subverting the principle of a commune, and Bernice and Cynthia and I called a meeting to complain.

Lysanne was (as always) apathetic, but the men said they had the right to do with their private money what they liked, that Lolly didn't mind doing this work and they did, so they would no longer do kitchen duty and that was that.

We were incredulous. "Brad!" Bernice protested, "You of all people to undermine commune principles! Everybody shares equally in work and reward, remember?"

"Marx said it: from each according to his ability, to each

according to his need," Brad intoned. *"Critique of the Gotha Program*, 1875. Kitchen work is not one of my abilities."

"And carpentry is not mine, but I do it!" Bernice exclaimed in fury.

"We all do everything!" Cynthia yelled. "We always have! Now that Bishop's gone you think you can ram things down our throats!"

Brad sat back and folded his arms. "Like it or leave it."

Bert looked on with a small smile on his face—Bert, who never smiled. Then Bert the Silent spoke: "What difference does it make to you?" he sneered. "You're not having to do extra work."

Everyone looked at Lolly, who was in part responsible for this coup. She sat looking up from under her eyebrows like a naughty child and said, in her child's voice, "Girls, I can't help it, I don't have any money and I don't have any skills except kitchen work. This is the best way I can pay for myself. Don't be mad at me, please."

We were, but we couldn't do anything about it.

The men won that battle, but they had unknowingly set in motion events that would lose them the war. It didn't happen right away. Brad savored his victory and what it meant to him. We women knew that he considered kitchen work women's work, and that was why he hated it so much. Once he no longer was subjected to the humiliation of the duty roster, he began to see himself in a new light and, gradually, began to carry himself differently. By January 1975, Brad was swaggering around like Big Daddy, and Bert had fallen into sidekick position, his enforcer. At family meetings, Brad was now acting as though he was in charge, when the whole principle was that we were all equal. But with Bert's support and the only other man weak-spined Stepan, trained by the USSR to obey in passive silence, he felt unthreatened. He had no respect for women, and no matter what we said, he treated us like unimportant servants and acted like a patriarch.

It was no longer pleasant to be there, and we women lived and worked under a cloud. Cynthia left: Mr. Howard had divorced his wife and Cynthia moved with him to California, where he bought a ranch they would manage. We got two or three letters from her before we lost touch. Stepan and I were still together but uneasy about it. I didn't trust his feelings for me, and he felt unmanned and blamed me for it. The sexual division at Pax was the same as it had been when I joined, three men, four women. But now one of the women was Lolly.

It was winter and I was deeply involved in my courses at Simon's Rock. I was reading Wallace Stevens and, in a philosophy course, Plato's dialogues. I went to school and worked at the market and did my kitchen chores at Pax, but I was as engaged with the kids at school and the people I worked with at the market as I was with the folks at Pax. There I was a fire down to the embers, barely present. In another month, I would have to plant seeds for my herb garden, but I couldn't even muster up the heart to look at catalogs. I kept putting it off. I rarely went to Stepan's room at night, preferring to read late and smoke in my room. Stepan had quit smoking, and he preferred I smoke elsewhere. If he entertained Lolly in my absence, I didn't know it.

At our usual weekly meeting on the last Friday in March, Brad said he had an important announcement. We'd been talking about budget matters, and we all stopped and looked at him, hearing the self-importance in his voice.

"I would like to put a proposal before the commune," he began. Then he read a long paragraph from a pamphlet he was holding, describing sexual customs at communes of the past. He looked up and said, "So I'd like to propose that Pax women be held in common."

"What does that mean?" Bernice wanted to know.

"Well, what it says, Bernice," he said sarcastically. "All women shall be available to any man," he said.

"What?" Stepan gasped.

"True communism! True communism, Stepan!" Bert snarled.

I cried out, "True communism! You mean sharing the wealth? So women are wealth? Possessions?"

Stepan looked troubled. I suspected, then hated myself for the thought, that what troubled him was the question of whether he counted as a man. Brad said we'd take a vote. He asked the men first. Bert nodded. Stepan said firmly, "Nyet!" Bernice said vaguely, "I don't think so," and Lysanne concurred with her. Lolly said it was fine with her. I emphatically vetoed the idea. Four against three: that was the end of it.

But it wasn't. The idea was out there, poisoning the air around us. We knew they wanted it, and we—Bernice and I—also knew that they wanted it not because they desired us but because they wanted to feel power over us. And then—what a shock! Bert began to come on to Bernice really hard, and Brad came on to Lysanne. It was a tactic, of course, but the strategy worked. Bernice almost swooned in surrender. She was a hard lover, as we knew, and all these years she'd been waiting for a master. And Lysanne, absolutely thrilled finally to be included in the sexual dance of the commune, poor thing, fawned on Brad with adoring eyes. I wondered how these women would feel when the bruises and black eyes started, and I decided they'd probably stick to their men, well trained in the myth as they were.

The day I saw Brad coming on to Lysanne I became very low. That night, I went to Stepan's room. We had not been together for over a week, and he was extremely happy to see me. I went into his bed like a kitten seeking warmth, hoping I had him, at least, as an ally in this war. He was loving and passionate, and I was grateful and loving to him, but after we'd made love—and he indulged me by allowing me to smoke a cigarette in his room—I told him what I'd seen. He shrugged. "Is good," he said. "Poor Lysanne never get love."

"Love?" I cried. "Is that what you think it is?"

He looked at me, bewildered and hurt.

The next day, a freezing April day, I was out in the fields digging earth to fill the boxes for my herb seeds, when I glanced over at the barn and the paddock and saw Lysanne clinging to Brad. I sat there stunned for a while, then walked slowly into the house.

Bernice had just come in from the chicken coops and was washing her hands. She turned toward me and her face took on an apologetic expression. "Oh, Jess," she said lamentingly. "Please don't feel I'm deserting you. But you know I didn't like Bert when he first came, and I was outraged at his idea . . . well, you know. But he's changed, he's become so . . . so . . . *masterful*. I couldn't bear him before, but suddenly . . . I just can't resist him! You understand, don't you?"

"Sure," I said. "And you won't mind him sleeping with Lolly too. And Lysanne, if he gets the impulse."

"Lysanne!" she said, screwing up her nose. She turned away, concealing her face as I started down the hall.

"Say, what's for dinner tonight?" she cried.

"Search me," I called back, mounting the stairs.

It was like the day I left Andrews. I didn't think then, but felt as if I'd been thinking all along without knowing it. I went up to my room and packed my gear. I didn't have much. The only things I'd bought in the past two and a half years were some cheap tops and underclothes and enough books to fill a couple of cartons. I found boxes for the books in the basement. I loaded everything in my car.

Bernice had gone back outside; the others were doing their usual chores. I debated whether to say good-bye to Stepan. But his behavior over the past weeks had soured my affection for him. They would know why I'd left. It pleased me that dinner would be late tonight: let them eat Bernice's millet. Lightness and harmony and democracy and virtue had disappeared from Pax. I had often heard that this happened at communes, but I had refused to believe it: we were different.

I wanted nothing from them. Pax had been my life for the past almost three years. I had learned an enormous amount here and been happy and loved them all. But the experiment had collapsed, as they usually do, when people tried to dominate. I thought how ironic it was that gentle Bishop, who never got angry or raised his voice, had been our major influence.

I put on my best jeans and sweater, my least scuffed boots, and set out for Cambridge.

14 **This was the second time** I had arrived home unannounced and unexpected, surprising Mom. Maybe she'd really missed me, because she was elated to see me. She fussed over me, kept touching me, smoothing my shoulders, exclaiming over my thinness. Her eyes kept tearing up. God, that Lithuanian weepiness! But I just laughed, I was so happy to see her and to be there. It was so *comfortable*. I'd forgotten. I rested for a week or so, taking long foamy baths (I no longer had to worry about having enough hot water), reading, marketing, spending Mom's money on meat and fish and butter and cream and wonderful desserts. Mom and I cooked luscious things I hadn't had for years: stews and blanquettes and sauces and soups made with stock. I was thin as an insect. I hadn't really known how skinny I looked, which was lucky.

It felt strange to have free time. I was used to constant work. It was much warmer in Cambridge than in Becket, and I thought of planting an herb garden in Mom's backyard, but it turned out that Mom was leaving Cambridge soon. In August, she was going to France, to Lyon, to teach in an exchange program for two years, and a French professor and his family were going to occupy our house. I would have to find someplace else to live.

I met Mom's new boyfriend, Moss, who was tall and gangly and loud and very endearing. He wandered around making jokes and being useless, as he constantly pointed out, but at least he took her out to dinner and a movie once in a while. He had promised to fly to France to visit her at least every other month. I wondered what it was about Mom that made guys commute for her all the time. Moss had an apartment in town, very modern and expensive looking, but to me it felt a little dark and cramped. It was on the first floor. I was used to the fields, the open air, and brightness. Even in winter, even when it was gray, Becket was full of light. I missed that, and the tremendous sense of satisfaction I used to have at Pax as I planted my garden or cooked something really good—good by our standards, I mean. But I determined that I would get those feelings back, somehow.

What surprised me and gave me a pang was that I didn't miss any of the people. What was the matter with me?

One Sunday after I arrived, Mom invited her old friends for brunch so we could see each other again. As they showed up, one by one, I realized that even though they were her friends, they loved me, and I loved them. It was a real pleasure to catch up with Alyssa and Eve and Annette and Ted. It was like old times—their affection caught me up and raised me high; at moments, I felt like a little girl again, a dependent child trying to please them. But on the other hand, I was different, older, and I now regarded them as equals. It was good to hear politics discussed by an older crowd—at Pax people thought that anyone over thirty was rigid and conservative and hopeless. It was good to hear different points of view for a change. We at Pax had almost given up on politics. I just listened. I no longer knew enough to argue; I'd stayed so out of things.

Alyssa hadn't changed at all; she was still so sweet she caught at your heart, but she was a walking ghost, filled with grief for Tim. Eve had recovered; she had a large practice and was becoming known for papers on a new therapeutic outlook, urging that therapists abandon their old silent, disinterested stance and replace it with interconnection and responsiveness. She was really interesting on this, and we talked for a long time.

And Annette and Ted were calm and contented now. Whatever they felt about their lost children, they were hugely proud of Lisa, a professor now, and a striking woman. They showed me pictures—the homely child had become beautiful, tall and blonde, with her hair pulled back in a chignon, long straight legs in narrow pants, a beautiful figure in a stylish jacket. She was standing in front of a building on her campus, carrying books and smiling. She looked like someone who had made peace with whatever devils she had entertained.

Ted and Annette were both active in their professions and had a cozy new house, which they couldn't have had before. Annette was teaching autistic children and taking part in some experiments with them. She told me about some of these, saying how much more we knew now than we had known when her kids were young. I guess that was a good thing, although it didn't help her own children. When I asked about them, she said they never saw them and she sighed, but she didn't cry until she told me that Derek and Marguerite had forgotten her and Ted, and that was better for them. I was remorseful that I brought it up.

Moss did well with Mom's friends. He was interested in them and knew what kinds of questions to ask. He seemed to be on their wavelength, and they responded to him. He helped Mom in the kitchen and even helped clean up! He acted interested in me, even. That was a treat for me: I realized that although we loved each other, no one at the commune had really been interested in me. They were at first, when Sandy and I were new there and there were things to be found out about us. But after a while, we all lost interest in each other; we just lived together. I had come to feel pallid; I had wilted in the thin air of Pax. Eve's and Annette's curiosity about me, what I felt and thought, what I was going to do, felt like dew on parched skin.

None of the clothes I'd left hanging in my closet at home fit me anymore, I'd got so thin. Mom insisted I go shopping. She gave me money and told me where to go. I asked her to please go with me and wondered how it had happened that I had lost all my worldliness and confidence. I even needed her to help pick out pants and tops: it had been so long since I thought about clothes or bought any that I didn't know what was in fashion or what looked good on me. But once I had new stuff, I felt pretty good. I went to Mom's hairdresser and had a haircut; I kept my hair long but had it shaped and edged. I bought mascara. Then I felt ready to face the world.

I called Philo. I'd never stopped thinking about him, imagining a future for us. Whenever I was annoyed with Stepan or we quarreled, Philo flooded into the space between us like seeping water, giving no notice.

He was so happy to hear from me, his voice choked up. He'd been thinking about me, he said; he regularly thought about me, how the hell was I? Damned fine, I said, picking up his tone, although of course I wasn't. Losing Pax was losing the center of my life, but I had not allowed myself to think about that at all. Leaving it had been worse than when my father left, worse than the day I left Andrews. It felt as if my life had vanished, I faced only blank space. I'd have to start all over again, creating a life. Creating happiness, as Mom had described it years ago. As if I knew how. I felt aged, but I was only twenty-two.

Philo was a root I could grow from, I thought. I had something with him. We arranged to meet on Sunday at the gate to Harvard Yard facing the kiosk and the Coop. Mom was at an anti-nuke meeting in Boston somewhere, helping to plan a march. It was a beautiful day in late May. I arrived a little before noon and stood there in my new jeans and a new top (but the same old scuffed boots). Despite the new clothes and haircut and the mascara, I felt old and used and unattractive. I suddenly remembered my first glimpse of Bernice and Rebecca in their babushkas, and realized I too had become a commune hausfrau. I wondered if Philo would even recognize me.

I spotted him coming from the T and walking toward me. He looked just the same, maybe even more beautiful than before—a little older, a little softer. His waist and hips were as thin as ever, his arms and shoulders muscled and shapely. He spotted me too and charged toward me and grabbed me in a bear hug and held on and we rocked and rocked as if we were in a cradle. We stood there wrapped together for a long time, both crying. Finally he pushed me away, holding on to my shoulders and gazing at me.

"My God," he breathed, "you're even more gorgeous than you were!"

I burst into tears. Damned Lithuanians. "You too," I said.

We decided to walk up to the Common, where we found a big tree. We sat under it and talked. And talked and talked. He'd been devastated when Mom broke up with him, he said; he even had trouble working, which was unusual for him. He could manage to teach, but he couldn't write for a while. Eventually, though, he finished his dissertation and got his PhD and was promoted to associate professor. He got a raise and could afford a tiny apartment in Boston, right in Back Bay. He was sometimes asked to speak at conferences, so he got to travel around the country. He gave talks about Marvell and Milton and had started to write a book on George Herbert, another poet he said I'd like. I'd never read him, but naturally he had a copy of Herbert's poems in his backpack and he read out a few to me. They were hard, I thought, but lovely.

"Have you been involved with anyone?" I wanted to know.

He grimaced. "A woman on the faculty at BU—Alicia Estevez. A dynamo, like your mother."

"Your age?"

"No. Older than me. But younger than your mom."

"And . . . ?"

"Oh she was great! Terrifically smart and she says what she thinks. She's had pieces published in *PMLA*. *PMLA*!" He rolled over on the grass and sat up again. "I'd give my eyeteeth to be published in *PMLA*. She works on a bunch of French guys—Derrida, Barthes, and Lacan."

"I know about them. Sandy's sister Rhoda worked on Derrida."

"He's starting to become really well known. He's part of a movement called deconstruction."

"Yes. Sandy said it was really hard."

"Well, the principles aren't difficult, but the way they write about them is." Philo laughed.

"So you don't follow it?"

"I'm starting to. You can't be in academia these days and not be involved in it."

"Are you still with Alicia?"

"No-o. We split up. Actually, she didn't like the way I acted with her kids."

"Why?" I was outraged. "You were wonderful with me!"

He shrugged. "I don't know. They were smaller, little kids. I thought they should do what she said, what she told them to do. They were kind of wild."

"I can't picture you being severe."

"I wasn't. I didn't think. Oh, I don't know. They were awfully hard to handle, and I insisted they do what she said. She was a fierce woman, but not with her kids. Well, she was fierce with her kids, but in a protective way. Whenever they cried, she let them do what they wanted. She was the opposite otherwise. She'd fly into rages at faculty meetings. They called her *La Passionara*." He laughed. "She was a peace activist like your mother, but she felt anybody who wasn't was morally deficient. And she went crazy at anything she thought was sexist. A faculty member, a guy known for patronizing women, said something insulting to her. He belittled her or something she wrote, I'm not sure which. To her face! In her office! He started to leave and turned back and laughed at what he'd said, and she was standing at the door with him smoking, and she raised her cigarette and put it out on his cheek. He screamed. He created a huge to-do in the department but he was so hated that she wasn't reprimanded."

"Wow."

"Yeah."

"Did you start to worry that one day she might do that to you?"

"No. I admired her. What guts!"

I wondered about that a little, but most of what we said to each other was conveyed by shining eyes and smiling mouths and glowing skin. We didn't touch. After an hour or so, we agreed that we were hungry and wandered back down into the Square and over to Bailey's, still there after all those years and looking just the same, except for its new banquettes and floor. My heart ached with all the past it held for me and the people I'd lost. I told Philo about the commune and Sandy and Bishop and Dolores, whom I hadn't yet looked up. I left out why I left Pax. He didn't ask and I didn't say. I brought him up to date about Alyssa and Eve and Annette and Ted. And Mom. He was weepy about these friends, whom he'd lost when he and Mom split up. Philo was as nostalgic and romantic as I was, and together we indulged in an afternoon of sentiment.

I touched his hand lightly a couple of times, and he did the same to me. Clearly it was up to me what happened next: he was giving me control. A surge of power lightninged through me, and my heart flew at the thought that finally Philo and I could be together.

But nothing happened. Affectionate as I felt, I could not bring myself to move toward him and he did not move toward me. We had sandwiches and coffee and sat over second and third cups for hours, until both of us were twitchy. We sighed and looked at each other. We knew.

So Philo signaled for the check and paid for my lunch, which was nice, since I was still broke, having left Pax with about fifteen dollars in my wallet. We stood up. I couldn't believe I was letting him go—Philo, my dream lover. But I had to: it felt almost like he was my brother. Slowly, we walked outside and stood in the warm air for a few minutes, and I remembered that the last time I'd stood like this outside a restaurant I was with Steve outside Sonny's, and Christopher was watching us. Philo and I clasped hands a final time, then he turned toward the T and I toward home.

All the way walking home and even after I got there, I was sunk in feeling. I felt loved, which I hadn't felt in quite a while. I don't know why—did Stepan not love me? I had thought he did. Maybe I didn't love him. Didn't the Pax people love me? Wasn't that the magic of commune living, being with a group of kindred souls connected by fellowship and good feeling? Where had the good feeling gone? When? How?

But I also felt hollow. For years now I had let myself dream or fantasize or imagine, or do something more profound than dream, about living happily ever after with Philo. Letting him go felt like letting go of the hope of happily-ever-after, and I almost couldn't bear it. My temptation was to brush it aside and not think about it, and I decided that was the right thing to do. Other people might make themselves stronger by facing things, but not me. I handled things by putting them in a cubby.

Our fireplace was on a wall that projected a couple of feet into the living room; around the bend from it, set in the floor like a big mousehole, was a cubby with a door, a brick floor, and plaster-finished walls. It was meant to hold dough during bread making, to protect it from drafts. In its warm shelter, the dough would rise to its yeasty fullness. I thought I did best in life when I put things that hurt me or made me uncertain in the bread cubby of my soul and let them rise in their own time. I stopped thinking of myself as a coward and just went ahead and hid things, certain that they would rise when they were ready.

The next day I went to Sonny's to get a job. Sonny wasn't surprised to see me; I was following a common female pattern. Women quit waitressing when they finish college or get a real job or marry or have a baby. But an awful lot of them come back, because things don't pan out—few jobs pay women decent wages and women always have to work around their responsibilities to children and men. Waiting tables allows them to do that. At least, this was the way it was then, in the 1970s.

I was just biding time. I had no idea what I would do when Mom left for France, but I would have to vacate the house on Kirkland Street. I thought vaguely of applying to UMass in Boston, not because I had a driving desire to learn—although I would have liked to take some poetry courses—but to pass time until I knew what I wanted to do. The thought drifted across my mind that I could maybe share an apartment somewhere with someone.

I called Dolores but couldn't find her. She had written me a couple of times at Pax, and I had intended to answer. But somehow we lost touch. The people presently at the halfway house didn't know where she was now; the director knew that she'd lived there and had completed her BA. He thought she had gone to graduate school somewhere, but didn't recall where. He hadn't personally known her and no one from her time there was still there.

I wondered if I'd ever see them again—Dolores, Sandy, Bishop, or Philo. Now I had to add the people at Pax. It felt as if my life had burned up, leaving no residue. But by the time June rolled around, a residue exploded across my calendar, changing everything for me.

I discovered I was pregnant. I don't know how it happened. Stepan had used condoms and I made him be careful, most of the time. But sometimes, he was broke and couldn't afford to buy any, and sometimes, when we were out in the fields working we would get hot for each other and just do it. He hadn't worn anything the last time, I recalled. It must have been that night I went to his room just before I left; or maybe it was that day when we fell in each others' arms on a shady bank of grass near the pond: green deeds in a green shade. When he didn't have a condom, he would withdraw before coming. He said that was what most men in Russia did, and that it worked dependably. I should never have believed him. It was mid-June before I realized I had missed my May period. I began to worry immediately, but in those days they gave you a really hard time when you wanted to find out if you were pregnant. *You weren't allowed to know.* You would go to a drugstore and give the druggist your urine sample and ask for a rabbit test but the test didn't work until you were two months on, and some druggists made you swear you were married before they'd give it to you. So you had to put a ring on your finger and reverse it, so it looked like a wedding ring, and lie. I didn't find out I was pregnant until early July.

Mom was beside herself. She kept cursing herself for agreeing to go to Lyon. She said she would cancel her trip, and if she couldn't stop the man coming to live in our house, she'd rent another house for us to live in. She said she would help me, take care of me, do whatever necessary to see me through this. Unless, of course, she added, I wanted an abortion. She didn't go further, but isolated as I had been, I did know that abortion had been legalized a few years before, and that there was a clinic in Cambridge. I didn't know what to do.

I had no desire to have a baby for Stepan, if that is ever a woman's motivation. I'd often seen plays and movies in which a woman wants to have a baby for a man, but by that time I'd realized they were almost all written by men who knew nothing at all about real women. I had never met a woman who wanted a baby for a man. I suppose it's possible, but I wasn't one of them.

What I had to decide was if *I* wanted a baby or not. My thinking on the subject consisted of pictures of me living with a baby. Since I couldn't imagine how I was going to live at all, I could invent stories at will, and I did. I lay in bed, night after night, envisioning myself taking courses at some college, being supported by Mom and, somehow or other, taking care of this baby. It seemed a grim life, hard and unrewarding. And Mom would have to do most of the work, and how could she? Her job was demanding. Besides, it wasn't fair: she'd already done her share of child rearing with me. This one was my turn.

I pictured Stepan leaving Pax to get a job and support me. He'd be sulky and raging. I pictured Stepan and me living together in Boston or Cambridge. It wasn't pretty. I did not and could not picture returning to Pax while Bert and Brad were there.

I then tried to picture myself without a baby. I went back to school. I got some sort of job. I asked Sonny to hire me as a cook. But these images all felt grim and empty too.

Whatever stories I told myself about my future, I was scrupulously realistic in my daydreams. I never let anything imaginary happen that couldn't happen in life or wasn't likely to happen. As a result, my visions were tamer than life, because in real life, things that can't happen, do—things you couldn't have predicted, that weren't probable. That was the most wonderful thing about life: magic was real.

But an odd thing: once I'd pictured my possible lives *with* a baby, and removed it, I felt this aching loneliness, a hole in my soul. I knew it had been there at least since Daddy had left, and maybe before. Nothing had ever filled it, not any of my girl-friends, not the Andrews boys, not Christopher, not Stepan, and not even Philo. I had the suspicion that it was never going to be filled. Girls think it will be filled by a lover or husband; I don't know what boys think—maybe they expect it to be filled by adventure or career. But I sensed that nothing would ever fill it for me—except for brief snatches of time, for example, when I was writing that paper on the Bible that thrilled me so much, or when I was cooking a great meal—like a baby would. It could only be filled by something I cared about more than my own life—and that could only be a child. I wondered if that was the reason older women often seemed content, and men not, and why so many men went from woman to woman all their lives. Maybe women who put a child in that space felt less empty, and maybe men didn't know they could do that.

But a woman could not fill that place for a man any more than a man could fill it for a woman. Children, not lovers, assuaged emptiness. I didn't know if that was a good reason to have a child, or if I would be able to be a decent parent, despite all the resolutions I'd made as a teenager. But I couldn't think of anything better to do right then.

I let myself remember what I had lost by leaving Pax: my garden, cooking for the commune, and a sense of mattering to others. I didn't miss writing poetry, because I could—and did—write wherever I was or whatever I was doing. I had written dozens of poems at Pax and a couple since I was back at Mom's, including one I liked:

Poppies
I feel thin,
thin as the skin
of the poppies,
rising on their thin

and crooked spines
as they step away
from earth.
The crepe paper
Blossoms cup
Their orange hands.
Burnished till translucent,
they reach up
and open—
as if begging
for emptiness.

I had been working on this for some time, adding "complete" to the last line, then removing it, changing the order of some words, and adding and removing spaces. I was working on another poem I had tentatively called "Anthurium," but I wasn't satisfied with it yet. When I was writing, it filled me completely, satisfied me; but I couldn't write every day, I didn't have the energy, the right kind of energy, didn't have the drive. Writing poetry was something I did for pleasure, not for a living. I also cooked for pleasure but I did not get the same kind of satisfaction just cooking for myself or for Mom and me. To get fulfillment from cooking, I had to cook for a lot of people. Cooking was like playing the piano or singing; it was something you did for an audience. So I thought I could cook for a living.

But I wouldn't want to work as a chef for Sonny, because I didn't want to cook the kind of food he served—hamburgers and French fries and chicken salad and bacon, lettuce, and tomato sandwiches. He served canned soup. That would not satisfy me at all, especially now that I was home and could use bones to make broth and was busy making delicious potato leek soup, cream of mushroom, cream of celery, or chicken broth with egg drop noodles—the Lithuanian, not the Chinese, kind.

So after a couple of weeks of waitressing, of being pregnant and knowing it, I called Dad.

It made sense. I needed shelter and someone who cared at least a little about my well-being. He was alone. He had land I could cultivate. There were lots of restaurants in his area that I could persuade to give me a chance. And who knew? He might be happy to see me.

He must have been a little sloshed when I called because he sounded as if he didn't know who I was. I told him I'd left the commune and needed a place to live for a while. Was he still alone? If so, could I come and live with him? He was sarcastic, his tone conveying the message, "So you finally call the old man. What happened, your mother throw you out?" I said Mom was going to France for two years. High dudgeon: what kind of mother is she, going off to Europe and leaving her child alone? Not remembering that I was twenty-two years old and had been, until the month before, safely ensconced on a commune.

I laughed. I said, "I'm a big girl now, Dad, but the thing is, I'm pregnant."

That stopped him.

"Well, come, Jess, of course! Live here as long as you like, think of this as your house, you know how I am, I just eat and sleep here. You can live here and do what you like. It'll be your house."

And so I went.

Dad's house looked unloved and uncared for. It was clean—his housekeeper, Mrs. Thacker, saw to that—but the straw flowers and pink bows looked dusty and tired. It looked like a house no one cared about. Houses can look that way, just like people—clean and neat, but abandoned. When Dad embraced me, he had tears in his eyes but he wasn't drunk. I hadn't seen him in three years, because he'd never visited Pax, although I'd invited him.

I drove to his house in the car he'd bought me, which by now was getting old, and he said, "Time we got you some new wheels."

But I hadn't come back here to be Daddy's little girl. "When I can afford them, Dad. The car goes fine. I love it. It's enough that you're letting me live here. I really appreciate it."

"Hey, you're my little girl. *Mi casa es su casa*. So how far along are you?" He surveyed my body, which of course showed nothing yet.

"Not far. I figure the baby will arrive at the end of January or early February."

"And who's the daddy?"

"A guy called Stepan, who lives on the commune."

"And what is he going to do about it?" He spoke peremptorily, the outraged father of a wronged innocent.

"He doesn't even know about it."

My father opened his mouth to expostulate.

I put up my hand like a traffic cop. "No, Dad."

He shut his mouth and stared at me.

I shook my head. "Let it be." I walked away from him to gaze out the big window facing the lake. "God, it's beautiful here."

"You're going to have this baby on your own?" he asked in a flat voice.

"No." I turned to face him. "With your help," I said.

His face changed; it grew softer and pinker, younger. "Well, that's a new one! I guess I can do that. Although it's really your mother's job."

"She did it for me. You'll do it for my child."

Did I imagine him puffing himself up? I walked over to the couch and sat down.

He bent over me, but only said, "How about a drink? You drink these days?"

"Not much. A little wine once in a while. But I'd love a Coke."

"Comin' up." He went into the kitchen, moving faster than usual. He came back with dark Canadian Club on the rocks and a Coke. He sat down across from me. And he smiled.

I smiled back. "You miss Julie?"

"Not really. She was a nice kid but a little tiresome. Silly. Something your mother never was. But much more agreeable than your mother."

"You won't mind having me here? With a squalling baby?"

"I won't mind having you. About the baby I can't say, haven't laid eyes on a baby for—how old are you now?"

"Twenty-two. I'll be twenty-three next month."

"That long. But I don't recall minding having you around twenty-two years ago."

"I really need your help."

"I'm in a much better position to help you now than I was then—young, broke, inexperienced, didn't know a goddamned thing . . . What do you need?"

"Well, a home. I'll get a job, so nothing else, except I'd like to plant some of your land."

"What?"

"Yeah. One of the meadows. I've been farming on the commune, raising vegetables and herbs. I'm good at it and I love it and you will love the organic food I grow . . ."

"I'm not much for vegetables. You know, steak and a baked potato is my dish. What the hell is organic food?"

"A few years ago, a few farmers began to experiment with growing things without chemicals. American farmers spray their crops with toxic chemicals to kill bugs and fend off certain diseases. Nowadays we have huge factory farms, and farming is business. So, those of us who don't like this have decided to try the opposite.

"We are trying to raise vegetables and fruits without using any of those methods. It's called organic farming. It's good for

— 255 —

people and good for the land, and what's more, things raised this way taste better than the other stuff."

"I haven't had a decent tomato or peach since I was a boy," my father grumbled.

"Right. It's kind of a movement. There are only a couple dozen farms in the whole country that do this kind of thing. But lots of people are talking about it. There's a woman out in San Francisco, Alice Waters, who started a restaurant that's become famous, Chez Panisse. Her meals are supposed to be luscious and she uses locally grown products. She urges what she calls sustainable agriculture. She's my hero."

My father was gazing at me. "Good, Jess," he said finally. "Very good. Of course you can have a meadow. Whichever one you want. There are three."

"The one facing Beaver Dam Road is the sunniest. And the most manageable for a tractor. Can I use that one?"

"Of course," said my suddenly benevolent father. Then his brow clouded. "You don't expect to make a living raising vegetables, do you?"

"No, of course not."

"It's a hell of a lot of work."

"I know. What I want is to plant some herbs and vegetables and find a job cooking and eventually maybe open my own restaurant. Isn't that a neat idea?"

He sat back and blinked. "You always were a good cook. Like your mother."

"Yes. I'm better now. I had a lot of experience at the commune."

"Really." He seemed impressed. Funny, because he never acted as if he thought about the taste of what he was eating or could tell good food from bad. And I never thought cooks were people he had respect for. I knew he respected men who worked with their hands building things or putting roofs on houses or laying concrete, but he always acted as if Mom should be able to just rustle up whatever he wanted as if she was dialing a number. He always admitted she was a good cook; he just hadn't seemed to think there was much to cooking. My father respected only men—men who did manual work, who dealt with real things, material stuff, not ideas. He hated ideas, said they were pernicious. But I could feel, I absolutely knew, that he had suddenly developed respect for me, and it was because I could cook.

It made me feel terrific.

I settled in. I had brought all my stuff with me; I'd had to empty my closet for the French professor and his family. I brought whatever clothes still fit me, and some that didn't, and gave all the rest to Goodwill. I'd brought my books, my favorite pictures, my few pieces of jewelry, and my omelet pan. Dad helped me empty the car and carry everything upstairs, and then he went out to his studio to work. After I put my stuff away—there wasn't much—I went around my room grabbing the fake flowers and cutesy vases and pretty pink bedspread that Julie had put in there and tossed them in a plastic garbage bag. I rolled up the flowered pink rug she had bought and hauled out my brown and orange Indian rug from the closet and put it down. I stripped the cutesy curtains and left the window bare except for its bamboo blind. The only bright color in the room now was orange—in the globe of my desk lamp, in my Hopi rug, and in a small Aboriginal painting Dad had bought me when I was a girl. So the room was austere once more. It was beautiful. It amazed me that I cared. Maybe living for three years among the shabby remnants of Pax furnishings had honed my taste.

When I showed the room to Dad he just looked and nodded. "Funny how little it takes to change so much," he said, standing there admiring it. I had the sense he knew exactly what had been taken away and what had been added. It seemed he did know the difference between cutesy decorating and good taste, yet he hadn't done anything to stop Julie. I wondered how many things he'd kept silent about over the years, not just with Julie, but also with Mom and me.

He had changed. He was older—of course, so was Mom. But she still looked good, healthy and full of life. Dad looked yellowish—except when he was drinking, when he became flushed—and his body looked frail. Yet he was only fifty. It seemed to me that he drank less, or maybe he started later in the day. He also went to bed earlier, so perhaps he didn't imbibe the same quantity in a day. My sense was that he didn't get as drunk. When I was a kid, I used to think he woke up drunk, as if the residue never left his system and his body was always carrying alcohol from the day before. Something was different now.

After I fixed up my room, I asked Dad if he minded my redecorating the house.

"Be my guest," he said. "It's a gift shoppe" (he pronounced this *shop-pey*) "now. A worn-out gift shoppe. Anything would be an improvement."

So I went around the house, systematically removing Julie's embellishments. She had tried to create a home. She had been trying to do a good thing, but I couldn't stand it. Dad seemed to like what I was doing. He'd come in for lunch looking haggard and see me taking down curtains, removing slipcovers, banishing vases, figurines, artificial flowers, fake plants, and watercolors of children, dogs, flower arrangements, Vermont barns, and birch trees, and he smiled. And when I hung his paintings on the walls and put some of his things on the mantel and on side tables, his chest expanded. Collected over the years on trips with Mom and later with Julie, and stored in bookcases in his studio, they'd been for years haphazardly jumbled together, covered with dust: pieces of pottery and sculpture from Mexico, Venezuela, India, Inuit country, Africa. There were only about a dozen pieces, but they reflected my father's eye, and they were gorgeous.

Once I stripped Julie away, the house looked terribly bare. She may have been kitschy, but she was alive and full of love, and without her or her stuff the house was neither. I'd looked down at Julie for her awful taste, but at least she had had some idea of how to decorate a room and I did not. Even with Dad's paintings hanging in it, his few collected objects placed around it, it didn't feel like a home. It was just a shabby place whose inhabitants had no idea how to live. The slipcovers had concealed the worn, torn fabric of the old armchairs and sofa, which Mom and Dad had bought used in the first place. Tables, shorn of their ornaments, were scratched and shabby; lamps without their fringed, bedecked lampshades were ugly and bare. I was befuddled; I really didn't know what to do to fix the damage I'd done. "What should I do?" I wailed to Dad.

"Go to New York and buy some new furniture," he said.

Well, that was simple. He gave me a couple of credit cards and told me not to worry about what I spent. I took them gingerly, having never handled such things before. Credit cards had always been taboo for me, symbols of a way of life I'd rejected.

With guilty glee, I drove to New York City. And there I, the virtuous nonmaterial girl, the austere pure commune member, proceeded to betray my principles and my past, like the most shameless turncoat.

I had done some research. I'd called Alyssa to see where I could stay and where I should shop. She'd offered to accompany me, which would make it more fun. I went to town like an army tank mowing down the enemy. Did I enjoy it! I stayed at Alyssa's apartment, which she'd inherited from her sister (who had moved to France), and which had three bedrooms and five bathrooms. We walked out the front door onto Central Park West, and as she'd told me it would, a cab came cruising along within seconds. At first I cringed inside when I handed my card over to the salesperson, but I was having such a good time that I forgot the joy I'd taken in planning my herb garden or making nettle soup. And best of all, Alyssa's going with me cheered her up, so I had the illusion I was doing a good deed.

Most of what I bought was Italian, and we had to wait months for it to be delivered from Milan. The main room was big, so I bought two couches and three armchairs and four table lamps and a standing lamp. In antique shops Alyssa knew that were sprinkled over the city, from Tenth Street to Madison Avenue to lower Broadway to Atlantic Avenue in Brooklyn, I bought five tables of different sizes, shapes, and nationalities.

By the time everything arrived, Dad's Vermont cabin had the same feeling as the house in Cambridge, only more modern. It had an almost Shaker austerity, and I liked it very much. So did Dad. But the process humbled me; I could never again tell myself that I was pure or unmaterialistic. After the first wave of disillusionment wore off, I thought it was probably a good thing, because I had likely been using claims of purity to mask envy. I had been well on my way to becoming a self-righteous hypocrite. Now I could never again feel superior on the grounds of not being materialistic (and I'd probably never again have such a spending spree).

Dad was only vaguely interested in what I was doing, but he liked the results. All his former bad feelings about me seem to have vanished, as if the poison that had entered his system when I reached thirteen had worked its way through his body and out during the years I was absent from his life. I tried to figure out why he had changed: maybe he'd been lonely since Julie left and was happy for company; maybe Mom and Julie both leaving him had crushed his ego and made him humble; maybe having two women leave him made him think about how he acted. Maybe loneliness had made him grateful for acceptance from anyone. Maybe he was getting older and worn out. Maybe, maybe, his life experiences had made him value other people, value love, in a way he hadn't known to do earlier. Or maybe he was just tired of yelling.

I didn't know, but I was grateful, and my old love for Dad began to flow like a long-clogged tap that was suddenly cleared.

I found a job cooking in a new restaurant called Artur's, a few miles away on a back road. Its owner, Artur, had escaped from the USSR, from Georgia.

Fascinated, at first I had asked Artur about his past, but I soon stopped, because he only talked about one thing. You'd never know he came from a country that capriciously arrested people for nothing, that had had a paranoid ruler who had killed millions of his own people, a country that censored newspapers and magazines, film and speech, literature and art and even music, a nation that had lost a vast portion of its population to a revolution, two world wars, and a dictator's whims. All Artur talked about was the deprivation. He had never been able to get a pair of shoes in his size but had to buy shoes whenever he saw them, whatever size they were, and then go from person to person trying to trade, to get something closer to his size. He talked with agonized recall about queues, shortages, no fruit, no meat, no soap, no washing machines, no paint, no sanitary napkins for his mother and sister, no anything. He told of his mother waiting in three lines to buy half a lemon, and having no vegetables except cabbage and potatoes for whole winters, having only occasionally a bit of sausage. Even in the hotel where he worked, he could not get provisions. Unless political leaders were coming for a meal (when provisions miraculously appeared), they served only chicken or sausage with cucumbers and potatoes. His entire life in the USSR had been, he said, an agony of deprivation. He described how they were forced to steal and to buy on the black market.

Artur had studied in a cooking school and become a chef in a hotel in Tbilisi, but his cooking did not improve, because he could not get the ingredients he needed.

Artur got out somehow, a lot of Jews did. I think the Russians let them go out of anti-Semitism. His sister had married an American and lived in Brattleboro, but there was no work for Artur there. He drove a cab in New York City for ten years and saved enough money to buy a run-down restaurant on a back road outside Brattleboro. His sister had passed this restaurant every day and knew that it was in a pretty good location, on a road that connected two major roadways. She took her husband there for dinner and saw that it was poorly run, and she suspected it would fail. When it did, she alerted Artur.

Buying the restaurant was the high point of Artur's life. He was elated—a penniless immigrant determined to succeed, who finally gets his dream. But he lacked capital and found himself unable to do things he wanted to do. With his sister's husband's help he had enough for the down payment, but carried a high mortgage. He insisted on decorating it in the Russian style—crystal chandeliers, red-flocked wallpaper, Victorian chairs in the dining room. He kept the ovens, sinks, dishwasher, mixer, and other equipment of the previous owner. They were not the most modern or efficient, but what did he know? They were better than what he had been used to in Tbilisi. What gnawed at him was the knowledge that he did not have the capital to hold on for two years if the restaurant did not become popular immediately. He knew that restaurants were the type of business most likely to fail.

He lived at his sister's. He planned to live someday in the rooms above the restaurant, but they were dilapidated and he put off renovating them for a while. His sister was kind to him and even slipped him money once in a while, when her husband's gaze was averted. Artur tried hard, but he did not, despite his ten years in America, understand American taste. The restaurants he'd frequented in New York when he drove his cab served pizza, hot dogs, and Chinese food, so he had learned nothing about what made a good restaurant in those years. What he knew was what he had learned in Tbilisi.

He developed a faithful following for his stuffed cabbage, beef Stroganoff, veal meatballs, and chicken Tbilisi, but it was not enough. He had been open for eight months and was expecting to have to close soon, when I arrived on his doorstep, led there by instinct, homing in on him after several days of driving around the area looking for restaurants where I might work. I scared him: he did not understand my confidence or the meaning of my experience—three years cooking at a commune? What did that mean? After studying his menu, I told him he needed more American dishes. He knew I was right and hired me on the spot. He was desperate, besides, and I agreed to work for a month for subsistence wages. He wanted to impress on me that he was the boss, the chef, and I the sous-chef, but he admitted his ignorance about American customs and taste and gave me more or less a free hand.

I understood his defensiveness and forgave it. By now, I understood the form anxiety took in men—men like my father, Brad, and Stepan. With Artur, as with them, image was everything. If I gave him something first, said he was right about something, or told him how delicious his chicken was, I could then offer some modification. If I always pointed out that I was referring only to local taste (he thought Brattleboro locals were all expatriate New Yorkers with tons of money and snobbery to match), I could get him to put almost anything I suggested on the menu. And of course I had to cook it, since it was unfamiliar to him.

He did his own things well—his borscht was inventive and his chicken delicious: cut in half at the breast, flattened out in a big skillet, weighed down with a brick, and fried in duck fat. It was a frequent main course at the hotel in Tibilisi.

At first, I added basic dishes that Americans expect: rib or loin lamb chops, pork or veal chops, leg of lamb or a fresh ham, several cuts of steak, a big hamburger—which I called hamburger, refusing to call it Salisbury steak as most restaurants with pretensions (meaning, tablecloths) did in those days. Then I added specials, dishes offered one or two nights only, that I loved to make: pot-au-feu, a navarin of lamb shanks, chicken broth, and mushrooms; Mom's chicken in broth with angel hair pasta; chicken paprikash from the recipe Philo had stolen from his mother. This last one became so popular, we had standing orders to telephone people when we planned to serve it. People didn't eat much fish in those days, and I didn't know much about cooking it, but I added shrimp cocktail and crab cakes as appetizers, and filets of sole, snapper, or salmon, and swordfish or halibut steak as specials.

I didn't try to be adventurous at first because we were aiming simply for survival and when I had experimented at the commune, I had sometimes failed. The restaurant gradually became more popular. After six months we were breaking even; after a year, we were making a small profit over my salary, which was still tiny. Artur took almost nothing for himself, just spending money. I was living with Dad, and Artur with his sister, so we were both being subsidized. But both of us were doing what we loved to do; we told each other that was the important thing. Artur was truly happy. He had what he'd dreamed about in Tbilisi.

After a few years, I had gained a certain fame in the area. When people hear you are successful, they imagine you "hit" overnight, but nothing happens fast; it takes time, and during that time you suffer, worrying, fearing ruin, seeing your empty restaurant and feeling terrified that it will never fill up. And some nights it doesn't. And when it does, it fills so swiftly that you can't breathe, and you're hustling like a madwoman, yelling at the helpers to get this or that done, nervous about burning the roast, and then you turn around and everyone has gone home; the place is empty again. What a business!

At the end of that August, I had Dad's meadow mowed for hay and plowed under. It would get weedy over the winter, of course, but I didn't want to have to do the deep plowing in the spring; I wanted to turn the soil over and plant as soon as the likelihood of frost had passed. My baby was due in early February and I knew I'd have my hands full next spring. It was just about as cold here as in Becket—it was in the same latitude, if lower in altitude. The growing season was equally short.

Fall was gorgeous in Vermont that October, the leaves especially brilliant in patches of gold and orange and crimson, and for the first time in my life, as I drove around the area, I looked out at the world with pleasure, without anxiety, serenely. I wasn't in need of anything or in fear of anything. I didn't even want anything. Even my perennial longing for a soul mate was in abeyance, maybe because of my pregnancy. I was easy in my soul. It was a different way of living, a way I'd started to learn at Pax, but had always fallen a little short of. I was always anxious about my garden, or what the others thought of me, or how Sandy or Stepan or Brad would respond to me. Dad didn't lean on me at all, and I was grateful. Caring so much about what people think is maybe the worst oppression I know. The only person whose opinion I might worry about was Artur, but I knew how to handle him, and before long, my opinions had as much weight with him as his own.

I found a gynecologist who felt solid, recommended by Mom and Dad's old friend Dan Templer. Dr. Bach was youngish and energetic and insisted on monthly checkups. I worked most afternoons and evenings, so Mrs. Thacker, Dad's housekeeper, still cooked Dad's dinner and cleaned the house. The restaurant was closed on Mondays, the only night I was home. I would give Mrs. Thacker a night off and cook something special for Dad and serve it in the dining alcove he'd put in near the new kitchen. He came to the table when I called him: there was an intercom between the kitchen and his studio now—and he would be sober. He ate politely and complimented me on the food—always—the old Leighton manners reasserting themselves. After dinner, he would pour his first drink and take it into the living room, where he sat in front of the television set. It didn't matter what was on, he just sat there watching numbly. Then he'd get sloshed. I worked in Julie's studio, which I'd turned into my office. On Monday nights I studied seed catalogs, read new recipes and articles on cooking, or took care of my accounts. Mulling over the catalogs gave me pleasure. I greedily picked out flowers and herbs and vegetables for the spring, but had to put a lid on myself when I actually ordered. I knew I had to pay attention to costs, try to be budget-minded, if I was going to make the restaurant profitable. I'd had plenty of experience being provident at the commune. Dad was usually asleep in his chair by the time I went to bed.

On the mornings I was home, I took care of my body—exercising, bathing, doing my nails (still a great luxury after the commune)—and did errands. Sometimes I had long telephone conversations with Mom in France. I'd had my own phone installed, so I had privacy and Dad couldn't complain about the bills, not that the new Dad would have. He refused to let me pay anything toward the house. I put most of my earnings in my savings account. I was saving for the baby and toward buying a restaurant of my own. By the new year I would have enough cash to buy seeds.

Artur's served only dinner, but I went in several mornings a week to do the ordering and help him with the accounts. Artur came from a country where women worked in the fields until the moment they gave birth, so it never crossed his mind when I came waddling in that fall that I should quit when I got big. I went in because I wanted to learn all the nuts and bolts of restaurant work—ordering, buying, the characteristics of different jobbers, hiring, dealing with staff and personnel problems—everything. A restaurant couldn't survive without good budgeting and prudent ordering of supplies.

Still, getting around started to get hard. I became huge, skinny as I had been. A customer told me one night that you can carry across your body or all in front, and I was carrying in front. She said that meant I had a girl, something I didn't necessarily believe. Dr. Bach had warned me that I might not be able to maintain my pregnancy because I had such a small pelvis. I didn't believe him, either. I refused to worry about it. I was sure my body would take care of what it had to take care of. My only worry was the weather: I didn't like the thought of Dad driving me to the hospital through winter snow and ice late at night after he'd been drinking.

I hadn't told Stepan about the baby. I didn't want to live with him again and he could not support the baby. When I'd told Mom I was pregnant, she asked if I was going to tell him.

"Why should I?"

"Well, he might like to know that he's a father. That he has a child."

"He might like to make a claim on it, too."

"And you don't want that?"

"I don't want to raise my child in an atmosphere of conflict and hostility."

"Like the one you were raised in."

I shrugged.

"Are you sure he'd be hostile?"

"No. But why take the chance? What does he have to add?"

"You think it's better for the child not to have a father at all than to have one who . . . causes conflict?"

"Yes."

She thought for a while. We were sitting in the kitchen, and she got up and poured herself a drink. "When you think about your own life, do you regret that your father was in it?"

I thought about that for a long time. Mom smoked. I didn't. Then I did.

At last I said, "Sometimes. Oh, I guess not."

"What did he add, besides trouble?"

"I don't know. A point of view maybe. Even if it was a crazy one. But I guess I'd rather have him in it the way he was than not to have had him at all."

"Why?"

"Because I love him." I wept.

Damned Lithuanian genes.

15 **In the end**, what I feared is what happened. In early February 1976, I went into labor around midnight on an icy night. I hadn't been able to sleep and had been pacing around downstairs in the cabin. Dad was in no shape to drive—he was sound asleep in his chair. I called a taxi. I thought about letting him go on sleeping, but I felt too alone. So I woke him, and as soon as he understood what was happening, he started yelling that he *could* drive me, *would* drive me, *insisted* on driving me. I told him to shut up (realizing that I sounded just like Mom) and to just come along with me if he wanted. Disheveled, his face marked with creases from the chair pillow, he lurched into his coat and charged out to the cab. He belched and farted and sighed and groaned and smoked all the way to the hospital. The smoke was making me sick. When we arrived, he staggered into the hospital holding on to me, thinking, I guess, that he was holding me up, though it was the reverse.

He waited for hours until the baby was born, and the next day he bought cigars and handed them out to every man he saw. I told him this was ridiculous, but I found it endearing, like all his behavior these days.

The birth wasn't fun. I had no idea. Was this what every woman had to go through for every baby that was born? Amazing. It was a wonder the human race had continued for so long. I wasn't alone in the delivery room; four women were giving birth that night. But I was extremely proud of myself: I didn't cry out loudly. One woman did; another moaned. After all the movies I'd seen in which women screamed their lungs out giving birth, I was surprised that not a single woman was shrieking. Even the one who did yell did not do so often. Mostly we grunted, stoically weathering the pain. I was proud of us, proud of our sex.

As soon as I recovered, I asked for a phone and called Mom in Lyon, and *she* screamed—with joy and excitement. She said she'd fly home the next day. I protested: she'd have to come to Dad's house! She said she'd rent a car and stay in a motel and that she'd deal with Dad and not to worry. But I did. My stomach turned over and I wanted to cry. I didn't want my baby and me to be surrounded by their fighting and shouting, to have my poor baby with her tiny pink ears that had just begun to hear the sounds of the world, a little bitty thing with no defenses who had never heard a fight, to awaken on the first day of her life to one of Dad's drunken rants. No! But I couldn't stop Mom.

I slept.

The next day, lying in my hospital bed, I picked up the phone and called Stepan at Pax. A stranger answered the phone. I'd left nine months ago; it could be anybody

"I want to speak to Stepan, please. Yes, it's important. I don't care! Call him in from the goddamned fields!"

It was ten in the morning; it wouldn't kill them to fetch him. But a long time passed before he came to the phone. "Da?"

Imagining a crisis in his hometown, I guess. "Stepan. It's Jess. I wanted you to know you have a daughter."

Shock can be transmitted in silence.

Eventually, he responded, "What?"

"Isabelle," I told him. "Her name is Isabelle."

He said he'd drive to Vermont to see me and the baby that very day. I said he didn't have to bother; I didn't need and wasn't expecting anything from him. He said he was coming anyway. I was still in the hospital, I told him. He should wait until the weekend, when I'd be home. I gave him directions to Dad's house.

So a few days after Isabelle was born I went home from the hospital with a belly emptied of baby but full of dread. I was carrying a tiny creature wrapped in a blanket the size of a bathmat, whom I didn't know how to take care of. My father, who had come to pick me up, was already asserting himself with vigor (if he couldn't take me *to* the hospital, he'd damn well fetch me *from* it even if he'd had a drink even though it was only ten in the morning). He hovered behind me as though he expected me to fall and drop the baby—as if he would be any help if that happened. And on my other side, not speaking to Dad and looking at me as if I were a one-year-old who could barely walk, was my mother, who if I fell would not only catch me and the baby, but also would find a nurse to tend to us immediately, mortifying my father and provoking an outburst that wouldn't end for a month. Newly arrived from France and dizzy with jubilation and jet lag, she couldn't keep her hands off the baby. Waiting for me in my father's recently redecorated Vermont cabin was my employer, who was regularly made a nervous wreck by the dinner hour, so heaven knew how he'd handle *this*, and the baby's father, who until three days ago had not known he had fathered anything, who had parted from me involuntarily but in a state of bad faith, and who had no reason to feel anything positive toward me or my child.

This quartet constituted my entire family, none of whom was actually related to any other member, except me, and none of whom could speak amicably to any other. I remembered my adolescent self insisting that, unlike my parents, *I* would have a happy family. What I had was the family from hell.

Still, there was nothing to do but deal with it.

Artur had brought a gift, a beautiful baby carriage, an old-fashioned British pram. Artur also brought his extreme anxiety about when I would come back to work. Nightmare complete.

The scene felt like a dream. I felt as though I'd taken a sedative, as I watched myself walk through my role, remembering to express joy at seeing Mom and Dad, and pleasure at seeing Stepan and Artur, and to appear to be taking care of the baby, when all the while I was totally disconnected from my body and the baby and didn't know what I was doing. I think Mom must have had some sense of this, because when we entered Dad's house and stood in his big main room, she took Isabelle away from me and laid her in the bassinet, an exquisite basket with an organdy skirt and hood trimmed with pink satin ribbon standing on wheels. She had gone to Cambridge, intruding on the French family now living there (who were thrilled when she told them the reason) to fish it out of the attic and bring it in her rental car all the way to Vermont. The bassinet had been passed down in the Leighton family for several generations: I had lain in it after I was born and, Mom told me, under the very same blanket, which she had knitted of white wool and threaded with pink ribbons, that now covered Isabelle. Mom wheeled the bassinet into my office, leaving the door open so we would hear Isabelle if she woke. I followed her with my eyes, lying on the couch where Dad had deposited me. I was inert. Everybody was sitting around with a drink; Dad must have made them. Even I had a drink, a scotch and water with ice in it; why did he think I would drink that? And at that hour of the morning? Was that how you took care of a baby? You got drunk? He must have been right about my preferences, though, because I drank it.

Mom came back and sat down and asked Stepan polite questions about Pax, while Dad looked at him with eyes that were black beads of rage and ignored Mom entirely. Stepan could barely speak, he was so terrified. Recognizing a man from his own region of the world, he kept looking to Artur for help, although he should have known that since he was Ukrainian and Artur a Jew from Georgia, there would be little forthcoming. Artur kept looking at me in outrage—a Ukrainian, the people who had been the worst persecutors of Artur's kind, daring to implore him for help!

I fell asleep.

I woke up thinking I had drifted off in the middle of a movie about radicals planning the Russian Revolution. Labor, I heard. I knew about that: I'd just been in labor . . .

"The basis of every economy, every political system, probably every religion," a sullen, stubborn, lazy voice was saying. "I know from youth," the thick voice continued. "Always I know. Of course Marx know too, is there in his writing, still is great secret, unspoken fact that everybody knows. That's why, when I come to this country, I say I will live on commune, not to make money, not to succeed American way, no, but to try for what Gramsci write about, to merge political society and civil society, to merge labor with intellect . . ."

"No! Smart ones should be in control, like Plato said," said a sharper, more metallic voice. "In my religion, we understand. We cherish scholars, we take care, they no have to work, we work, support them, they read Torah, Talmud . . ."

What was the name of that movie anyway? *Ninotchka*. Greta Garbo . . .

"Intellectuals always claim to be part of an elite," a scornful voice pronounced. "First, they took over as priests and rulers, making the laws *and* enforcing them; look at the Hebrews, they didn't even have a king at the beginning. Look at Sumer: one guy, a guy with a powerful family, a commander, a military man, a killer, takes over all property and turns everybody else into bondsmen and -women. The leader appropriated everything, ran the church and the state. The priests of Sumer were the guys who invented prostitution . . ." My father knew history?

"Yes," a woman's voice interrupted. She sounded vaguely like my mother. What was my mother doing here? "Except they weren't just intellectuals; they were primarily *men*. Whether they were the priests, who I guess would have been the intellectuals, as in Israel, or the soldiers, as in Sumer, they wanted men to be an elite with rights over women; they forced women to be a servant class and eventually made them property . . . Elite men will do whatever they have to do to avoid manual labor . . ."

"No, lady!" Artur cried. "Intellectuals are close to G-d, they must avoid soiling their hands! They must devote selves to learning and to guide us! In the Middle Ages everybody knew this! They had a sliding scale! Angels, archangels, G-d!"

"What the hell is G-d?" the woman's voice snarled.

"Different god, Artur," Stepan challenged. "Middle Ages god not your god, my god. Or what should have been, if I had one. But Marx and Lenin believed that everybody should be involved in the process of production, everybody should do the hard work, the intellectuals as well as the peasants . . ."

"Marx! Marx's daughters cleaned his fireplace and built his fire every day; they made his tea, and his wife cooked dinner while he lolled around studying and thinking like a good Jewish scholar. The women did his fucking laundry, and cleaned his fucking room. Equality! Don't make me laugh!"

By now I was sitting up and looking around the room. I saw Artur blanch at my mother's language. It surprised me, to tell the truth. She didn't used to talk that way.

Stepan charged in. "What place more elite than Russia, *tovarisch*? Even special lane on highway, just for intelligentsia, for nomenklatura! Not have that even in England, where is queen."

"Damn straight. The few claim privilege and foist systems of ideas on everybody else, systems that are horrible, inhuman, evil, but nobody can stop them once they get going. Here they invented racism to justify slavery! The Arab countries too! They wanted to justify keeping Muslim slaves! And look what they did to your country, Stephen—Marx and Engels and Lenin! Turned it into a nightmare! Who wants to live there, huh? Stephen's right, everybody should have to work with their hands, everybody! Huh, Stephen?"

My father, arguing about ideas! My father, being friendly to Stepan!—although he called him by the wrong name.

Mom spoke fast and low. "What you are all refusing to see is that the basic paradigm is male/female. That's how it started, and you've put your finger on why it started. No one wants to do the shit work, so a few men said they were descended from gods, superior to other men, and didn't have to labor, but when the other men complained, they said, Well, you are superior too, guys, just not as good as us, but you're better than the women, look at them, they labor whether they want to or not, it's inherent for them, they give birth . . . Why don't you admit that that's the real reason for discrimination? Look at yourselves!" my mother cried, standing up, preparing to fetch the baby, who was mewling in the next room.

They paid no attention to her. They were arguing hot and heavy. I got up too and followed her into my office and watched her pick up the baby. She spread some receiving blankets across my desk and removed Isabelle's diaper.

"Can you get me some warm water, Jess?"

I went into the kitchen, found a pitcher, and filled it. I brought the pitcher back and poured water onto a washcloth, rubbed a little soap on it, and handed it to Mom. Isabelle was gazing at the ceiling. I couldn't tell if she could see us. When her eyes lighted on Mom or me, she stared for a moment, wondering at us, meanwhile kicking her little legs and throwing her arms around. I could see she didn't know us yet. I wondered if it was a delight to her to be able to move around after all those months confined in a womb. Although God knows she did enough kicking in there. I thought she looked happy.

Mom cleaned her little bottom, then rinsed it and folded a clean, dry diaper up over her. Isabelle paid no attention to what Mom was doing, too busy looking around, studying her world. She she kept making tiny bleating sounds, like a baby lamb.

"Hungry, you think?" I asked.

"Probably. How long has it been? Three hours?"

I nodded. "You could try," she said, lifting the baby to her and holding her close, her hand firmly held against the back of Isabelle's neck, fingers splayed up to protect her head. She headed toward the living room.

"I'll stay in here," I said, feeling uncomfortable.

My mother lifted her head. "You will not! You are not going to hide yourself! You're going to be part of civil society!"

We went back into the main room and sat down on the couch again and, miserably, I opened my blouse and lowered the cup of my bra and began to nurse Isabelle. She *was* hungry; she sucked avidly. Her tiny fingers clenched, her little toes curled. She was entirely concentrated on the act of sucking; she was ecstatic. Feeding was the most profound experience of her little life.

The men paid absolutely no attention to me. Artur was angry now, defending the pious scholars of the Jewish community and the customs that maintained them; Stepan alternated between sullen silence and the explosive outrage of one who knows he is right and thinks the others know it too but refuse to admit it. My father was drinking hard, spitting scorn at Artur's arguments, agreeing with Stepan but disapproving of him at the same time, and withdrawing into his drug of choice. None of them had even listened to Mom's arguments. Civil society—was she kidding?

I looked over at Mom and raised my eyebrows. She shrugged. We were not part of this conversation, even though she had tried to enter it. "I think I'll start dinner," she said. It was only three thirty in the afternoon. "I bought a brisket." she said. "I'll make pot-au-feu."

"Okay, when she's done feeding, let's cook," I said.

Having a new baby is supposed to be a happy time. All the books I'd read to prepare for it emphasized this, and all the accounts I'd read described it that way. But I found it a time of huge anxiety and dread. Not only was my whole family gathered uneasily like a bunch of government officials after a calamitous security leak— searching each others' faces for evidence of who had done it—but suddenly this . . . creature . . . had appeared and was screaming its tiny lungs out, expecting me to do something about her misery, when I couldn't even understand what she was communicating. One of the nurses had said that having a baby was like being in love with someone you hardly know. Yes, I loved this creature absolutely, but didn't know her *at all*.

What was worse was that this tiny living thing, whose head barely filled the crook of my elbow, was horribly vulnerable. Babies died in their sleep; no one knew why. The top of her skull was still soft, and if something happened to her there, she could be badly injured or even die. Her neck was so weak she could not hold up her head by herself. And she was helpless. Animals at birth can at least stand. They know how to find where to go to nurse; she didn't. She knew when she was hungry and she could pee and shit, but she had a hard time belching on her own. I had no idea what was going on inside her, and yet her very life depended on me! She'd cry and I'd think she was hungry, and she'd start nursing as if she was starved, but after five minutes she'd pull away from my breast and start looking around, waving her arms and legs, or fall back to sleep. Ten minutes later she was hungry again. She'd cry and cry until I nursed her again; she'd start to suck, then pull away and scream bloody murder. I didn't know what to do. Mom said maybe she had gas, and I'd hold her up against my chest and pat her back and bounce her a little, but she'd just keep crying. Oh, God.

At first she cried in tiny bleats, but as she grew, her cries became louder and more demanding. Sometimes she sounded as full of rage as my father at his worst—in fact, she reminded me of him. But at other times she cried with such sorrow that I wondered what she could possibly be feeling, since she had experienced so little. What did she know? The impulsion of birth, the discomfort of hunger and dampness, the satisfaction of eating, shitting, and peeing, the pleasure of arms enfolding her. Birth may not have been fun for her, but did it cast her into such sorrow? Was she aggrieved at leaving my warm, pulsing belly? I held her close and tried to calm her with my mouth soft against her head, but nothing sufficed. It was tragic. I wanted to cry with her.

Mom was a help. She calmed me down when I got crazy, and taught me things I didn't know. When things, or I, calmed down a bit after the first couple of weeks, and I could address the stuff I'd been ignoring—Dad looking at Mom as though she was the snake in Eden, or at Stepan like a man who'd been robbed, or Stepan staring in horrified fascination at my materialistic warmonger elitist capitalist parents, or Artur looking at me as if I was the corn-and-oil goddess who could confer huge favors upon him but just wouldn't—I decided to retreat back into my daze. I couldn't deal with it all; it was enough I had to deal with the baby, who bothered me more than anybody because she barely looked at me at all.

Somehow everything passed without any explosions. I'm not sure how Mom kept Dad in abeyance; he sat every night at the dinner table like a chastened little boy, saying little and never looking at her. And every night after she'd made dinner for all of us, and eaten with us, and cleaned up the kitchen, she kissed me on the forehead and went back to her motel. Dad would then relax into his third drink of the night and fall into his usual stupor in front of the television set.

Dad let himself like Stepan a little bit because he too believed in manual labor, and had spent his life doing it, but he hated him because he wasn't taking responsibility for me and Isabelle, which a man should do, my father believed, much as he had repulsed it himself. Stepan, who rose at five even when he was away from Pax, at nights went directly from dinner to my office, where he spread out his sleeping bag and fell into a coma. Artur, who had managed to alienate both my father and Stepan, was, thank heavens, not with us daily.

Days were better: Dad was in his studio all day; Mom helped me bathe and otherwise care for the baby. Mom showed me how to boil diapers—the paper ones were, I felt, ecologically toxic, so I wouldn't use them. She took care of Isabelle during my brief sojourns away from her. I only went out for a half hour each day, for a walk along the lake, just to stay sane. It was too cold to take out a canoe, and some days the wind was vicious.

When Isabelle was a week old, I risked taking her out with me. I put her in a pouch with shoulder straps that rested on my chest, and Mom and I went shopping in town. Mom outfitted the baby for the rest of the year (Dad paid for this; they must have talked to each other some). It costs a fortune to equip one of these tiny creatures. She bought Isabelle a snowsuit for next winter—little dresses and shoes, sunsuits, a bathing suit, pajamas, and undershirts in three different sizes. I wondered how fast she expected her to grow. She also bought a car seat, a crib, a playpen, a high chair, a stroller, a jump chair, and a record player and some records: nursery rhymes, *Peter and the Wolf*, *The Young Person's Guide to the Orchestra*, some Haydn symphonies, and Bartók's and Debussy's piano music for children. She said, "Just play them while you're bathing her or dressing her." Did she think I had the time to put on records in the middle of bathing and dressing her? Was she crazy?

Yet I found myself doing it. The music calmed *me*.

Stepan stayed for only a week. He wanted to be involved with the baby; you could see that. But he was even more intimidated by her than I was. He'd hold her when I let him, but the minute she cried, he was terrified and handed her back. Mostly he just hung around. He had to stay at Dad's, not having money for a motel, and Dad treated him like a parasite, though he was somewhat sympathetic to this Communist defector. There wasn't room for Stepan in my bedroom along with the baby's crib, and besides, I didn't want to sleep with him. On my office floor in his sleeping bag, he was out of Dad's way, but I imagine he heard Dad rousing himself at three or four in the morning and stumbling drunk to his bedroom. I didn't care. I hadn't forgiven Stepan for the way he'd acted at Pax after the Brad-Bert takeover and I never would.

I was curious about Pax, and one afternoon when I was halfway back to my old self, I cornered Stepan at lunch. Dad was working in his studio and Mrs. Thacker had already left. I'd already fed Isabelle and put her down for a nap. We were eating pea soup I'd made, with bacon and elbow macaroni in it.

"So how's Pax, Step?"

"Uh, okay," he said.

"Anything new?"

"Bernice left."

"Bernice left! Really! She left Brad?"

"Bert. Brad. Whoever. She left."

"Why?"

He shrugged. I remembered the joys of holding a conversation with Stepan.

"Why did she say she was leaving?"

"She say she sick of being bossed around by two assholes and doing all the scut work."

It took many more questions and much probing to discover that Bernice had gone back to California. She had returned to her mother's house and was helping her mom sell real estate in Orange County. Bernice was going to get a broker's license herself and planned to make a fortune. She told Lysanne in a letter to "tell that anus Bert" that she was driving a Thunderbird. This had puzzled Stepan. He had no idea what a Thunderbird was. After ten years in the United States, he was completely ignorant of the joys of capitalism.

"And Brad and Bert? Still sleeping with Lolly and Lysanne?"

"No."

Laboriously, he explained that Brad had met a girl in town one day and brought her back to the farm. Eunice was a runaway from an abusive father, with no place to go, a waif who was full of terror. She brought out the best in Brad, apparently, and he treated her delicately. Her fragility excited Bert, but Brad wouldn't let him touch her and didn't touch her himself. That led to an explosion and Bert rebelled. He left, taking Lolly with him. The rest settled down to a more peaceful existence. Stepan was now happily coupled with Lysanne, and Brad was with Eunice. Another couple had joined them, she a horse person, he a farmer, and they had two kids. So they were eight people now, and all were content. The townsfolk seemed to regard them as respectable members of the community and called the place Pax Farm. They were thinking of buying goats and establishing a chevremaking dairy.

I liked this ending a great deal—I hoped it was an ending and not just a pause. It sounded like happily ever after. But I wondered what had happened to Bert. Much as I disliked him, he seemed a tragic victim, destroyed by forces he couldn't control, namely, an indefensible war.

Stepan had borrowed the Pax truck, and they would be needing it back. I could see that he was unhappy at the prospect of staying and at the idea of leaving. He wanted to be part of the baby's life, but I didn't want him to be part of mine, and he didn't want to be part of mine, and it seemed impossible. I told him he could visit her again in the summer and that I'd try to take Isabelle to visit him in the fall. He had to be satisfied with that. That was the first, and only, time in my life when the difference in people's treatment of the sexes fell in the woman's—my—favor.

I can't deny that Mom was a big help to me, but her presence made me terribly anxious. Dad tried to zombie out, but his intense involvement with her remained and I was relieved when after a month she said she had to go back to France. She made the announcement on a Thursday, said good-bye that night, and went back to her motel. Friday morning, she packed her bag and drove to Boston, turned in her rental car, and booked a midnight flight to Paris. I must have spoken to her on the phone almost every hour during this process. She was distraught at leaving me, and part of me felt wrenched too.

But I also felt relief, ease. I was as fickle as ever.

I think Isabelle noticed Mom's absence, though I couldn't be sure. Once I was freed from the nervousness I always felt when Mom and Dad were under the same roof, I felt utterly abandoned. Without her help, I had to spend the whole day, day after day, doing nothing but taking care of the baby! This was no life for a person! When Mom was there, we got the chores done and could sit down with a cigarette and a cup of coffee and have an intelligent conversation. We could go shopping or to the market or read together in the living room, looking up at each other when the baby cried in silent consultation. Now I had no one to consult with. Dad was pathetically willing to help me, but he had no idea at all how to take care of a baby. He'd never in his life changed a diaper or fed a baby. I had asked him once to change Isabelle when I had to go to the market; it was raining and I didn't want to lug her out into the cold damp weather. I came back to find her fussing and miserable, her bottom red and raw. Dad was watching a ball game on television. He looked at me shamefaced, but then laughed. "Aw, honey, I just couldn't do it," he said.

The next three months were without question the hardest time of my life. I wasn't miserable, I was nonexistent. I had no life at all. I was only a servant, a slave to this baby. I trudged through a round of labor from a two a.m. nursing to a six a.m. nursing to a ten a.m. nursing, a two p.m. nursing, a six p.m. nursing and one at ten p.m., after which I put her to bed. I thought that was bad; I didn't know that all too soon, I'd have to cook cereal for her twice a day, and soon after that, boil an egg, and soon after that, bake a potato for her two o'clock feeding. And soon after that, I'd have to puree meat and vegetables every day in a blender, since I would not feed her bottled baby food, loaded as it was with sugar and salt. But by then, she would have given up the two a.m. nursing and would be on a six-hour schedule with a bottle at midnight, and I would be on my way out of servanthood.

Between nursings I sterilized bottles, which I left for the baby when I went to the market and took with me when I took her to the doctor for her monthly weighing and checking. Every day I did her laundry—an amazing amount because of spit-up and spill and leaked effluent. And I had to boil diapers every three days or so. I also bathed her every day, which was, I have to say, a delight. I soaped her gorgeous shiny skin, oiled and powdered her, and dressed her in fresh clothes. I burped her, soothed her, held her, and walked her when she cried, which was often. I surprised myself with my steely endurance, my patient fortitude. When she screamed unendingly and I could find nothing wrong, I just held her in a kind of mute sorrow and thought about how easy it would be to smother her. I didn't feel guilty about these negative impulses. They seemed to me just a function of human nature, and of course I went on carefully cradling her fragile, defenseless little head and neck. Even when I couldn't stand the screaming, even when I was exhausted, even when my life seemed mere servitude, I could feel myself loving her more than I loved myself, her little finger more precious to me than my own arms and legs or anything else on earth.

That's how these little creatures get us, I thought. They know how we feel and they know we'll put up with anything to save them.

My life seemed utterly given over to things I didn't love doing but had no choice about. The snatches of time I had to myself were so short and interrupted that I couldn't use them for anything. I tried to read, but kept losing the thread; I couldn't concentrate on any of my books until one day, in a drugstore I picked up a murder mystery. It occurred to me that this was something I could read in snatches—a hard way to read Adrienne Rich or Günter Grass or Doris Lessing, whose books were presently on my bedside table. It cost only a couple of dollars, which even on my budget I could spare. And it worked: I could read for half an hour then put it down, and I needed only a little rereading to recapture the plot eight or twelve hours later. After that, I always had a mystery at hand to pick up when I had a half hour to myself. I knew I was wasting my mind, but at least I was entertaining myself.

In May excitement returned to my life as I planted my garden. The plot Dad had given me was big, almost as big as my plot at Pax, so I needed help with it. I pinned up a note on the post office bulletin board and a woman offered her services. Kathleen Martinelli, who lived nearby, was married to a local dentist; she had three kids now in their teens and a big house with a garden of her own, but she was bored. She missed the farm in Georgia where she'd been raised. She was perfect for me. I hired a man to plow, and Kathleen and I planted seeds by hand, row after row.

I had an automatic watering system installed; that left me broke and in debt. After that there was weeding to do, but we had put mulch on everything, so a couple of hours a day by us both was enough to keep it under control.

I would set Isabelle in her stroller, which had a little canopy. I wheeled it under a tree, with a bottle of water tied to the metal support of the carriage. She regularly knocked it too far away to retrieve and would start to wail, and Kathleen and I got lots of exercise running over to her. Her lungs got some exercise too. But mainly she was happy sitting in the outdoors, watching us pull weeds, kicking her arms and legs and babbling to the wind.

The deep winter months, January and February, were the slowest time at the restaurant, so Artur had been only mildly upset by my absence. For Artur, mild upset meant moderate hysteria. The restaurant did not do nearly as well with me absent, and as spring approached his hysteria heightened, with accompanying outbursts. But I had been trained by an expert, and I could shrug it off, not even getting angry with him. Since he was overwhelmed with guilt after each tantrum, this worked to my advantage: his debt to me grew with every episode. Still, after three months, I was itching to go back to work, but the baby was still too demanding: she ate five times a day. I could not leave her with Dad even for a few hours.

Stepan came back at the end of May and by this time he could play with Isabelle a little. At four months, she knew us all. She could play peekaboo and enjoyed being lifted and swung around. She was just starting on pureed food and I let Stepan feed her. He held her in his left arm and fed her with his right, as I did, but in the process revealed his moral deficiencies. For Stepan was shocked by Isabelle's certainty about what she wanted to eat and what she didn't. He profoundly disapproved of this. Maybe he grew up hungry enough to be willing to eat whatever he was given and felt that she should do the same. But Isabelle had never been hungry for very long; her screams might sound as if she were dying of starvation, but she was always fed within twenty minutes of their starting. She might be vague about most things, but not her tastes: she loved lima beans, green beans, any kind of beans mashed into a puree. She adored tiny bits of bacon on her tongue. But she hated peas and merely tolerated baked potato and cereal. Fussy little bit, she was. He tried to fight her on this, forcing mashed peas into her mouth. She just kept spitting them out. In this fight, like most struggles of will between parents and small children, he was not just wasting his energy but was also teaching her things like rage, hate, and rebellion. I told him parents invariably lose power struggles with infants, if not immediately, then in the long run. This got me nowhere. So then I told him if he didn't stop he couldn't feed her anymore.

By the end of May Isabelle was down to four meals a day—milk at six a.m., cereal at ten a.m., a baked potato and vegetable at two p.m., and another meal at six p.m. She was sleeping through the night! Hurrah!

I started planning to go back to work. I would stop nursing; I prepared to take her with me. I would go in about three, after her lunch. I'd only have to feed her once during my working hours, at six. I could use the restaurant blender to puree. Also I would have a larger choice of fresh foods and the kitchen staff could help me.

There was an unheated back room in the restaurant holding mainly junk. One Monday when the restaurant was closed, I got rid of the trash. The next day, I went in early and scrubbed down the walls, ceiling, and floor before work. Monday and Tuesday of the next week, Artur painted the room white and bought an electric heater for it. I bought a lined window shade and a white curtain for the window and took in an old bookcase from our house.

Artur painted that too, and I used it to store Isabelle's baby oil, baby powder, diapers, diaper rash cream, safety pins, and suchlike. I bought a covered diaper pail for the stinky things.

I bought a second baby seat, one of those little bouncy canvas chairs they had then, and sat her in it in the kitchen. She was enchanted by all the activity. The staff adored her, of course; every one of them made a fuss when they passed her, and soon she loved them all, crying out and hurling into the air whatever she had in her hand whenever she spotted them. They helped me puree varied things for her to eat, and eventually she ate like a restaurant critic, sampling pineapple and butternut squash and mango and brook trout and capon and whatever else we had. She turned into a gourmet, with extremely sophisticated tastes, and she stayed that way.

When I started back to work, I would go in early in the day, leaving Isabelle with Dad for an hour, and plan the menu and order the food. Then I would go back home and take care of her. I would change her, dress her, and drive with her to the restaurant, set her in her bouncy seat, and start cooking. She was deliriously happy, entertained by six staff members plus Artur; sometimes a customer would come back to visit.

The staff helped me fix her dinner, and they took turns feeding her, fighting for the privilege. After that she would play for a while, then I'd steal a half hour, take her into her little room and clean her up, powder her, and put her in the English carriage Artur had given me, with a bottle of warm milk to keep her company. The carriage was solid and had a brake; it was high enough not to break my back when I bent over to put her in it or pick her up the way the car seat or bouncy chair did. She nestled under her blanket, ecstatic with her bottle, and closed her eyes. The room was chilly even in June, so I would turn on the electric heater. She seemed to be in bliss. She slept better there than she did at home.

Before I left home every day, I made up a batch of formula. I kept the sterilizer at the restaurant and sterilized the bottles every day. I kept bottles in both refrigerators. When she went to sleep, at naptime or in the evening or late at night, I propped the bottle on a soft little holder next to her. I worried that she would be unhappy at missing my breast, but she didn't seem to mind and fussed only when she lost the bottle. These days she was feeding well, filling herself up and sleeping well afterward. And with so many people in and out of the kitchen, someone always heard her if she fussed.

Her only bad time was when I was leaving work late at night and had to bundle her up even more to carry her to the car; she always woke in a rage and would start to cry. But the cool outside air hitting her lungs made her pass out almost instantly—which always made me laugh, which then always made me feel like a monster.

Artur was humbly, satisfyingly grateful for my return. Business always picked up in the summer, his best time. People thronged to visit their Vermont vacation houses or spend long weekends at local bed and breakfasts. The busy season lasted till the end of October, when people stopped coming to see the leaves, so there was no way I could take Isabelle to Pax in September, as I'd promised Stepan. I called him to apologize. He was nice about it, being busy himself with the harvest and pruning, and came to visit us in November instead, braving Dad's contempt to see her. I respected that. And in time I came to trust him with her—he had stopped provoking power struggles with her. He fed her sweetly, didn't try to force her or get annoyed with her slowness at eating. She would hum and look around the room when he fed her, take her time mashing her mouthfuls with her tiny gums and tongue, while she studied the kitchen ceiling and walls and the pots hanging over the stove, the pictures on the walls. He changed her promptly and well, and he picked her up immediately when she started to cry. So for the week he was with us, I left her with him when I went to work.

Her absence when I was working made me realize what a strain her presence created: it broke my concentration and I didn't cook as well. But I thought, Hell, so what. It's more important to take care of the baby than it is to cook perfectly. My next thought was, That's why men seem more dedicated than women. To art or whatever. They won't break their concentration for a baby or a child, they'd rather let it scream. Or sit in shit. Like Dad. Their art or their work, or even just television, comes first. But I didn't want to be like that. No matter what, for me the baby would always come first. When Stepan left, I went back to taking Isabelle to work with me.

16 **She grew so fast**. I could cry with sorrow that Isabelle grew so fast, remembering how adorable she had been crawling around discovering the world of carpets and chair legs, shoe buckles and cigarette packets, especially the cellophane. Then suddenly she was on her feet, running in triumph to our outstretched arms, so proud of herself she couldn't stop grinning and exploring tabletops and objects she could bang on. She lurched around the rooms, more surely than Marguerite, the Fields' child, but reminding me of her, and I suddenly understood how Annette and Ted could have loved their little bundle, despite the problems. Isabelle launched herself from table or chair and ran in tiny staggering steps as far as she could before falling or managing to reach some handhold, a chair arm or table, which she would then pound in triumph like a tiny Tarzan. She loved the kitchen and explored it at every opportunity. She would open a cabinet and remove its contents, pot by pot. She'd carry each object across the room and present it to me, then go back for another, with the utmost seriousness of purpose. When the cabinet was empty, she would start on the next; when they were all empty, she would replace the objects, but in such disorder that they didn't fit. I had to redo the job, but I waited to do that until she'd gone for her nap. She would babble all the while she did this, and in time, the babbling turned into words, though not words I could fathom the meaning of. The satisfaction of utterance made her face beam with complacency. *She knew what she was saying.*

By the time she was a year old, I could understand her. Recognizable words—*no, poppop* (for my father), *gone* (also usually for my father), *car.* No *mama*, not for a long time. But once she mastered those syllables, she was off and running, sentences pouring out of her. She was a fierce little thing, intense whether in a state of joy or enduring the profound tragedies that beset childhood. I tried to understand. I stretched myself as far toward her as I could reach. And she grew into a beautiful child, a good child—all children are good—wanting to be loved, wanting approval.

By 1979 the restaurant had become a fashionable place in our part of the state; we were completely booked most summer nights and now were in the black even in the winter. Artur was ecstatic. Success was good for him. It made him generous with praise and less subject to panic. Success did for him what it is supposed to do but doesn't always, put him in a mellow state of mind. At this point I could tell him I wanted to be a partner in the business without fearing a hysterical explosion. He knew I could leave if I was unsatisfied, that Dad would back me in a place of my own if I asked him to. By now Artur loved Isabelle and me; we'd become his family and he couldn't do without us. I didn't just cook, I co-managed the restaurant; I ran the kitchen and, with Kathleen's help, supplied it with fresh organic vegetables and herbs, at least in late summer and early fall. So he agreed, asking that I put some cash into the business. The restaurant badly needed redecorating. I had saved most of my wages, so I could do that.

The restaurant was really tacky looking, with its crystal chandeliers, flocked wallpaper, a red flower-patterned carpet, heavy red velvet draperies tied back with gold braid, and Victorian chairs cushioned in crimson velvet.

I knew it would break his heart if I simply tossed everything out. After much thought, I decided to persuade him to renovate the upstairs into a real home for himself, so he could live somewhere other than in his sister's damp basement room. I redesigned the space, five tiny bedrooms and an ancient bathroom, into a sitting room and a bedroom with a big luscious bathroom. When he saw the drawing I had made for his bathroom, I could see that he was thrilled.

I guess poor Artur had completely given up any hope for a personal life. He'd lived with such deprivation earlier in his life that simply eating well was a luxury. He relished being greeted as an important person by the guests who frequented his place and being complimented on his food. But now something new began to ferment in the Artur brain.

We closed for a month in January while the construction work was done, by local workers my father had met when he built his studio and expanded his house. I moved the chandeliers, the Victorian chairs, and the dusty drapes upstairs. Artur hung the chandeliers and the drapes in his sitting room, set some of the chairs around his new round dining table (the rest went to a dealer in fake antiques), and reused the salvageable parts of the downstairs carpeting. He pored over catalogs for his bathroom and with my help chose modern fixtures and a Jacuzzi. When it was finished he was exceedingly pleased.

The work took months, but Artur was not in a hurry, being as wary of the new life he pictured as eager for it. He began to make eyes at a customer from New York who came in from time to time with her brother and his wife, with whom she spent frequent weekends in Brattleboro. She had dyed red hair and was somewhat hefty but shapely. Mildred Hildrein was a widow. She worked as a bookkeeper for an importer of silk flowers and was a trusted employee, earning a good salary, but lonely and afraid of growing old alone. I had long seen that she found Artur attractive, and I knew that he was drawn to her too. Artur was handsome, though a little heavy, and his manners were polished. He was courtly in the European manner, which American women are starved for. Most of the women patrons adored him. I smiled, watched, and waited.

The money I had invested paid for the restaurant renovation, which I designed. I had the painters steam off the flowered wallpaper and paint the walls a warm pale cocoa and the molding that framed panels of the wall beige. I hung bright brass sconces in the center of each panel and chose a cocoa carpet with a waffle pattern that would disguise dirt. The tablecloths were beige and the napkins cocoa, and I put chocolate-colored candles on each table. I hung pleated beige linen shades at the windows and bought bentwood chairs the color of maple syrup covered in beige. It looked classy.

For about a year, once or twice a month, I had been putting Isabelle in the car—she loved to ride around, babbling in her car seat, with a little bottle of water, some toys in hand, and a few cookies in a waxed paper bag—and had been driving to small farms in Vermont, Massachusetts, Connecticut, and northern New York.

The technological revolution had brought us tomatoes with thick skins that would not break when transported thousands of miles across the country. Our fruits and vegetables now lasted longer after harvest, making it worthwhile to ship produce raised in warm California to chilly Maine, so everyone could have strawberries in winter and oranges in summer. Pigs were bred to have less fat because people were dieting, and chickens, sheep, and cattle were fed hormones and antibiotics, which kept them healthier and reduced waste and also created a race of giant animals. This revolution was supposed to make the United States the best-fed country in the world, with the cheapest food. That it probably had.

But farms containing ten thousand pigs stank for miles and produced so much pig shit that disposal was a serious problem. And without fat, pork was tough and tasteless. The new vegetables and fruit also had no taste. People like me stopped buying pork and lamb, and did without tomatoes that were not grown locally. We bought meat and produce from local farmers, whose numbers were decreasing. (In the winter, only potatoes, cabbages, and turnips were available locally, so we had to have other options.) Locally raised food tasted much better than the other stuff. A movement had arisen to promote organic food.

By 1979 there were maybe a dozen and a half organic farms in the area that I could reach by car in an afternoon. For the past year, I had been looking at farms that raised foods I would want to serve in my restaurant. One couple in Monterey, Massachusetts, had started a goat farm and cheese-making business, set up in such an organic, sanitary way that they became a model for other aspiring cheese producers across the country. I wanted to buy their products: not many people ate goat cheese at that time, but it was starting to become popular. Inspired by Greek salads, which always contained feta cheese, I introduced goat cheese in the restaurant in a salad of baby greens (also unusual then). People liked it, so later I used goat cheese with scallions and parsley in a risotto, which also was popular. Alice Waters had invented a salad with a baked goat cheese that was delicious.

Then I heard about a chicken farmer in Rhode Island who shunned the antibiotics that other chicken farmers used. He also did not feed his chickens feed made out of chicken parts (which was common). He gave them natural feed and the meat tasted so superior that I served it exclusively. In Vermont, these things mattered: many of the people who lived and visited there cared about things like that. So we continued to thrive, and I continued to seek out better sources of food.

I had earlier pressed Artur to build a solarium out back, behind the kitchen, where I could grow herbs and spices and lettuce all winter. He had put this project off, but in 1979, during the upstairs renovation that winter, I finally got my greenhouse. This made it possible for me to stop planting Dad's meadow, which had become too much work for me. Between taking care of an increasingly demanding Isabelle, searching out natural foods, and trying out new recipes to keep the restaurant fresh, I was overwhelmed.

Kathleen, my assistant, now paid Dad a nominal rent and kept the field going. The following year she rented another field from someone else and organized an organic farm on her own. She was so happy with her project that her marriage improved.

Artur and I got along well; we rarely argued, and working together in the restaurant every day was really a pleasure. With the experience of the commune behind me, I knew how to disagree diplomatically and how to be delicate when I needed to overrule him. He had learned to tell me without shrieking when something mattered strongly to him, which was not often. When something mattered strongly to me—which *was* often—I knew how to ask for agreement without servility, and he would pat my back and say, "Of course, of course, my little Jess." He adored Isabelle, even after she started talking. Once kids can talk they say things adults don't like, demanding what they want and objecting when they don't get it. This period of childhood loses kids some of their most effusive admirers, but Isabelle did not lose Artur, who, had I not taken him in hand, would have had her fat as a pig, sneaking her bits of bacon, avocado, and chocolate candy.

We were thriving now, and I had a good enough sous-chef that I could take a winter vacation (I could never take one in the summer). I went only as far as Cambridge, to Mom's, where I spent three weeks. After she came back from France she had visited me in Vermont, staying at a motel again and avoiding Dad's house, but we never saw enough of her. I wanted Isabelle to get to know her better, so we went to her that February. Isabelle and Mom and I went to museums and playgrounds (very sparse on the ground in Vermont) and to Boston Common, with its swan boats, which enchanted Isabelle, as they had me a generation earlier. We ate at restaurants almost every night—Cambridge was now full of wonderful new ethnic places—and Mom got to know her granddaughter.

When in the spring of 1979 I set off on my round of visits to organic farms, I found most of them through word of mouth; there was no register of these farms. I visited a small pig farm in Connecticut that produced pork with some fat and some flavor, and happily signed on a new supplier of chops, roasts, and bacon. Then I wasted my time on a disappointing series of farms whose claims to organic vegetables were exaggerated. I found some potential sources that would have to be visited again in the late summer, one promising organic corn, another tomatoes. The tomato farmers told me about an organic mushroom farm in Vermont, up near Springfield. Many people found mushrooms to be bland, but reading about food constantly, as I did, I had encountered some interesting new ones—shiitake, cremini, and cèpes. I knew that my never having been to Europe was a drawback for a person who specialized in food, and I didn't know when I could possibly take the time to go. This organic farm in Vermont was supposed to grow many kinds of mushrooms, and I decided to visit it.

Springfield, Vermont, is halfway up the state and colder than the area around Brattleboro, where we lived. That May when I drove up, the fields were still brown, only slightly tinged with green. I was almost past Springfield when I saw a small sign reading "Champignons Jacquet" beside a driveway, which led through masses of trees, still only in bud, to a plain old Victorian house.

I got out of the car and undid Isabelle from her car seat. At three, she was getting heavy, but whenever I picked her up, she would throw her arms around my neck and grapple my body with her little legs. This always sent hot lava pumping through my heart, and I held her close against my body as I walked to the door. A large man with a long, pale face, a broad forehead, and dark hair opened the door. He had the good looks that caught a person's attention, but I kept my face immobile.

"Mr. Jacquet? I'm Jess Leighton. I have an appointment."

"Hello, come in." He tilted his head toward the room. I put Isabelle down and led her by the hand inside the house. The front room was an office, with a desk, a typewriter, a telephone and Rolodex, two standing file cabinets, and some charts pinned to the wall. I recognized them as planting charts; I had made similar ones for myself at Pax. There were also a couple of shabby armchairs, but he didn't invite me to sit.

"Artur's, right?" he asked.

I nodded.

"You're getting well-known. The restaurant and you." He smiled down at Isabelle. "But I don't know this young lady."

Isabelle bristled. She hated to be called a young lady. It signaled a demand for formal deportment.

I put my hand on her shoulder. "This is Isabelle."

He bent toward her. "Hello, Isabelle."

She pressed her face against my leg. "Isabelle would say hello if she weren't hiding," I said, ruffling her hair.

"She's a beautiful child. Your husband is a lucky man."

"I have no husband," I said in a frigid tone.

He flushed. "Sorry. Stupid of me."

I stood in cold silence. I didn't like the intended compliment.

It sounded as if he were praising some man for owning such fine property as Isabelle and me. I said this aloud.

He changed color again, to white. "Terribly sorry." But his voice was cold too.

I nodded.

"I was trying to say—actually, I had a pang of envy for whatever man was in your lives. Yours and Isabelle's," he said.

"No serious harm done," I said, relenting.

"Just minor harm?" he asked.

"Let's forget it and start over," I said.

"I can't—I have this need to defend myself. I have to insist, to tell you what I was trying to say: looking at the two of you does give a man pleasure. This man, anyway."

"Okay," I said dubiously. "I guess that's different. Thanks." Then I added, "I guess," and laughed.

He laughed too. He was standing, arms akimbo, between the door and me and for a moment I felt trapped by him, with him. He was tall, much taller than I, and full bodied. And I had Isabelle. But he moved slightly to one side, waving me before him, and my body eased.

"Shall we go?" he asked.

I tried for a lighter voice. "I want to warn you, I'm totally ignorant about mushrooms. Eager to learn though," I added.

"Most of us in America don't know about mushrooms," he said. "We still have a frontier palate, frozen by the Depression; we eat Corn Flakes and beefsteaks, Wonder Bread and Velveeta cheese. We know nothing about wine, cheese, fish, herbs, or vegetables. But I hear you are an herbalist and serve great vegetables. That's your reputation."

"Oh." My face became warm; I was afraid I was blushing. But it thrilled me to hear that I had any reputation at all, that people actually talked about me, especially in such a way.

We left the house and walked toward some large sheds. They

were two across and three deep. Around them was open land—room for expansion, I deduced, and beyond that, along the perimeter of the property, deep woods, evergreens that cast their shade across much of the plot and helped to keep the sheds cool.

He continued, "When I was fourteen, I spent a couple of years in France with my grandparents. They lived in the Périgord and would go walking in the countryside, picking mushrooms. They'd take a bottle of wine, a baguette, some *saucisson*, and fruit. We'd meet other people doing the same thing and compare notes. My grandparents knew every type of mushroom they saw, including the poisonous ones, and they taught me as we went. It wasn't like learning in school, it was just conversation, you know? Afterward, we'd go home and make mushroom crêpes or mushroom omelets or mushroom soup or just sauté them. Delicious! We'd have that with great French bread and a hearty red wine for Sunday dinner. It was a happy time for me."

"So you decided to grow them yourself," I said.

"Not right away. I did time in a corporation after college."

So he was a dropout too.

"You didn't like corporation land?"

"I have no objection to the idea of business," he said, somewhat pedantically. I wondered if he always pronounced on things. "But I do have objections to big business. People say it's more efficient, but to me it's more oppressive and inefficient and slow. Slower even than small businesses can be. And I object to the fact that in this country small business is becoming impossible. In a small business, you know your customers and they know you and trade is a fair exchange. But the way things have evolved, you have to do things in a big way or you can't survive." He laughed a little, without humor. "The big fish swallow up the little fish, or drown them."

"Yes. I know what you mean," I said. "I had a little plot of ground, you couldn't call it a farm, it was too small. I grew herbs and vegetables, just enough to stock the restaurant for a couple of months of the year. But it was costing me too much to keep it."

"You raise vegetables *and* cook in the restaurant?"

"Well," I admitted ruefully, "I was paying someone to help me plant, weed, and water. That was part of the problem. I couldn't do it all. Too much work, and it didn't pay."

"It never would have been worth your effort if you didn't have the restaurant," he guessed. "You had your own distribution network."

"Yes. You're right." I laughed, thinking that *distribution network* was a ridiculous name for my tiny operation. "Artur and I love what we do, but we earn barely enough to live on. I'm sure I don't earn enough to live on: I live with my father and have a low overhead."

"Poppop," Isabelle chimed in.

My guide perked up. He leaned toward me a little, as if he was making an intimate statement. "I understand. If I'm going to survive in my business, I'll have to expand."

"Yes, probably." I understood that he was telling me something that he felt mattered, to *me*.

Isabelle was looking around with alert and interested eyes. She rarely spoke on these outings but she noticed a great deal and would comment and question afterward. She'd say, "Man have funny eyes, Mommy," about someone whose stray eye I'd barely noticed, or, "Lady fat, Mommy" about a pregnant woman.

We reached the first concrete shed. I could hear the roaring of a huge fan that must have been mounted around the corner on the outside of the building. There was another fan just above our heads as we entered. I looked at it questioningly.

"The shed has to be airtight. Air is pushed in by the big fan, and out by a smaller one, so there is always too much air coming in. When it is pushed out, that seals the building. There can't be insects or other contamination. Mushrooms are very demand-ing. A lot of varieties can't even be raised; they only grow wild—cèpes, for instance, and chanterelles.

"They have to have light." He pointed to the fluorescent lamps mounted on the ceiling. "The temperature has to be maintained at around seventy degrees and the humidity at 90 percent. The air has to be cooled in summer and heated in winter. They are one pain in the neck." He laughed. "But I love them. Like having a baby, I guess," he said ruefully.

I smiled at him. His expression was sweet, unassuming, a little self-deprecating. Nice.

"These are portobellos and cremini. They grow in compost and soil. I make the compost myself of horse manure and chopped-up straw."

I saw raised boxes full of mushrooms, row upon row of broad, flat, brownish mushrooms and beyond them, little golden ones. The shed sprawled at least seventy feet.

He walked forward and picked one of the brownish ones, which he cleaned with a damp rag taken from his pocket. He handed it to me. "Portobello."

I broke off a piece and tasted it. Isabelle watched me in the utter horror of children in the face of strange foods. One would never imagine that for the previous year, she had put absolutely everything she encountered into her mouth. "Delicious," I said, and offered her a piece; she recoiled.

"I predict they'll become very popular," Jacquet said.

We walked down the long center aisle toward the other mushrooms. They were shaped like button mushrooms but had a golden color. "These are cremini," he explained.

I tasted the sample he gave to me. "Good. Much tastier than buttons, moister and with more flavor."

He smiled with great pleasure.

Isabelle watched me warily. I didn't offer her a piece this time.

"Want to see some more?"

"Of course!" I was enthusiastic now. Oh, what I could do with those portobellos! They tasted like steak, chewy and juicy and meaty. A whole mushroom would provide a small meal. A first course. Sautéed with butter and maybe some scallions and cilantro, on toast, its juices seeping into the toast . . . It would be a sensation!

We left the shed and walked to another one next to it. It was open sided, its roof supported by uprights. Inside were logs stacked crosswise; mushrooms sprouted from the logs.

"I make holes in the logs, which have to be replaced every two years," Jacques explained. "I plant spores in the holes. These are oyster mushrooms." He pointed. "And over there, those are shiitake. The oysters mature in four weeks, but the shiitakes take eighteen months."

We went through the tasting process again. I found the flavors haunting. The mushrooms were each a little different and would lend themselves to different treatments, I thought.

The next shed was open too and was filled with plastic bags about two feet high, stuffed with straw, with mushrooms sprouting out of tiny holes in the sides. These were oyster mushrooms also, a lesser quality, he said, and black poplar mushrooms, which he grew in limited quantities.

The last shed contained button mushrooms, his biggest seller. He broke one off and offered it to Isabelle this time. She hid her head against my leg again, so he popped it into his own mouth, then picked another and offered it to me. It was okay, just an ordinary mushroom. A letdown after tasting the others.

"You sell a lot of these?"

"That's all most places want. They've been selling well, especially since I discovered a new marketing wrinkle—I wipe them down and sell them clean and white, wrapped in plastic. Worst thing in the world for mushrooms, plastic. Makes them go bad really fast. But people snap up those clean mushrooms in plastic, I swear. Americans like their food clean." He laughed. "They care less what it tastes like."

I didn't tell him that I stored mushrooms in plastic.

As the afternoon wore on, Isabelle became whiny and clingy, a real pain. She finally started to cry and insisted on being carried.

I think she comprehended that she had now encountered competition. I picked her up and whispered in her ear that I had to work and if she didn't calm down, I would put her in the car. It was warm enough for her to sit in the car and I had brought along some toys, a thermos, and a cassette tape of some music she liked. But in those days, for her any separation from me was banishment to Siberia, and she shut up and let me get on with what I was determined to do.

"So, Mr. Jacquet . . ." I began, "should we talk about quantities and prices?"

"Sure. But let's go back to the house, it's more comfortable. And my name is Philip. My friends call me Philo."

My heart stopped. Philo. "I have a good friend named Philo."

"Really?" He seemed incredulous and maybe a little put out. "It's an unusual name."

"Yes."

"Come on back and I'll make us some coffee. Maybe Isabelle would like a cold drink and to watch television."

Isabelle's face appeared from its nesting place in my shoulder. She studied him.

He gazed at her with a slight smile. "And if Mommy allows, we could even dredge up a cookie," he said. She stared, wary but tempted.

"Do you think you can walk, Isabelle?" I was tired of carrying her. She was big to be pulling this routine, but I always figured she knew what she needed better than I did.

She nodded her head, still not speaking, and I put her down on her feet. Together, we followed Philip—Philo!—out of the shed and back to the house. We walked through the front office. Philo slid open an oak pocket door, which opened to a living room with a fireplace. He asked if I wanted coffee or tea and what he could give Isabelle. I okayed cookies and milk, and he turned on the television set that stood in a corner and fiddled with the dials until he found a show about animals. Then he disappeared through a swinging door.

Isabelle floated to the floor and sat cross-legged (as she always did) in front of the TV. I studied the room. The furniture was old and varied, comfortable. I saw nothing screamingly ugly, nothing cutesy (suggesting a female occupant) or macho (suggesting ego problems). While he prepared our snack, I did some accounting. On the negative side were his sexist assumptions. They might not be serious. His pedantry could have been aggravated by nervousness. It might be permanent, but it was probably something I could live with, albeit with constant criticism. Stacked against the current I felt emanating from him and the responding current I felt in myself, the intense heat I felt radiating from his large, musky body, and the response my own made to it, these were minor objections. Was the sexism accidental, and could it be eliminated?

I continued my examination of the room. A bookcase held a hundred or more books, many on mycology, others on history and politics—no novels or poetry. Too bad, and maybe not remediable. There were a few sculptures I recognized as Inuit. Excellent. Prints hung on the walls, most of them careful depictions of mushrooms in muted pastels. Good if not great. But—some artistic taste. You couldn't expect everything, could you? But I knew I wasn't at my most alert: my heart was beating too fast, too hard.

Philo came back with a tray. He was clearly used to doing this; he probably did it for all his customers. He was easy and comfortable now, even with Isabelle; he had dropped the pedantry. She watched him as he handed her a snack. In a tiny voice, she said, "Thank you." I could see exactly how she was going to be with him: stubbornly hard to win but seducible, and once won, fiercely attached, as jealous of him as she now was of me. I smiled grimly, privately, at her perverse little heart. Not so different from mine.

"So," I began, when he was settled in the chair opposite me, "how long have you had the mushroom farm?"

"It's three years since I opened it. It took a year before that to get it going. The hardest four years of my life, but I've loved every day of it."

"You've done this all alone?"

"Yeah." He sighed. "I started out with my girlfriend . . ."

Heart swoop.

"Debbie. We met when we both worked for Crumper Strauss in D.C. after law school. Crumper Strauss—I don't know if you've heard of it—it's a huge law firm, hundreds of attorneys. We did wills and estates. God, did we hate it! It was so boring. The three years I worked there were the most miserable time of my life. Hers, too. We both started having daydreams—me about mushrooms, her about theater. But somehow mushrooms seemed more possible than theater; a mushroom farm was more tangible . . . She'd acted in some undergrad productions, but she hadn't studied acting. She wasn't even sure acting was what she wanted. I think my enthusiasm for mycology sort of swept her up . . ."

He was sipping coffee from his mug as he spoke, and I was staring at him with intensity. I was surprised at what was coming out of him, and yet I wasn't. He was telling me this personal stuff as if I had a right to hear it, as if he knew I would care, and he wanted me to know it all. I did care, I did need to know it all, but how did he know that? In what exchange of looks had that been settled between us?

"We earned great salaries for this deadening work, and both of us saved it right from the beginning. We knew immediately that we'd have to get out. On the third anniversary of our being hired, we both quit and took off for France. We went to Paris, to the Sorbonne. I spoke French fairly well, but hers was shaky. I signed up for a course in mycology; Debbie wanted to learn French well and immersed herself in French culture.

"During the year we were there, my grandmother died—my grandfather had died some years before—and left me her house. Real estate values in France were horribly low but it was a gorgeous big old house in an area where tourists were starting to come, and I was able to sell it for a good price to a group that wanted to open a hotel. I couldn't have afforded to keep it up, and I thought my grandmother would have loved that I used her house to buy a mushroom farm.

"I came back and looked around. Debbie stayed in Paris a while longer. I have a cousin who lives in Rutland. He urged me to look around this area because property was relatively cheap here, and the land is rich. It's so rocky that it hasn't been farmed much, and it has retained its nutrients. I was going to strain it anyway, to put it in boxes, so the rockiness didn't matter. Anyway, eventually I bought this house and land and built the sheds. There were a lot of expenses—the seeds and spores, the automatic overhead misting system, the huge fans, the heating system—and my inheritance and my savings together didn't quite cover it. I had to get a bank loan for some of it. I'm still paying off that loan.

"Debbie came back when I started operating. I don't know what she thought mushroom farming would be like: I don't know what *I* thought it would be like, for that matter." He laughed. "We knew it wouldn't be like real farming, where you're utterly subject to the weather and the work is backbreaking. It seemed safer, more protected, somehow. But it *was* very hard work—planting, harvesting, they're laborious, but you know that." He laughed wryly.

"Debbie didn't care for it. She liked Vermont, the trees, the greenness. But I was occupied with building the sheds and planting and worrying about soil and nourishment and water and humidity, and she hated all that and refused to participate. And once winter came—well, it's tough up here, you know that—she began to hate it.

"She'd met some people in Paris, Americans involved in a national theater based in D.C., a couple of gay men she liked very much. She called them and asked if they knew of any job she could fill. They'd liked her—she's smart and witty—and told her to come down and they'd find something for her. She went. She said she'd come back every other weekend, but I sort of sensed . . .

"Anyway, by then . . . It's funny, I don't know if you've found . . . if you have enough differences with someone, even if you still love them, you don't mind parting from them, like you've had enough despite the love . . . Or maybe I'm just a cold bastard." He eyed me hard. "What do you think?"

"Yes," I said tentatively, thinking of Stepan. "Differences can stretch love too thin. That happened to me too. I used to think I was fickle . . ."

"Yes!" he exclaimed, as if I'd solved a problem for him. "That's how it feels! She left most of her stuff here and flew down with just an overnight bag. They found her a job at the National Endowment for the Arts as somebody's assistant. Within six months she was running a department. She came back a couple of times, but then she packed her stuff and said good-bye. We're still friends but nothing more: we talk on the phone once in a while. She's been successful and she loves what she does. She works for Lincoln Center now."

Finally I could breathe out.

He offered me a cigarette and lit one for himself, and the two of us sat there smoking in silence. I don't smoke anymore but I miss it because of the way you could sit with someone and smoke and not have to talk yet feel you were doing something.

"How long have you been alone?" he ventured.

"Four years."

"And how old is Isabelle?"

"Three."

His eyebrows went up. I laughed at the way it sounded.

"No, she wasn't an immaculate conception. I left her father before I knew I was pregnant. I was living in a commune."

"Really!" His eyebrows went up again. "I always wanted to do that! How did you like it?"

"I loved it until . . . These things work until somebody decides to dominate."

"Yeah," he said as if he knew all about it. But did he?

I wondered how old he was. Could I ask? "I'm twenty-five," I said. "How old are you?"

"Thirty-three."

Born in 1946, started college in 1964. "College got you out of Vietnam," I suggested.

"College. And then a high number."

"Did you march?"

"Of course. You?"

"Yes."

Then, as if continuing something, he asked, "So you live with your father . . . ?"

"Yes. Since I left the commune. It was in Becket, in the Berkshires. Isabelle's father still lives there."

"What's his name?"

"Stepan. Stepan Andropovich. He's from the Ukraine."

"And he has no interest in being a father?"

"Actually, he'd like to see more of Isabelle." Her head turned when I mentioned her name. However engrossed she was in the baby leopards she was watching, she was keeping watch over me.

"He loves her. But we don't want to be together anymore, and he doesn't want to leave the commune, and I don't want to be there anymore, so . . ."

He nodded with what seemed like real understanding. And I knew that everything was as I thought: things did not need to be spoken.

But we did have to talk business. Philo and I came to an arrangement for him to deliver a half dozen boxes of mushrooms every weekend. His prices were fair and I began to get excited, thinking about the dishes I could invent. When I mentioned this, he rifled through a drawer and handed me a stack of photocopies. "I'm sure you don't need these, but I offer them to all my customers—some of my grandmother's recipes for mushrooms. I know you're an inventive chef. Just throw them out if they're useless to you," he added apologetically.

"Oh, I'm fascinated by recipes!" I exclaimed. "They're what I read for pleasure. And they're your grandmother's! How great!" I gazed at him fondly, about to ask a crucial question. "Do you have a delivery person?"

"No, I do it myself. I spend Thursday and Friday on the road, making deliveries."

I sat back, satisfied. It was time to go. It was starting to get late and I'd have to drive home in the dark if I didn't leave soon. But I sat there, unable to move.

"How did you happen to become a chef?" he asked, as if he really wanted to know. "I mean, you don't look like a chef."

"What does a chef look like?"

"Oh, I don't know. But not like you. You look like a model, or an actress. In the first place, you're too thin to be a chef!" He laughed. "Chefs look more like me." He patted his stomach.

"I started out to be a poet. But I always liked to cook. And when I joined the commune . . . The food was so bad there, they were vegetarians and couldn't afford butter or cream or even fish, and their food was so bland and boring, I just had to do something about it!" I laughed. "I'll tell you when you come to Brattleboro," I said. "I have to get this tired child home." Isabelle glared at me. I forced myself into a standing position.

He rose and came over to me. He stretched out both his arms as if to embrace me. My heart stopped for an instant, but I took his hands, sidestepping the embrace.

"I'm so happy we met," he said.

Isabelle stood up too. She put her glass and napkin on a table like the good little girl she was, and ran to repossess me. I had to let go of Philo's hand to take hers.

"See you in two weeks then," he said.

"Right. Call and tell me what day you're coming."

I went through all the usual motions as I installed Isabelle in her car seat, speaking sweetly to my baby, but all the while, my mind was whirring. I was thinking, If he comes on a Thursday or Friday, I'll plan something special, crispy duck, maybe, with my delicious mushroom soup, or a *blanquette de veau* with mushrooms. I'll insist he stay for dinner, maybe I can even eat with him if I can steal the time, set up a table on the back porch. Or maybe I can get him to hang around until nine thirty or so, when most of the customers are gone, and then we can eat together. Or maybe I can persuade him to come on a Monday, when we're closed. I could go in and cook a meal just for him. I could leave Isabelle at home with Dad.

I still took Isabelle to work with me. She didn't get tired until seven or so, and I left around three. I didn't want to leave her with Dad, who worked until around nine. She was really good; she didn't run around the restaurant, but stayed in the back rooms or in the yard, with the staff keeping an eye on her. She had plenty of toys and her own cup and bowl and high chair, and I'd bought a crib to keep in the restaurant. I put her to bed about seven, and she slept soundly there, being so used to it. I would pick her up to go home around ten thirty or eleven, and she would wake momentarily but go right back to sleep.

I didn't want to entertain Philo at home. I didn't want Philo to meet Dad just yet.

Isabelle spent the drive home asking questions about "the man," about whom she harbored terrible suspicions, all of which were right on target: he was about to wreck her world. He would, if things went as I hoped, compete for my attention. She would fight to the death to avoid this, I knew, but she was doomed. She could have no idea that "the man" would also enrich her life, although why I thought that, given my experience of daddies, I don't know. Unless "enrich" simply means "make more complicated."

It was Monday. I didn't have to work that night, and I pulled into the driveway of Dad's house full of secret happiness.

17 **Philo called a week later** to say he was changing his delivery schedule; some of his customers were experiencing bigger Friday crowds and wanted their mushrooms earlier in the week, so they could plan their Friday specials. He would now be delivering on Wednesday and Thursday, so could he drop my mushrooms off Wednesday evening? Would I mind if he made it his last delivery of the day? Because given the direction he traveled, east, then south, then north, it would be on his way home. Was that all right?

It was perfect. Tuesday and Wednesday were our slowest days; I might be able to spend a little time with him. And the last delivery of the day would be at what time? Oh, maybe seven thirty or eight. Maybe a little later?

Great. Why didn't he stay for dinner?

He'd love to.

He didn't sound surprised.

I had already planned a popular special for that night, linguine with scungile, shrimp, scallops, calamari, and mushrooms in a sauce of olive oil, fish broth, and saffron. I would serve it to him with a salad of buttery lettuce, red onion, and avocado, with lemon and olive oil. For dessert, we would have crêpes with orange segments, orange jam, and vanilla ice cream. I had a wonderful pastry chef now who specialized in things like that.

It was amazing how much attention was required for this one simple special, on this particular day. I absolutely needed a haircut; I hadn't had a professional cut in three years and my hair looked it. I also suddenly perceived it needed a little brightening. Just a few blonde streaks. And I desperately needed a facial. How had I let myself become such a mess! And I had to have something decent to wear. I had no clothes! I needed new shoes! And I had no time!

Isabelle chose that week to be cranky and whiny, which she almost never was. Oh, she knew, she knew, the little pest.

Saturday morning was always the busiest time of my week. I went in early to examine the deliveries and make sure the meat and fish and produce were all top quality. Then I ran into town and shopped. I found a really cute black top, with long sleeves that were not too tight, so my arms would be able to wrestle with heavy pots. The top was moderately low cut in front. I also bought a tight pair of black trousers, and some neat black shoes with buckles and a pair of silver hoop earrings. Altogether I was quite happy and got through Saturday and Sunday somehow. We had easy specials, baked salmon and rack of lamb, so I didn't get too tired, and on Monday I was able to run into town again and get my hair cut and have a facial and buy some makeup. I needed everything. My entire makeup kit contained only the Kmart lipstick I'd worn for the past three years. I bought mascara, blush, eyeliner, and a shiny metallic lip gloss, and when I put it all on, I have to say, I thought I looked . . . Well, I didn't know who that was in the mirror. An actress or a model, he'd said. Yes!

When I got all dressed up on Wednesday and was ready to leave for the restaurant, I asked Dad how I looked. He looked up from his newspaper—he came in from the studio for lunch these days—and said, "You look fine. Why?"

But Isabelle noticed the difference and she didn't like it. "You have stuff on your face, Mommy!" she protested and tried to climb up on me. Then she started to cry, and Mrs. Thacker said, "Why Isabelle! Why are you being such a baby!" because of course she didn't understand. This only made Isabelle howl louder, and inside I was laughing, but I hugged her and as I carried her out to the car, I told her I would never ever stop loving her, whatever happened. It was a grand drama.

Isabelle and I went to Artur's, and once we reached the restaurant and everything was just as it always was, she calmed down and ran into Artur's arms.

I worked and waited.

And worked and waited.

As it approached six, customers started to drift in. By seven, we had four orders of rack of lamb, six linguine-and-seafood specials, a crabmeat salad and an osso buco, a roast chicken, and a strip steak, and then it was eight and he still wasn't there. The restaurant filled up and I forgot about him—the bastard.

It was nine o'clock before I could breathe calmly enough to look at the clock. My makeup was gone and my blouse spotted and my feet hurt in my fancy shoes with the buckles that I'd worn instead of my usual sneakers, and my hair was damp and trying to escape from my cap, and most of the seafood was gone, the rack of lamb was finished, and then the back door opened and this big guy pushed his way in carrying huge flat boxes.

Of mushrooms.

I turned, barely able to muster a smile. He didn't seem to expect anything, just stood there chatting with Eberly, one of the assistants, who took the mushrooms, put them in the cold storage room, and checked them against our list and then asked Artur to pay him. Artur went over to Philo and talked to him— of course, I'd told him all about Philo and the mushrooms—and finally I could take a breath. I went over and chatted with them and offered Philo dinner. Was I sure? he asked. He didn't want to bother me. I insisted, and we set up the staff table in the alcove and I had Eberly pour him a drink. He took bourbon, a Jack Daniels on the rocks.

Isabelle was sound asleep in her crib, and things were beginning to close down outside; there were only about a dozen people left in the dining room. I had told Manuel early in the evening to be sure to reserve two orders of the pasta with seafood for Philo and me. Artur sat with Philo, drinking a vodka and water, continually hopping up to go out and say good night to patrons. Philo looked exhausted. He admitted that deliveries tired him; he was happy to relax with a couple of bourbons. By nine forty-five, no new customers were arriving and the staff was cleaning up.

I sat down across from Philo with a Glenlivet. I smiled, and he smiled, and he asked how Isabelle was, and my heart felt like a leaf folding because he'd asked about her, because he'd remembered, because he was saying that he knew that she was the most important thing in my life.

After the last customer left, Manuel finished the cleanup and Artur came in and sat down with a great sigh. I signaled Eberly to serve the three of us. He poured wine for us, a Pinot Grigio, and assembled the salad so it was ready when we finished the seafood. Then I told him he could go home. The pastry chef, Lou, had already gone, leaving behind three portions of orange crêpes.

Artur talked eagerly with Philo about mushrooms. The two of them got along famously, but Artur could see what was happening as well as Isabelle could, and as soon as dinner was over he busied himself with what I call polishing the kitchen, ordering me not to help but to sit and rest and talk to Philo. Artur went into the dining room to check it over. It would be vacuumed and polished tomorrow. When he returned, he yawned—rather theatrically, I thought—and asked if I would mind closing up, he was tired. I agreed, acting as if this were normal, when in fact I had never closed up before; Artur always did it.

"Nice to meet you, Philo." He pronounced it "Pheelo." "We talk again about mushroom . . ."

"Nice to meet you too, Artur," Philo said, standing and reaching out his hand. "Sure, anytime."

"You go beck to farm now? Is far?"

"Yes. No, it's not far. Less than an hour's drive."

"Okay," Artur said, as if he were approving something, and turned away and went upstairs. I knew perfectly well that he would wait until I left and come down again and check that everything was locked, but I could not bring myself to leave quite yet.

We were both tired, but mellow. Philo talked about college, the Périgord, Paris, and the Sorbonne. I talked about the commune and Sandy and Bishop. Eventually, out of sheer weariness, we sadly agreed we had to leave. He stood around while I locked up, then walked me to my car and waited while I settled the still-sleeping Isabelle. We stood there together. He took my hand in his.

"See you next week," he said.

When I looked at myself in the bathroom mirror that night, I had to laugh. All my plans and fussing, and I looked as bedraggled and hot and sweaty and messy as I did every other night. Raspberry sauce had splattered on my blouse. My new shoes were spotted with grease. My face was bare of makeup and my hair was limp. But it didn't matter. We'd had a special evening, we'd touched each other someplace. I was full of hope.

Every week, Philo came down from Springfield with a half dozen boxes of mushrooms, eventually raised to a dozen, then two. Artur began using black mushrooms in a beef Stroganoff he'd only imagined in the USSR. I put mushroom omelets on the menu as a first course, added mushrooms to many of our salads, and invented salads and hot vegetables with some form of mushrooms in them. My mushroom soup (thickened with a puree of mushroom stems and finished with cream), already famous among my customers, became a standard, and I started to make it with a variety of mushrooms.

For my soup, I sautéed shallots in butter, then added chopped mushroom stems and half the caps, sliced. When this was liquid, I poured in quarts of chicken broth and a little salt and pepper and simmered it. After about forty minutes, I pureed the whole thing in small batches in the blender. That was the base. When someone ordered it, I heated a small amount, added a dollop of cream, and sprinkled a few raw mushroom caps and chopped chives on top. Sometimes I made croutons from rich white bread toasted in a ton of butter. When people were on a diet, if they requested no cream, I skipped it and the croutons, using nonfat milk to thin the soup. We noted on the menu that our mushrooms came from Champignons Jacquet in Springfield, Vermont, and Philo's business gained some fame too.

It stayed easy between us; he was never again as stiff and sexist as he had been that first day, although sometimes his assumptions needed . . . enlightening just a little. We talked about our families, our old friends. Philo had had a younger brother who had died of a heart attack when he was only twelve, when Philo was fifteen; and an older brother, who lived in California and worked in computers. The older brother was very successful; he lived in a fourteen-room house with a pool. He was married, with a son and daughter. He'd done everything right, Philo said, with chagrin.

Philo's parents lived in Florida; his father was retired and played golf all day. His mother liked to go to the pool. Both played bridge. They were tan year round. Philo acted dazed when he talked about them, as if they were people he had only heard about. He visited them in Florida once a year, at Christmas.

I told him about Mom and Dad, who fascinated him. He said they sounded real; he felt that his parents weren't real. It had never occurred to me that I might be lucky in my parents, given the misery of our household when I was growing up. But remembering Sandy's home environment, which I had envied, yet felt off balance in, I thought that maybe domestic tranquility was not the greatest good. But I still wanted it, for myself and Isabelle.

I told Philo about my old friends, of whom I had occasional news. Sandy still lived in Northampton and worked in a clinic there. We wrote each other a couple of times a year, and I knew that she lived with her partner, Louisa, who taught chemistry at Smith and, like Sarah, played a mean game of tennis. Sandy did not live as comfortably as her parents had, but she felt she was much happier. She and Louisa had built a whole world in the Connecticut River Valley: tons of friends, tennis and swimming and string quartets—Louisa's best friend was a violinist. They felt useful.

Bishop and Rebecca had gone back to Cambridge, where Rebecca was in med school. She planned to do her residency in pediatrics at a hospital in Boston that catered to a largely black population and they were buying a house on the fringes of Roxbury, where Bishop had opened a children's book store. He also sold toys—high-quality, educational toys—and was in his element. They were obviously not rich, but someday they would be comfortable. And they too were very happy in their lives. Bec intended to get pregnant when she finished her residency. I didn't know if Bishop ever saw his mother and father; I wanted to ask, but because we spoke only on the phone, I felt hesitant bringing up possibly uncomfortable subjects.

Dolores, who had finally written to Mom, was in New York, going to graduate school at NYU. She was becoming a therapist specializing in incest, and had already published a paper. She was elated about that.

Philo—my Philo, not Mom's Philo—hardly ever heard from Debbie, and he never called her, which made him feel guilty. I tried to sympathize, but the truth was, I was pleased. I seldom spoke to Stepan; we called maybe twice a year, and when he visited, it was to see Isabelle. He was involved with a new woman at Pax, Elissa, who was also from the Soviet Union. For the first time in his life, Stepan was overwhelmed with passion and thinking of marriage. This was fine with me, and Isabelle was not jealous when on one visit, he brought Elissa with him. They brought a tent and sleeping bags and stayed out in the woods, which gained Dad's respect, and he stopped sniping at Stepan.

There was a problem, however. Stepan had decided he wanted partial custody of Isabelle and spoke about going to court to obtain it. I was outraged and furious with myself for ever telling him about her. I was prepared to fight him to the death over this, but Philo, calmly, rather sweetly, persuaded me that it would not be so bad. It wasn't, he said, as if Stepan wanted her every other weekend; he wanted her for a weekend once in a while and for a month in the summer. Philo said it might be good for her to live on a farm for a month in the summer, and I had to concede that he was right. And Isabelle liked Stepan. He was kind to her, affectionate. The first time she went to stay with him, she was five. Philo and I drove her out to Becket. She took one look at the farm and ran, wide-armed, into paradise. By then they had a couple of dogs and cats, besides the horses and chickens, and Isabelle made herself at home. She loved the animals, and the smell of hay, and all the folk about, and the two older kids, whom she followed around on their chores.

After we'd known each other for a few months, I asked Philo to come up on a Monday night to meet Dad. I made an everyday sort of dinner, purposefully; I didn't want Dad making snarky comments on the bloody artichokes he had to eat because we had company or Isabelle crying and refusing to eat the skate or bream she wasn't used to. So I made a dish I knew both Dad and Isabelle would eat with gusto, the plainest possible meal, spaghetti Bolognese—pasta with chopped beef, tomatoes, garlic, and basil. I also made Mom's salad: lettuce, avocado, and red onion, with a vinaigrette. All the vegetables and herbs came from Kathleen's garden.

Philo showed up exactly on time, at seven o'clock, and Isabelle ran to the door when the bell rang. We sat outdoors on the porch looking at the lake. Dad offered Philo a gin and tonic, which he accepted. It was hot, but there was a breeze off the lake, which was beautiful, framed by pine trees. Dad talked about the horrors of Harvard; Philo talked about the horrors of Penn. I did not even bring up Andrews.

Isabelle sat on the floor, coloring, looking up every once in a while at me or at Philo. I know I was looking at him more often than at her or Dad, and after a while she stood up and climbed into Dad's lap, a rare event. He was thrilled, and he put his arms around her, cuddling her, and she lay against him, sucking her thumb. I talked about gardening, which interested Philo. When he talked about mushrooms, Dad listened and asked questions. Isabelle then slid off Dad's lap and walked off, as though in a huff. I called her but she ignored me. I followed her indoors. I grabbed her hand. "Want to help me make dinner, Isabelle?"

This thought delighted her; she loved to help her mommy. I fastened her tiny apron around her, then put on my own and started dinner. It didn't take long—I'd made the sauce earlier, and set the table. I just had to boil the pasta and put the salad together. I found things for Isabelle to do—I had her put napkins at each place, and she put rings of red onion on each salad plate with great care, concentrating.

The food warmed everybody up. We all began to chatter. I poured more wine. I gave Isabelle a drop, with water. I said it was a special occasion. Her mood improved even more. By the time dinner ended, she would look at Philo, and when I took her off to bed, she hugged her grandfather and let Philo kiss her on the cheek. Warily.

Success.

Philo and I got married the next year. Philo wanted to have a child, and we thought we should be married, for the child's sake. We started out living in his house in Springfield. We had a guest room for Dad to stay in, but he never came to stay. He'd come for dinner once in a while, then scurry home. Mom did stay, though, and often. The next year, I had a son, whom we called William, after Philo's brother who had died.

By that time Isabelle was five and going to kindergarten. I had to take three months off from the restaurant; William was born in January, so once again I was away only in the slow winter months.

Isabelle fought Philo off as long as she could, but by the time we were married she had given in and was glued to him like his shadow. She fought me for his attention. She cuddled the new baby and played with him the way the dog played with her. Philo adored her, while his own son terrified him—for the first year, anyway. I had to teach him not to provoke power struggles with William, and he had to teach me to let him have his own relationship with him. The two of us had to deal, once in a while, with the kids' jealousy of each other. We were, in other words, a relatively happy family. And this had happened without my consciously doing anything.

Soon after I married Philo, Dad went to New York for an opening and met a rich woman from the art world and married her. He moved to a New York loft and became part of the art scene in the city, and I didn't see him anymore, but would see his name in newspapers and magazines. He left the cabin empty, saying he would come up summers. He probably did, once in a while, but he didn't call me. Mrs. Thacker still went in one day a week to clean the place and make sure nothing had leaked or broken or exploded, and Philo and the kids and I went over occasionally to swim or canoe in the lake. We'd wash in the outdoor shower and sit on the porch, and put our soda in the fridge, but we didn't disturb things in the house.

We were mostly happy. Philo did housework along with me, automatically. He was used to it, having lived alone. Sometimes I felt frustrated with him because he had trouble being interested in anything but mushrooms; he didn't make much conversation and I was often parched for it. I couldn't get it from other women, because with the restaurant, the children, and the housework, I didn't have time for friends. Only after the kids were older did I have time to form friendships with smart local women who were fun to talk to.

The zest went out of our lovemaking after some years, but by then I wasn't as hot as I had been and the longing for something more was rare. I think Philo still felt the same longing, which of course made me feel terrible. But once in a great while, we'd have an intense desire for each other, and those times made up for a lot. One evening at the restaurant when dinner was over, Mildred, Artur's girlfriend, came out to the kitchen as we finished cleaning up and caught me and Philo looking at each other. That was all—we were just looking at each other across the kitchen table, both tired after a heavy night, me of cooking, Philo of delivering—and thinking what we'd do in another hour or so. When Mildred appeared it broke the connection, and Philo went to take the garbage out. Mildred came over to me and said softly, "There is nothing sexier in the world than a mature couple as handsome as you and Philo looking at each other with lust." She stepped away with a secret smile, then grabbed Artur's arm as he walked past her with some pâté to be refrigerated, and he stopped and kissed her.

Philo and I both developed some fame in the food community. I was often mentioned in the same breath as Alice Waters and Chez Panisse in San Francisco, which she founded in 1971. I was asked to be on panels and was written about, and I wrote articles about organic foods and farmers' markets. Philo was famous for his mushrooms. He now had a large farm and several helpers; he no longer made his own deliveries, and he turned over huge sums of money every year. But none of that translated into great personal wealth. We had enough to live on without worrying, that's all. And that's enough. Having too much money ruins your children and spoils you for life. The kids were my deepest source of satisfaction. The kids grew, our house was comfortable, we loved our work, and we felt that was the most people could get from life. It was enough.

It still is enough. I am now fifty-one, still cooking at Artur's, which I now own, poor Artur having succumbed to lung cancer a few years ago. I suppose it was to be expected—he smoked so heavily. He lived into his early seventies. Dad died at fifty-nine, from the same disease, in 1985, right after he left his third wife. He left most of his money and paintings to this woman, who already had everything. Mom was the most distraught person at the funeral. She stayed downstairs; she couldn't stop crying. Yet when he was alive, she'd hated him.

I felt terrible, not because I missed him—I'd hardly seen him in recent years—but because I felt that he had never lived the life he'd wanted. Many people came to his funeral, but none of them knew him at all, really. Only his family knew what he was like. I'm not sure that even he truly knew himself.

He left me the cabin in Vermont, and everything in it, and the three meadows, and the sailboat and the rowboat. Philo and I added rooms onto the cabin so we had four bedrooms and baths, a dining room, and two offices, one for each of us—a far cry from the old cabin. We put in a huge kitchen and a greenhouse. Dad's paintings and pre-Columbian sculptures were all in places of honor.

Mom died of cancer too, in 1992. I cried, but at least I felt she'd had a full life, had done what she wanted, become who she wanted to be. When she got sick, I stopped smoking and made Philo stop too. I tried to get Artur to stop, but he couldn't. It might not have made any difference—it seems to get you even years afterward. It was hard for me when Artur died; after all, I saw him every day. A lot of customers came to his funeral, which was nice and would have made him happy. His only relatives were his sister and her kids. He and Mildred never married, although they were together for years. She came up for long weekends almost every week, staying in his apartment over the restaurant. They took a cruise together every winter to some warm place where French was spoken. Artur used to say that the last twenty years of his life had more than made up for the first fifty. Mildred wept at his graveside, and so did Philo and I and Isabelle and old Loren Rosenberg from town, who had played chess with him on Monday nights.

I had a letter from Dolores around Christmas in 2000. She said she always thought about me at Christmastime. Her practice was really satisfying, she wrote; she felt she was helping so many girls, and she was writing a book about girls who'd been raped by relatives and what they needed to heal. She felt she was of use in life. Maybe that's all there is.

All this looking back caught me in the throat in 2002, when I found out that Sandy had died—the first death in my generation. She had died of breast cancer. Her mother had died of it just a few years after her father's suicide; Rhoda had died of it, and Naomi was in treatment for it. It was as though a massacre had occurred in her family. I kept feeling as though Sandy was sacrificed, but I couldn't get my mind around by what or to whom. I vaguely blamed the government, which hadn't done enough research on breast cancer, and I vaguely blamed her father. Sandy had never gotten over her father's suicide. It just undercut everything in her life. She seemed to feel that his killing himself had made their lives together as a family meaningless.

I was really down after I heard about Sandy. September 11, 2001 had happened, and now Sandy, cut down in midlife. She who had dedicated herself to helping others, to alleviating poverty, and to other good deeds.

Philo tried to make me feel better. He made me strong tea and put whiskey and sugar in it and made me drink it. He offered to go out and try to find some weed for me. I told him not to bother. I was crying all the time. The kids weren't there, so I could let myself cry openly. Isabelle was in England, doing graduate work in biology, and William was at college in Amherst. Philo and I were alone again after all those years and I had been thinking about writing a cookbook. But not that night.

"It was the war that doomed us," I cried. "My generation has never gotten over that war—the protest against it, the anger against the protesters, the fear of another one."

"I think our generation was great," Philo said. "Greater than our fathers'." Philo called the so-called "greatest generation"— our parents—the alcoholic generation, the heavy-smoking, heavy-drinking generation, the angry men.

"Look what they did. Sandy spent her life helping poor women get medical care. She didn't try to become famous or rich; she did real good in life. It's hard to do good. You start out wanting to do something good but somewhere along the way your dream twists into something profitable, something that serves your ambitions. But she stuck with it, all her life. She chose that way over a conventional life, over seeking money and status, over being wild and druggy and having fun, over being an artist, over . . . anything else!

"And look at Bishop and Rebecca. She's a pediatrician in a poor neighborhood: what a great thing! Pediatrics is not a branch of medicine that makes you rich, like surgery or dermatology or oncology. It's *good*. And he—what could be better than selling books for children? What a great thing to do! Good people do it.

"And Dolores. She tries to heal girls who've been abused. That's a heartbreaking job, imagine how many failures you must encounter. And there's certainly no money in it.

"You spend your life trying to make people feel good through food that you make sure is as healthy as it can be. You make just enough money to get by, but you foster an ecologically healthy world. I do too in my way.

"Our generation chose these things. A lot of my friends from college who started out working in corporations, the way I did, dropped out, the girls especially. And they started to do things that don't pay a lot, that help other people, that make life better.

"All those things we shouted back then, Make love not war, peace and brotherhood—or sisterhood—whatever. We meant them."

I sat up. Philo never talked much, and this was extreme eloquence for him. It surprised me.

"You think we produced a generation of saints? Then how come the world is worse than it ever was?"

I sat back and sipped the tea he'd made me. It did make me feel a bit better. I loved what he was saying about Sandy and Bishop and Dolores—and me. I loved thinking about us that way. It's true, we had lived our lives so as to do some kind of good. Even me, just cooking. In articles in fancy cooking magazines they talked about me as if I were some kind of prophet who had brought health back to the American diet. But all we'd done was what we loved doing: we cooked what we loved to eat. It was selfish, after all.

But the world is as terrible a place as ever.

The most famous of any of the people I knew was still my father, who never even thought about doing good or doing anything for anyone else, and who, poor broken soul, hardly even did anything for his own pleasure, much less profit, as far as I could see. He's so famous now that they're talking about building a museum just for his work. The paintings of his I own give me a great sense of security—I know I'll be okay in old age because I can always sell them if I'm in need. And they are there for Isabelle and William. As a chef, I have no retirement plan except my own savings, and they are sparse after putting two kids through college. But I have a dozen of Dad's canvases.

And here we were about to be at war again, bogged down in a country we had no business being in, with no clear way out. *Again!* This time they would take us to war *after* huge protests. The shots of the antiwar marches in London and Berlin and other cities, everywhere in the world, would be the most inspiring photographs I'd ever seen.

I think about the millions of people starving, working for starvation wages, or dying of AIDS in faraway places; I think of millions of people in my own country who work hard but have no place to live, have no health insurance, spend their lives sick with worry. And then I think of my friends and me, and Philo, and poor dead Sandy, and Bishop and Bec and Dolores, and how we found a way to live in contentment, to have the thing I wanted so much when I was a girl: happy lives. And I wonder: Does it matter? Is it important in the scale of things that a few people achieve happy lives? Does it change the balance for the rest? Does it create a usable example? I only know that I want my happy life, I want to keep it, I want it more than anything. And that if I were to live again, fifty times over, that is what I'd want.

The Feminist Press

at the City University of New York

is a nonprofit literary and educational institution dedicated to publishing work by and about women. Our existence is grounded in the knowledge that women's writing has often been absent or underrepresented on bookstore and library shelves and in educational curricula—and that such absences contribute, in turn, to the exclusion of women from the literary canon, from the historical record, and from the public discourse.

The Feminist Press was founded in 1970. In its early decades, the Feminist Press launched the contemporary rediscovery of "lost" American women writers, and went on to diversify its list by publishing significant works by American women writers of color. Beginning in the mid-1980s, the Press's publishing program has focused on international women writers, who remain far less likely to be translated than male writers, and on nonfiction works that explore issues affecting the lives of women around the world.

Founded in an activist spirit, the Feminist Press is currently undertaking initiatives that will bring its books and educational resources to underserved populations, including community colleges, public high schools and middle schools, literacy and ESL programs, and prison education programs. As we move forward into the twenty-first century, we continue to expand our work to respond to women's silences wherever they are found.

For information about events and for a complete catalog of the Press's 300 books, please refer to our website:

www.feministpress.org